The Man from Banner Lake:

Hero Blood

(Revised Edition)

By Tim Black

Freedom never descends upon a people. It is always bought with a price.

Harry Tyson Moor

I would like to thank my sister-in-law, Nancy Bre Miller Black, for her help and advice with the German language that appears in the novel. I would also like to thank my Beta readers who offered suggestions on the manuscript and helped with proofreading. They include "The Box Lady," T.H., J.G.

A note on the vernacular used in the novel. African-Americans in the 1940s were referred to as "colored" or "Negros." The term "nigger" was used widely during the Jim Crow era.

Other Books by Tim Black

Daydreams & Diaries (with Taylor Black)

Eye

Tesla's Time Travelers

Gettysburg: The Crossroads Town

Jamestowne

Abolition

Once Again with You

A Song of Love and Loss

Boyhood, Baseball, Bobby and Bill

For Bette

Prologue

Henry Morgenthau, Jr., United States Secretary of the Treasury, sat with his wife at Violins Restaurant on Park Avenue. He peered over his glasses at their bill for the lunch, checking the math as meticulously as he did a Treasury Department report.

His wife, a quizzical look on her face, asked him: "Shouldn't we be getting over to the NBC studio for Toscanini, Dear?

"Uh huh," he mumbled, double-checking the bill.

"Henry, we need to go to the studio. The Defense Savings Bonds drive...that is why we are here, Dear."

"Uh huh...it looks okay," he said, referring to the bill. "Okay, Elinor, let's get going."

The Secretary of the Treasury towered over his wife; indeed, he was taller than most people. Henry Morgenthau, Jr. was one of Franklin Roosevelt's oldest friends and closest advisors. Morgenthau agreed with the president's assumption that it was only a matter of time before the United States was once again pulled into a European war. He was in his hometown of New York City, promoting the sale of Defense Savings Bonds for that eventuality.

Morgenthau stopped at the coat check and helped his wife with her overcoat. It was a bit nippy for early December, with a predicted high for the day barely above freezing. A waiting limousine was idling at the curb in front of the restaurant.

Morgenthau's driver opened the car door for the secretary who let his wife precede him. "Mr. Secretary?" The driver whispered.

"Yes?"

"The Japanese attacked Pearl Harbor, sir."

Morgenthau, his face suddenly ashen with shock, looked at his driver. He paused a moment and then replied: "That can't be right, James. They might have attacked the Philippines, but not Pearl Harbor…that's impossible."

The Secretary of the Treasury was stunned. He had always assumed the Germans would attack; not the Japanese. The president had moved the fleet from San Diego to Hawaii as a deterrent, not as a provocation. This meant war, but with the wrong enemy. The Germans were the real threat. Now, the only way the United States would fight Germany would be if Hitler were rash enough to declare war on America to honor the treaty Germany had with Japan. F. D. R. couldn't be that lucky would he?

Congress would certainly declare war upon Japan for attacking the United States, but Henry Morgenthau doubted that the president would ask for a declaration of war against Germany. Germany hadn't attacked us, and there were too many isolationist congressmen who didn't want to get into another European brawl.

"To the studio, sir?"

"Huh?" said Morgenthau as he came out of his thought. "No, James, take us to the Waldorf Astoria. The president's train is on track 61."

"The Ferdinand Magellan?"

"Yes. We need to get back to Washington as soon as possible."

"Very good, sir."

Chapter 1

The gray *Unterseeboot* rose to the surface in the late evening off the Florida coast, breaking through the water with a *swoosh* of rippling waves. The submarine's captain didn't wish to waste torpedoes if he could finish off a cargo ship with his deck gun. He preferred to surface when it was safe and he felt certain there was nothing to fear from the incompetent Americans. Also, there was the matter of dropping off an agent for a mission of which the captain knew nothing.

The captain's orders were too simple: drop the agent and his inflatable rubber boat off at the proper coordinates and then proceed on and troll for easy pickings along the Gulf Stream. With any luck he would sink a tanker or two.

From the conning tower of the submarine, the captain could see the outline of the coast and a few lights from the houses that hugged the shoreline. He was surprised that the Americans didn't patrol the waters or engage the U-boats. The lights from the shore made the silhouetted outlines of ships easily discernible. These Americans hadn't been ready for war nor, the captain assumed, did the Americans ever imagine that their homeland would be attacked. They were thousands of miles from Europe. But the cargo ships were Britain's lifeline, and Britain was Germany's enemy, and the captain would go anywhere to fight an *Engländer*.

On deck, the agent in a wet suit, his face blackened so that even the scar on the left side of his face didn't show, finished inflating his rubber raft. He put his Uncle Rudolf's Lugar pistol in a waterproof bag and looked up at the conning tower for a "go" signal from the captain. The captain nodded, and the agent lowered the raft over the side of the submarine.

"*Das Meer ist ruhig*," the captain called down to the agent who nodded silently but thought, in English, *the ocean is indeed calm tonight*. He had to remember to think in English, or he might say something in German and draw suspicion. It was, after all, his first espionage mission, a special assignment to please the *Führer*. Because the agent had gone to school in America and had a good American friend who had been a member of the American Nazi Party, he was selected over more experienced agents for a most sensitive mission: *To kill the most prominent Jew in Roosevelt's Jew government*. It was probably a suicide mission, but the agent was willing to give his life for his country and for a chance to see his friend and lover one more time. And for a chance to redeem the Hess family's honor.

The captain watched as the agent paddled the rubber raft toward the shoreline then he turned his head, and with his binoculars, scanned the eastern horizon. A fat tanker was waiting a few miles to the North. It would be an easy shot and the tanker's captain wouldn't have a lookout on the shore side of his ship since he'd never suspect that a submarine would fire from that direction. It would be a nice kill and serve as a diversion for the agent. Although considering the lights from the shore, the captain doubted if the Americans even had beach patrols or spotters out. They had only been in the war two months, and the Americans were learning the rules the hard way. Many a ship off Florida's coast had been sunk by German submarines. The captain would give the Americans another lesson this night.

Chapter 2

"Old Tom" Burk stood beside the parked black 1934 Buick sedan at the Hobe Sound railroad station awaiting the arrival of the passenger whom Mr. Barry instructed Burk to pick up and drive to his home: a Jupiter Island home known as *Gate House.*

Jupiter Island was a barrier island accessible by way of a two-lane drawbridge that spanned an appropriately named Bridge Road. Philip Barry, famous playwright, was gone for a few days and only the day before, Tom had picked up a white lady, a red-haired actress who had been in one of Mr. Barry's plays, *Without Love.* Although many of the winter visitors were normally picked up at the Hobe Sound railway station by the small yellow bus, a 1937 Ford Deluxe Touring Sedan, the islanders' conveyance was in the shop for repairs, and Tom had his regular clients on the island.

White people and their plays, Tom thought, removing his black beret and replacing it with amore traditional chauffeur's black cap with a brim. The beret was a fashion accessory he had adapted from the French after his *visite* to France decades before, but he found that white people expected him to dress in a servile fashion; hence the chauffeur's cap. White people really liked their play-acting. But Mr. Barry was different from most of the white folks. He always called Old Tom, *Mr. Burk* not *boy* or *Tom,* but *Mr.* Burk. He was the *only* white man on the island who did that. But then Mr. Barry was from New

York City: Broadway. It seemed appropriate to Tom they nicknamed it "The Great White Way." Broadway was for white folks. White folks' plays. Except for Paul Robeson in *The Emperor Jones*. Robeson was a rarity, Tom thought.

Still, Mr. Barry was an odd white man; he sat on his porch in nothing but a towel writing his plays. Tom knew *The Philadelphia Story* had been Mr. Barry's big hit, but he couldn't imagine Langston Hughes writing his poems sitting in nothing but a towel.

Tom remembered the time he dropped another white man off at Gate House and Mr. Barry was sitting on the porch with nothing but his towel and what the Good Lord gave him, and the other man had shouted, "Barry, if you lose that towel, the whole world will see your shortcomings." Not a bad joke as Tom recalled. Mr. Barry had laughed at the teasing.

Mr. Barry was a nice man, unlike most of those rich folks. Most white Jupiter Island men were paternalistic. Banner Lake was built for the colored folks and then set up as a school to train the residents how to serve rich white folk. But Mr. Barry was different from the others, as different as that red-haired actress lady from the day before. She was kind of odd. She sat in the backseat, fiddled with the strings on a tennis racket and talked to Tom Burk in a husky voice, as she ogled the yachts moored on the river side of the island.

"Did you know, Mr. Burk," she had called him *Mr.* Burk, as well. "Spencer thought I was a lesbian. Imagine that. He said I had dirty fingernails. Hah! He knows I'm no lesbian now, that's for sure. Do you go to the pictures, Mr. Burk?"

When Tom had answered, "No ma'am," the red-haired lady drew a scowl across her face that was visible in the rear-view mirror and then she hadn't, thankfully, said another word to him. She had pouted like a spoiled child. White folks and their play-acting! Although, if Tom were honest, he would admit that he occasionally went to the movies if a movie had colored actors. He admitted that colored folks liked play-acting, too. There just weren't as many movies with colored folks in them.

He smiled to himself, realizing that *he* was an actor in real life. Tom Burk was always play-acting around the white folks: acting the part of the good, colored *boy*. He didn't want the white folks to know how well-read he was. He was a self-educated man and among his own people, Tom Burk had the freedom to be articulate. Around whites, he downplayed his intelligence and played the role of *Stepin Fetchit,* for in Florida, a smart colored man was a dangerous colored man, especially to the illiterate redneck white trash of which Martin County had more its fair share.

Tom Burk went to France in the Great War to fight for his country, hoping that things would change for the colored man when the war was over. Hadn't the colored man risked his life in the Meuse-Argonne? Tom Burk had. But when he returned to the United States after the Great War, nothing had changed; Jim Crow was still the rule. Segregation was the law.

Now, the white folks on Jupiter Island were different from the rednecks. They could be nice to their colored servants if their servants didn't get "uppity." They weren't threatened by educated colored men. Speak with a British accent, and the rich folks, true anglophiles, thought you were from the Bahamas, as Tom Burk's father had been. Although his father lost his British accent by the time Tom Burk entered the world, a colored man with the trace of a British accent was considered a higher class of colored servant to the white folks.

The rich had no reason to fear the *Negro,* as some of the Jupiter Islanders referred to the colored, although Tom preferred the more commonly used term *colored* to *Negro.* The colored man, or *Negro,* would never live on Jupiter Island. The Jupiter Islanders didn't even allow Jews, not even the rich Jews, to live on the island. Tom wondered if that would ever change and whether even a Jew or a colored man might live on Jupiter Island someday.

The white man, whose arrival he was awaiting, was a Hollywood film star of whom Tom had never heard as he didn't go to the Lyric Theater in Stuart, the only theater in the county. Coloreds had to go up the back stairs to take their seats in the balcony, away from the white folks. He hadn't told the red-haired lady one reason he didn't go to the pictures was that he didn't want to feel like a second-class citizen at night-time too. Unless, that is, they showed a Paul Robeson film. Then, he would go. He would to *any* movie that starred Paul Robeson.

Tom Burk had been one of six hundred colored officers in the Great War, a member of the courageous 93rd Infantry that fought with the French, because colored combat troops were not permitted to fight in the American Expeditionary Force. He was awarded the French Croix de Guerre and the Legion of Merit for valor in the Meuse-Argonne Offensive, the military operation that finally defeated the Kaiser's troops. But Tom Burk, a hero in France, was a second class citizen in the United States of America. Presently, his only son was in Fort Huachuca, Arizona, a soldier in the reactivated 93rd Infantry Division which would soon fight the Germans all over again, barely more than twenty years later.

Tom did not understand why we were fighting the Germans harder than the Japanese when it was the Japanese that bombed the United States at Pearl Harbor. He felt the

Japanese should be dealt with first. Some politicians, especially the president, determined the Germans were the bigger threat; but they weren't going to invade, like the people in California thought the Japanese might. Oh, the blackouts that were rarely enforced at night had more to do with German submarines than German airplanes, and there had been a number of ships torpedoed off the Florida coast. As the headlines of the *Stuart News* stated:

Subs Sink 3 U.S. Tankers off Coast,

38 Missing, 75 Are Saved.

That was the other night, and the weekly paper was just getting around to coverage. Now, finally, there was talk of patrols on the beaches and a tower being built to spot submarines.

Still, Tom admitted, unrestricted submarine warfare was the reason the United States entered the Great War, Tom Burk's war, and here it was all over again. Now it was Thomas Burk *Junior's* turn to fight for a country that denied freedom to the colored man.

His son thought his contribution in this new war would help change things after the war was over, just like Tom had thought his contribution in the Great War would help change the segregated world. He didn't have the heart to tell his son he was being as naïve as he, himself, had been. Like father, like son, when it came to optimism. But these Germans of 1942 seemed worse than the Germans Tom had fought in 1918. These Germans seemed crazy; more like mad dogs than men. Hitler was a megalomaniac; he was even worse than the Kaiser who was merely a narcissist. A few short years ago, people had laughed at Herr Hitler for his silly little mustache, the absurd raised-hand salute and the robotic greetings of "Heil Hitler," but no one was laughing any longer. Hitler had conquered most of Europe.

He walked over to the newsstand and scanned the magazines. There were some pictures of Nazis killing unarmed civilians in the Soviet Union. A caption on the photograph mentioned the victims were Jews.

Tom overheard a good deal of anti-Semitic comments while driving his cab for another pair of white folks, winter guests who were visiting Jupiter Island. The two men hated President Roosevelt. One man said the president was "a traitor to his class" and wondered if Roosevelt had Jewish blood in his veins. The other complained about one of Roosevelt's advisors, Henry Morgenthau, being a Jew. Having a Jew as a cabinet member was wrong, the man complained. Never trust a Jew. He suggested somebody ought to do something about the dirty Jews, to which the other man replied: "Maybe they will."

Tom heard a great deal when he drove the white folks around as they seemed to treat him as if he wasn't there or he wasn't listening. Certainly, a colored man was too dumb to know what the white men were discussing. But he was listening. Tom Burk understood. He understood hate very well. Very well indeed.

Tom had seen more than his share of hate in his life. He remembered what the Klan did to the town of Rosewood in Levy County shortly after the Great War as well as the night Sam Nelson was lynched down in Palm Beach County in September of 1926. Pure hate. Nothing ever happened to the white men who murdered Sam Nelson or attacked Rosewood. That was justice in the state of Florida.

The whistle of the approaching train brought Tom back from his reverie. He took the black and white photograph out of his pocket and looked at the white man in the picture. Nothing special about him, Tom thought, unlike the snooty red-haired woman he had dropped off the day before at Mr. Barry's Gate House. The inscription on the photograph: *To Phillip Barry with best wishes, Spencer Tracy.*

On the platform, awaiting the train stood a tall, athletic-looking young white man in a chauffeur's uniform and cap, smoking a cigarette. The only blemish in the man's appearance was a scar on the left side of his face. Tom thought the man must be a new chauffeur for one of the island's wealthy winter residents. Tom watched intently as the chauffeur smoked his cigarette; a memory tried to surface, to focus. The stranger held the cigarette in an odd way, as if he were pinching it. Tom Burk was certain he had never seen the man before, nor had he seen any smoker he knew who held his cigarette in such a way. But his memory was trying to sharpen a hazy image of the Great War. What was it that was strange about how the stranger smoked? It seemed to Tom to be foreign. European perhaps? Perhaps he was British.

Then the memory came vividly back to Tom with crystal visual clarity. He remembered the way a captured German soldier had held a cigarette Tom had offered him. He remembered looking at the soldier curiously, wondering why he held it so differently than an American smoker. This man on the railway station platform held his cigarette in the same manner.

For a brief moment, Tom Burk was in the Meuse-Argonne again, and it was 1918. He didn't want to go back there, not this morning, not today, and he tried to shake off the thought. But the image persisted. His intellect

intervened and overrode his emotion: The chauffeur was
just another stranger to the area. It was nothing more, he
assured himself. He saw enough Germans in his dreams;
he didn't need to see them while he was awake. Just
another stranger to the area, he assured himself. He shook
off the memory.

Quite a few new people had entered little Martin
County since December 7, 1941, and an army camp was
being built; the installation named for a Signal Corps
officer named Murphy who had recently died in the Pacific
theater of the war. Soon, there would be thousands of
soldiers, and his cab business would thrive. Mr. Reed, of
Jupiter Island, was a captain in the army now. Even the
rich white folks were joining up. That was different from
the Great War as the U.S. Army had relied on Woodrow
Wilson's draft.

The Florida East Coast Railroad's train rolled to a stop.
Henry Morrison Flagler's engineering triumph cost the
Burk family its livelihood in 1912, when the railroad
connected to Key West, and cheaper Cuban pineapples
began replacing the pineapples of Martin County with
imported Caribbean fruit. Pineapples were the reason that
Tom Burk's father had left the Bahamas to head for the
United States and settle in Martin County.

Two white men descended the train stair steps, one
middle-aged and the other in his twenties carrying a
briefcase. Both men sported fedoras. The fedora seemed to
be the most popular hat for white men this year.

The chauffeur with the cigarette stubbed his butt with a
heel, smiled, and said something softly to the younger man
in a phrase that sounded to Tom Burk like German. But he
didn't know what *Liebchen* meant. He thought the word
was German. He had heard enough German during the

Great War to remember a bit of the language. *Liebchen* might be German, but he had never heard that particular word. He shook off the thought, dismissing it as his mind flashing back to some irrelevant combat memory. He turned his attention to Spencer Tracy. The movie star was carrying an overcoat and a suitcase in one hand. His fedora was off and in his other hand.

Tom Burk tipped his black chauffeur's cap and introduced himself: "Mr. Tracy, I am Tom Burk. Mr. Barry hired me to drive you to his house."

The white man smiled. "Fine, Mr. Burk. Lead the way."

"May I take your bag, sir?" Tom asked.

"That won't be necessary, Mr. Burk. I'll carry it with me in the back seat."

"As you wish, sir."

The white man replaced his hat. "You can call me Spencer."

Tom Burk sensed that Spencer Tracy was a good man and he could chance being frank with him. Tom smiled. "No, sir I can't. This isn't California. This is Florida. This is Jim Crow's country."

The white man looked at Tom curiously. "Sorry, Mr. Burk. I forgot. Got to play by the Southern rules I guess."

'Yes, sir."

"Don't want to cause you any trouble, Mr. Burk."

"Thank you, sir."

"Seems damn silly to me," Tracy added.

Tom Burk didn't reply.

In the rearview mirror, Burk saw the white man's apologetic smile. Maybe he was a decent man, Tom reasoned, but there still was only so much that he would confide in a white man. Oh, there were one or two in Martin County he might trust, but that was about it. And that trust wasn't absolute; it was guarded.

On the drive to the island, the movie star asked Tom if he had ever seen his movies.

"No, sir," Tom replied.

"Why not, Mr. Burk?" Spencer Tracy grinned. "They aren't *all* bad."

Tom hoped the white man could see his smile in the rearview mirror. Here seemed to be a white man who didn't take himself too seriously. That was different. He was an odd one that was for sure.

"No, sir, I guess they all can't be bad or you wouldn't be here." Tom said.

Spencer Tracy laughed. "Very true, very true…Mr. Burk, they say this Jupiter Island is a pretty private place. Is that so?"

"Yes, sir."

"'Where the rich go to be rich together,'" Tracy said.

Tom Burk didn't let on that he knew the white man was quoting F. Scott Fitzgerald in *The Great Gatsby.*

"Yes, sir," Tom replied.

"I'm just here to see a lady, Mr. Burk. I heard what the Germans did the other night. Did you hear the explosions?"

"Just one, sir. But you could see the tanker burning out in the ocean. It lit up the sky,"

"They think the *Japs* may bomb California, Mr. Burk. They shelled an oil facility in Santa Barbara and have sunk a few ships off the coast. I guess we've got the Japs, and you've got the Nazis."

Tom said nothing. He nodded. Spencer Tracy quickly changed the subject back to women.

"She's a real little spitfire too, Mr. Burk. I think it's the red hair. You know red-haired women are all spitfires, Mr. Burk."

"I didn't know that, sir."

"I didn't either, Mr. Burk. I just made that up," he laughed. "But this one, this little filly, she is a spitfire, let me tell you."

"Yes, sir."

As they approached Gate House, Tom didn't see the red-haired lady. Only Melda May, an elderly colored lady who cleaned Mr. Barry's house was visible. She was busy sweeping the porch. He stopped the car on the crushed shell driveway.

"Looks like she stood me up, Mr. Burk."

"I don't know, sir, perhaps I can ask Mrs. May, the lady on the porch. She may know where the lady is."

"I'd appreciate that, Mr. Burk."

"Mrs. May?"

The old lady didn't respond.

"She's a bit hard of hearing," Tom explained. Then he raised his voice.

"Mrs. May," Tom said loudly when he was out of the driver's seat.

"Good day, Mr. Burk. Is that the actor fella you have with you?"

"It is."

"The lady said for Mr. Tracy to bring his bags into the house. She is playing tennis down at the Jupiter Island Club."

"I see."

"Take me to the Jupiter Island Club, Mr. Burk."

"Yes, sir. Let me take your bag in for you, though."

"Fine," said the actor, who remained in the back seat as Tom took his bag into the house. Mrs. May came over to the cab.

Spencer Tracy smiled. "You know who I am, Mrs. May?" He shouted.

"You don't have to shout at me, sir...I can hear close up."

"I'm sorry. Have you seen any of my pictures?"

"Ain't you the white man that kissed Scarlett on the bridge in *Gone with the Wind?*"

Spencer Tracy laughed. "I wish I was, Mrs. May. I wish I was."

"Only picture I've seen in the last five years."

Tracy smiled. Tom Burk returned and thanked Mrs. May. He drove on to the Jupiter Island Club.

"She thought I was Clark Gable, Mr. Burk. That's the first time anyone ever mistook me for Clark Gable."

"Uh huh." Tom knew who Clark Cable was from the movie posters, but he hadn't seen Gable's movies either. He also knew that Melda May thought all white men looked alike. He was not about to tell Spencer Tracy *that.*

"Looks like the folks around here have a lot of money," Spencer Tracy observed. "They always dress up like this?"

"Yes, sir."

"Sure isn't California."

"No, sir, it sure isn't," Tom agreed.

Tom knew the conservative dress code. Most of the men who sashayed around the Jupiter Island Club wore blazers, many without ties; but other men wore suits, and the women wore cotton print dresses with a hemline below the knee. He seemed incongruous to be in such clothing near the beach. And the white women in their modest, one-piece bathing suits were certain to add bathing caps when wading into the Atlantic Ocean.

There were a number of couples gathered around circular tables in wooden deck chairs with awnings unfurled should there be a hint of rain. Colored waiters in white jackets brought trays of iced-drinks to the chattering members of the upper class. The scene itself smelled of money, Fitzgerald might have written. Tom thought. The Jupiter Island Club smelled of money.

They drove down Beach Road. Tom swerved into the left lane to avoid hitting a couple riding a bicycle built for two. A man in a brown summer suit, who was out strolling, meandered onto the road and Tom navigated away from him. They passed the well-manicured golf course and a number of well-kept hedges which provided a barrier to keep snoopy souls from spying on one's neighbors. Finally, they pulled into the Jupiter Island Club.

"Here we are sir." Tom parked by the tennis courts where two women were volleying. The red-haired woman, whom Tom had transported the day before, was in a white tennis skirt with a matching white top. When she saw the actor exit the cab, she threw her racket into the air as if she had just won Wimbledon and went racing across the tennis court.

"Spencer darling, you came! You're here!" she shouted in a gravelly voice.

Spencer Tracy smiled wryly and said to Tom Burk, "She's recovering from a play. She is overly dramatic. Will this cover it, Mr. Burk?" He asked, handing Tom a fifty dollar bill.

"That's too much, sir. I can't make the change."

"Keep it. You made me laugh, Mr. Burk. It was worth it. They pay me much too much money in Hollywood, believe me." He didn't say another word for Katharine Hepburn flew into his arms, and his lips were busy elsewhere.

Chapter 3

After depositing the film actor for a close-up with his co-star, Tom Burk returned to the train station to await the next train and another fare to the island. He was in no hurry. He had fifty unexpected dollars in his pocket – two weeks wages-and he splurged with a nickel and bought a copy of the *Stuart News* to read the story of the submarine attacks. The article didn't declare that the submarines were German, but that was assumed. The Gulf Stream was a shipping lane for the Allies, and most of the cargo ships were headed to Great Britain, Germany's enemy.

Germany and Japan were winning the war. The Germans had invaded the Union of Soviet Socialist Republics; they controlled most of Europe, except for Britain, and the Japanese seemed unstoppable in the Pacific. Wake Island fell after a valiant defense. Guam was gone. The Philippines were near surrender. There was widespread paranoia on the West Coast, fear that the Japs would invade Hawaii, as well. American citizens of Japanese descent in California were being detained and herded into *relocation camps,* which Tom Burk considered a euphemism for concentration camps. Tom saw it for what it was: racism. During the Great War, German-Americans had experienced some discrimination. German names were changed. Heck, even the English royal family changed their German name of Saxe-Coburg and Gotha to the more English-sounding *Windsor.* In America, dachshunds became "liberty pups," sauerkraut became "liberty cabbage" and hamburger became "liberty sausage," but the white German-Americans were never rounded up *en masse* and put in *relocation* camps. They were white.

In the Great War-what everyone was now calling *World War I-it* looked like the Kaiser's German Army was unstoppable. But it wasn't. The Americans made the difference in 1918. The Meuse-Argonne Offensive proved that.

Meuse-Argonne: That's where Tom Burk was wounded. He caught a machine bullet in the leg, but continued to fight in the battle that day, ignoring the pain. To the French, he showed great *élan*, as the certificate stated. The French awarded him a medal for his valor. Tom Burk hadn't thought about the pain during the battle, he just didn't want to be let his men down. An officer had to set an example for his men. He'd been taught that in his training in Des Moines, Iowa. Tom Burk was one of 170 Negro soldiers who won the French Legion of Merit, for the colored soldiers in the United States Army were assigned to French divisions by John "Blackjack" Pershing. General Pershing was the commander of the AEF who, ironically, had earned the nickname, *Blackjack,* when he commanded a colored unit of Buffalo Soldiers in the West, as well as commanded a heroic colored unit in the Spanish

-American War unit which fought beside Teddy Roosevelt's Rough Riders at the Battle of San Juan Hill. T.R.'s heroic infantry charge up San Juan Hill on July 1, 1898, what he would call his "glorious hour," led the lieutenant colonel to the political summit of the United States: the White House

Tom would not have obtained officer status -no colored officer obtained a rank higher than captain-had it not been for W.E.B. Du Bois and the organization he founded: the National Association for the Advancement of Colored People.

The NAACP put pressure on the politicians. In regard to rank, the congressmen gave in, but the Southerners demanded that the colored troops be assigned to the French and not be allowed to fight side-by-side with white Americans. The French, who had recruited thousands of troops from their African colonies, were accustomed to working with colored soldiers and appreciative of the extra men. The colored American troops were more than welcome in the French army which recognized their bravery while the United States of America, did not.

Earlier in the week, when Tom Burk saw the pillar of fire in the sky emanating from the burning tanker off the coast, it reminded him of artillery explosions in the Meuse-Argonne: the flash of fire as a shell detonated on impact, sending dismembered body parts of unfortunate soldiers scattered into the air. On the night of the submarine attack Tom dreamt once again that he was in the Meuse-Argonne: a moonscape of bomb craters and a defoliated forest with shards of craggily timber, where once, straight and noble trees had lifted to the sky. The tattered woodland resembled daggers of driftwood which had been stuck vertically into the soil of a wounded Mother Earth. Broken bodies littered the ground: severed, lonely limbs, reaching forlornly for their non-existent bodies. Then the chlorine gas invaded his dream, and the choking gas felt so real he woke up in a cold sweat gagging and coughing. Thank God, Rachel had been there to hold him, to comfort him, to ease his nightmare. Rachel was his angel, his anchor. He was blessed to have her by his side.

Ten years after the Great War ended Tom Burk read Erich Maria Remarque's antiwar novel, *All Quiet on the Western Front.* He came to the scene where the author described a direct hit by an artillery round on a trench. Paul Baümer discovered the remains of his buddies to be nothing more than what he could scrape off the side of the trench with a spoon. Tom Burk knew that was not hyperbole; Remarque had been there. Remarque knew combat. Heck, Tom figured, the soldier in the Tomb of the Unknown Soldier was probably just a collection of body parts from the Meuse-Argonne. It wasn't a coincidence that led Hitler to order *All Quiet on the Western Front* to be burned with other pacifist books. Hitler had been a corporal in the war and had won an Iron Cross for heroism; he had been at the front, and he had been gassed. Hitler knew the accuracy of *All Quiet on the Western Front* and the power of its pacifistic message. The novel was a dangerous book to a man determined to lead his country once again into war.

Tom's mind drifted as he thought of Remarque's middle name, *Marie.* He remembered a more pleasant interlude of his time in France: his brief affair with a French widow, *Marie,* whose husband had been killed at the meat grinder known as the Battle of the Somme. He had met her at a café in Paris while on weekend pass. He spent the night with her, challenging his own axiom on white women: "Once you go white, nothing goes right." And nothing had. Maria died of the Spanish Flu in 1918, one of millions of victims around the world who succumbed to the deadly virus during and after the war. The pandemic of influenza killed more people than all the machine guns in the Great War had slaughtered.

He shook away the images of the Great War and tried to concentrate on the newspaper story of this new war. He often regretted that he and his wife returned to Florida after the Armistice. Rachel Burk had a good job in New York City, where she lived during the Great War, raising their son while Tom Burk was overseas with the army. But when Tom Burk returned from overseas, she begged him to return to Florida so she could be near her mother, who wanted to help Rachel raise her first grandchild. After confessing his infidelity with a white woman and seeking forgiveness by an understanding wife, Tom gave up his dreams of a career as a businessman in Harlem. The little family returned to Martin County before the Florida land boom. Tom had also toyed with the idea of writing a book about his combat experience in the conflict and Harlem seemed to be a center for creativity after the war. Yet he acquiesced to his wife's wishes due to his own guilt feelings. It was his penance for his infidelity. Besides, there was a rumor that Hobe Sound was to be "Picture City" and movies would become a big business for the area. Unfortunately, the mosquitoes, no-see-ums and sand flies, among other pests, chased the movie men to California, where the weather was more predictable and the insects less annoying. Hobe Sound might have been *Hollywood* save for the insects.

Then the hurricanes of the 1920s killed the Florida land boom, and the Sunshine State got a head start on the Depression. Tom Burk and his family struggled through the late 1920s. Zora Hurston had written a great book about the hurricane and its victims from the Lake Okeechobee flood. Tom Burk made extra money after the catastrophe, burying the corpses from the hurricane and the subsequent flood that Hurston wrote about in her novel. What was the novel's name? C'mon, Tom, he told himself. Why can't you remember that? You aren't even fifty. But he knew he looked older than fifty; the Great War had aged him, as it had many men. Many veterans felt like they were on borrowed time, that they shouldn't have survived when so

many others were in eternal rest in Flanders fields. He
recited John Mc Crae's poem in his mind.

In Flanders fields the poppies blow
Between the crosses, row on row,
That mark our place; and in the sky
The larks, still bravely singing, fly
Scarce heard amid the guns below.

We are the Dead. Short days ago
We lived, felt dawn, saw sunset glow,
Loved and were loved, and now we lie
In Flanders fields.

Take up our quarrel with the foe:
To you from failing hands we throw
The torch; be yours to hold it high.
If ye break faith with us who die
We shall not sleep, though poppies grow
In Flanders fields.

He had committed that poem to memory in honor of his
fallen comrades, even though they were interred in the
Meuse-Argonne Cemetery and Memorial and other
cemeteries. Had he broken faith with the Dead?

Tom Burk sometimes felt that he had. He felt guilty;
guilty for being alive. And when the guilt overcame him, he
drank. Sometimes he drank too much. For many folks,
Tom Burk, wizened by war, seemed elderly, and he had
acquired the sobriquet, *Old Tom Burk*. The nickname stuck.
Their Eyes Were Watching God, he smiled, finally recalling
the name of Hurston's book. Old man, he told himself. Just
an old man. Some days, he still felt frisky, and Rachel
could attest to that. He smiled, remembering the night

before and the satisfied look on his wife's face. I'm not dead yet, he mused. Nor was Hobe Sound.

Ironically, with Mr. Barstow's purchase of some land west of the island and Mr. Joseph Reed's development of Jupiter Island and the erection of the Banner Lake community, the area began to make a comeback after the Florida land boom fizzle, at least in *the season*. But now, with Camp Murphy about to open, things would finally pick up. Or so Tom Burk hoped. He lived in *Hope* Sound, he liked to say, but the town was actually named after the tribe of native Americans, the Hobe Indians, who were long gone thanks to the white man. Had to hand it to the white man, Tom mused. They knew how to get rid people who weren't white. Maybe somewhere a few white folks might be upset with what Hitler was doing to the Jews, but white Americans did similar things to the Indians, as well as enslaving the colored people. Same white folks who felt like Hitler was a monster probably had an ancestor who killed an Indian or two or owned a slave. From the white man's viewpoint, the Indians were as racially inferior as the Jews were to the Nazis, but neither group, Indians or Jews, was as trainable as the coloreds. Death or a life of slavery? Wasn't much of a choice for a man who wasn't white.

Tom conceded he would be 50 in April, no matter how much he preferred denial. He saw the reflection of a withered-looking face in the mirror in the morning. His face resembled a hide of tan wrinkled leather, but then he had looked 'old' since the Great War. He had seen enough on the battlefields to age a man's face and his heart, but he knew he was actually in good physical shape and unlike some of the redneck crackers, Tom Burk could easily pass an army physical, even at his age. He even had all of his original teeth. He smiled at the thought.

Tom's experience in the Great War had led to his friendship with William Slocum Barstow, a part-time Jupiter Island resident, who was a multi-millionaire inventor. Barstow developed the electric meter and had worked with the late Thomas Edison. When Barstow learned about Tom Burk's heroic service in the war, it reminded him of his only son, Frederic Barstow, who served overseas as well, but whose health had been ruined by the conflict, leading to Frederic's premature death in 1931. Mr. Barstow and his wife even funded a school in Vermont in memory of their son. Mr. Barstow sprouted a large handlebar mustache that Tom thought helped the old man cover the sorrow of etched on his face. A generous man, Mr. Barstow had been the major source of Tom Burk's books for the last few years, providing a number of volumes for the wooden bookshelves of the little library which Tom maintained in his home. Tom often wondered if it was this bond of the first war that led Barstow to buy the land which would later be turned into Banner Lake for the colored servants who worked for the Jupiter Islanders. Barstow was appalled at the lack of adequate housing for the colored servants in segregated Martin County and wanted to give the servants a chance to own their own property.

Tom often drove Mr. Barstow to and from the railway station and his winter home on Jupiter Island. On these cab rides, Tom had conversations with a white man in which he was respected and treated as an equal. On one such occasion, Tom asked Barstow about Edison, and the millionaire electrical engineer replied that the *Wizard of Menlo Park* was superstitious; one time turning his hands over in a photo opportunity for magazine editor Hugo Gernsback for fear that the fortune tellers might read his palms if Gernsback's photo of Edison's hands appeared in the magazine. Mr. Barstow had known Edison until

Edison's death and had spent time with Edison in Fort Myers, Florida at Edison's winter quarters. On a Florida visit, Barstow arrived at the idea of his own winter home in the Sunshine State. While Barstow was a positive presence in Tom's life, he was not the only salutary influence.

Tom's Christian faith kept him strong along with his Christian partner, Rachel, his wife since 1916. Rachel had assumed they would have a dozen children, but the Good Lord had only given them two: Thomas, Jr., named for his father, and Phillis Wheatley Burk, a daughter named for the famous colonial poet. Unlike her father, Phillis Burk left Florida for the friendlier streets of Harlem in 1940. Thankfully, Rachel hadn't tried to stop her daughter from leaving for Tom had encouraged her to move to New York. He had told too many stories of the wonders of Harlem to his impressionable little girl; she could hardly wait to grow up and leave Florida. He missed her though, for he had been close to his beloved daughter. He cherished her letters, epistles which had grown less frequent over the past year. Rachel sensed their daughter was in love and that another man had replaced her daddy in her affections. Tom, like many a father before him, felt crushed to be relegated to second place by the apple of his eye. But yesterday, after a long silence from Rachel, Tom Burk finally received a letter, which he kept in his pocket unopened, waiting for an appropriate moment during his day when he could be alone with his daughter's words. With a break between train arrivals, Tom was finally able to be alone with his daughter's letter.

Dearest Papa:

I know I have been remiss in my correspondence and I beg your forgiveness. Recently, I met an older gentleman who said he knew you in the Great War. I met him in a restaurant in Harlem. His name is Eugene

Bullard, but he prefers to be called Gene. He is pretty old, probably near fifty, but he said he met you in Paris in 1918. He claimed that he was a combat pilot during the war, but I never heard of a Negro pilot in that war. I thought the Tuskegee airmen were the first colored pilots. Anyway, when he found out my last name was Burk he asked if I was any relation to a man named Tom Burk and I said that I was his daughter. Well, his eyes lit up and he asked me if I might add a note from him to you in my next letter, which I thought was odd, but since he seemed to know you-he mentioned your wound and your medals and the Meuse Argonne and I remembered those things as you had told me those stories when I was a little girl. He wanted me to add a note from him to you and he agreed to pay the additional postage as he seems to be a bit wordy. It is quite a lengthy "note."

Love, Phillis.

Good Lord! Tom thought. Gene Bullard. What was he doing in New York? He stayed in Paris when the war ended. Opened a club. Tom had heard stories about his nightclub. Bullard entertained Hemingway, Fitzgerald, dancer Josephine Baker. He was surprised that Bullard remembered him from all those years before.

Dear Tom:

I met your charming daughter in a restaurant in Harlem recently where I was dining with my own two daughters as my oldest daughter knows your daughter Phillis. Just a chance meeting. Your daughter was there with a handsome well-dressed young man, but I suppose you already have met her beau.

Tom smiled- so, Rachel knew Phillis had a boyfriend, but his wife had been trying to break it to him gently.

My daughters and I had a good life in Paris until the Nazis arrived in 1940. France was everything my father had said it would be; a place where men are judged on merit and not on skin color. I believe I told you that my father had been nearly lynched in Georgia in 1902 and after that incident my father kept encouraging me to go to France when I was older. I don't believe I told you that I was only twelve years old when I stowed away on a ship bound for Scotland. I did a lot of odd jobs in Glasgow and trained to be a prize fighter, working my weight up from bantam weight to lightweight. I was trained by a well-known boxer named Dixie Kid. With a better diet and better training I soon became a welterweight. It was boxing that finally allowed me to make it to France when I was 18 in 1913. I knew as soon as I stepped foot in France that it was the place for me. I learned French and German as well and the chance to live in France was a fulfillment of my father's dream for me. I also served as interpreter for the English boxers when they were in France. It seems to me that the French democracy influenced the minds of both white and black Americans in Paris and helped us all to act like brothers as near as possible. It convinced me too that God really did create all men equal, and it was easy to live that way.

When the Great War started in 1914, I had to wait until my 19th birthday in October to join the army. I joined the French Foreign Legion and after only five weeks of training I joined the Moroccan Division, an outfit that contained 54 nationalities. I remember talking to you about the meat grinder of the Somme and I remember your stories of the Meuse Argonne. I think we were very lucky to have survived the war, especially considering all the bullets they took out of us. I never mentioned Verdun but in 1916 at Verdun I was severely wounded and while in hospital the doctors said I would never walk again and that even if I did

*I was unfit for the infantry, but my military record was
decent enough that I was given the opportunity to join the
French Flying Corp. An American friend, who shall
remain nameless, bet me two thousand dollars that I could
not become a pilot. Honestly, that was quite an incentive.
I won my wings and collected the bet.*

*After a few holdups, I was finally assigned to the now
famous Lafayette Escadrille. I was treated with respect and
friendship even by those pilots from America. Then I knew
at last that there are good and bad white men just as there
are good and bad black men. I think you remember the
Spads. That was the plane I flew. I painted a red bleeding
heart pierced by a knife on the fuselage of my plane. I also
put on an inscription in French "Tout le Sang qui coule est
rouge" which means roughly- "All Blood Runs Red."*

*When the United States entered the war, I wanted to
transfer to the U.S. Army's air corps but they wouldn't take
me. They ignored me, because I was a Negro. So when I
was discharged from the armed forces of France in
October, 1919 I decided to remain in Paris. I wound up
marrying the daughter of a French countess. The French
considered me a war hero, but my home country considered
me a second class citizen. Staying in France was an easy
choice. The marriage failed, but since we were both
Catholics we never divorced. I had three children, but my
son died soon after he was born from complications of
pneumonia. My wife died six years after we separated and
I raised my daughters. My nightclub was called Le Grand
Duc and I was the host and part owner. I even entertained
the Prince of Wales one evening. When this second war
broke out in 1939, I joined the French underground and
resistance movement. Spying for France was natural for
me. However, when the Nazis entered Paris I was a man
wanted by the Gestapo and I fled the city with my
daughters. In Orleans, I was badly wounded, but my*

*woman resistance partner patched me up and smuggled my
daughters and me into Spain. From Spain we came to New
York where I now run an elevator in Rockefeller Center.
Makes me laugh. I ran a nightclub in Paris and now I run
an elevator.*

*I would love to hear from you, Tom, whenever you
get the time to write. Your daughter told me your only son
is in training out West. May God bless him and keep him
safe.*

Gene.

And then Eugene Bullard posted his New York City
address on East 116th Street in The heart of Harlem.

Eugene Bullard, Tom thought. "The Black Swallow of
Death." The world's first colored combat pilot. He had
met him by chance at a Paris café when he was staying with
Maria. It was Maria who had first met Eugene Bullard and
introduced the two countrymen to each other. She had
known Bullard from the early days of the war when she had
worked as a nurse in a military hospital. Tom felt he owed
it to Eugene Bullard to tell him about Maria's death, but
Tom realized that Bullard probably knew about Maria's
demise.

Tom managed two more fares to the island before
calling it a day. He stopped by a florist in the colored part
of Hobe Sound and bought some daisies for his wife. He
didn't often have extra money for such luxuries, but today,
Tom Burk had a fifty dollar bill burning a proverbial hole
in his pocket. He would buy Rachel flowers and use the
extra money to buy tires for his car for he heard a rumor
that rubber would soon be rationed and gasoline would be
restricted, as well. He had already begun filling gas cans
for the day that gasoline was rationed. Of course, he had a

feeling people who lived on Jupiter Island or worked for the rich white folks, might be exempt from gas rationing, but he wasn't certain. This war seemed different from his war.

Rachel had a day off from her employer and, as always, when she was off, she concentrated on cleaning the house. A person could eat off the carpet in the three-bedroom, Dade Pine, framed structure.

Rachel, in apron, was indeed tidying up the house when Tom Burk arrived home: dusting with a feather duster. Lord, he knew she liked to dust, to neaten things up, and to "straighten up the nest," as she often referred to her household routines. Tom was not allowed to help. He was assigned responsibility for the outside: the garage and the yard. He looked at his rotund wife. There was certainly more of Rachel than the day he married her, he mused with a smile. She was quite a bit wider than she had been on their wedding day, but he wasn't fool enough to say that to her. She nibbled on too much rich food on the island, he thought, wishing that his wife still had the shape she had at twenty. Then he smiled: Maybe she wished the same about him. Although he hadn't gained weight, as she had, his age showed in his leathery face.

By comparison, Rachel's visage remained younger than her years. Tom attributed her youthful face to her attitude; Rachel was the most upbeat person he had ever known. She rarely had a negative thing to say about anything, or anyone. She thanked God every morning and again every night. She began the day with a reading from the *Holy Bible*. It was Rachel who had led Tom Burk to Jesus, and Rachel's Christian happiness seemed to resonate on her face; her smile was a testament to salvation. It was Rachel who listened to his horrible memories of the war, weeping for him, asking God to help take her husband's pain away.

The memories weren't gone, but they had become
manageable. Rachel had saved her husband's life, but
more importantly, from her point of view: his soul.

Even with Rachel's help, the nightmares hadn't ended,
but one night they seemed to lessen in intensity. The
change was sudden and welcome, and although he still saw
Germans in his sleep and on occasion, like the night of the
submarine attack, the dreams seldom reverted to nightmare
proportions. But now Tom could cope with the memories,
thanks to the intercession of his wife and to what Tom
attributed to be the Holy Spirit. Faith, Rachel reminded
him, had been the way the colored people had survived
slavery. Rachel was the descendant of a slave from
Georgia, a woman she knew only as her great grandmother.
So when Tom had a true nightmare of the war and cried out
in anguish, Rachel, as she had the night of the submarine
attack, was always there to wake him from his sleep and
comfort him until the images dissipated. Tom Burk
realized that he would be lost without Rachel. He owed her
everything. If she had wanted to move to the moon, he
would have gone along with her. He realized he had more
with her than he would ever have had alone in Harlem.

He sat at a checkerboard-covered kitchen table as
Rachel served him a plate of biscuits and gravy. She sat
down across from him and asked about his day.

He wondered for a moment if he should hide the fifty
dollar tip from her, but he was a lousy liar and Rachel
would catch any deception in his voice. He was glad that
he hadn't been like other men and strayed from his wife
after he returned from France. Part of that was fear, fear
that she would cut off his manhood if he put it in the wrong
place, again. She had forgiven him for his infidelity with
the French white woman. A white woman was no threat to
Rachel. Had he broken his marriage vow with a colored

woman, he might be singing soprano in the church choir. He smiled at the realization that he could fear his sweet wife more than the memories of the Meuse-Argonne.

"I got a fifty dollar tip," he confessed. It hadn't taken two minutes for his confession. Confession was good for the soul, but lousy on the wallet.

Her eyes lit up. "Let me see," she said.

He hesitated. He knew if he gave her the bill, he would never see it again.

"Let's see it," she persisted, her hand outstretched.

He resigned himself to his fate and took the fifty dollar bill out of his pocket. He held it up, looked at it and said, "Goodbye, President Grant. It was nice to meet you." Then he handed his wife the fifty dollar bill. It was a sudden transfer of wealth.

"Praise, Jesus!" she said as she examined the bill. He wondered if she was going to bite into it to see if it were real.

Tom Burk smiled. The fifty was long gone. Tom guessed Rachel was already planning what to do with it. He knew she would tithe five dollars to the church. Some would go to her useless sister who had three children by three different men. Tom would never see a dime. He smiled. He would have to get some new tires another way.

The money snapped safely into a small change purse, Rachel suddenly switched the subject "Tom, who is Henry Morgenthau?"

"He is the Secretary of the Treasury, Rachel. He is one of the president's top advisors. Why do you ask?"

"Is he a Jew?"

"I believe he is…why?"

"There were quite a few people at dinner the other night that seemed to hate him. Is it because he is a Jew?"

"I would imagine so."

"The white folk can be so strange, Tom."

"God's truth, Rachel. God's truth."

"Aren't Jews white people, too?"

"Pretty much. For the most part anyway."

"I don't understand white people, Tom."

"I know what you mean."

He listened as his wife told him of a dinner the previous evening where her employer declared to his guests that Hitler was doing a good thing ridding Germany of the Jews. Most of the people at the dinner party had agreed with the very rich white man; a man whose daddy had made millions by insider trading in the stock market and enslaving poor immigrants with starvation wages in his factories, forcing them to work twelve hour days, six days a week. As far as Tom Burk knew, the son and heir had never had to work a day in his life. He was the beneficiary of a lucky birth. Many of the residents of the island, unlike the self-made William Barstow, had been born into wealthy families.

Jews, Tom thought. Was God telling him something? But what was He saying? Tom had had too many revelations of a spiritual nature not to believe that Rachel might unconsciously be giving him a message from God.

He had these revelations since the day he heard a voice in the Meuse-Argonne, tell him that everything was going to be fine, as he initially writhed in pain from his wound. Suddenly, he could stand the pain. That voice; such a soothing voice. But no one had been near him. Tom didn't become a Christian that day; his acceptance of Jesus Christ as his Savior would take Rachel's missionary work, but the seed had been planted by that voice in the Meuse-Argonne in 1918. After he studied the Bible, Tom Burk came to believe he had been visited on the battlefield by the Holy Spirit.

Later that afternoon, Tom Burk sat in the front seat of his car rereading Hurston's *Their Eyes were Watching God,* as he awaited the arrival of the train from New York City. Most of the people on the train would be headed for Palm Beach or Miami, but one passenger, Mr. Harriman, would be getting off at Hobe Sound for a cab ride to Jupiter Island. He was the younger brother of Mr. Averell Harriman, a man whom Tom often drove from the Hobe Sound station. He had met the younger brother, E. Roland Harriman, the previous year when the two Harriman brothers arrived together on the train. Tom knew Harriman's close friends called the younger brother, *Bunny,* but Tom had no idea why. The senior Mr. Harriman was a diplomat who was overseas on behalf of the president, and the younger brother, a businessman, was going to use the Jupiter Island house for a few days for a short vacation. Tom Burk hadn't expected *Bunny* to have company, but two men arrived on the train.

E. Roland Harriman was wearing his customary dark blue business suit. He was accompanied by a taller man, similarly dressed, who seemed to stagger as he walked as if he were intoxicated. As the stranger drew closer, Tom Burk could smell the alcohol emanating from the taller man's body. He seemed to reek from his pores, and a whiff of the man's malodorous condition nearly knocked the cabdriver over, reminding Tom Burk of his own terrible drinking days shortly after the Great War concluded.

Tom Burk opened the rear seat door for the two men and placed their suitcases in the trunk. "Hold on a second, Bunny. Gotta mail a letter," the taller man said and walked to a nearby mailbox, deposited an envelope and then deposited himself into the sedan.

"Morgenthau did us in, Bunny," the taller man explained to Mr. Harriman. "So I wrote him a letter. Didn't sign my name though…" Tom Burk noticed the dazed look of the glassy eyes in his rearview mirror. Why were they talking about Morgenthau? Tom wondered. Was it *Henry* Morgenthau? The man Rachel asked him about? That was a coincidence and didn't Rachel always say: "a coincidence was the Good Lord's way of getting our attention." What were the chances of hearing Henry Morgenthau's name twice? Maybe it was a different Morgenthau, he thought.

"Are you sure you didn't sign it? That was a dumb thing to do. You are drunk aren't you?"

"So? What of it? Henry Morgenthau closed down the company, Bunny, the damn socialist and his Social Security system…"

Tom Burk's ears lit up. *Henry* Morgenthau? That name again. What was going on? He listened closer to the conversation. God was sending him a message…but what was He saying? Was He speaking through a drunk? *God moves in mysterious ways, His wonders to perform. He plants his footsteps in the sea and rides upon the storm.*

Tom thought, remembering the opening of a William Cowper poem. Why not a drunk then?

"You had too many in the bar car, Preston. It was only one company. We are doing well with the others. So you go and send him a letter?"

"Damn Jew. I didn't sign the damn letter, Bunny. Christ!"

"I hope not…okay, he pissed me off, too. But Christ, Preston, that was really dumb to write him a letter. That's all I am going to say…There's a goddamn war on. Oh fuck it. Let's forget about it and have a good time."

"Good idea. Well, at least it's good to be away from the wife and my father-in-law."

"Daddy Warbucks," Mr. Harriman chuckled. "Your father-in-law reminds me of the cartoon character from *Little Orphan Annie,* Preston. Your wife is a sweetheart. You married *up,* Preston, and sometimes when you are shit-faced, you seem to resent it. Why does Papa stick in your craw?"

"He's a pain in the ass."

"Look, Preston. He made you rich. Don't knock it. Didn't hurt with Skull & Bones either; that he liked you before you ever married his daughter. Preston, my dad made me rich. Nothing I did. I was just a member of the lucky sperm club."

"My head is hurting, Bunny."

"I wonder why. Does it feel as bad as Geronimo's?"

"The skull?"

"You got that when you were stationed at Fort Sill, right?"

"Yeah. Best 'crook' at Skull & Bones." Somehow, the taller man seemed to be sobering up, Tom Burk thought, but he never expected him to begin to sing. "We're poor little lambs, who have lost our way…"

"Baa baa baa," Harriman chimed in, a bit off key.

"We're little black sheep who have gone astray…" the taller man continued.

"Baa baa baa," Mr. Harriman sang and then they both sang:

"Gentlemen songsters off on a spree, doomed from here to eternity,

Lord have mercy on such as we. Baa baa baa."

"God, Bunny, I miss those days, sometimes….Will we beat Harvard this year? Lost the last two."

'There is talk about canceling the game, Preston."

"Why, for heaven's sake?"

"The war."

"Hell, Bunny, football builds character. Makes better soldiers. You know my boy is talking about going in the service when he graduates from boarding school in June. Wants to be a flyer. Navy… off carriers for heaven's sake. Averell is Roosevelt's pal; he can do something about my boy. He's only 17. I'd like to see him go to Yale first. Put in a word with Averill for me, will you, Bunny."

"Let the boy grow up, Preston. This is his war. You had yours. It's his rite of passage. Let him have it."

"His mother doesn't want him to sign up."

"She's a mother, that's understandable. He can go to Yale when the war is over. I still regret I wound up with pneumonia in the first one and was discharged."

"That's not your fault, Bunny. Averell didn't put on a uniform. He made a tidy profit with those ships. War may be hell, as Sherman said, but war is also hellishly good for business...if that damn pipsqueak Senator Truman doesn't fuck things up. We were in the last war for less than two years. How long do you think it will take this time?"

"I don't have any idea, Bunny. You know, at Yale they still believe that whopper I told during the first war."

Harriman laughed. "Oh, the one about how you saved Pershing, Foch and the Limey Sir Douglas Haig by deflecting artillery shell with a bolo knife?"

"My mother wrote an apology letter to the newspaper after the paper ran the story," the taller man replied.

"They still believe your story in Connecticut."

"Not my fault. I wasn't a hero, that's for sure."

"Now, Preston, our cab driver actually *did* win the Croix de Guerre from the French. Isn't that true, Tom?"

Tom Burk didn't want to answer. But he knew he had to. He said softly: "Yes sir, Mr. Harriman."

"Well, I'll be," the stranger said. "A colored boy. I didn't think we had colored troops fighting in the AEF. What was your division, boy?"

Tom Burk hated the word "boy," but he offered his fake smile and replied: "I was assigned to the French army, sir."

"A colored boy. Well, I'll be."

Tom Burk turned into a driveway lined on either side by a protective hedge which provided privacy for the wealthy Harriman family.

"Here we are, Preston," Harriman said to his companion, who still seemed to be struggling with the fact that a colored man had been more courageous than he in the Great War. His own "heroism" had only been one of his trademark practical jokes which he referred to as "fooling" and he seemed a bit embarrassed that he had run into a genuine hero in the colored man who carried his suitcase into the Harriman cottage.'

Tom Burk sensed the taller man's discomfort, and this time his smile was genuine.

Chapter 4

Wolfram Hess, in a charcoal grey chauffeur's uniform, stood ramrod straight on the Hobe Sound railway station platform awaiting the arrival of his American contact. He relaxed his stiff posture to light a cigarette, and out of the corner of an eye, he noticed an African man looking at him curiously. He looked away and then back in the direction of the African, but the African wasn't looking at him any longer. Why had the African looked at him, he wondered? Wolfram thought his disguise had made him appear to be an American. He had tried diligently to follow the instructions and dress appropriately. Maybe all these American *niggers,* as his American friend called them, looked at white men with curiosity, wondering what it was like to be a member of a superior group, the Aryan race. Poor mongrel breed, he mused. Why didn't the Americans do something with the Africans like the Führer had done with the Jewish filth? His eyes scanned the headline of a newspaper on a newsstand rack.

He smiled momentarily when he read the headline about the submarine attack the night he arrived via submarine. The attack had worked as a diversion so Wolfram Hess could come ashore on Jupiter Island, undetected. Sinking the Allied ships had been a bonus; the submarine captain would certainly be pleased about that. The explosions to the north had caused any wandering eyes looking out at the ocean to rivet to the burning ships.

Because of the diversion, an unseen Wolfram Hess paddled a rubber boat to shore, deflated the craft and carried it with him as he crossed the dune line on the island. The hand-drawn map he carried was precise and accurate, and with the help of the moonlight and his military training in night vision, he could read the map and quickly find the Jupiter Island house. The house key was just where he was told it would be, as well as fresh clothes, including a chauffeur's uniform and a train schedule on a table in the foyer to the living room. The shoes were the correct size, as was an additional blue suit which hung in a closet. He smiled for the color of the suit matched his eyes. It was a typically thoughtful gesture of the man he loved.

Three years before on spring holiday from Yale, Wolfram stayed at the house on Jupiter Island and he remembered the dwelling. But so much had transpired in those three years. Too much. The passenger he anxiously awaited at the railway station owned the house or, rather, his parents did. The passenger he awaited was his lover, as well as his contact for the upcoming mission.

A good night's sleep calmed him after his long journey the night he came ashore. He hadn't slept in a comfortable bed in weeks, not on *das Boot*. *Think in English, Wolfram*, he corrected his thought. *Das Boot: the boat in English. Think in English or you might slip up and reveal yourself,* he told himself again.

His uncle, Rudolf Hess, had once been Deputy Führer of the Third Reich, second only to Adolf Hitler until Uncle Rudolf took it upon himself to fly to England and when he was over the island, he parachuted into the enemy's homeland in an effort to end the war with England. After all, England, like Germany, was an Aryan nation. It made no sense to Uncle Rudolf that Aryans should be fighting and killing each other when Jews and Communists were the real threat. Unfortunately Uncle Rudolf was captured and imprisoned by the English and the Hess family was disgraced.

Wolfram was in America to atone for his uncle's foolish misjudgment. He was going to kill Franklin Roosevelt's most important Jewish advisor. He was set on redeeming the family's honor or die trying. He was going to kill Henry Morgenthau, Jr., the Secretary of the Treasury of the United States of America.

Wolfram thought he knew America. He had spent two years before the war studying at Yale, but didn't return for the fall semester in 1939 after the vermin Poles attacked a Deutschland radio station forcing the Führer to declare war on Poland. *Germany, not Deutschland, Wolfram, Germany*, he told himself. *Think in English.*

At Yale, he met a number of Americans, most of whom were good Aryan stock, and it genuinely surprised Wolfram when the Führer declared war on America after the Japanese attacked Pearl Harbor. Wolfram never understood how the Fatherland would be allied with the racially inferior Japanese. It seemed to be a flaw in the racial superiority theory. But he was reluctant to doubt the Führer's decision. Doubting would only get him into trouble.

Still, the Americans hadn't declared war on Germany. In fact, from what Wolfram had gleaned, it was possible that had the Führer not declared war on the United States, America would have never joined the war against Germany. But America was forced to in reply to Hitler's declaration. Sometimes, Wolfram wondered if Uncle Rudolf had been so stupid after all. Nonetheless Uncle Rudolf still disgraced the family name by failing to commit suicide when he was captured.

During his matriculation at Yale, Wolfram became the best of friends with a classmate, a Nordic boy of German heritage who had been a member of the pre-war German American Bund and who spoke fluent German. Wolfram didn't even allow his mind to think of Hans' surname, as he was afraid that if he were captured, he might divulge his contact. It was Hans' family's winter vacation home where he was hiding out on the island, and it was Hans whom he awaited at the train station while masquerading as a chauffeur.

Wolfram had missed Hans in the time they had been apart. The nights in Hans' college dormitory room were filled with a passion he had never been able to replicate. Hans was his first lover, and he had been Wolfram's best. Oh, the S.S officer Lutz had been delicious, but it was only physical with Lutz; he had only been attracted to Lutz because of his ring with the skull and crossbones. Lutz reminded Wolfram of Hans and his insignia for Skull & Bones secret society at Yale. The night he paddled ashore and entered the house, Wolfram turned on a light in the living room and looked at Hans' family photos. Hans had spent a summer in a German American Bund camp, Camp Siegfried, in Yaphank on Long Island. It was at this Bund camp for boys that Wolfram first met Hans. As it turned out, both of them were headed to Yale University the following fall as freshmen. Two young Nazis.

While they were at Yale, the pair kept their Bund activities secret, although when they were sophomores they did travel together to Madison Square Garden for George Washington's birthday celebration hosted by the German-American Bund. They heard Bund leader, Fritz Kuhn, referred to Roosevelt's New Deal as the "Jew Deal." Nearly twenty-thousand Bund members in attendance applauded Herr Kuhn. The boys hadn't participated in the beating of the few anti-Nazi protestors who showed up, but they eagerly cheered the muggings along with most of the crowd. That night, aroused by the Bund rally, the beatings, and the invigorating shouts of *"Heil Hitler,"* the two boys began their physical relationship in a Manhattan hotel room, exploring each other's bodies. For Wolfram, it was a revelation. Hans' pale, milky skin had aroused Wolfram. It had been the best night of Wolfram's life.

After the Madison Square Garden rally, the Jew, Morgenthau, would have his revenge: Bund Leader Fritz Kuhn was convicted on phony charges of embezzlement of party funds. The boys were certain that the Jews, led by the "Top Yid" Morgenthau, had invoked revenge for the Madison Square Garden Rally. Certainly, Herr Kuhn was above reproach.

Wolfram walked upstairs to his lover's bedroom. He quickly remembered which room it was. He flicked on the light switch. There was a framed cartoon of the comic strip *Smiling Jack* signed by a cartoonist named Zack Mosley. Wolfram remembered that Hans loved that comic strip, for Hans read it to him daily at Yale. The cartoonist was someone Hans knew in Florida. Hans had read the comic strip, *Smiling Jack,* since he was a boy. There was also a Yale pennant in his lover's room as well as the skull and crossbones insignia of the secret Skull & Bones society and a robe for the fraternity's hush-hush ceremonies. It was believed that Skull & Bones had started at a German university.

Among the other items in Hans bedroom was a Yale yearbook; Hans was the Class of 1941. Next to the Skull & Bones insignia was a miniature ceramic skull. Hans told him it was a replica of the real skull of Apache Indian chief Geronimo, an artifact at the Skull and Bones society at Yale. Near the ceramic skull was, incongruously, a

baseball glove. Hans had played baseball for the Yale team
and he had been very adept at fielding.

Wolfram sat on the bed, leaned over, and sniffed the
bedspread. He felt like a hound dog. He smelled Hans.
Or thought he did. Images of what they had done in that
bedroom flooded back to him. He shook them off
momentarily, lest he become aroused. A poster on the wall
was a photograph of the Madison Square Garden Bund
rally in February 1939. Wolfram smiled wistfully, his
mind filled with images of that memorable evening at the
hotel and his first intimacy with Hans. They had been so
clumsy; two virgins fumbling together. Looking at the
poster, he remembered the background banner on the stage:
an enormous portrait of George Washington in his
Revolutionary War uniform. Herr Hitler, to Wolfram, was
Germany's answer to George Washington.

With the American entry into the war with Germany,
the German American Bund was outlawed by the United
States government, although some members felt a greater
allegiance to Germany than to the U.S. Wolfram realized
that the real reason he was so disturbed with the Führer's
declaration of war against the United States was personal.
For Wolfram, war with the United States would make visits
with Hans difficult, if not impossible, unless he could find a
way.

Before America's entry into the war, Wolfram learned
Hans had been working undercover for the Nazi regime
since 1940, and to Wolfram's surprise and relief, American
entry into the war didn't change Hans' allegiance. Like
most Americans, Hans thought Jews were dishonest and
greedy. Hitler's policies toward the vermin appealed to
Hans as it did to Wolfram. The Führer was right when he
said that America was a mongrel nation. Putting a Jew in
charge of the nation's money as Secretary of the Treasury?

That was too much for Hans to take. It was a threat to his class, the rich of America.

Hans corresponded with Wolfram through 1940. When Wolfram was granted leave after the quick German victory in Poland, and before returning to his unit for the spring offensive in Western Europe in 1940, Hans sailed to Spain to meet him for a holiday. It was in neutral Spain where Wolfram learned the depth of Hans' loyalties to the Third Reich. Hans, not Wolfram, dreamed up the idea of killing Henry Morgenthau, Roosevelt's trusted Jewish advisor. Hans instructed Wolfram to return to Germany with the idea and deliver it to Wilhelm Canaris, the head of the *Abwehr,* the German espionage service. Wolfram, whose uncle Rudolf had been a friend of the espionage chief, was able to obtain an audience with the spy master and propose the assassination. It was a plan that would appeal to Hitler, and Canaris knew it. Killing Roosevelt's top Jew advisor: it was a wonderful concept, Canaris told Wolfram.

Canaris took credit for the assassination idea and ran it up the chain of command. Hitler loved the idea and, after the fall of France, Wolfram was reassigned from his infantry unit and recruited to be an *Abwehr* agent. Wolfram was delighted to leave the infantry and overjoyed to accept the mission. Wolfram told Canaris that he *would* redeem the family name, but at the time, if he were truly honest with himself, Wolfram really only wanted the chance of getting to see Hans again. He was perfectly willing to let Canaris take credit for his idea in exchange for a trip across the Atlantic Ocean to kill Morgenthau and see Hans. To have sex with Hans again was worth a dangerous trip across the Atlantic by submarine.

The train slowed at the Hobe Sound station, and Wolfram stubbed out his cigarette with heel of his shoe. Two men emerged down the stairway steps of a railroad car. One was young and handsome, the other, middle-aged and rumpled. Wolfram felt his heart race. There was Hans. Smiling. Hatless. His blond hair jostled by the soft, balmy breeze of a South Florida wind. His blue eyes twinkling and promising mischief. Hans might have been a model for a Nazi recruiting poster or a Leni Riefenstahl propaganda film: the beautiful, ideal, ideal Aryan man. But when Hans noticed Wolfram's scar, he grimaced.

Wolfram wanted to rush up to Hans, to embrace him, and kiss him, but he was a chauffeur. *Act like a chauffeur,* he told himself. He took Hans' bag. "*Liebchen,*" Hans whispered to Wolfram to assure his lover everything would be fine. They would only have to continue the masquerade for a little while longer. In a short time they would be behind closed doors and in each other's arms once again. Wolfram's heart raced with joy, such joy that he thought his heart might burst. He had risked everything to be here, to be an agent in an enemy land, but it was all worth it to be with the man he loved.

Wolfram smiled contentedly, but out of the corner of his eye he noticed the African man again. He was staring.

"Who is the African?" Wolfram asked his friend, as the two young men walked to the car. He corrected himself, remembering the white American term: *nigger.*

"Him?" Hans replied. "That's Old Tom Burk, a local nigger who drives a cab in the colored section of town. No one to worry about. We keep the niggers in their place around here. Every now and then we have a lynching or two to keep them in line."

"That's good," Wolfram replied. He began to hand the car keys to Hans.

"No," Hans whispered. "You are the chauffeur. Don't draw suspicion." He said this softly, but with a hiss.

"Sorry," Wolfram blushed. He looked around. The African wasn't looking any longer, but he had unnerved him. If a harmless *nigger* could unnerve him, what kind of agent would he be? Let alone an assassin? What would happen when he ran up against a suspicious American of English descent?

In the car, Hans asked, "How did you get the scar on your face?"

"A Belgian's bayonet," Wolfram said in a matter-of-fact tone.

"I'm sorry, *Liebchen,*" Hans said.

"Don't be. The Belgian is dead."

Hans was taken aback by the coldness of his Wolfram's voice. Wolfram had killed a man and his voice sounded like he might have just said: *I wonder if it will rain today.* Well, Hans told himself, Wolfram had seen war. Wolfram had been in combat. Combat, he had read in books, could change a man. Hans would try to understand. He would try to be sympathetic to the man he loved.

The two men said nothing more until they were on their way to the island. Wolfram stopped the car for the raising of the drawbridge on Bridge Road. A small sailboat, with a mast too tall to pass beneath the bridge, floated leisurely through the opening. When the boat cleared the upraised span, the bridge tender lowered the drawbridge to accommodate the traffic, both pedestrian and automotive.

Finally, Hans broke the silence between the two lovers:

"Did you find everything you need, Wolfram? Was there enough food?"

"I haven't seen so much food in a year, *Liebchen*."

"You'd better not call me 'lover,' Wolfram. Your German might slip out and then you are done for...and so am I."

"I've missed you," Wolfram said, his eyes trying to catch Hans' expression in the rearview mirror. Hans showed no emotion.

"We will make love once, and then we will discuss the plan, Wolfram. Do you understand? We must keep our emotions in check, or we may fail. We cannot fail. The Führer is counting on us. You don't want to wind up like your uncle."

That was a cruel thing to say, Wolfram thought. Had Hans changed? That comment seemed cold. Perhaps Hans was just focused, Wolfram thought. After all, the assassination of Roosevelt's top Jew was Hans' idea.

Wolfram began to wonder about Hans. Was he still his lover? Had this trip been futile? Yes, he would kill Roosevelt's top Yid, but that was only the secondary reason for his risking his life on a spy mission. Seeing Hans meant more, so much more to Wolfram than the mission. More than the war, more than life itself. A small tear escaped his right eye. Behind them on the bridge, a car beeped its horn impatiently for Wolfram to proceed while the bridge was down.

Hans finally noticed the tear on his lover's face. He took a handkerchief from his pocket and handed the silk cloth to his lover, who gently wiped the moisture from his face.

"I am sorry, *Liebchen,*" Hans said. "That was a cruel thing I said. Forgive me, please," he added, patting Wolfram's shoulder.

Wolfram sighed. Everything was fine. Hans still loved him. It had all been worth the risk.

Chapter 5

Upstairs, on the second floor of the White House, the luncheon table was set. The steward had been told by Mrs. Roosevelt to expect six, but the steward had set eight places in anticipation of an additional guest, or two, that the gregarious Mrs. Roosevelt might lasso for lunch during her daily walk down Pennsylvania Avenue. She had invited perfect strangers she met on the street so often for lunch that the steward just added two places to the number of guests Eleanor said would be there. There were only seven chairs around the table as the president had taken to staying in his wheelchair in case something came up during the lunch and he had to leave on short notice. It seemed easier than having a Secret Service agent carry the crippled president from the room. The war had changed things. The abnormal had become the normal.

Mrs. Roosevelt was always up to some mischief, the steward thought, remembering the lunch in which the president was entertaining a congressman from Mississippi and Mrs. Roosevelt invited colored singer Marian Anderson as a guest. The congressman, who was lobbying F. D. R. for a naval base in his district, couldn't just up and walk out so the congressman had to smile and squirm the whole lunch. The congressman's constituents never learned that their congressman violated Mississippi's segregation laws by sharing the same table not only with the president, but with a colored woman as well.

The steward had admired Mrs. Roosevelt for a number of years, especially after she resigned from the Daughters of the American Revolution when the DAR refused the

Marian Anderson permission to sing in their Constitution Hall due to her race. Eleanor nagged her husband for an alternate site for Anderson's concert until he granted permission for Anderson's concert to be held at the Lincoln Memorial on Easter Sunday 1939. The steward had adored the first lady ever since that magical day he joined the 75,000 other people lining the Reflecting Pool to listen to the famous contralto sing an angelic version of *Ave Maria*. He heard white people say that Marian Anderson was "a credit to her race." He hated that phrase. They had said the same about Jesse Owens. Marian Anderson was a credit to a race alright: *the human race.*

Even though he respected Mrs. Roosevelt, the steward couldn't gather the courage to tell her that the president entertained Mrs. Lucy Mercer Rutherford when the first lady was out of town touring the country for the Roosevelt Administration. Nor could he tell her that her daughter, Anna, was the one who arranged the rendezvous' between the former lovers. He knew enough to keep his mouth shut, wondering what in Heaven's name the president saw in Mrs. Rutherford when he had such a devoted wife. Walter Burk would never cheat on his own wife, Mary. He was devoted to her.

Walter Burk had been a steward at the White House since Calvin Coolidge was President of the United States. Like many "colored" born in the Deep South, he had left during World War I for the job opportunities in northern cities, settling in the District of Columbia which was, in its way, a very Southern city. Washington D.C. practiced segregation: in housing, schools, transportation and nearly every facet of life. There were numerous colored servants working in the White House, but the steward wasn't able to land a position there until after the death of President Harding. And, of course, colored servants made less than white servants. That was just the way it was.

Walter Burk started as a doorman at the Washington residence of a congressman from his home state of Florida. After the congressman retired, he provided a letter of reference that helped Walter Burk acquire a position at 1600 Pennsylvania Avenue. He realized he was lucky to have obtained his position and in his position he overheard and saw much more than the white folks ever realized. He discerned who Franklin Roosevelt really liked and who he actually loathed. Walter knew the president even ordered the rich Joseph Kennedy to drop his trousers for him.

"You know, Walter," the president once remarked to the steward. "Orson Welles and I are the two best actors in America. The president has to be an actor, Walter. I bet even Lincoln was an actor. Of course, the poor chap was shot by one. Ha!"

It was odd, Walter thought, how white people could say things to their colored servants, thinking the servants would never repeat what they said. It was similar to the way the president talked to his dog. Franklin Roosevelt didn't expect his dog to talk to anyone. Not that stupid spoiled little Fala at any rate. That little Scottie followed F. D. R. everywhere and sometimes wound up underfoot at luncheons, a scavenger for table scraps. The dog was the gift of his distant cousin, Margaret Suckley, who went by the nickname "Daisy." Daisy, the White House maids told Walter, was another of F.D.R.'s girlfriends.

True to form, Mrs. Roosevelt walked into the dining room with her personal secretary and two additional luncheon guests: a white, middle-aged couple from Illinois that she had met while strolling the sidewalk on Pennsylvania Avenue with her secretary. The first lady was nearly as tall as Walter Burk, and he was 6'1". She had the kindest blue eyes, and her light brown hair was done up in a bun.

"Walter, we will need two…" the first lady began and, noticing the extra places already set, she stopped in mid-sentence and smiled at her colored steward. "Please welcome Mr. and Mrs. Miller from Alton, Illinois. Their son is at the Naval Academy in Annapolis, and they took the day to see the sites in here in Washington. I thought they might like to meet the president."

"Yes, ma'am," the steward replied. He said to the Millers: "Pleased to meet you." He understood that the Millers from Illinois were overwhelmed to be in the living quarters of the president of the United States and about to have lunch with him. They seemed to have trouble closing their mouths. The steward smiled for he had seen the same reaction on numerous occasions from strangers the first lady recruited for her lunches. But it was the first lady's own unorthodox way of keeping President Roosevelt in touch with the real American people and not letting the president isolate from the common man.

Mr. Miller said, smiling. "It's nice to me you, Mister…?"

"Burk," Walter offered.

"Nice to meet you, Mr. Burk."

The steward showed the Millers to their seats on the first lady's end of the table and distracted their vision from the president's entrance. When the Millers sat down, Franklin Roosevelt, an ivory and wooden cigarette holder in his mouth, was already seated at the luncheon table having wheeled his chair into the room. He had been dutifully followed by Fala, the most famous Scottish terrier on the planet. F. D. R. was also accompanied by three men in business suits.

"Walter, what's for lunch?" the president asked, peering over his pince-nez.

"Baked chicken, Mr. President."

"That sounds deee-lightful," the president replied as he took the cigarette holder out of his mouth. "Harry, park your posterior in a chair."

To the steward's amusement, two of the men sat down. The steward knew Harry Hopkins, one of Roosevelt's top advisors, but he didn't know the other man. He had only been informed that he was a senator from Missouri. The steward was also familiar with another intimate advisor, the Secretary of the Treasury, Mr. Henry Morgenthau, Jr., for the cabinet member had been to lunch with the president quite often, more so since the war commenced. As the two men took seats, Fala jumped up onto the First Lap and F. D. R. petted him.

"Senator Truman," Eleanor smiled. "It is so nice of you to join us."

The bespectacled Senator Truman managed a smile. "Thank you, Mrs. Roosevelt."

The president just let Eleanor chatter on. He seemed to be a bit amused. "Franklin, I would like you to meet Mr. and Mrs. Miller from Alton, Illinois. I believe that is across the Mississippi River from your home state, Senator Truman."

Senator Truman nodded.

The president came forth with a campaign–wide smile, grinning from ear to ear. "Nice to meet you, folks. Where did my wife Shanghai you?"

The Millers seemed dazed.

"We met while I was walking on Pennsylvania Avenue, Franklin," Eleanor answered for the star-struck couple

"Fine, fine," the president said. "Did you get a coat check slip downstairs, Mr. Miller?"

Mr. Miller sensed the president was kidding. "No sir," he said. "Should I be worried?"

The president laughed. "Didn't Lincoln and Douglas have a debate in Alton, Mr. Miller?" He asked with a characteristic grin.

"Yes, Mr. President," Miller replied. "That debate was about the biggest thing that ever happened in the town. That and when slave holders from Missouri crossed the river to kill Elijah P. Lovejoy."

"Yes, the abolitionist. I think I recall the history of Lovejoy. Correct me if I am wrong, Mr. Miller. The slaveholders came over from Missouri and threw his press into the Mississippi River, as I recall..."

"That's right, sir," Mr. Miller said.

F. D. R. seemed pleased at his own erudition. "Mr. and Mrs. Miller, allow me to introduce you to Fala," he smiled. He held the dog up above the luncheon table for a moment and then put the Scottie down. Fala took his place beneath the table and curled up beside the president's shoes.

"Fala is so cute, dear," Mrs. Miller gushed to her husband. "He's even cuter than in the newsreels."

"The movie producer Pete Smith thinks so too, Mrs. Miller," F. D. R. beamed. "He wants to do a movie about

Fala for *MGM.* I think it won't be long before *MGM* replaces its lion symbol with a Scottie, ha."

There were a few chuckles around the table. The president smiled at his wife.

Eleanor frowned. "Franklin, don't you think you should introduce your *human* companions as well?"

"Ha, indeed," F. D. R. chuckled. "Mr. and Mrs. Miller, allow me to introduce Senator Truman, my advisor, Mr. Hopkins, and the Secretary of the Treasury, Mr. Morgenthau. Senator Truman is the man investigating the waste in the war effort and doing a bang up job of it. I sent one of my Secret Service boys undercover at a new base down in the South. The country appreciates all that Senator Truman is doing."

Senator Truman smiled. "Thank you, Mr. President."

"Franklin," Eleanor interrupted. "I'd like to say a word about the Jews…That magazine article about what the Nazis are doing…well, what are we going to do about it? It is worse than Ambassador Dowd warned us about years ago." Walter Burk knew the first lady was referring to William Dodd who had been the United States Ambassador to Germany during the 1930s, and a diplomat who reported the growing anti-Semitism in Germany to the president. Mrs. Roosevelt had invoked the neglected warnings of the late ambassador on more than one occasion.

The president lost his smile. "Eleanor, I'm afraid there isn't much we *can* do about the Jewish problem. Right now we are just trying to keep Russia and Britain from being overrun by Hitler. We have no troops in Europe and won't for some time. It is terrible, but we have bigger worries. Right, Secretary Morgenthau?"

The steward, of course, knew Morgenthau was a Jew, and he had seen the president enlist Morgenthau to thwart his wife's criticism of his seeming indifference toward the Jews on more than one occasion.

"Mrs. Roosevelt," said Morgenthau. "I am afraid I agree with the president. We are not in any military position to do anything to help."

"It's because the American people don't care about the Jews, isn't it, Mr. Secretary?" The first lady persisted. "Are you still getting those letters, Henry?"

Morgenthau looked uneasy. "Yes," he answered.

"Really? How many?" F. D. R. asked.

"Just one this week, Mr. President."

"That's not bad, Henry. How many hate letters did I get this week, Eleanor?"

"Five," the first lady replied.

"Five? Fala gets more fan mail than I do."

"No one is threatening to shoot Fala, Franklin," Eleanor observed.

"Hmm," the president began. "Mr. Miller did you know Fala gets so many letters I had to hire a secretary for him? People are always asking about his name. I shall tell you... I named him after a Scottish ancestor of mine: Murray the Outlaw of Fala Hill. When they make a movie about Fala, I think Rin Tin Tin may have some competition."

"Really, Franklin, must you go on about Fala?"

"Quite right, dear. Quite right. Mr. Hopkins, let's have someone look at Secretary Morgenthau's mail as well as mine."

Harry Hopkins nodded.

"You didn't bring it with you by chance did you, Henry?" the president asked.

"Yes, sir, Mr. President." Morgenthau replied. He retrieved an envelope from his suit jacket.

"Are you going to play detective again, Franklin?" the first lady asked. "Really, Franklin, you are not a Hardy boy." She had a hard time holding back a smile for she knew her husband enjoyed playing detective. "Perhaps you should call Captain Midnight and ask him to send you a decoder ring."

Franklin Roosevelt pretended to ignore Eleanor, but his smile betrayed him. He enjoyed it when Eleanor teased him. "Ha," the president said as he examined the letter addressed to Henry Morgenthau. "No return address. That's typical. Sloppy handwriting. Let's look at the post mark…hmm, Florida. Hobe Sound."

"Hobe Sound?" the first lady said. "Doesn't one of the staff have a relative there?"

Roosevelt shrugged. "I don't know, Eleanor." He turned to the Millers and asked, "Is that a union pin, Mr. Miller?"

"Yes, Mr. President. I am a machinist at the Owens-Illinois glass factory. That's local 95 of the Glass Bottle Blowers Association, located in Alton."

"Yes, the G.B.B.A. Good, solid trade union," the president replied. "I really appreciate labor's support, Mr.

Miller. I met your International President, James Maloney. A good man. From Scranton, as I recall. As I said, I appreciate your union's support."

"We appreciate *you*, Mr. President."

F. D. R. smiled. "Mutual admiration society. Ha!" F. D. R. had no problem with the A. F. of L; it was John L. Lewis and the C.I.O. that was bothersome. Even though the C.I.O. had pledged not to strike for the duration of the war, the president didn't trust the bushy-brows union leader. F.D.R.'s charm failed to work on the old coal miner.

The steward and a waitress brought the food for lunch. President Roosevelt was about to attack a chicken breast when the first lady bowed her head to say grace. His fork stopped as if suspended in space by his wife's blessing. When Eleanor reached "Amen," the fork continued its descent, joined by a knife, to do battle with the baked chicken. When his wife wasn't looking, he slipped a small piece of chicken to Fala beneath the table. Fala quickly ate the evidence, leaving no incriminating scrap.

"You know, Mr. Miller, since you are from Illinois, you might like to know that Senator Truman found some defense shenanigans at Carnegie-Illinois on the quality of steel for our Navy vessels."

"That was in Pittsburgh though, Mr. President," interjected Truman.

F. D. R. grimaced. He wasn't fond of being corrected. He forced a smile. "Senator Truman, it is an Illinois company," the president replied with an icy smile. "I thought Mr. Miller should see how his government is doing a good job. What do you say, Mr. Miller?"

"It's fine to me, Mr. President…and my wife and I would like to thank you for lunch," Miller replied.

"Thank Mrs. Roosevelt, Mr. Miller," F. D. R. smiled. He turned to the steward. "I will have another cup of coffee, Walter."

The steward poured the president another cup. It was a shame that as a resident of the District of Columbia, Walter Burk couldn't vote in a presidential election. His inability to vote was something similar to his brother's inability to vote in Florida, although Tom was kept from casting a ballot by the white folks and their Jim Crow rules. Tom had passed the literacy test, but the white folks still wouldn't let him vote. So neither of the Burk brothers could vote for president; one because of the law that applied to residents of the District of Columbia, and the other because of segregation.

It was ironic that Walter Burk couldn't vote for president, because he probably knew more about what was going on in the White House and in the Unites States government than most people in the country. He overheard discussions as well as arguments, and he inadvertently listened like the time when the first lady told the president her plan to visit the Tuskegee airmen. She even informed the president she was going to take a flight with one of the colored airmen. The president wasn't too pleased about her flying with a colored pilot, as he feared the repercussions it would have for him politically in the South. Nevertheless, a few weeks later the first lady took a plane ride in a southern state with a colored man at the controls. Then they posed for photographs. The fuss that followed was something to behold. But Mrs. Roosevelt was no dummy; she went up with "Chief" Anderson, the flight instructor who ran the Tuskegee program. Anderson had more experience in the air than ninety-nine percent of the white pilots in the country. The picture that was on the front page of many newspapers was worth those proverbial thousand words. Yes sir, the first lady was all right by Walter Burk. He wished he had been able to tell his brother what Mrs. Roosevelt was about to do before she did it, but he suspected all the phones in the White House were tapped by Mr. Hoover, plus the fact that his brother in Florida had a party line at home, subject to all the listening ears of the gossip grapevine of the Hobe Sound colored ladies beauty shop.

The president turned to the Secretary of the Treasury. "You know, Henry, you can never be too careful. J. Edgar can't catch all the spies in the country. You might want to assign one of your Secret Service men to guard you."

"They are for *your* protection, Mr. President, not mine. Besides, we have to keep an eye on counterfeiters; the Germans are trying to print our money. I'm sure Mr. Hoover can catch the spies, Mr. President."

"Hoover's an idiot," Harry Hopkins chimed in. "He can't catch anyone by himself. He takes all the credit and publicity for his agents' work."

Franklin Roosevelt laughed, then turned serious. "Mr. Miller, do you remember a mayor of Chicago named Anton Cermak?"

"Wasn't he shot?" Miller replied.

"Franklin, please…" Eleanor began, but the president ignored his wife.

"Sure was," said the president. "Miami in '33, a month before I took office. Mayor Cermak was shot by a short little man of Italian lineage who was crazy, they say. Giuseppe Zangara was his name. He had stomach problems he blamed on presidents. But I guess it was too warm in Miami in February to leave and travel to Washington to shoot Hoover. Not when there was another president visiting Miami."

"It might have put Herbert out of his misery," Hopkins quipped.

The president laughed. "Anyway, this Zangara fella read in the paper that this other president, yours truly, was going to be giving a speech at a park in Miami. Why go to Washington when a president was coming to him? Zangara got off a few rounds and missed me, but he got Anton. Got to hand it to Florida- they tried Zangara right away and executed him shortly thereafter. So what I am saying, Henry, is to be careful out there. There might be some crazy guy who wants to kill the Secretary of the Treasury. Ha!"

Morgenthau laughed along with the president. "You had me going there, Mr. President."

"What I am saying is, Henry...a guy who wants to kill you doesn't send you a letter. Still, it is strange that an assassin would go after a Secretary of the Treasury. Nothing personal, Henry, but doesn't this assassin have bigger aspirations? Maybe shoot a Vice President at least?" The president laughed at his own morbid humor, but the laughter at the table seemed a bit strained. Eleanor frowned at him.

"Assassination is not funny, Franklin," she scolded. "Remember Mr. Long? And that Mr. Trotsky in Mexico?"

"There's a red that's dead," Harry Hopkins joked. The former Foreign Minister of the Soviet Union, Leon Trotsky, had been axed to death two years prior by one of Josef

Stalin's agents. "Said Uncle Joe, Leon's got to go," Hopkins added, finishing his joke.

The president roared with laughter. The Millers looked at one another confused. Eleanor assured the Midwesterners that Trotsky was an evil communist.

"But aren't the communists our allies against Hitler?" Mr. Miller asked.

Eleanor was a bit flummoxed by the question, but quickly regained her composure. "Well, yes, but they are the good communists." Her voice sounded insincere. She quickly changed the subject. "Franklin, I don't think it is funny to tease Henry."

"Of course not, Dear," he replied with a campaign-wide grin, "Just joshing, Henry."

"He gets letters because of his religion, Franklin," Eleanor persisted. "Not because he is Secretary of the Treasury."

"I know that, Eleanor."

"You know how Hitler prattles on about your Jewish advisors; it's bound to get our anti-Semites riled up."

"Uh huh. Mr. Miller," the president began, ignoring his wife and speaking to the tourist from Illinois. "May I ask what your religion is?"

"We are Lutherans, Mr. President?"

"I see. Good for you. What do you think about Jews?"

"I don't know any, Mr. President."

"Well, now you do. You met Mr. Henry Morgenthau... The Secretary of the Treasury...have you seen the Lincoln Memorial, Mr. Miller?"

"Yes, Mr. President. It's majestic."

"'Majestic'...that it is, Mr. Miller. A perfect description for the monument. Abraham Lincoln was the only good Republican president I think."

"What about your cousin Theodore, Franklin?" Eleanor asked, referring to her Uncle Teddy Roosevelt who was not only her uncle but a distant cousin of Franklin Roosevelt, too.

"Yes, yes, your Uncle Teddy was okay. You know I liked Cousin Theodore. I thought he was better as a Bull Moose though."

"You should. You stole his whole platform," said the first lady with a mischievous smile. "Uncle Theodore's platform from 1912 is the New Deal, and you know it. You would think just once you would give him attribution."

The president smiled in response, seeming to enjoy the sparring with his wife. His grin only made her huff in response. But Walter Burk knew that Mrs. Roosevelt was playing at being mad. The Roosevelt's didn't get along well; there was always a friction. But on occasion, there still seemed to be something of a spark between them, for the president truly respected her opinion and knew that she was as smart, if not smarter, than he.

The steward had waited on Franklin Roosevelt many a morning when the president gave him a pile of notes from Eleanor that she left in a wicker basket beside his bed. They were ideas and suggestions, many of which the steward read and concluded would be good for the country.

But the president discerned that Eleanor's ideas, while brilliant, would never pass muster in *The Cave of the Winds,* as F. D. R. sometimes referred to Congress. The only change a congressman liked was the change in his pocket. Especially the Southern Congressmen.

The Southern Democrats posed the problem. F. D. R. had to walk a fine line with the Southerners on the race issue, because the solid south was essential to the Democratic Party's congressional majority, and hence, its' governing ability. Eleanor lobbied for an integrated military, but the president knew he would lose the South if he pushed too hard for that. And he needed the Southerners in the fall elections if the Democrats were going to retain control of the House of Representatives. No, perhaps after the war was won and everyone was in a good mood, F. D. R. might accomplish the goal of integrating the military services, for he agreed with his wife in principle. But integration wasn't practical in the middle of the conflict. She had the freedom to be the idealist; he had to be the pragmatist. "I have to be a compromiser, Walter, a very good compromiser, like Senator Henry Clay of Kentucky," the president said to the steward on more than one occasion, as if to reassure himself.

The first lady thought it was ridiculous that colored people in the South couldn't vote because of poll taxes and literacy tests, but Franklin Roosevelt knew he couldn't press for equality. That set up the hypocrisy of fighting for democracy overseas while denying it to colored citizens at home. The irony was that the white man would deny that there was any hypocrisy at all in the nation's foreign policy.

After Franklin Roosevelt and his guests finished, they left the table and departed the room with Fala trotting dutifully behind the president's wheel chair. Walter Burk began to clear the table. Mrs. Roosevelt, who had led the Millers downstairs, returned and approached the steward. Walter watched her curiously.

"Mr. Burk?"

"Yes, ma'am?"

"Don't you have a relative living in Hobe Sound, Florida?"

"Yes, Mrs. Roosevelt. My brother Tom."

"I see…Hobe Sound isn't very large is it?"

"No ma'am, Tom probably knows just about everyone there."

"Thank you, Mr. Burk. You were very informative."

The first lady left the dining room and left Walter Burk to wonder what the conversation was all about. *Had Tom done something wrong?* He thought he should probably call Tom that evening, but Tom had that darn party line, and the nosey neighbor, Mrs. Birdstock, would be listening in on any calls. The next time the old biddy went to the beauty parlor, she would repeat their conversation. No, he would have to write Tom a short letter.

Chapter 6

Even though Hans told Wolfram that they would make love only once, the two lovers continued with few encores, until both of the young men were exhausted. They fell asleep in one another's arms. This time, when Wolfram wept, his tears were tears of happiness. He had risked his life to see Hans again and it had been worth it; the seasickness, the cramped quarters of a submarine, and the wretched diarrhea of the voyage across the Atlantic Ocean had been worth it. If he could die in his lover's arms he would die happy. It was as wonderful as that first night in the Manhattan hotel after the Bund rally in 1939. And now, at this moment, he had no desire to kill anyone; only a desire to stay in his lover's embrace forever.

Hans, on the other hand, was not about to tell Wolfram that he was seeing a girl from Vassar College and that he had sexual longings for her, as well. She, of course, realized Hans's lust for her and guarded her virginity with a figurative chastity belt. With firmly crossed legs, she knew her maidenhead was her gateway to a good marriage with someone of her class. She might engage in some heavy petting with Hans, but only enough to whet his appetite for the main course, which he would have to pay for with a wedding ring. She was a proper Catholic girl. Her promise of chastity was her physical dowry, although her family was wealthy, as well.

Hans's parents approved of the girl, as her family was of the same social class-although Cynthia's people wintered in Palm Beach, near the Roman Catholic Kennedy clan. Hans hadn't thought highly of the Kennedy clan until the family patriarch, Joseph P. Kennedy, as United States Ambassador to Britain, encouraged the United States to stay neutral in the war and not come to Great Britain's aid. Franklin Roosevelt's Jew advisor, Henry Morgenthau, had probably been responsible for Kennedy's removal as Ambassador to the Court of St. James in November 1940, Hans thought. One more reason the Jew, Morgenthau, needed to die.

But first, Hans owed Wolfram a nice vacation. It was the least he could do for his awful comment about Wolfram's uncle, Rudolf Hess. That the Deputy Führer could have been so naïve to think the British would welcome him with open arms to negotiate a truce with the Reich was obviously an embarrassment to Wolfram. There was no reason for Hans to rub it in. For a German family that had risen so high, the Hess family had fallen even further with Rudolf's bizarre flight. What was his uncle thinking? Was he insane? That's what most people thought. Rudolf Hess was insane. For a brief moment, Hans wondered if insanity ran in the Hess family.

The two young men spent the next few days enjoying the Florida sun, tanning on the beach, playing a bit of tennis at the Jupiter Island Club, lounging around on the patio of the club and drinking a few beers. Wolfram, accustomed to real German *Bier*, detested the American brews. Hans found Wolfram's discriminating tastes amusing, considering his own family's fortune stemmed from its American beers. But after the first day of beer drinking, Wolfram ordered Bahamian rum drinks. Hans, attempting to be agreeable, switched from beer to rum, as well. Hans cautioned Wolfram not to get too intoxicated, as he might give away his cover.

Hans introduced Wolfram socially, whenever it was necessary, as an old school chum from Yale down visiting on a holiday. Wolfram was instructed to say as little as possible, but most of the club members were elderly and merely polite to the younger generation. They didn't ask questions. They hadn't been that curious about Wolfram, as many had seen him with Hans a few years earlier when both boys were enrolled at Yale. If anyone asked about Wolfram's accent, Hans was prepared with a background story of Wolfram's Swiss citizenship.

The young men spent the balmy nights on Jupiter Island listening to Bob Hope and other radio entertainers. When torch singer, Frances Langford, sang *I'm in the Mood for Love*, the two lovers found passion once again, consummating their ardor on the floor of the house's Florida room. For Wolfram, who had witnessed the horror of combat and the brutality of war, America seemed a surreal oasis where the inhabitants went on with their normal lives. They seemed oblivious to world catastrophe, as if the war would never touch the cities and towns of the United States. For the rich of Jupiter Island, life seemed to go on as usual. *Steward, I will have another gin and tonic.* Yes, a few ships had been sunk off the coast, but there was no threat of German invasion for the wealthy of the golden island.

The days passed as the two lovers dawdled, lounging about in this paradise of privilege, drinking more rum, sun bathing and playing a few more sets of tennis at the Jupiter Island Club. One morning, as the two men were waiting for a tennis court to open, Hans pointed out a woman serving in the near court.

"That is Katharine Hepburn, the film star."

Wolfram seemed intrigued. "She is famous?"

"Yes."

"She is good player," Wolfram observed.

"She is *a* good player," Hans corrected his lover's syntax. "Add the article to avoid suspicion."

Wolfram nodded. "I will remember," he replied. "Who is the old man watching her?"

"That looks like Spencer Tracy…another movie star…I wonder what he is doing here?" Hans asked, more for himself than Wolfram.

"Maybe he is…how do you say it…screwing her?"

Hans smiled. "That's how you say it all right…well, that is interesting. The far court is open. Let's go."

Wolfram was an adequate tennis player, but he was only able to take two games from Hans, who won the set six to two.

"Want another set?" Hans asked.

Wolfram smiled. "*Nein*," he replied.

Hans, alarmed, swiveled his head to see if any of the club members noticed Wolfram's gaffe: German had slipped from his mouth. The coast was clear, although off in the distance, Hans noticed Old Tom Burk, standing by his cab. He seemed to be writing something in a notebook. Probably just a record of his pickups, Hans thought, as Katharine Hepburn approached the colored man's cab. Tom Burk opened the back door of his sedan and the actress took a seat, followed by Spencer Tracy. Then Burk drove off. Yes, Hans thought, Tom Burk hadn't heard anything, and even if he had, Tom Burk didn't know German. He smiled to himself. That nigger barely knows English, he concluded. Old Tom Burk was just another dumb, harmless nigger. You're getting jumpy, Hans, he told himself. The mission is going to call for steadier nerves.

A colored servant in a white coat brought Hans and Wolfram separate Jupiter Island Club towels to wipe off their sweat. As they walked to the shower in the locker room, Hans took a moment to whisper.

"Be careful…German slipped out."

"I know…I am sorry. I am relaxed, I think."

"Yes," Hans said. "I think we both are. We are too relaxed. I think perhaps it is time to try to plan the mission."

"Yes, shoot the Jew," Wolfram whispered. "I will shoot the Yid with my Uncle Rudolf's Luger."

"We will both shoot him," Hans said.

Wolfram nodded. "*Ja,*" he whispered.

They rode bicycles back to Hans's house. The Florida breeze gently tickled their faces with a warmth that had contributed to their lethargy. The weather in early March was decidedly vernal, without the oppressive humidity that plagued Florida in the summer and caused the rich to retreat to Newport, Maine, and other points north. Hans knew they needed to snap out of their idleness; they had a mission to complete. The Führer was counting on them. The Jew Morgenthau must die!

Chapter 7

The first lady of the United States, adorned in robe and slippers, walked down the corridor in the White House which led from her bedroom to the president's sleeping quarters. Eleanor and Franklin Roosevelt had not slept together since the day she discovered her husband was having an affair with her social secretary, Lucy Mercer, many years before. Eleanor threatened to divorce her husband, an admonition which would have ruined Franklin's promising political career. She relented on a divorce when he promised to end the affair and not have any contact with Lucy ever again. He swore to end the affair, but Eleanor stopped sleeping with him anyway, for his violation of her trust. A few years later, Franklin contracted infantile paralysis and Eleanor, the dutiful wife, helped nurse him back to health. It was ironic that polio had taken away his legs, but given her husband a backbone, as the man who was hobbled by polio was more of a man than he had ever been on two good legs. For his courage and perseverance Eleanor loved him, but she had not forgotten his betrayal. Nor had she truly forgiven him. Forgiveness, thought Eleanor, was the Lord's domain, not hers.

Their celibate marriage became an intimate political union, for Eleanor thought that as his wife, she could influence Franklin and push and prod him to do great things. She would serve as his legs, his eyes and his ears, going around the country, visiting people while he stayed in Washington running the government. Eleanor wrote a syndicated column, *My Day,* which ran in scores of newspapers across the United States. It was a popular feature and good public relations for the administration. Eleanor had the leeway to say things which the president never could utter, especially with the 1942 congressional elections hanging over his head. Franklin Roosevelt was an astute politician who listened to his wife, and while their physical marriage was in ashes, the state of their political union burned bright. Eleanor, he admitted to himself, would make a fine president. Too bad she was a woman.

There was a Secret Service officer sitting on a chair outside F.D.R.'s bedroom when Eleanor approached the president's door.

"Good evening, Edward," the first lady said with a toothy smile.

"Good evening, Mrs. Roosevelt."

"Is the president awake, Edward?"

"I just took him in a few minutes ago, ma'am."

"Thank you." She knocked on the door. "Franklin, Dear, may I come in?"

There was barking in response.

The first lady smiled. "Fala, may I come in?"

"Eleanor...yes, come in, please."

The president was sitting atop his bed smoking a cigarette, a long ash dangling from the end of his ivory cigarette holder. He was looking idly at the photographs of ships that adorned a wall, perhaps reminiscing of the first war when he was the Under Secretary of the Navy for President Wilson. He was also petting Fala.

"Franklin, you shouldn't smoke in bed. You might burn down the White House."

The president chuckled and smiled. "The old place needs a renovation anyway, Eleanor. We should do that before we leave, don't you think?"

"Yes, Dear, but you should try to win the war first."

"Ha ha, good one...I enjoyed your column today about Mr. Gunther in London. Very good. What brings you down the hall...I have your suggestions in your basket," he said, pointing to the little wicker basket by his bedside.

"Mr. Morgenthau."

"Henry?"

"Yes, the letter he received."

"Oh that...Eleanor, no one is going to shoot the Secretary of the Treasury. Assassins go for presidents or kings like that Zangara fellow."

"Franklin, it is because he is a Jew, not because he is Secretary of the Treasury. And you know it. People criticized you for appointing a Jew, but when you appointed him Secretary of the Treasury, I thought the Wall Street bankers were going to go apoplectic."

"Yes, some of them did," the president smiled. "It made it all worthwhile."

"Well, I think someone might actually want to kill Mr. Morgenthau, and you underestimate the anti-Semitism in our country. You should do something about it."

"The anti-Semitism?

"No...Mr. Morgenthau's safety."

"Me? What do you want me to do, Eleanor?"

"Give him a Secret Service man to protect him."

The president thought for a moment. He could try to coax Henry into letting his men guard him, but he would only refuse again. Still, it didn't hurt to placate Eleanor. "Okay, I could do that-it can't hurt. Anything else then, Eleanor?" He knew there was another shoe to drop; there always was with Eleanor.

"Did you know our steward, Walter Burk, has a brother in Hobe Sound, Florida?"

"Huh? Well, no, I didn't... what does that have to do with Henry?"

"The letter originated in Hobe Sound. I bet it came from one of those snobs on Jupiter Island. Have Mr. Hoover check the fingerprints on the letter, Franklin."

"Too many people have handled that letter, Eleanor. Jupiter Island? We are of the same class as the Jupiter Island people."

"Yes, but we aren't snobs."

The president smiled and placed a gentle needle into his wife. "No, just traitors to our class."

"That silly statement again, Franklin. It is so trite. So passé. I think it would be interesting to enlist Walter Burk's brother to keep an eye out for suspicious people in Hobe Sound. He seems to run a taxicab service and often takes people to Jupiter Island from the railway station. He could be the perfect spy. Who would ever suspect a colored man, a Negro?"

"Really, make a colored man a spy, Eleanor? Really?" The president thought a moment and then said. "Go on, Eleanor," he said with a smile, for he knew there was more. "Tell me what is on your mind."

"Don't patronize me, Franklin Delano," she snapped. "I'm serious. Why not a colored man? Most of the colored people are servants for whites, and they overhear a great deal. I daresay Walter Burk knows more than we suspect," she added. "Whites don't even think about their colored servants when they are talking. It's as if the colored folks wouldn't ever repeat what they hear. Rich people are dumb, Franklin, you know that."

"A colored spy," the president smiled. "Reminds me of James Armistead in the Revolution. I can just see J. Edgar now. You know he won't allow a colored agent in the F.B.I. Eleanor, you accused me of being a Hardy Boy, and you are acting like Nancy Drew. Did you have a glass of port before bed?" A smile came over F.D.R.'s face and a twinkle to his eye.

She frowned at her husband. "I'm serious, Franklin."

The president paused to contemplate the idea, odd as it seemed on the surface. It was fun being president, he always claimed. A little skullduggery might be great fun. It might take his mind of the war a bit. At the very least, they might obtain some good gossip on those Jupiter Island high hats; find out who was sleeping with whom. But he couldn't say that was his reason for the spying. Camp Murphy, the new radar base, was a good reason. It was near Jupiter Island.

"Might not be a bad idea with Camp Murphy about to open up down there, Eleanor. Going to be working on some of the latest radar equipment, and we wouldn't want that to fall in enemy hands. Let me think about it, Eleanor. Let me sleep on it. Is Walter's brother a good man?"

"He won several medals in the Meuse-Argonne, Franklin."

"Really? We treated the colored soldiers shabbily in the first war, Eleanor. That's for certain. We are going to make sure the Negros see combat in our army in this war...I just have to do it in stages, like Lincoln did in the Civil War."

"So you will think on it?"

The president smiled once more. "Yes, Dear, I will think on it. It is an interesting idea. I'm glad you didn't write it down though."

She walked over and kissed him on the cheek. "Thank you, Franklin," she said.

As she returned to her room, Eleanor knew she had him. The Hardy Boy in Franklin would find it fascinating to see if there really was some rich man's plot to kill his Jewish advisor. She knew he loved to get the gossip on folks, as well. It would serve as a diversion from a war that wasn't going all that well. And he needed a diversion, *or* this war would kill him, she thought.

Chapter 8

Dulcinea adjusted her neck scarf against the bracing, March, Manhattan wind and stopped by a curbside newsstand. She glared at the headline.

JOE K. SPY RING ON TRIAL: LUCY TELLS ALL!

"The stupid little cow," Dulcinea muttered before she walked on to the consulate. 18 year-old Lucy Boehmler, had taken the stand in the spy ring trial and implicated many of the German agents who had been arrested shortly before the United States entered the war. Dulcinea read the names of the accused and was relieved to see the F.B.I. hadn't arrested *everyone.*

At the Spanish Consulate in New York City, brown-eyed, brunette, beauty, Dulcinea Martinez was known as a single girl from Puerto Rico, an American citizen, who was fluent in English, Spanish, Italian and German. She told the charming, if fabricated, story of how her father so loved the book *Don Quixote* that he named his only daughter after the female character in the Cervantes novel. It was rumored that Dulcinea had been the lover of Don Julio Lopez Lido, who was accidentally run over by a cab driver while crossing 7th Avenue in March 1941. Miss Martinez, whose real name was Gretchen Schwartz, had indeed been Lido's lover, but Lido was not who people thought he was.

The late *Señor Lido*, in fact, had actually been a German agent: Captain Ulrich von der Osten of the German *Abwehr*. The F.B.I. believed von der Osten was the head of a group of Nazi spies working within the United States. The car accident in New York had led to a discovery in the diplomat's briefcase of sensitive information on U.S. factories.

What really intrigued the F.B.I. agents was the information in the briefcase was in German, not Spanish, rather odd for a Spanish "diplomat." Von der Osten's death led the G-men to arrest Kurt Ludwig and his associates and put them on trial for espionage. The New York City newspaper tabloids covering the trial were calling Ludwig and his gang the *Joe K. Spy Ring*. When the late von der Osten adopted the alias of *Lido*, he brought Gretchen along with him to the consulate. She served as his secretary.

Gretchen had been recruited by von der Osten from a list of German American Bund members in the New York City area. Born after the Great War on January 11, 1921, she grew up on Long Island in a German-American immigrant family that had strong ties to Deutschland. Her father served in the Kaiser's army in World War I, before bringing the family to the United States in 1920. All of Gretchen's cousins still lived in the Third Reich, and she visited the Fatherland with her family during the Olympic Games that were held in Berlin in 1936. Some of her cousins spent summers with her family on Long Island and attended German American Bund meetings while in the United States. Upon graduation from high school in 1938, Gretchen joined the German American Bund, accompanying her father to the meetings. On one occasion, she accompanied her German cousin Helga to a meeting in Madison Square Garden. She wore her swastika stickpin proudly until von der Osten enlisted her as a German agent;

as an agent, she had to appear inconspicuous and not call attention to herself. Now, Gretchen wore her swastika pinned to her bra, invisible to others but close to her heart.

When the war in Europe broke out in 1939, Gretchen's older brother, Rolfe, returned to Germany and joined the *Wehrmach,* the Germany army. Rolfe was subsequently killed by a British sniper when the Germans overran France in 1940. Had Gretchen been a boy, she would have joined her brother in serving the Fatherland, but after Rolfe's death, Gretchen hated all things French and British. She seethed when President Roosevelt aided the British after the Battle of Dunkirk by sending the British small arms to replace the ones they left behind when they fled from France, across the English Channel. Up until the moment that Franklin Roosevelt sent weapons to the British in June 1940, Gretchen had been a loyal American, but with F.D.R.'s outrageous aid to the people who killed her brother, she joined her father in calling the president, "Jew-loving Roosevelt."

At an Oktoberfest celebration in 1940, Gretchen met von der Osten and was recruited as a German spy. She became von der Osten's lover on an impulse after some champagne on New Year's Eve. Their cover as diplomat and secretary in the Spanish consulate was provided by a friendly Franco government, which was technically neutral, but pulling for its fellow fascists and von der Osten was able to convey espionage information via diplomatic pouches. Up until that unfortunate accident, the information had found its way to Berlin. Now, Gretchen was waiting for orders, and she spent her days in the consulate translating meaningless messages from Spanish into English. She felt as if she was wasting her talents, as well as her time. She craved excitement, adventure and a way to strike back at the "Jew-loving Roosevelt." Surely, she could still be of service to the Fatherland and the Führer.

As Gretchen walked into the consulate that morning, a small man in a grey fedora and matching trench coat was awaiting her. She hoped that this was the day, the day when she would meet von der Osten's replacement; She knew him only by his code name: Klaus. He motioned for her to follow him into a small room off the entrance. A small conference table with six chairs and a few Spanish language newspapers and magazines on a small oak book case was the only clue that this was the reading room which doubled as a waiting room.

The small man indicated for Gretchen to sit at the conference table. She obeyed. He closed the door.

"I am Klaus," he said succinctly in German before switching to English. "You are being transferred, temporarily, to the Spanish embassy in Washington. You have a new mission."

"A new mission?" Gretchen asked.

"Yes. You are to meet two agents coming from Florida who are on special assignment."

"What is the special assignment?"

"The information is in the envelope," he said giving her a small, manila package. Don't open it here; put it in your pocketbook."

She nodded. "I see...when do I leave?"

"Tomorrow on the first train to Washington. Your ticket is inside the envelope, as is money for lodgings. The information on your meeting place with the agents is inside the envelope. Heil, Hitler!" he said, raising his right arm in ritual Nazi salute.

The prospect of excitement and adventure sent a thrill through Gretchen's body. She smiled, raised her right arm in ritual Nazi salute, and replied, "Heil Hitler!"

That evening, after dinner with her father and younger brother at their Mineola home, Gretchen descended the stairs to the basement where her father often retired in the evening to the shortwave radio. Father and daughter hoped to pick up a pre-recorded speech by Joseph Goebbels or Adolf Hitler on German radio. If the atmosphere was just right, the basement would fill with the shouts of *Sieg Heil* from the shortwave. Her father sat amid his collection of prize possessions: a swastika flag, a picture of the Führer and a photograph of Charles Lindbergh beside *The Spirit of St. Louis.* Gretchen could remember that glorious morning in 1927 when she accompanied her father to Roosevelt field to watch the great, German-American aviator take off for his flight across the Atlantic. To think Reichsmarshall Goring had awarded Lindbergh *Verdienstkreuz der Deutschen Adler,* the Service Cross of the Order of the German Eagle in 1939! Lindbergh was one of Papa's heroes. How often she had sat with her father in his basement den, listening to the shortwave radio.

In 1940, Gretchen and her father had listened to the CBS broadcasts of Edward R. Murrow from London and cheered as Murrow described the bombing of the British capital. The British were paying for killing Rolfe, her father claimed. Sadly, the Führer postponed the invasion of the wretched little island to turn his fury against the Soviet Union. The attack on the Soviet Union had confused Gretchen, as only two years prior, Rippentrop and Molotov the two foreign ministers for Germany and the Soviet Union signed a non-aggression pact. It was part of the

Führer's bigger plan, her father assured her, for it was the Jews and the Bolsheviks who caused Germany to lose the first war. It was all outlined in Hitler's masterpiece, *Mein Kampf.* Hitler's *My Struggle* had become hers.

On a cork peg-board beside an oak-paneled wall in the basement, her father was obsessed with a map of Europe, moving various colored stick pins around the continent. The pins represented the different armies, and the Nazis were represented by black pins; the Soviets by red. The black pins progressed as far as striking distance from Moscow, but they hadn't moved forward in months. In fact, the black pins had even retreated a bit. Her father, who had fought on the eastern front in the first war, knew of the Russian winter; nothing much would happen, he assured his daughter, until the spring thaw.

The roads were terrible in Russia he explained. He went into details how bad roads slowed

the German *Blitzkrieg,* the "lightening war," that had so quickly had defeated Poland, Belgium and France. Come spring, however, the German Army would once again roll across the Soviet Union. Moscow would be theirs by May, he assured Gretchen.

Gretchen took a seat at her father's desk as he moved from his map and stood by his shortwave radio set, attempting to find a German station. He shook his head. "Bad atmospherics tonight, Gretchen," he groused.

Gretchen took a deep breath. Her father knew she was working for the Fatherland. He approved of her doing so, but the transfer to Washington might unsettle him. Her mother had died two years earlier, and if Gretchen left for Washington there would be no woman to look after her *Vater.* And he was approaching *50.* He was overweight .

He smoked too many cigars. When her mother was alive, she watched Papa's weight but since her death, Papa had gained 40 pounds. A simple walk up the staircase from the basement caused her father to become winded. His shortness of breath concerned her.

"Papa?" she began.

"*Ja?*"

"I have been transferred to Washington, Papa. I leave tomorrow."

He smiled. "Can you tell me why?"

Gretchen hesitated. She knew she could not tell her father. It was too dangerous. If she were caught they would come after Papa, and he couldn't have any knowledge of her mission. If Papa knew, he might be arrested.

Curious, she opened the envelope in the bathroom on the train from Manhattan to Mineola. Two hundred dollars! Her eyes widened when she saw the money. She hoped it wasn't counterfeit, but she assured herself the German *Abwehr* wouldn't risk passing counterfeit notes with its agents. *Would they?* The agents she was to meet in Washington were named Wolfram and Hans. One of the agents would be wearing a white carnation. The white carnation would be the signal.

Were those real or code names? Gretchen wondered, realizing it really didn't matter. One of the agents was an American man, a Yale Law School student, the other a German, a nephew of a former Nazi leader. There were no photographs of the men.

Klaus had mentioned that there was an American man who had traveled south to meet the German agent. The

German agent arrived by submarine and had slipped ashore in Florida. Dulcinea/Gretchen was to find lodging not far from the Spanish Embassy and offer the agents a safe house from whence they would conduct their mission: a mission to assassinate Henry Morgenthau, Jr., the Secretary of the Treasury.

Gretchen's eyes stared at the name in disbelief when she read it. Kill Morgenthau! Roosevelt's top Jew! *Wunderbar*! She mused in German. She was to meet the agents three days later at the Rideau Restaurant at 1306 H Street, NW in Washington. The reservation would be in the name of Lido, in honor of her fallen comrade and lover. She never thought of him by his given name, *Ulrich,* for he had never called her Gretchen. She was always Dulcinea, to him and he was always Lido to her. A small sadness for her dead lover overcame her for a moment, but she shook it off. Lido had hated sentimentality and he had warned her to be careful with her feelings. She looked at her father and smiled.

"No, Papa, I cannot tell you about my mission," she said.

Her father smiled. "I understand. I am proud of you, Gretchen."

In a corner of the basement stood her father's gun cabinet. Her father walked over and unlocked the cabinet. He returned to his daughter carrying a snub-nosed .38-caliber revolver with a pink handle.

"This was Mama's" he said. "You may need a gun in Washington with all those niggers," he suggested.

She knew that her Papa had an irrational fear that his daughter would be molested by either "Kikes" or "niggers," as he often referred to Jews and colored people. He had long ago shown her how to use firearms. She checked the chambers on the pistol: five bullets, one empty chamber to prevent an accidental discharge. Papa had taught her that. She smiled at her father. Only Papa would think of giving her Mama's gun, instead of her mother's jewelry. She had had to ask for her mother's necklaces, broaches, bracelets and earrings. She began to feel tears coming at the thought of her mother. In her mind, her mother was piercing her ears for her first earrings when she was a little girl, because Gretchen had become so insistent on pierced ears. In her memory, Gretchen was beginning to cry, but her mother's soothing voice calmed her. She took a deep breath and exhaled.

Don't cry, she told herself. *Do not cry. Do not be a silly woman, Gretchen. Not in front of Papa.* She took another deep breath and regained her composure. "I'm worried about you, Papa. How will you and Franz get along without me?"

"We will survive, *Töchter*," her father assured her. "Now, get your rest for your trip and say no more about Papa," he added, kissing her on the cheek.

Herbert Yardley's lunch meeting with William Donovan at his own Rideau Restaurant in Washington, D.C. did not go well. Yardley had expected Donovan to ask him to restart the Black Chamber and return to his expertise in cryptography. Instead "Wild Bill," as he was known to espionage professionals, brought the bad news that Henry Stimson, the Secretary of War, had blackballed Yardley. Again. Just like in1929. Yardley despised the sanctimonious Stimson.

During the First World War, Herbert Yardley ran MI-8, Military Intelligence Section 8, a secret, off-the-books, spy agency which deciphered all the German diplomatic and military codes within a few months after the United States entered the conflict. After that war, Yardley's small group continued its clandestine operations in peacetime, deciphering various foreign government cables until the goody-two-shoes, Henry L. Stimson, was appointed Secretary of State by Herbert Hoover. When he learned about the Black Chamber's existence, a morally outraged Stimson declared: "Gentlemen do not read each other's mail."

Stimson shut down the American Black Chamber in 1929, throwing Yardley out of work. Unable to find employment with the onset of the Great Depression, Yardley turned his considerable talents to writing a book, *The American Black Chamber.* The book became a controversial bestseller and made Yardley a pariah in the intelligence community for divulging too much information to the public.

Hollywood called, however, and Yardley's book was made into a movie entitled, *Rendezvous,* a sensationalized account of Yardley's own work in the Great War. It was a box office hit and starred William Powell and Rosalind Russell. The film, as well as the book, estranged Yardley even more from the intelligence community.

Still, Donovan, who was putting together an organization called the Office of Strategic Services, or simply, O.S.S., considered Yardley for a top position deciphering codes. But once again, Yardley's nemesis, Henry L. Stimson, now Secretary of War, vetoed Yardley. Stimson realized he no longer could worry what gentlemen did or did not read, since the country was at war; but

Roosevelt's Secretary of War thought Yardley was a headline-seeking liability.

Donovan tried to explain the situation to Yardley as they sat in a booth in his restaurant beneath a movie poster of *Rendezvous,* with actor William Powell on a telephone while both Rosalind Russell and Binnie Barnes were looking at the hero with adoring eyes. Of course, debonair leading man William Powell didn't look a thing like Herbert Yardley, but Yardley, who suffered from narcissism, loved the poster, had it framed and proudly hung it on a prominent wall in his restaurant. Only the year before, Yardley had been in China deciphering Japanese military codes for Chiang Kai Shek, and now here he was, reduced to running a restaurant in the nation's capital. What a comedown. During the lunch, Donovan explained, as politely as was possible, that Yardley's book, the movie and his love of publicity, contributed to a feeling that Yardley's public persona made it difficult for him to work in secrecy again. What Donovan didn't tell Yardley, however, was that the F.B.I. was investigating his restaurant as a possible "rendezvous" point for Axis agents. That was another strike against Yardley.

The lunch crowd was beginning to finish up. A number of employees from the nearby Treasury Department often lunched at the restaurant as the eatery was a few blocks from their offices. As the clock approached 12:30, a number of the Treasury Department workers lined up to pay their bills. Yardley moved to the cash register to collect the lunch checks when a young brunette-haired woman approached him and asked for "the Lido table." He pointed to the hostess a few feet away.

"Helen," he said, speaking to the hostess. "Will you help this young lady?"

Even though Yardley was still seething from the conversation with William Donovan, he watched attentively as the young brunette walked over to Helen. She had a fine ass... he evaluated with an easy eye... a very fine ass. Whoever this Lido was, he was a lucky man.

Yardley's eyes followed her to a booth where two young men sat waiting. Good-looking young men, but why two? Yardley wondered. *Ménage a trios?* Why was one man glancing furtively around the restaurant? He appeared to have a scar on the left side of his face. Yardley wondered if he were a fencer. The scar resembled a fencing wound. The man certainly seemed ill at ease. Yardley smiled when he noticed the other man wore a white carnation in his lapel. He was the boyfriend of the girl, Yardley assumed.

Maybe the fencer was an AWOL soldier, Yardley thought. Who else would be looking around so nervously? *Well*, he thought, *I won't turn the boy in. If he has the balls to not want to work for Henry Stimson...* well, that was fine with Herbert Yardley. Maybe he should buy the boy a drink.

Chapter 9

A few days before in Hobe Sound...

Melda May had the white movie stars' suitcases ready on the porch at Gate House when Tom Burk pulled his cab into the driveway. She didn't approve of unmarried couples sleeping together, but she kept her thoughts to herself. She assumed the movie stars weren't church people. What white movie stars were?

Tom Burk turned off the car and waved to the old woman.

She smiled at him as he approached the porch.

"Didn't see you in church yesterday, Thomas," she said, still thinking about the movie stars and their behavior.

"No, Miss May, you didn't," Tom smiled, making sure to add volume to his voice for the hard-of-hearing woman.

"I hope you weren't out with the devil."

"No, ma'am. I was picking up my brother at the train station."

"Walter? I do declare! I thought he was working in the White House." Finally, the movie stars were out of her mind.

"He is, Miss May. He was in town for a short visit. He has to get back to help the president though."

"You must be right proud of him, Thomas."

Tom smiled again. "Yes, ma'am."

"How long will your brother be here?"

Tom realized she had misunderstood him. "He went back this morning, Miss May," he explained patiently.

"So soon?"

"Yes, ma'am. The president needed him."

"Your brother's an important man, I guess," she said.

"Yes, ma'am. Where are Mr. Barry's guests?"

"She's down at the club playing tennis, and he's there, too. They've been two peas in a pod. I could tell you a few things…"

"Now, Miss May, the Lord doesn't want us to gossip, now does He?"

"Ha…" she laughed. "You're right, Thomas. I bite my tongue a lot with white folks, but you are right. Gossip is the devil's work. Do you need any help with the bags?"

"No, ma'am, I can handle them." Tom concluded that, in spite of the old woman's best intentions, it was only a matter of time before Miss May told the old biddies in town everything she had seen between the movie stars. But the white movie stars would be safe with their naughty secrets as colored women would never tell the white folks what they saw. But the women would tell one another at the gossip mill of the beauty shop.

Tom picked up his brother, Walter, while Rachel was in church on Sunday. The telegram he had received on Friday caught him by surprise. He hadn't seen his brother Walter in three years. The Burk brothers weren't particularly close and they had grown even more distant after their mother died in '39. Still, Walter was his brother, and he sensed that it must be important if Walter was coming all the way from Washington on the train.

The railway station was fairly deserted, as there were no regular stops that Sunday morning. The Miami Express was scheduled to stop at West Palm Beach at 11:02, and its last stop had been Fort Pierce. But Walter said he would be on that train and that the train would stop to let him off. To Tom, that sounded a bit preposterous; an express train stopping to let off a colored man at one small station. But sure enough, as Tom waited, the express train did indeed stop to let off the president's steward. Tom was amazed. He had seen the express stop for a Jupiter Islander, but never for a colored man, who had to sit in the back car due to the segregation laws.

The astonished looks on the white faces in the train's windows made Tom smile. He knew they were wondering how a colored man could make the train stop to let him off. The looks of astonishment on their faces amused him.

Walter, carrying a small suitcase, approached Tom and offered his brother a smile and an extended right hand. Tom shook it and asked Walter, "How in the world did you get the Express to stop?"

"Someone at the White House made a phone call, Tom."

"Must be nice, Walter," Tom sensed the "someone" was Franklin Roosevelt. "To have friends in high places."

Walter Burk smiled. "It is," he said.

By habit, as a cab driver, Tom took his brother's bag and tossed it in the back seat of the cab. He was about to open the back passenger door, but Walter grabbed the door handle to the front passenger seat.

As they rode away from the train station toward Banner Lake, Walter asked Tom about Rachel, daughter Phillis, and Tom's son, Thomas, Jr., who was off at army training in Arizona. Tom realized his brother was getting the necessary family questions out of the way before divulging why he was in Florida. He assumed Walter's wife, Mary, had made the list of questions for Walter to ask. Otherwise, Walter would never have asked about the family. Women asked, men didn't.

Rachel was in church, and the house was empty when the Burk brothers arrived. Tom took Walter's suitcase and placed it in a guest room, a room which normally served as Tom's library and study. A fold-out couch doubled as a bed for guests. Walter made himself at home at the kitchen table. When Tom returned to the kitchen, he sensed Walter was about to tell him why he was here, as it had always been a Burk family tradition to discuss important matters at the kitchen table.

"Will Rachel be gone long?" Walter asked.

"She'll be gone most of the morning. She has Sunday School to teach after the service. Would you like to go to Sunday School, Walter?"

Walter laughed. So did Tom. As boys, they had snuck out of Sunday School on more than one occasion to go fishing together.

"I'm sorry we haven't kept in touch," Walter said.

"Yes, Mother would have wanted us to keep in touch. If we had a sister, I think we would have. She would have made us."

"Women do that, don't they?"

"Sure do."

"Tom, the president sent me here to see you."

"Come again, Walter?"

"President Roosevelt sent me here to see *you*. That's why the train stopped. I am on a mission for the president."

"President Roosevelt wants you to see *me?* Why on earth, Walter?"

"He wants you to serve your country."

"I'm too old for that, Walter. I had enough of country-saving years ago. Didn't do me a heck of a lot of good, as I recall."

"No, no, Tom. Not military service. He wants you to be his eyes and ears in Hobe Sound. I told him how you know everyone around here and with Camp Murphy, he just wants you to report if you see or hear anything suspicious. "

"Me?"

"Yes, you."

"That's ridiculous."

"Is it?" Walter replied. "You have access to people and to white areas that other colored people don't."

"So why not a white man?"

"White folks don't pay attention to us, Tom. You know that. We watch them and listen, but they don't even think we have brains, let alone ears. The president knows that...or Mrs. Roosevelt does, at least. I think it was more her idea than his."

"That's true, the white folks don't pay attention to us," Tom agreed. He thought for a moment. Maybe it wouldn't be so hard to write down suspicious behavior. Maybe he could make a few dollars, too. He certainly could use that new set of tires for his car. "What's in it for me?" he asked Walter.

"A 'B 'sticker, for starters."

"Sticker...what are you talking about?"

"Voluntary gasoline rationing isn't working, Tom. The president is going to ration gasoline for civilian automobiles. So they are coming up with a decal system for cars. Trust me, it's going to happen. An A sticker gets 4 gallons of gas a week; the B sticker gets 8 gallons a week. You'll get a B sticker. Plus, the government will pay you one hundred dollars a month. It will be in cash so there is no trace of the payments. You'll have a Secret Service contact..." He handed Tom a hundred dollars in small bills

Tom looked at the money. He held a twenty up to the light. It appeared genuine. "This is from the government, Walter?"

"Actually," Walter admitted. "I think the money is from the first lady. I think it is from her money for her newspaper column. Seems it was her idea: spying on Jupiter Islanders."

"Mrs. Roosevelt's idea?" Tom was perplexed.

"Yes. She's afraid someone may try to harm Mr. Morgenthau, the Secretary of the Treasury. He's a Jew."

"Yes, I know. I've heard people around here complain about Secretary Morgenthau. Rachel heard a group of white folks complain about him at a supper party."

"It seems the white people hate Jews as much as they hate us. Well, nearly as much as they hate us, I guess."

Tom smiled. "Oh, I think we are still on top of the white man's hate list, Walter. So let me get this straight... I just report suspicious activity in the area to a Secret Service man and just who is this Secret Service agent?"

"His name is Allan Kane, and he will have the cover of Captain Carver. Refer to him as Carver, not Kane. He will be assigned with Mr. Reed ...Captain Joseph Reed... to make the Jupiter Island Club a getaway for officers from Camp Murphy. Captain Reed is unaware that Captain Carver is actually a Secret Service agent.

"The first lady is concerned about Secretary Morgenthau, but the president thinks the most important thing for you to keep an eye on is Camp Murphy. The president feels the enemy would like to know about Camp Murphy and the Jupiter Lighthouse, I think. It is probable that enemy agents are in the country. "

"This sounds crazy, Walter."

Walter Burk smiled. "Maybe. Maybe it is. Maybe everyone is being paranoid. Nothing has been normal since the Japs sneak-attacked us. Oh, another thing. You can't tell Rachel anything about your mission or where you got the money. Or what you are doing with it."

"I'm okay with that," Tom smiled.

"Mary," Walter said, referring to his own wife. "Has no idea either. She thinks I am just paying you a social visit. She didn't even ask to come along. She said you and I needed time together to heal or something like that."

Tom smiled. Walter didn't tell his wife. That was good. Otherwise, it was only a matter of time before Mary told Rachel everything she knew. While the men didn't communicate, their wives, on the other hand, always seemed to share information. The female grapevine ran from Washington to Florida and back. By not telling Mary, Walter had Tom covered. He wasn't allowed to tell Rachel about the cash. So he could keep the money. Finally, he could get some new tires before all the rationing began.

"Don't use the telephone in your house. You have a party line. If you have to call Agent Carver, use a pay phone. Your code name is…"

"Code name? Are you kidding me?"

"No, I'm not," said Walter in a serious tone. "Your code name is 'James Armistead.'"

"Huh?"

"It's the president's idea. He said he admired James Armistead. Who was he?"

"He was a slave who was Patriot spy during the American Revolution," Tom replied. "He actually served as a double agent. The information he gathered on the British led Washington to lay siege to Yorktown which led to the British surrender and the consequent founding of the United States. He was a slave and a hero who worked under Marquis de Lafayette. When the war was won, Armistead was sent back to slavery even though the information he provided helped win the war. When the

Marquis de Lafayette heard about Armistead's return to enslavement, he intervened and helped James obtain his freedom and Armistead took Lafayette as a surname."

"How do you know all these things?"

"I read a great deal, Walter," Tom laughed. "There were a lot of colored men fighting in the Revolution. For both sides. Peter Salem was at Bunker Hill, Walter. He was on *our* side, though. So what is *your* nickname?"

"Murray."

"Murray?"

"Not my choice. It is one of the president's Scottish ancestors."

"Where's your kilt, Walter?" Tom teased. "This all sounds a bit like white people craziness. What am I supposed to look out for?"

"Things which seem out of place, people who don't belong. Foreign accents. People with a lot of cash…whatever you see or hear. I know you listen to your passengers in your cab when they talk to each other. Listen closely. Take notes of anything suspicious. Hawaii is worried about Japanese spies, but the east coast needs to worry about German and Italian spies. Well, maybe not the Italians, but certainly the Germans. They have sunk too many ships off the coast with their submarines. They could land enemy agents, too. That's what the president says."

"The war isn't going well is it, Walter?"

"No, it's not. We're losing, Tom. That's what everyone is whispering."

"The president, too?"

"No, not the president. He seems to holding up well. The other day I was wheeling him down to his bedroom.

"Wheeling him?"

"Oops."

"What do you mean, wheeling him, Walter?"

"Tom, I will tell you this, but you can't tell anyone, not even Rachel. The president is in a wheelchair."

" The White House doesn't allow photographs of the president in the wheelchair. Oh, he has braces on his legs. That helps him stand. If you see photographs of him standing, he usually has a hand on something to steady himself."

"That's incredible. I didn't know he was crippled."

"His Polio is worse than they let on. He can walk with steel braces on his legs, but only if he is holding on to someone or to a rail. His pants cuffs hide the braces from view. The only reason I know about this is because I work there."

"That doesn't seem right; the people not knowing."

Walter smiled. "What does that mean to us? I live in the District, and I can't vote for president, and you live in Florida, and you can't even vote for dogcatcher."

"We don't vote for dogcatchers here, Walter," Tom replied with a smile. "Just nigger catchers. But it seems the people should know about his handicap."

"Why? No one is asking the president to lead troops into battle. There is nothing wrong with the president's *mind*. That's what the nation needs: his brain. Look, Tom,

I need to go back tomorrow. So we need a good story about why I came for so short a visit. How about mother's estate?"

"Mother had an estate?"

"No, of course not. There is just her house, but our story can be that I came down to talk to you about mother's estate. We can say I found some bonds she had. We'll say they mature in 1950 or so. That would give you a cover in case Rachel found out about your extra money. You could say you cashed a bond in early. If Rachel is anything like my Mary, it will be difficult to hide a thing from her."

"That's the truth," Tom said, thinking of the fifty dollar bill that had so recently slipped from his fingers into Rachel's.

"Well you have to, Tom. It is a matter of national security. You have to zip your lip. As they say, *loose lips sink ships*," Walter smiled.

"And bank accounts," Tom agreed.

Walter laughed and said, "So now, why don't we go to the river and catch a few fish? You still have our old cane poles, don't you?"

"Sure." Tom smiled. He hadn't gone fishing with another man in a long time; not since his son went off to training in Arizona. Most of the time, Tom Burk just went fishing by himself to get away and think, and to read the books he received from Mr. Barstow. He loved Rachel, but he needed some time alone now and then. Just like she needed to be away from him when she went to church on Wednesday nights. She never asked him to accompany her on Wednesday nights. Fishing was just as spiritual for Tom as church was for Rachel. If he caught a catfish or a largemouth bass, that was fine, but it didn't really matter. What he enjoyed was the solitude and the peace of the river. God's river. Tom found God in nature. Yes, he normally went to church on Sundays, but for Tom, God wasn't in church; God lived in nature. As boys, the brothers fished together for long hours in the summers. As boys, he and Walter had been close, very close. But they weren't so close anymore.

"What's biting?"

"Catfish mostly," Tom answered.

"Let's catch a few for supper then…just like the old days," Walter smiled.

Their luck was good, and in the late afternoon the two men returned to the house, proudly displaying their string of catfish to Rachel Burk.

"I moved Walter's bag into the other bedroom," Rachel said as the two men came in. "Your brother doesn't need to sleep on a fold-out couch, Tom."

"Sorry, Dear."

"Men," she sighed. Then her eyes brightened when she saw the fish the brothers had caught. "Good eatin' tonight!" she said. "Tom, you boys clean 'em and I'll cook 'em."

Rachel fried a mean catfish, and the two men stayed up late, reminiscing after Rachel retired. In the morning, Tom drove his brother to the Hobe Sound railway station. Walter gave Tom a small pocket notebook to chronicle any suspicious activity he observed. He was to keep a record of the things he saw or heard that were out of the ordinary; no matter how trivial. Time and dates. This diary, Walter assured Tom, would be useful in helping to apprehend possible spies.

"If anything goes wrong, Tom, you are to send me a telegram at the White House. It should mention 'fish are biting' or something like that. Don't use your home telephone to call me with those women listening in. You send me a telegram with 'fish are biting,' and someone will contact you."

"Nothing much is going to happen around here, Walter."

Walter smiled. "I don't think so either, but these are the president's instructions. I think this is some kind of diversion for him. A little bit of fun. He needs it, Tom. Mrs. Roosevelt thinks it will help the president relax." He offered his hand to his brother and Tom shook it. "Ask Rachel to have the congregation pray for the president, Tom. He needs all the help he can get."

As Walter's train pulled away from the station, Tom waved to his brother and returned to his cab. He was scheduled to pick up the movie stars from the Gate House in two hours so they could catch a later train. He decided to read for a while and retrieved a book from under the driver's seat in his cab. William L. Shirer's *Berlin Diary: The Journal of a Foreign Correspondent 1934-1941*. After two hours reading Shirer 's book, Tom was convinced that the Nazis were evil. He found it hard to put the book down, but he had customers to pick up.

When he arrived at the playwright's home, Mrs. May informed him Miss Hepburn and Mr. Tracy were down at the Jupiter Island Club. Tom picked up their bags and stored them in his trunk, then drove off to the tennis courts to find the movie stars.

It hadn't been hour since his brother had given him the notebook before he put in his first entry: *A strange man, who just the other day had been dressed as a chauffeur, was playing tennis with one of the members of the club. I heard him utter two German words, "Nein," which means 'no,' and "Scheissese," which means 'shit' or 'crap.' I will keep an eye on him and the club member, as well...*

Chapter 10

After Tom Burk dropped off the movie stars at the
Hobe Sound railway station and pocked it another fifty
dollar bill from Spencer Tracy, he drove to a colored
section of Hobe Sound to use a pay phone. He dropped a
nickel in the coin slot and dialed the number Walter had
given him. A woman came on the line.

"Extension, please," she said.

"Captain Carver, please, 4721."

"Thank you. I'll connect you."

A man's voice came on the line. "Carver."

"Captain Carver, I am Tom Burk...ah, James
Armistead."

"Yes, yes, Mr. Armistead," an eager voice said. "Do you
have something for me?"

"I might, sir..."

"Good. Good. You're the cab driver, is that correct?"

"Yes, sir."

"Good. I want you to come over to Camp Murphy and
pick me up. Take me to the Jupiter Island Club to meet this
fellow, Reed. Do you know where the camp entrance is?"

The entrance to what everyone said was a *secret* government base was the worst kept *secret* in Hobe Sound. The racket from the erection of the wooden barracks was impossible to ignore. Construction had been going on for two weeks now. "Yes, sir I know where it is. When do I pick you up?"

"Why, now, of course. I'll call the guard at the gate and tell him you are coming. Just tell him your real name and that you are picking me up."

At the guard shack by the entrance to the base, Tom Burk stopped, and an MP came to his car window.

"Name?"

Tom began to say "James Armistead," but caught himself.

"Tom Burk. I'm a cabbie. I'm here to pick up Captain Carver."

The MP consulted a clipboard and read down a list of approved people. Unsmiling, he looked Tom over and then finally said in a dismissive voice: "Proceed. Building 12. Take the road to the left. Fourth building on the right."

A cacophony of construction noise permeated the air like a bad *Spike Jones and his City Slickers* instrumental medley. Hundreds of men were busily building scores of wooden structures for the new base. When the wind was right, Tom Burk could hear the hammering and the buzz saws from his Banner Lake home. Camp Murphy promised boom times for both the white and black folks of Hobe Sound. There would soon be a lot of soldiers in camp with a good deal of money to spend.

Tom drove slowly and marveled at the scope of the camp's construction; dozens of one floor wooden buildings were rising from the hundreds of acres of cleared scrubland, an area that only a few weeks before had been a hodgepodge of Florida foliage. Gone was the tangled jungle of underbrush, vines and slash pines. The bulldozers cleared the land in a matter of days. Posted wooden signs indicated where a bank was to be erected as well as the location of a future movie theater. Camp Murphy promised to have more inhabitants than the town of Hobe Sound, and Tom realized that he might make a good living shuttling officers back and forth between the camp and the Jupiter Island Club. Rumor had it that the rich islanders were going to patriotically open the Jupiter Island Club to the white boys of Camp Murphy. Of course, only the officers would be welcome. Patriotism did not extend to the enlisted ranks, Tom thought cynically. There would be no riffraff hobnobbing on Jupiter Island with the "Swells." Yes indeed, the cab business, along with the spy business, promised to make Tom Burk a pretty penny.

A uniformed officer stood outside Building 12, smoking a cigarette, expertly puffing smoke rings into the air. Tom saw the officer's two silver bars on his left shoulder, glistening in the sun. He deduced it to be Captain Carver. Carver wore his hat loosely on his head, titled a bit backward, but the eagle insignia above its brim reinforced his status as an officer. He waved for Tom to stop.

"James Armistead?"

Tom felt silly answering to the code name.

"Yes, sir." He blushed.

"I'm Captain Carver," he said as he opened the back door of the Buick and slid in.

"You are the brother of the President's steward, is that correct?" He took a small notebook from a side pocket on his officer's jacket, flipped it open and began to scan its contents. He waited for Tom to answer. When Tom didn't, he repeated his question.

"Yes, sir." Tom Burk turned around and looked at the captain. Fearful of a flat tire from a nail in the road as he always was around a construction site Tom didn't hear the captain's question, initially. He noticed the large ring that the officer wore; it was a college ring. Carver realized Tom Burk was looking at his ring. He smiled. He had a friendly face.

"College class ring. I went to the University of Texas."

Tom Burk nodded. "Yes, sir," he said. "It is really nice looking."

Carver smiled again and consulted his notebook. "Thank you. You served in the first war?"

"Yes, sir."

"Where?"

"With the French Army in the Meuse-Argonne," Tom replied, wondering why he was being questioned.

"What is your Christian name?"

"Thomas Burk."

Carver nodded and consulted his notebook, flipping through its pages. "What medals did you win?"

Tom listed his awards, wondering why the captain was conducting an interrogation.

"Okay, you check out," Carver explained. "Sorry, but we have to be very careful. I hope you understand."

Tom smiled. He admired thoroughness. "I understand, Captain Carver."

"Good. Now, what do you have for me?"

"A young man was speaking German at the Jupiter Island Club."

"German? You know German?"

"A bit of it...from the war."

Odd, Tom thought. He still thought of his war as *the* war. *The Great War.* He hadn't become accustomed to people calling his Great War, "World War I." It wasn't the Great War any longer, just one conflict in a string of many wars. Too many wars. Tom Burk resented his war being demoted to a mere number; it was like a corporal losing one of his stripes and being busted to private.

Carver nodded and took a *Lucky Strike* from its white package with the red circle and lettering that had replaced the cigarette's prewar, iconic, green package. He tamped down the cigarette in his palm, clicked open a Zippo lighter and fired up the smoke.

"Okay...what words did you hear?"

"He was playing tennis, and he missed a shot and shouted 'shit' in German."

"Shit?"

"*Scheissese,* which means shit or crap, and he also shouted, '*Nein,*' which is no."

"Anything else out of the ordinary?"

"Yes, that particular man is a chauffeur. Chauffeurs do not play tennis at the Jupiter Island Club, Captain Carver. Not even white ones."

Carver blew a smoke ring and tried to picture the scene in his mind. When he envisioned it, Carver said. "I see. Is there anything else?"

"He smokes."

"So do I. What does that have to do with anything?"

"It's not that he smokes exactly. It's the *way* he held his cigarette, the way most Europeans hold it, pinching it. Not between two fingers, like you do. I don't think he's an American."

"You are very observant, Mr. Burk. You don't care if I call you Burk instead of the Armistead nonsense?"

"I'd prefer that, sir."

"Good. So how did you become so observant, Burk?"

"I learned that in O.C.S., sir."

"Officer Candidate School?"

"Yes, sir."

Carver leafed through his notes. There it was. Tom Burk had gone to OCS at Des Moines in the First World War. *Lieutenant.* Unlike Lieutenant Burk, Captain Carver would never see combat in this war. Up until this assignment, Carver, real name Allan Kane, had been stationed at Warm Springs, Georgia, on a rather permanent basis as Secret Service security for F.D.R.'s visits to the spa; visits which had become less frequent as the war progressed. "Take me to this Jupiter Island Club, Lieutenant Burk," Carver said, acknowledging the cabdriver's former rank.

Tom Burk smiled. "Yes, Captain," he said, as they crossed the bridge to Jupiter Island. He decided he liked this white man.

"Where is this chauffeur staying on the island?"

"He is staying with a young man whose family has a winter home here. They call it *Flamingo*. Mr. Reed, excuse me, Captain Reed, named a number of the cottages: Bamboo, Hibiscus, his own home is Artemis. Do you want me to drive you to Flamingo, sir?"

"Drive by the house, so I know where it is and then drive me to the Jupiter Island Club and then I want you to drive me to meet this Captain Reed."

Tom parked on the side of the road to give Carver a good look at the home named Flamingo.

"Is that cement construction?"

"Coquina rock. Shell fish. Very strong. Very expensive."

After showing Captain Carver the residence, Tom Burk drove on to the Jupiter Island Club, explaining that the club had once been the Olympia Beach Hotel, before the Reed family purchased the building and converted it into a club.

Burk noticed the two men playing tennis were the same men who had been playing the day before. He slowed the car and pointed to the tennis court.

"Those are the men I was telling you about, Captain Carver."

"Really? That's fortuitous...ah, lucky, Burk."

"I know what fortuitous means, Captain," Tom smiled. *I'm a smart nigger,* Tom thought to himself. He smiled. Carver was blushing.

"Sorry. I, ah..."

"*Scheissese!*" came a shout from the tennis court, as one player missed a return shot.

The other player drew his hand across his throat in a "shut up" gesture to his opponent.

"Park the car, Burk. I want to watch."

"You heard the word, sir?"

"'*Shit*' in German? You betcha."

Chapter 11

Allan Kane was born in 1912 in League City, Texas, a tiny town near Galveston, on the Gulf of Mexico, the youngest son of Newton and Helen Kane. Newton Kane worked as an accountant for J. C. League, the man who laid out that Texas town and then named the town for himself. Allan's father, Newton Kane, had the honor, or dubious distinction, of being among the first men selected in the draft by President Wilson during the Great War. The U.S. Army, in its bureaucratic wisdom, ignored Newton's accounting background and trained him as a foot soldier in the United States 1st Infantry Division. That division went into battle in France at Cantigny in May 1918. The Battle of Cantigny was a win for the green troops of the American Expeditionary Force, but it was an irreparable loss for a little boy from League City, Texas.

Oh, the local paper proclaimed that Newton Kane died a hero, but Allan's father's body had never been returned to Texas. When the Tomb of the Unknown Soldier was dedicated at Arlington National Cemetery on Armistice Day 1921, nine-year-old Allan Kane believed the body in the tomb to be his missing father. When, as an adult Secret Service agent stationed in Washington D.C., Allan Kane made frequent visits to the Arlington tomb as his way to remember his dad. As an adult, he knew, of course, that the corpse in the tomb was not literally his father, but while stationed in Washington, Allan visited the tomb at least once a month, and he never missed a Father's Day, when he would wear a white rose to signify his father was deceased.

His father had not only been a good accountant, but a wise investor, leaving Allan enough money to complete his education. After graduating from the University of Texas, Allan sought a job in the F.B.I., a government agency which had become highly popular through the publicity of its crime-fighting director and master of public relations, J. Edgar Hoover. He was turned down, but he was advised to try the Secret Service as one F.B.I. agent suggested that the Secret Service's requirements were not as demanding as the stringent prerequisites for Hoover's acolytes. Whether or not the F.B.I. agent told him the truth or his F.B.I. application was rejected by the segregationist director due to Allan Kane being a quarter Quapaw Indian, he was never able to discover. The United States Secret Service, on the other hand, was delighted to hire the young, University of Texas graduate.

For the next six years, Allan Kane spent his days trying to catch counterfeiters before being reassigned to protective services. He was given the night shift at the White House. Not much went on during the midnight shift; no well-mannered assassin would attempt to assassinate a sleeping president, or so Allan thought. Over time, he became a favorite of the often-sleepless, Franklin Delano Roosevelt, who would invariably chat with whichever agent had the graveyard shift by his bedroom door. In 1940, Allan began a torrid love affair with a female secretary from the State Department, an indiscretion which was reported to priggish Secretary of State, Cordell Hull. In turn, Secretary Hull reported the agent's entanglement to the president, who assured his cabinet member that he would take care of the matter.

One night while Allan was on duty by the president's bedroom door, F. D. R. called for him to enter. As Allan walked in, the president greeted him with a mischievous smile and asked about Miss Vivian Wisler.

Allan Kane was certain his face turned crimson, and in response to his change of color, the president laughed. Then F. D. R. broke out into a grin, not a campaign grin, but rather, a shit-eating grin, like a man who had been caught in a dalliance of his own during his privileged youth. Franklin Roosevelt understood the discomfort the young Secret Service agent was experiencing at that moment. Allan remained tongue tied.

The president dropped his grin and said in a sober tone, "You planning to do the right thing and marry the girl, Agent Kane?"

"I can't, Mr. President," Allan Kane recalled his heart racing.

"Oh...why not?" The president frowned.

"She isn't *Miss* Wisler, sir. She's *Mrs.* She is already married, Mr. President."

"What? Secretary Hull told me she was unmarried."

"No sir, she lied to them. She's married. You know how difficult it is for a married woman to get a job. So many employers think married women belong at home. Mr. President, I think her husband found out about us. She is really scared. He's a traveling salesman, and he's coming back next week."

"Har," the president slapped his knee. "That's a twist on the old traveling salesman story. The salesman is cuckolded." F.D.R. laughed anew. "So, Agent Kane, you are a bit worried about the husband?"

"He has a temper, I'm told."

"Yes, I believe husbands can get a tad upset when their wives stray. Hmm...maybe we need to get you out of town, Agent Kane. Special assignment."

A day later, Allan Kane was assigned to be the lone agent at the presidential retreat in Warm Springs, Georgia; until the war changed everything. In a roundabout sort of way, and with Secretary of War Stimson's help, Allan Kane's identity was changed and "Captain Carver" was created: a United States Army officer complete with a plausible back story. Kane was sent undercover as "Captain Carver" to Camp Murphy in Florida to check on construction and possible waste of government money, and to report to Senator Truman's office if he found anything irregular. The Missouri senator was chairing a Senate committee investigating contractor fraud. The fact that Allan Kane was at Camp Murphy working undercover as "Captain Carver" when Eleanor came up with her idea of enlisting Walter Burk's brother in skullduggery was nothing more than a fortuitous coincidence.

At the Jupiter Island Club, "Captain Carver" watched the two men intently as they played a set of tennis. He heard no more German words or phrases from either man. He wasn't sure what to make of it, but he sensed there was something odd about the two young men. He wondered if they were "fruits," his slang for homosexuals.

"Are those two, *fruits*, Burk?"

Tom Burk, a baffled appearance on his face, looked at the agent. "I'm not sure I understand, Captain..."

"Homosexuals, Burk? Are the men homosexuals?"

Tom Burk's face turned to disgust. "I don't know, sir. Maybe."

"Okay, I'll see what I can find out about those two. Now, I would like you to take me to meet Captain Reed."

"Yes, sir."

Tom Burk drove his cab to the Reed's *Artemis* property and waited in the car as the captain was ushered into the house. A half hour later, Carver emerged from the home and instructed Tom to return to the mainland.

"That was easy," he said. "Reed is an amiable fellow."

"Yes, sir."

"Should be good for your business, Burk."

"Sir?"

"Camp Murphy officers will be allowed at the Jupiter Island Club."

Tom Burk smiled politely at something he already knew.

"You should have quite a few fares, Burk." Carver was quiet for a moment and then changed the subject. "I want you to keep an eye on those two men we saw, Burk. I think it will be easier for you to find out information on those two than it would be for me. Keep a record of anything you hear or see that is suspicious. I may make an official visit to them myself. Now… take me into Stuart to the office of the *Stuart News*. Folks in Washington are not real happy about the paper publishing stories of submarine attacks. They want them censored."

Tom Burk remembered the censorship in the Great War. He heartily approved of censoring the local newspaper about military matters.

Tom drove his cab past the last remnants of Picture City: the unlit, cement lamp posts that bordered the road, pillars of a would-be-movie-dream factory town that turned into a developer's nightmare when the Florida land boom went bust. Tom Burk sometimes wondered what Hobe Sound might have been if had developed movie studios. Bigger, that was for sure. He smiled. Bigger wasn't always better.

He drove his cab through the whistle-stop known as Gomez and then on through the small town of Port Salerno. The penetrating odor of fish in Salerno lingered in the air, and Carver commented on the smell.

"It is a fishing village, Captain. Men make their living from fishing," Tom Burk explained to the Texan.

"Downtown" Stuart was a misnomer for two streets of an eclectic mixture of shops which seemed collectively nestled next to the railroad tracks, as if the tiny town drew its lifeblood from the iron artery that pumped commerce from Miami to New York. The portion of the Florida East Coast Railroad from Jacksonville to Miami was the work of Henry Morrison Flagler, the man who *invented* Palm Beach. Less than a decade before Flagler's railroad had stretched all the way from Jacksonville to Key West, across the open water and down to the Florida Keys, as if the Gulf of Mexico was merely a mill pond and the keys little more than lily pads for Flagler to run his rails across. The overseas extension of the railroad to Key West was one of man's greatest engineering feats of the twentieth century, but some saw it as an affront to Mother Nature who, it seems, had *Her* own plans.

In 1935, a Labor Day hurricane blew two hundred mile per hour winds across the Middle Keys, dismantling the railroad with the ferocity of a spoiled child destroying his toy train set. Ironically the sound of the hurricane's winds reminded survivors of a freight train rumbling past one's ear. Flagler Avenue in Stuart was named after the great railroad baron, who had died long before Mother Nature pronounced a death sentence of excessive hubris on his engineering feat.

Tom Burk drove past the Lyric Theater, which was showing *Woman of the Year* with Spencer Tracy and Katharine Hepburn. That was an odd coincidence, he thought.

He pointed to the marquee. "The two movie stars were just on Jupiter Island, Captain. I drove them around."

"Really? They were together? As a couple?"

"Sure seemed like it."

Carver smiled. "Boy wouldn't Hedda Hopper like to know that."

"Who?"

"A Hollywood gossip columnist…never mind, Burk. Take me to the *Stuart News* office. If you would."

Tom Burk parked the Buick outside the newspaper office and waited in the driver's seat as Carver entered the building. After about fifteen minutes, he returned, his business finished.

"Okay, Mr. Burk. Let's get back to Camp Murphy. I don't think you will be reading any more stories about submarines. The publisher is a really cooperative fellow."

"Mr. Menninger? Yes, sir, they say he is."

"He has an idea for a bus revive for Camp Murphy which he calls the Red Bus Line. The army is going to hire quite a few local people who will need transportation to the base."

"A bus service will help," Tom agreed.

Early that evening, *Captain Carver* (aka Allan Kane) in uniform, signed his fictitious name to a checkout sheet at the Camp Murphy motor pool. He was assigned a Willys GP, general purpose vehicle, which had been nicknamed *jeep,* as that was what *GP* sounded like when soldiers slurred the initials together. He enjoyed driving the jeep with its simple H shifts and its ability to traverse any terrain. They weren't fast vehicles, but they were dependable. Like the rest of the United States Army, the little jeeps were colored olive drab.

Carver drove the jeep from Camp Murphy to the Jupiter Island property that Tom Burk identified as the place where the two young male tennis players were staying. *Flamingo,* as the house was named, was a two story wooden house constructed of solid Dade County Pine and featuring paddle fans and jalousie windows, which allowed a cross-breeze to blow through the building and cool the structure. On the walkway from the driveway to the door, the requisite porcelain statue of a flamingo welcomed visitors. Carver parked the jeep, adjusted his hat with the brown visor and eagle insignia, and walked up to the porch of the two-story wooden house. He knocked on the front door. There was no immediate answer, but he faintly heard the crackling sound of what he took to be a shortwave radio receiver and the unmistakable guttural voice of Adolf Hitler, a voice he had heard much too often in newsreels at the movies. He assumed it was a recording of a Hitler speech, as it was past midnight in Germany. They were probably listening to the English language Nazi broadcast, *Germany Calling*. Suddenly, a cold feeling coursed his veins: he realized he might have been better off if he had carried a sidearm. He sensed danger. But the feeling came too late.

A sharp, sudden pain disabled him. He couldn't breathe. Blood was rushing up from his throat. He buckled and collapsed to his knees. His hat dropped from his head. A second sharp pain cut through his body. He toppled over. His consciousness was ebbing. "Mother," he mumbled. The last thing he saw was the man from the tennis courts who had uttered the German profanity. He was wiping off the blade of dagger, a dagger made of good Krupp steel, a dagger that had once been the property of his uncle, Rudolf Hess. Atop the man's head, Agent Kane noticed his captain's hat.

Then there was a white light, and he was at the Tomb of the Unknown Soldier. A World War I "Doughboy" whose face resembled the only photograph he had ever seen of his deceased father, Newton Kane, approached him. He was smiling. "Welcome, son. I am here with you." Then he faintly heard voices from below; two men were on a porch surveying his bloodied body. One had a foreign accent. Was he going with his father or was he waking up? Allan Kane wondered. He felt the blood rush out of his body and felt a sharp pain in the back of his neck. He couldn't catch his breath, and he let go, let go of the earth. He was back with his father at the Tomb of the Unknown Soldier.

The two men walked together toward the tomb, and as they approached the monument, the tomb opened and the shrine was bathed in white light. Hand in hand, with his father, he ascended. He felt an overwhelming peace.

Chapter 12

Hans Hoffman III was born into privilege as the second son of a man who was the grandson of a 19th century Milwaukee *Bier* baron, the *original* Hans Hoffman. According to legend, the original Hans Hoffman spoke only German even though he was fluent in English. He prospered in the brewery business and when he died of cirrhosis of the liver at the age of 57, he bequeathed a multi-million dollar brewery and distribution empire to son, Heinrich. Heinrich expanded the business and later turned it over the reins of the company to his son Hans II. Hans II would be the family scion that built the family's winter vacation home on a Jupiter Island.

Hans II was the first Hoffman to graduate from college, having matriculated at Yale. He later informed Hans III that he was going there as well to train to become an attorney for the family business. In the tradition of Old World primogeniture, first son Heinz would inherit the family business and was given paternal permission to skip college. Hans III was shipped off to boarding school at Phillips Academy, Andover, a feeder school for Yale University, which was why his father chose the prep school for "Three," as Hans III was nicknamed. *Three* was a sobriquet that young Hans despised but as the youngest of the children-there were three sisters as well- Hans III was powerless to end the teasing. Hans III seethed silently for years, often wishing that his older brother would die, become disabled or, at the very least, get arrested; anything to take the loving glow that radiated from his father's eyes when he gazed upon his first born and heir apparent. "Heinz the Wonderful," so wonderful that he made the United States Olympic Team that went to Berlin in 1936. The whole family trekked to Germany to see Heinz compete, and "Three" was mesmerized by the beauty, the cleanliness and above all, the order which was Hitler's Third Reich. *Deutschland*: he loved the sound of the word. Even though he was fluent, he was besotted by the German language, a tongue so much more expressive than English, Hans III thought. He became a Hitler fan and then, upon his return to the United States, an ardent supporter of the German American Bund. If there was any consolation for Hans III, it was that big brother Heinz won no medal in canoeing. In fact, "His Majesty the Crown Prince," as Hans called his older brother behind his back, didn't even finish his race. And with the war in Europe starting in 1939, the 1940 Olympics were canceled, and Heinz's dreams of an Olympic gold medal vanished as well. Hans once even gathered the courage to taunt his older brother by saying to his face, "Even that nigger Jesse Owens could win gold medals, but you didn't even finish." That sarcasm garnered Hans a black eye, but it had been worth it.

Hans had no girl friends in high school, and his first sexual encounter was a bit of experimentation with another boy in which they engaged in mutual masturbation. It wasn't until Hans met Wolfram that he developed what could have been labeled a "relationship and it was not until he kissed the girl from Vassar that he discovered he liked boys *and* girls, a sexual secret he feared to share with Wolfram. He understood Wolfram had a jealous streak, and he was fearful Wolfram might turn ugly. Wolfram was not a man to betray.

In fact, as Hans rushed out of the Jupiter Island house onto the porch, he saw his lover standing over an apparently dead army captain and wearing the dead man's hat. Suddenly, Hans felt fear course through his veins; fear not only for their predicament, but a fear of Wolfram, as well. He had never seen that hardened face on Wolfram: a killer's face. His eyes seemed suddenly cold and distant, as if his mind had drifted to some battlefield. Belgium? The *dead* Belgian? Wolfram's appearance frightened Hans. That face, he realized, a face that he loved, that face had been in combat and had killed men before. It was etched on his visage, like the face of a soldier on a Roman coin.

Hans could only ask his boyfriend. "Is he dead?"

"*Ja.*" Wolfram tipped the captain's hat to Hans.

"Oh, shit."

"Scheissese?"

"Yes, Wolfram. We are in deep shit!"

Wolfram looked at Hans coldly. "This is not game, Hans. This is war. People die in war, *Liebchen,*" he warned.

It hit Hans: He was officially a traitor to the United States of America. This mission was no longer some fantasy for the Führer, a privileged rich boy's romantic adventure with his lover; this was real. A United States Army officer was dead, and the United States government executed traitors.

Hans unbuttoned his neck collar as suddenly the shirt felt tight around his neck, like a noose. *My God! My God!* He thought. What should they do with the body? An idea came to him quickly, although the thought gave him a queasy stomach: *Shark chum.*

Thank God Wolfram hadn't shot the captain; someone would have heard the shot. The sound carried well at night on the island. Thank God for small favors. Looking at Wolfram's satisfied face, however, Hans realized that God had nothing to do with it.

Nervously, Hans went to the side of the house and unlocked his father's tool shed. He extracted a McCullough chainsaw, the latest model, a model which his father had received as a gift from the company president before the device was even sold to the public. Gas fed and fairly light, the new chainsaw was an improvement over McCullough's earlier models. Hands shaking, he splashed gasoline into and over the gas tank. He nervously walked back to the captain's body. The chainsaw would make a racket, and the neighbors might ask what he was doing cutting at night. He had to cover the sound. He noticed the dead man's name tag: Carver.

Hans laughed at the man's name. He was going to carve up "Carver." It was a sick laugh; a hollow, sick laugh, for Hans really wanted to vomit. He could feel bile backing up in his throat, but he held it together. He feared showing weakness to Wolfram. Hans instructed Wolfram to go inside the house to the laundry room and retrieve a laundry bag. He, in turn, returned to the living room and dialed a different radio station. The announcer was introducing Glenn Miller's hit, *In The Mood.* He turned up the radio to full volume and returned to the porch where he began work on Captain Carver's corpse, using the swing song blasting on the radio to cover the noise of the chain saw.

While Glenn Miller's orchestra blared into the night, the chainsaw roared. As Hans began to cut Carver's left leg, a geyser of blood gushed forth, splattering his face. Was Carver still alive? He hadn't checked the man's pulse. Dammit! He turned off the saw and checked the man's pulse. Faint, but there.

"He's still alive, Wolfram."

Wolfram shrugged, unsheathed the dagger and thrust the knife into the back of the captain's neck. The body's legs twitched for a moment, like a frog being dissected in a high school biology lab, and then the body stilled. He was truly dead.

Wolfram said coldly to Hans, "Try pulse again."

Coldness ran through Hans' veins as he looked at Wolfram. He hoped his fear did not show in his eyes. He checked the pulse a second time. Nothing. Glenn Miller's orchestra changed its tune to *Chattanooga Choo-Choo*.

Wolfram picked up the chainsaw. "I cut, you bag," he instructed Hans, tipping the dead captain's hat theatrically. Hans made no protest. He watched as Wolfram, acting like a nonchalant butcher on a side of beef, expertly cut the late captain into shark-sized nibbles. The scene was bizarre with Wolfram still wearing that hat, like a wild Indian parading around with a scalp, Hans thought. Wolfram could be just as savage.

As Hans readied his father's Bermuda sloop, Wolfram lugged the two laundry bags containing the remains of the late Allan Kane, alias "Captain Carver," onto the little boat. Allan Kane was reduced to shark bait. Fishermen called such bait *chum,* and Hans thought of the irony of that word's normal friendly usage, but then the captain was never their chum, their pal. Hans wondered if the captain had been married and had a family. Maybe there was a little boy who would be without a father. Maybe that boy would be better off if his father were dead. Hans certainly would have been better off if his father would have died years before. He hated his father. He hated his brother. He hated his country. Sometimes he was surprised by the depth of his hatred; he sensed it could turn to rage if properly provoked.

Hans adjusted the sail, caught the wind, and the boat moved quietly away from its mooring into the ocean. It wouldn't take long to reach the Gulf Stream where they would dump the remains of Captain Carver into the ocean's current. Either the sharks or the current would take care of the rest. Surprisingly, Wolfram said a short prayer for the departed Captain Carver, and when he finished, he offered a short German eulogy for his deceased enemy, as well. Then Wolfram unloaded the contents of the first laundry bag into the Gulf Stream, sending the remains of United States Secret Service Agent, Allan Kane, on the same ocean route that returned Italian sailor, Christopher Columbus, to Spain on the completion of his famous first voyage.

The deed done, they returned to the Hoffman's island dock and tied up the sloop. As they walked back to the house together, Hans noticed the ring on Wolfram's left hand.

"What is that?"

"*Kapitane* ring," Wolfram said in German.

"The captain's ring? Let me see."

Wolfram took it off and handed it to Hans. Hans realized it was a college ring, University of Texas. "Why did you keep it?"

"Souvenir, you call it."

"But you have his hat?"

"*Ja*. I have two souvenirs. My first American. I have two Belgian fingers back home."

Hans tried not to visualize the dead Belgian's fingers, but he failed. Images of dismembered fingers crowded his mind; he felt as if they were going to poke or prod him. One finger made an accusatory gesture to Hans and he grimaced. He shook his head to rid it of the fingers. What was the point?

There *was* no point arguing with Wolfram. Hans sensed he'd better return the ring to Wolfram or there might be trouble. He handed the ring back to his lover and thought: *What about the jeep?* He decided to wait until after midnight and drive the jeep off his family's property. But where to put the jeep? On the beach? No, no, that wouldn't work. Then he got an idea: *the railroad station parking lot.* Make it look like the captain took a train and went AWOL. Absent without leave. He wouldn't be the first man to do that. That might work, but they needed to get out of town on the morning train. Hans also sensed it would be a difficult night and that he would be sore in the morning. Wolfram had that look in his eyes, more the look of a conqueror than a lover. Hans wondered what he had gotten himself into. Was he in over his head? Was Wolfram insane?

He shook off the thought. "We need to move the jeep. I'm going to drive it to the train station and then walk back. Can you pack so we can leave first thing in the morning?"

"*Ja.*"

"Will you clean the blood off the porch while I take the Jeep to the station? "

"*Ja.*"

The jeep was surprisingly easy to handle, and Hans motored down Beach Road to Bridge Road. The bridge was down, the bridge tender appeared to be asleep and at 1 AM, there was no one at the Hobe Sound railway station. He knew there wouldn't be anyone at the station until 5

AM. He left the jeep and walked back across the bridge. The calmness of the night belied the violent crime that he and Wolfram had just perpetrated. They had killed a man, an officer of the United States Army. They had no choice but to leave town as quickly as possible. Hans was surprised how calm he was about everything. Was he in shock? In his head, he worked out the rest of the plan.

A year before, snooping through his father's desk, he discovered the combination to his father's safe written on a slip of paper. His father kept a few thousand dollars in cash in the safe. On a previous spring break, Hans stole fifty dollars from the safe. His father never noticed. Father probably wouldn't even miss a thousand or two, Hans rationalized, and they were going to need money.

When Hans returned to the cottage, he didn't notice that Wolfram had done a sloppy job of cleaning. Han didn't see the few blood stains still left on the porch. He was obsessed with money, knowing they would need cash. He opened his father's safe and retrieved some cash. Noticing one of his father's revolvers in the safe, he grabbed the *Smith & Wesson* Victory Special, a .38-caliber special that he had shot at a shooting range with his brother. He loved the weapon's balance, but he hoped he wouldn't have to use it. Killing made him want to vomit. He understood now, the expression: "He had no stomach for it."

Before he had traveled to Florida, Hans stopped in New York City and met with his German contact, who was working at the Spanish Consulate as a Spanish "diplomat." Hans would need to send him a telegram to arrange for the Washington contact to meet them. Hans and Wolfram would take the morning train north to the nation's capital and check into a hotel under assumed names. Hans knew the restaurant rendezvous spot to meet the contact as it was a favorite of Axis agents, run by a former, and now disgruntled, American spy. All they would need was a day and time to meet their Washington contact. Hans didn't want to walk to the Hobe Sound station and drag luggage across the bridge, so he decided they would drive the car to the station and ask the ticket master to hire the nigger cab driver, Old Tom Burk, to drive the car back. Ten dollars should be more than enough. It was more than some of those niggers made in a week. He had noticed on the train station chalkboard that the first northbound train was a daily at 5:32 AM. He and Wolfram would be on it.

The two murderers were up before dawn, dressed in civilian clothes with topcoats for the cold March winds of Washington. Mr. Seaman, the elderly station master, was the only soul at the train station at 5:20 AM when Hans and Wolfram arrived in the family car. Hans parked the car in the lot next to the depot and walked up to purchase two tickets.

"Mr. Seaman?"

"Ah yes, Mr. Hoffman the younger, I believe?" The white-haired station master replied.

"Yes…May I have two tickets for a stateroom to Washington. Can you find that nigger Old Tom Burk to drive the car back to my father's house?"

"Sure, no problem."

"Here is twenty dollars for your trouble and ten dollars for the nigger," Hans said as he handed the station master two tens and two fives.

The crusty old station master registered a thin smile as he took the money for the tickets and the favor. "I'll find the nigger, Mr. Hoffman, don't you worry."

The train stopped, and a Negro porter descended the stairs, smiled, and took their luggage. A conductor walked by, examined their tickets and directed the two young men to their stateroom. He ordered the porter to follow the men with their luggage. In the stateroom, the porter placed their luggage in a closet. Hans slipped the man two dollars; the man tipped his porter's cap. "Breakfast is being served in the dining car, sir," he informed Hans.

Hans nodded.

It wasn't until the train accelerated that Hans finally relaxed. It wasn't until then that he was able to sit down and feel how sore his bottom truly was. Wolfram had been a brute. Wolfram had also been alongside Hans when he opened his father's safe and calmly counted out two thousand dollars. When Hans was ready to close the safe, Wolfram reached in and took the rest of Hans' father's cash. Between them, they had over five thousand dollars.

"Not coming back, *Liebchen*," he had said to Hans in such a cold voice that even as he sat in the railway car, Hans could feel a chill. This was, Wolfram implied, a one way journey, a suicide mission. That was something which Hans had never considered. He always thought of this mission as a romantic adventure, but that fantasy had ended the night before with the grisly death of the army captain.

There was nothing romantic about a chain saw. Not until they had finished their breakfast in the dining car and they passed the awakening town of Vero Beach did Hans remember the blood on the porch. Wolfram had taken care of that, hadn't he? Oh shit, Hans thought, trying to remember the porch; if Wolfram hadn't cleaned up all the blood he was fucked. Royally!

And it wasn't until they passed Jacksonville that Hans realized that Wolfram had not packed Hans' diary. But that wouldn't matter, he assured himself. Who was going to find his diary, anyway? His parents, perhaps? His father would be angry, but he would never tell the authorities what his son had done. That would hurt beer sales.

He looked at Wolfram's hand. He wasn't wearing Carver's ring, but Wolfram packed Captain Carver's hat in his suitcase. At least Wolfram had agreed to pack his uncle's Luger, instead of carrying it in a shoulder holster. Both of their weapons were in their suitcases. Hans felt better because the guns were packed, although he had to cajole Wolfram with the promise of more sex on the train to Washington.

When they made a twenty minute stop in Jacksonville, Hans sent a telegram to his contact at the Spanish Consulate: Klaus.

Staying at Willard. Contact Smith and Wesson.

He had drawn a blank on cover names, and Smith and Jones seemed too suspicious. But there was no way he was going to use his own name. Somehow, he would have to figure a way out of this mess.

Chapter 13

After breakfast, Tom Burk drove Rachel to her
employer's home on Jupiter Island, then returned via the
draw bridge to the mainland and the Hobe Sound railroad
station to await some morning business. He noticed two
vehicles in the parking lot, one of which was an U.S. Army
vehicle, what everyone was calling a *jeep*. What was a jeep
doing in the parking lot of the railway station? Had a
military man taken a train that morning? It was odd. He
shrugged off the thought and walked up to the station
master's booth, doffed his hat in a gesture of subservience
and asked:

"Any work for me, boss?"

"Yes, boy, there is. Do you know the Hoffman house?"

"Yes, sir. The house they callin' *Flamingo?*" Tom
replied in his best "darkie dialect" for the white man.

"Yeah, that's it. Interested in five dollars, boy?"

Tom gave the racist station master a phony smile and an
obsequious reply. "Why yes, boss. Old Tom would sure
like that." Tom thought the man was an ignorant fool, but
the station master was a white man, so Tom had to hold his
tongue in deference to the man's pigmentation. *The Good
Lord must like stupid white men*, he thought rephrasing
Lincoln's comment about God's love for the common man,
for He made so many of them.

"You drive that there car to the house, boy," he explained, pointing to the Hoffman's vehicle. "The two young men took the northbound train this morning."

Tom wondered why they left. Wasn't it sudden? Odd, the one man was the chauffeur one day, a tennis player at the Jupiter Island Club another, and now he goes North with the rich Hoffman boy as a traveling companion. Something wasn't right. Still, a job was a job. Tom knew he would have to walk two miles back to the station. But five dollars was five dollars, a day's pay for many men. As he accepted the car keys from the station master, he wondered how much money the old man had been given by young Hoffman and how much the old man had cheated him. Maybe the station master wasn't an ignorant fool after all. Maybe he was just a cheat and a double-crossing cracker. He shrugged. The five dollars was easy money, and it might be a slow day.

It was a treat to drive the Hoffman's fancy car. The black Rolls-Royce Phantom III sedan handled so much more smoothly than his Buick. It was a shame that the war had stopped production of the iconic vehicle. As he drove the V-12 across the bridge, Tom slowed down to a crawl. He was in no hurry to take the car back. He spotted Miss Melda May walking to work, trudging on the pedestrian sidewalk that ran across the drawbridge down toward the beach, and he stopped.

"Miss May, do you want a ride?" he offered.

Melda May stopped as Tom slowed the car down: "Tom Burk, what are you doing driving that white man's car?"

"Gave me five dollars to drive it back to their house."

"White people's so lazy," she said. She shook her head. "You go on now, Tom Burk. Don't want white folks to get upset seeing two niggers driving a fancy white man's car. They'll think wee'z taking over," she laughed.

Tom Burk nodded. It was sound advice. Melda May would rather walk than cause any problems for Tom. Or herself. That was how Melda May survived. Heck, it was how Tom Burk survived. Old Jim Crow, that damnable blackbird, he made a man do things he shouldn't have had to do. Jim Crow made him belittle himself. Jim Crow made Tom angry, but he kept his anger hidden from the white man. A fawning facade was a matter of survival. Jim Crow wasn't right, but that was how things were.

He drove the car up the Hoffmann driveway, stopping a few yards short of the porch to the house named *Flamingo*. He hadn't been instructed what to do with the car keys. He wondered if he should remove the keys or leave them in the ignition, or walk up to the porch and knock on the door. Maybe a servant would know what to do. But from what Tom had learned by asking around, none of the local people were working as servants at the Hoffman house. That was just another strange thing. Word around Tom's neighborhood was that the hermit-like Hoffman family brought their own servants with them when they came down from the North: white servants. But no one had seen the senior members of the family since January. Then a son and his friend/chauffeur showed up.

Tom removed the car keys from the ignition and walked up to the porch, nearly losing his balance on something slippery. Something slick seemed to be on the porch. He looked down. A chill ran through him. He knew the sight. He had seen it too often in the Argonne Forest in 1918: caked, dried blood. The stain on the wooden porch appeared to have been a great deal of dried blood that someone haphazardly attempted to clean. What happened? Had someone butchered an armadillo on the porch? Was it animal blood or –he shivered- was it human blood? If it was human blood, whose blood was it?

Suddenly, Tom Burk was fearful. It was as if he were back in the Great War. It was the same feeling, the same anxiety. He knew he had to fight through his fears as he had back in 1918. The Great War taught him that courage was facing your fears and pressing on, even when you thought you were going to shit your pants. He wasn't the only man who shit his pants during combat the first time under fire. Combat was bloody *and* smelly.

He took a deep breath and knocked on the front door. There was no answer. He sensed he should let it be, leave well enough alone… whatever happened was for the white folks to sort out. But then he had a foreboding that the dried blood might have something to do with Captain Carver. Tom Burk hoped it wasn't Captain Carver's blood. In his mind, he thought: *Why was the jeep in the railway station parking lot? That wasn't right. It was out of place. Was it Carver's jeep from Camp Murphy?*

"Anyone home?" he called out.

There was no answer.

He turned the front door knob ever so slowly and was surprised to see the door was unlocked. Nervously, he entered the white folks' home. In the vestibule, he stopped and hesitated. Then he called out once more:

"Anyone home?" He shouted. "I have brought the car back. Is there anyone home? I have brought the car back."

On a small rattan end table in the vestibule, Tom Burk noticed a set of keys and a ring. He placed the car keys on the table and leaned over to look at the ring. It seemed familiar. He picked it up: *University of Texas*: A chill returned through his body. He knew immediately: it was Captain Carver's ring. What had happened to Captain Carver? He tried to think of Secret Service Agent Kane instead of Captain Carver, but Carver's name persisted in his mind. Had Carver paid the two young men a visit, like he said he would? But why did the jeep wind up at the railroad station? Was it Carver's jeep? Carver wouldn't abandon a jeep there, would he? That made no sense to Tom.

He noticed a telephone. As he picked up the receiver, he realized it was a private line, not a party line. Just a dial tone; no other people talking. No one would know if he used the phone. He wanted to call his brother at the White House, but that would take an operator. It was long distance. No, he couldn't call his brother from the house. Maybe he could make a person-to- person call from a pay phone. He would need a lot of change. A few of the operators knew his brother was at the White House so that wouldn't draw suspicion.

In the meantime, he called Camp Murphy via a local call and gave the switchboard operator Carver's extension number. He let it ring ten times before hanging up the phone. Something *had* happened to Captain Carver. Had Captain Carver been kidnapped? Then the thought came to him, Carver was dead. Carver had been murdered. The blood on the porch. That was Carver's blood. He felt a chill run through his body, the same kind of chill he had experienced in France the first time he shot and killed a German soldier. It was the feeling of death. Death was near; he knew death. He knew death well. Tom Burk cringed.

Chapter 14

Instinctively, Tom Burk removed a handkerchief from his pocket, retraced his steps and wiped his fingerprints from doorknobs and the University of Texas graduation ring. Nearly twenty years before, J. Edgar Hoover's F.B.I. had centralized a national file of fingerprints. The only thing which the Martin County Sheriff's office would need was Tom's fingerprints on the ring and he'd be strapped into *Old Sparky,* the nickname that most folks, both whites and colored, used for Florida's electric chair. For Tom Burk concluded Captain Carver had been murdered and if a Martin County deputy discovered Tom's fingerprints, Tom feared he would be charged for the crime. A colored man couldn't get a fair trial in Florida. Not with all white juries. Too many colored men had wound up as *Strange Fruit,* as Billie Holiday sang: colored men dangling by a rope from tree limbs. Sure as shooting, a cracker sheriff would arrest a colored man if he had a fingerprint.

Word around Hobe Sound was that the Martin County's Sheriff's officers shot and killed bank robber John Ashley and his gang back in the 1920s, after the criminals had already surrendered. And the Ashley Gang was white. *If they shot white men, they'd let a lynch mob hang a colored,*

Tom concluded. It had happened enough times around the state of Florida.

What had the station master said? The two young men rode North on the early morning train. Tom Burk wondered what he should do. He presumed Carver was dead, and Tom didn't know if the commander of Camp Murphy knew Carver was actually a Secret Service agent. The only other person who knew Carver's true identity was his brother, Walter. Walter would be at the White House already this morning. He *had* to call his brother. It was Walter who had involved him in the first place. *Thanks a lot, Walter*, he said to himself, and then he smiled.

For some peculiar reason, this whole mess was making him come alive. What was that about? He wondered: what would Philip Marlowe do with this case? Tom Burk enjoyed Raymond Chandler's mystery novels. He preferred Chandler's detective to Dashiell Hammitt detective, Sam Spade. He thought Marlowe was the more cerebral of the two fictional private eyes.

Tom Burk, certain that the house was unoccupied, decided to sleuth about to see if there were anything he could pick up in the form of a concrete clue. He knew the house belonged to the Hoffman family, although he didn't know the family except by its eccentric reputation. They were a family that kept to themselves. He had he never driven any member of the family to or from the Hobe Sound railway station. He was a bit surprised to find, however, that during the height of the winter season, there was no one looking after the property. That made the Hoffman's different from the other Jupiter Islanders that traditionally had employees maintain their properties year-round even though the rich folks might only spend a few months in Florida every winter season.

Tom discovered an empty package of *Lucky Strike* cigarettes and recalled that was the brand Carver smoked. But it might be only a coincidence. The cigarette butts he examined in an ashtray were worn down to the nubs. That too was odd for a Jupiter Islander, a person who could afford cigarettes by the carton. A Jupiter Islander wouldn't want to stain his or her fingers. One didn't see yellow smoker's fingers on Jupiter Islanders, Tom thought. He looked through the bedrooms. The master bedroom was undisturbed, as was another boudoir. The third bedchamber was in shambles. Had both men slept in the same bed? He wondered. He winced. Tom Burk was homophobic. He couldn't help his prejudice; he had been brought up that way. The bed wasn't made. The sheets were visibly stained. Tom shuttered to think what had gone on in that bed.

Tom Burk noticed the poster on the wall; he had seen that picture in a magazine a few years before. It was the Nazi rally at Madison Square Garden in honor of George Washington's birthday. The German American Bund, a vile group, Hitler's little brown shirts in America. Tom remembered. So, the Hoffman's' were members of the Bund. Tom Burk walked over to a desk in the bedroom. On top of the desk was a journal with an imprinted name,

Hans Hoffman III, Yale University.

Tom Burk leafed through it. A letter slipped out. It was in German. Tom Burk scanned the letter and caught a few words, including one he thought was for *lover.* It was addressed to Hans Hoffman from Wolfram Hess. Tom wondered if Wolfram Hess could be any relation to Rudolf Hess, the crazy Nazi who flew to England in 1940. Probably not, wasn't Hess a common German surname? Carefully, Tom wiped off his fingerprints and placed the letter down on the desk. In a manner of Philip Marlowe investigating a crime scene, Tom picked up the journal with his handkerchief and began to scan entries, looking for anything that might be a clue to the whereabouts of Captain Carver. It didn't take long. There, in a scratchy, shaky handwriting was:

My God, Hess killed an army captain. Wolfram scares me sometimes. I love him, but I don't know what he will do! Is he as unpredictable as his crazy uncle Rudolf. Has the war changed him that much? We had to cut up the captain and dump the body parts in the ocean. I am doomed. We are leaving in the morning for Washington to kill the Top Yid, Morgenthau. Wolfram is asleep, and I am tempted to- he is waking up...

Top *Yid*. What did that mean? "Yid" was another name for a Jew, wasn't it? Yiddish? Yid? The term for Jews that Nazis often used. Who was the top Yid, the top Jew? It was Morgenthau, wasn't it? He copied the diary entry into his notebook, wondering for a moment if he should steal the diary. He decided against snatching the journal, fearful that he might be caught with a white man's journal on his person. If he were stopped with the diary in his possession, Tom was certain to be charged and held as an accomplice in a murder, the murder of a white man, a United States Army officer. It would not end well, he realized. Tom heard Billie Holiday singing in his head: "*Black bodies swinging in the southern breeze, Strange fruit hanging from the poplar trees.*"

He pondered the question of "Top Yid" in his mind as he walked back to the train station. Should he tell the station master what he saw? No, good heavens, no, he told himself. Play the dumb nigger. As he walked into the station, he doffed his hat and said to the station master, "Took the car back, boss."

The station master nodded and handed Tom Burk a five dollar bill without even looking up. He was looking down at a *Daily Racing Form*. He was probably checking the races at Hialeah Park, Tom assumed.

"Thank you, boss," Tom Burk said in deference, but he let slip a smile that the station master didn't see. Asshole cracker, he thought. He hoped the station master owed his bookie a bundle. Maybe the guy was just a stupid *bolita* player, hooked on the Cuban game of picking three numbers out of a thousand. Six hundred to one if you won the one-in-a-thousand bet. Tom Burk knew the station master could play a *bolita* bet in Hobe Sound any time of the day. But Tom wouldn't. He didn't gamble, at least not with money.

He put the five dollars into his pocket and walked to his parked cab. He unlocked the driver's side and clicked the coin changer for a few dollars to use a pay phone. Then he remembered what his brother had instructed:

"Send me a telegram at the White House."

Yes, that made sense. Send the telegram. Don't even risk someone overhearing the conversation at the station. He was skeptical that Mrs. Patterson wouldn't eavesdrop, even if the phone call was long distance, person-to-person. Tom Burk didn't want to risk getting arrested. No, the smart thing to do was to go to Western Union.

What was the phrase he was supposed to use to alert Walter? "Fish are biting," he remembered. He wouldn't mention Carver in the telegram, so he tried to recall the Secret Service officer's real name. Walter had mentioned it, but Tom was suddenly drawing a blank.

Carver was actually....think, think. He shook his head; he couldn't remember the man's real name.

As Tom walked into the Western Union Office, he took a slip and filled out the form. He knew it would raise an eyebrow. Walter Burk, White House, Washington D.C. Why wasn't he able to remember the name? *Able? Abel?* No, not Abel, his brother. The brother who killed Abel. Cain! That was it! But it wasn't spelled with a *C*. Then he remembered, Cain with a *K*. Kane. Allan *Kane*. He wrote out his message in pencil:

Walter, Cousin Kane died. STOP

Too bad fish are biting. STOP

Tom

Chapter 15

Before leaving the Spanish Embassy in Washington, D.C. for her restaurant rendezvous with the German agents, Gretchen Schwartz, alias *Dulcinea Martinez*, went into the ladies' room, removed the swastika pin from her bra and slipped the good luck charm into her pocketbook, next to her pink-handled revolver. According to her instructions from Klaus, two men would meet her at the Rideau Restaurant, a favorite haunt of many government workers in Washington, as well as, it was rumored, Axis spies. One of the two men would be wearing a white carnation in his lapel. The reservation had been made in the name of Lido, in honor of her lost lover.

Gretchen walked into the Rideau Restaurant unescorted. She approached the cash register where an older, refined-looking, balding, gentleman was counting money.

"Excuse me, sir," she said sheepishly. "Can someone direct me to the Lido table?"

Yardley smiled thinly and pointed to the hostess a few feet away. "Helen," he addressed the hostess. "Would you help this young lady?"

The hostess smiled at Gretchen. "Yes, miss. May I help you?"

"The Lido table?"

The hostess smiled again. "Yes, miss. Follow me."

The hostess led Gretchen to a booth where two men in business suits were seated. Gretchen was relieved to see one of the men was wearing a white carnation. The other man, who wore no carnation, seemed to be eyeing her suspiciously and she registered an uncomfortable feeling. The scar on his face unnerved her momentarily, but something in his manner put Gretchen on alert, as well. The carnation man, the American agent she guessed, was handsome and blessed with a winning smile. Mr. Handsome widened his smile for her as the two men, minding their manners, stood for her until she was seated. "Thank you, gentlemen," she said.

Gretchen slid into the booth next to the man with the carnation: Mr. Handsome. She felt a bit of a tingle as she brushed against his knee before excusing herself. The hostess placed a third menu down and retreated to her station.

Silence. The man wearing the carnation continued to smile, and the other man continued to eye Gretchen suspiciously. Such cold eyes, she thought. Of the two, she guessed Cold Eyes was the assassin. Were they waiting for her to speak? Was it her move? She wondered. Careful, she cautioned herself to be careful of Cold Eyes. She remembered seeing photographs of soldiers at Dunkirk in a magazine; they had the same cold eyes. Eyes that seemed to be looking for some lost horizon: forlorn, hopeless, lifeless eyes.

She looked around, and certain that no one was watching, she retrieved the swastika pin from her purse.

"*Ja,*" Cold Eyes mumbled, but this time he offered her a short smile. It only lasted for a second then his cold eyes returned.

"I am Dulcinea," she said softly. She wasn't about to tell the two men her real name. She assumed the men would give her code names, as well.

"I am Hans and this is Wolfram," Mr. Handsome said, extracting the carnation from his lapel and giving it to her.

Giving her the carnation was part of the cover, as well as the signal. According to the information Klaus gave Gretchen/Dulcinea, the carnation man was to act as if he was her boyfriend. That was a pleasant thought, Gretchen mused. A nice fantasy. Hans, a nice name. In her mind, Hans had already replaced Mr. Handsome. She was struggling to replace Cold Eyes with Wolfram, but it was more difficult. Too bad the boyfriend bit wasn't real. She had craved a man after Lido died, but none had appeared to fill that void. Lido had not only taken her virginity, but he had introduced her to sex as pleasure. Sex as pleasure was a revelation for her. That first orgasm! Heavenly! Lido knew the map of her body like some carnal cartographer who had mapped every every pleasure stop, every side trip of her desires. She missed Lido, but she missed her pleasure even more. She was like an alcoholic craving another drink. She never would have thought that sex could become addictive. *Get control, Gretchen*, she told herself. *Get control.* She drove the thoughts from her mind. She had a mission to accomplish, after all. But she so wanted a man, and this Hans would do nicely.

She smiled at the men and responded to Han's introduction: "Hello, Hans. Hello, Wolfram. I have an apartment rented not far from here. It is close to the Treasury Building," Gretchen said softly. "We will go there after lunch. It would be a good place to keep a lookout for *Uncle Henry.*"

"First we need to go to our hotel and retrieve our bags," Hans offered. Using the *Uncle Henry* code name for Treasury Secretary Henry Morgenthau, Hans asked. "Does our Uncle Henry dine here?"

"I am told he does eat lunch here on occasion," Gretchen replied. "He comes here with some of his subordinates."

"I have seen photos of him in the newspaper," Hans said. "Do you have better photos of him for us?"

Gretchen looked around to see if anyone in the restaurant was watching them. Sensing it was safe, she withdrew a black and white photo of Henry Morgenthau from her purse and passed it to Hans. Morgenthau was on the steps of the Treasury Building. He towered over the other man in the photograph.

"He is a tall man," Wolfram offered.

"Yes. Uncle Henry is athletic, as well," Gretchen added. "He sometimes walks alone outside his office."

"That is very good. We will have to see if there is a pattern," Hans said. Even though Wolfram implied that their mission was a suicide mission, Hans had not given up the idea of escaping after the deed was done. Escaping with or without Wolfram, if need be. For the first time, Hans toyed with the idea of sacrificing his lover. He loved Wolfram, but he loved himself more. He also he feared Wolfram was mentally unbalanced. He had asked Wolfram to keep his Luger in his suitcase, but Wolfram refused. Since they had checked into the Willard Hotel and unpacked their suitcases, Wolfram carried his uncle's

handgun inside his suit jacket in a shoulder holster. He
wasn't going to go around unarmed in the capital of an
enemy nation, he told Hans. That made sense, of course,
but Hans still thought Wolfram was unpredictable. If, at
that moment, Secretary of the Treasury Henry Morgenthau
had walked into the restaurant, Wolfram would have
jumped up from their table and shot him dead on the spot,
probably yelling, "Heil Hitler!" and giving a stiff-armed
salute to the Führer. If that happened, there would be no
escape for Hans; there would only be death or life in prison.
In his mind, he saw a school blackboard with the words
Death or Life in Prison. Suddenly, a large, disembodied
hand holding an eraser rubbed out the words *Life in Prison,*
leaving only *Death.* Strange images, like Belgian fingers or
disembodied hands, often invaded Hans' mind, but he was
reluctant to tell anyone. He didn't want to be declared mad
like his second sister, Greta.

The young woman continued to talk about
Morgenthau, but Hans was having a problem concentrating
on her briefing, as he was distracted by her beauty. She
was an attractive, young woman. He undressed her in his
mind. He could feel a stirring in his pants. His growing
erection was an indicator he was having trouble with his
bisexuality. He thought: with a woman he could be the
dominant partner; with Wolfram he could never be the
dominant, only the submissive. Wolfram always initiated
their sex acts. Hans was Wolfram's submissive, and he
was tired of that role. He wondered what it would be like
to have a woman.

"That about covers it," Dulcinea/Gretchen said, as she
concluded her briefing for the two would-be assassins.
"Uncle Henry is all yours now. Like I said, my apartment
is not far from here and within a short distance of Uncle
Henry's house," she said in code for *Treasury Department.*
You will stay at my apartment. I have told the landlord that

my cousin and his friend are coming to visit me, so there will be no questions asked."

"Good thinking," Hans said. *Damn,* he thought, he had a boner. He was glad that Wolfram couldn't see his little pup tent below the table top. *That would be bad,* Hans thought. *Very bad.* Wolfram's jealous nature was why Hans had not mentioned his Vassar girlfriend. Hans wondered if the young, Vassar undergraduate, woman would ever let him *go all the way* with her. That intrigued him, for he was still a virgin. At least with women. He needed to rectify that embarrassing situation. Perhaps the girl next to him wasn't as big of a prude as the Vassar virgin. He wouldn't have to marry *her,* Hans thought.

Their meals came, and the three conspirators ate in silence, for they had concluded their initial business and did not wish to speak any more in public, fearing a slip-up. After the waitress cleared the table and handed Hans the check, Wolfram fired up a *Lucky Strike,* took a deep drag and let out a whiff of smoke which he formed into a momentary smoke ring. Wolfram had so enjoyed the late captain's cigarettes that he bought a few packs of *Luckies* on the train.

Wolfram pinched the cigarette, European-style, and in the distance, Hans could see that the balding man by the cash register was watching. Or was he watching Dulcinea? Yes, Hans assured himself, the guy was a dirty old man, sizing up a young girl, a girl that an old man could never have. But that Hans might, if he played his cards right.

Hans looked over the bill as Wolfram continued to smoke and Dulcinea sat quietly, patiently waiting to show the men her apartment before they retrieved their suitcases from their hotel. When they walked out of the Rideau Restaurant, none of the three conspirators noticed a tall older man and two younger men, for they had entered through a back entrance and proceeded through the kitchen to the dining area of the Rideau.

"Hello, Yardley, do you have a booth available?"

"Yes, Mr. Secretary," Yardley replied with a smile. "Helen, would you show Secretary Morgenthau to his table?"

Secretary of the Treasury Henry Morgenthau had no idea that day was his lucky day or that he had escaped assassination by only a few moments. In fact, had one of his men not needed to use the restroom at the Treasury Department, delaying the group, the men might be lying dead in their own blood on the floor of the Rideau Restaurant.

Chapter 16

Walter Burk read the telegram from his brother and knew instantly that something was amiss in Hobe Sound. What in the world had happened? What should he do? Should he inform the first lady or President Roosevelt? He folded up the telegram and placed it in a pocket of his white waiter's jacket. He concluded that he needed to talk to the president right away, but he thought it best to run the telegram past Mrs. Roosevelt first.

As Walter oversaw the place settings for that day's luncheon, the first lady, followed by her personal secretary, sauntered into the dining room of the White House private residence, pausing to consult the lunch menu.

"New England clam chowder...yes, that will do very well. We have that congressman from Massachusetts today. He's a Republican, but he is one of the decent ones, Tommy," Eleanor Roosevelt said to her secretary, Malvina Thompson, whom everyone knew as *Tommy*. Malvina had acquired the nickname *Tommy* from Eleanor's daughter Anna when Anna was a girl. Malvina was more than a secretary for Eleanor Roosevelt; Malvina was Eleanor's closest confidant and her gatekeeper, an assistant who protected the soft-hearted Eleanor from suspicious people or unworthy causes.

"There may actually be one or two who are decent," Eleanor added with a smile.

"Yes, ma'am," Tommy replied.

"Have you had a chance to type tomorrow's column yet, Tommy?"

"Yes. I even corrected that run-on sentence," Tommy smiled.

Eleanor feigned irritation. In reality, Malvina Thompson protected Eleanor Roosevelt's image, even down to a run-on sentence for her daily newspaper column. "Thank you, Tommy," she said. "I don't know what I would do without you." It was a sincere statement.

"Excuse me, Mrs. Roosevelt?" Walter Burk ventured.

Eleanor resumed her smile, and ever gracious, replied: "Yes, Mr. Burk?"

"Murray heard from James Armistead, ma'am," Walter began, his voice indicating he was nervous. "All is not well in Hobe Sound."

Walter's shocking comment had the effect of erasing the smile from Eleanor's face; her visage followed, forming a quizzical look. Without looking at her personal secretary and with her eyes on Walter, she said: "I will meet you downstairs, Tommy; I must speak to Mr. Burk alone for a moment."

When the room was cleared, save for the steward and the first lady, Walter noticed that Mrs. Roosevelt appeared nervous. Walter was surprised. He had never seen her nervous before. She was always poised; but not now.

"Please explain, Mr. Burk."

"Something has happened to Captain Carver…ah, Agent Kane, Mrs. Roosevelt," he said. "I received a telegram from my brother."

"Heavens! Oh my, what is the matter?"

"Agent Kane is missing, and my brother thinks he may be dead."

The first lady was stunned. Her face turned pale. She staggered as if someone had hit her in the stomach. "I must tell Franklin… the president," she corrected herself. Walter had never heard Mrs. Roosevelt refer to the president by his Christian name when talking directly with a staff member.

"Yes, ma'am." Walter replied.

"Come with me, Mr. Burk. Please."

They took the elevator down to the first floor, and Walter followed the first lady as she marched rapidly toward the Oval Office. The president's secretary, Grace Tully, smiled as the first lady approached her desk. Grace had replaced longtime secretary, Missy Le Hand, after she suffered a major stroke. Walter knew that a depressed Missy had attempted suicide during the Christmas season. All in all, and in spite of the reasons for the secretarial change, Eleanor was delighted that Grace was secretary. Eleanor had liked Missy, but she was jealous of her as well. Franklin's female admirers, Missy, Daisy and the others, were the wood that formed the cross that Eleanor bore as Mrs. Franklin Roosevelt. Eleanor had no such misgivings about Grace Tully. Grace Tully could be trusted.

"Is he alone, Grace?"

"Mr. Hopkins is with him, Mrs. Roosevelt."

"No one else?"

"No, Mrs. Roosevelt."

"Tell him I'm here, please. Tell him it's urgent. Tell him we have a message from *James Armistead.*"

"Yes, ma'mm." She turned to the intercom.

The president's voice crackled over the intercom. "Yes Grace?"

"The first lady is here, Mr. President. She says it is urgent. A message from James Armistead."

The president's intercom voice seemed enthusiastic: "Show her in, Grace."

Walter Burk marveled at the enormous globe the president had in the Oval Office. The giant globe was a good way to keep track of the war, he thought, especially since the conflict had broadened to become a true, worldwide war.

F.D.R. remained seated with Fala on his lap as his wife entered the room, but the president's close advisor, Harry Hopkins, stood up, greeted the first lady and exited the room, closing the door behind him as he left.

"Franklin," Eleanor began. "Mr. Burk has some news from Hobe Sound."

"What is it, Eleanor?" the president inquired.

"Murray heard from James Armistead," Eleanor said, knowing that the Hardy Boy in her husband preferred code names.

The president brightened up. "Oh yes, skullduggery." He looked at Walter Burk. "What have you got for me, Murray?" he asked using Walter's code name.

"Mr. President, Captain Carver…Agent Kane, is presumed dead." He handed the president his brother's message which he had copied from the telegram.

Walter, Cousin Kane died.

Too bad fish are biting.

Tom

"Fish are biting?" the president asked.

"Our code phrase, Mr. President, for something wrong. *Cousin Kane* can only be agent Kane as we have no cousin named Kane."

"Oh, Good Heavens, Eleanor. What have we done?"

"Franklin, I'm worried. Something is going on down there. Shall we speak to Mr. Burk's brother by telephone?"

"Yes, good idea, Eleanor. What about it, Burk? Can we call you brother?"

"He has a party line, sir, and within ten minutes, every woman in town will know that the president called."

"But we must know what your brother knows."

"Perhaps another agent can talk to him, Franklin. Or one of Mr. Hoover's men."

The president frowned. "I don't want J. Edgar to know about this, or we will all end up in that damn file of his for doing something off the books, Eleanor. That twerp… no, Eleanor, we can't tell Mr. Hoover. If he found out about this, and the Republicans win the House in the fall, I might get impeached. Burk?"

"Yes, Mr. President?"

"Can you get your brother up here? Make up some excuse for him to come visit you?"

Walter thought for a moment. He remembered the brothers' cover story of their mother's "estate." Yes, that might work. Have Tom come up to Washington to go over "mother's will."

"I believe I could find a reason, Mr. President."

"Good! Eleanor, you know this can't get out," Franklin Roosevelt cautioned. "We have to keep a lid on this."

"Yes, Franklin. But something is amiss. Why would anyone want to hurt the dear Mr. Kane? He's such a good boy." She couldn't find it in herself to use the past tense for Agent Kane.

The president inadvertently raised his eyebrows, then ignored his wife and looked directly at his steward, saying in a command voice: "Burk, you send a telegram to you brother and have him take the next train to Washington. Do you understand?"

"Yes, Mr. President."

"When your brother gets here, I want to meet with him...and you... right here in my office. Eleanor, inform Grace and *only* Grace on your way out. You are sworn to secrecy as well, Burk. That will be all, Burk."

Walter Burk and the first lady began to exit when the president said, "Not you, Eleanor.

Would you stay a moment, please?"

"Of course, Franklin," she replied.

"Have a seat, my dear," he offered.

"Thank you, Franklin."

"Now, it would seem that our little skullduggery may have gone awry, or it may have discovered some real threat. Hobe Sound. Why Hobe Sound? Refresh my memory. I have quite a bit on my mind today. Especially in the Pacific."

"One of the letters threatening Secretary Morgenthau was from Hobe Sound," Eleanor replied. "At least, it was postmarked from there."

"The whole thing sounds preposterous, threatening a Secretary of the Treasury…"

"It's not his position, Franklin. It is that Henry Morgenthau is Jewish."

"Yes, yes. You've said that a dozen times if you've said it once, Eleanor. Still seems like a stretch though. "

"Franklin, my women's intuition tells me that someone or some group is trying to kill Henry. I think we may need to call Mr. Hoover in after all, Franklin."

"Eleanor, I had to cajole Stimson into giving Agent Kane an officer commission as Captain Carver, and now, how am I to explain to Stimson what we did? Let alone Hoover. I am sorry Agent Kane is dead, but we can't have this come out."

"That agent Kane was killed or that you employed a colored man as a spy?"

The president blushed. Once again, his wife had spoken truth to power. She always detected his true motives. She was his barometer; she knew which way the political winds were blowing as well as he did. "Well, that too," he admitted. "We can't lose the South in the fall. I need their votes. I can't lose Congress."

"Did you assign a Secret Service agent to Henry, as I asked?"

"Ah, well no, not yet. Henry is in charge of the agents, and he won't assign an agent to guard himself."

"I would like you to do that today, Franklin. Tell Henry to do it."

"Yes, Dear. But actually, I was thinking of Frenchy?"

"John Grombach? That old Olympic boxer?"

"Yes. Frenchy owes me a favor. He's a colonel in G-2, Eleanor. Frenchy knows how to keep a secret. Plus, he is looking for some more funding for a project which I like. He calls it *The Pond* or The Lake or something like that. This is all off the books, Eleanor; we would be better served by Frenchy Grombach. Trust me on this. Frenchy detests Hoover nearly as much as I do. So, Hoover will never learn about this."

"But Mr.Grombach is *such* an anti-communist, Franklin."

F.D.R. laughed. "I won't ask him to kiss Uncle Joe, Eleanor," he said, making a reference to Josef Stalin, the leader of the Soviet Union, an ally of the United States. "Frenchy is discreet. I think we need a bit of discretion, don't you? We can't have this getting out. We didn't exactly do things in an orthodox manner."

The first lady could not argue with her husband. She felt responsible for this mess. It had been her idea, after all.

Chapter 17

Changing her mind, Gretchen escorted the two would-be assassins a few blocks from the Rideau Restaurant to the agents' hotel where they retrieved their suitcases. Then the trio walked the few blocks from the hotel to her second-floor, walk-up apartment. Situated in a row house, her apartment was a short walk from the Treasury Building. She rented the apartment on a week to week basis with her alias of *Dulcinea Martinez*. A two-bedroom, furnished apartment, the loft included two double beds, one in each bedroom, and a fold-out couch in the living room. She had stocked the *Philco* refrigerator with an assortment of foods in anticipation of her two male houseguests.

"The apartment isn't much, but it is close to the Treasury Department. You can each have a bedroom, and I will take the couch," she said.

Wolfram smiled. He checked both bedrooms and chose the one with the window and a view of the street. The other bedroom had a window, but it led to a fire escape and a back alley. To Gretchen's surprise, Wolfram then carried both of the men's suitcases into the room he selected. Gretchen didn't understand at first. She looked at Hans as if seeking an explanation of Wolfram's action. Hans smiled at her sheepishly. Suddenly, it hit her: The two men were lovers. She was a bit unnerved by the realization.

Wolfram watched Gretchen's eye contact with Hans suspiciously, then declared, "I need sleep." He went into the bedroom and slammed the door.

Gretchen was startled.

"He didn't sleep well on the train," Hans explained. "He is a bit grumpy. He spent too much time in the submarine, I think."

"Uh huh," Gretchen said, trying not to show her anxiety. She was a bit disappointed to discover the assassins were homosexuals. She was under the impression that Nazis were intolerant of homosexuals. She hoped she was hiding her shock at the revelation. "I understand," she said mildly, not really understanding at all. "Would you like some coffee?"

"That would be delightful," Hans replied. He went out to the circular kitchen table, ironically covered with a patriotic tablecloth of a bald eagle, its talons raised in a menacing manner, ready to swoop down on a buck-toothed Japanese soldier. The caricature of the Japanese solider was a racist, stereotypical, portrayal that was prevalent on a number of consumer items after the attack on Pearl Harbor. The eagle's head reminded Hans of the *Screaming Eagles,* the menacing birds which decorated the arm patches of the 101st Airborne troops, many of whom had been on the train to Washington. Two German agents were about to eat breakfast on an American symbol: the bald eagle.

Hans chuckled when he noticed the tablecloth. "Who is your landlord, Uncle Sam?" He asked in a low voice, fearful of Wolfram overhearing. It was doubtful that Wolfram could hear a whispered conversation as he was behind a closed door, but Hans was not about to take a chance. Hans even had misgivings that Wolfram was actually asleep. He sensed his lover was angry, not sleepy. What had he done to anger him? Hans wondered. Smiled at a girl?

Gretchen smiled at Hans. *Such a lovely smile,* he thought. Too bad, Wolfram had messed things up for him with her. Or had he? She had such nice, firm, breasts, he realized, his eyes drifting down from her face to her chest. Again, he began to undress her in his mind.

The gesture was not lost on Gretchen. So maybe Hans wasn't queer , she mused. Men noticed her breasts. Or, maybe he liked both men and women. It might be challenging to discover what that type of man was like. He certainly would have been places on the human body that she had never visited.

"My landlord's name is Mr. Fabrizzi," she replied. "I find his taste in tablecloths to be rather racist, but I don't think I should make a fuss. Frankly, I have no idea why the Führer made an alliance with non-Aryan people. The Japanese remind me of little monkeys."

"That confused me as well," Hans admitted. "I trust that the Führer has a plan in mind, something which he hasn't disclosed. You know that my companion, Wolfram, is the nephew of Rudolf Hess."

"The traitor who flew to England?"

"Yes. But for your own safety, do not mention Deputy Führer Hess. Wolfram does not like to talk about his uncle. He is embarrassed by him. Wolfram is here to restore the family honor by killing Roosevelt's head Jew."

"The Jews are such filthy people," Gretchen offered. Like her *Vater*, Gretchen was an anti-Semite.

"Have you read *Mein Kampf?*"

"Of course," Gretchen said. "Twice."

"Then you know what the Führer's plans are for the Jews."

"Yes."

"He is doing that in Poland and Russia," Hans said. "Wolfram told me of a meeting in January at Wannsee, a town outside of Berlin where the top men in the Reich government decided on a final solution to the Jewish problem. Our job is to merely kill one Jew, the head Jew of America. Our job is a great deal easier than killing a million Yids. Don't you think?"

"Yes," Gretchen agreed, as she placed a coffee mug in front of Hans. She made sure to brush him with her breasts when she poured the coffee. It was a little test to see if she was correct and if his glance at her breasts was more than merely accidental. As she finished pouring, he snatched her hand and gave it a quick, gentlemanly kiss. She knew she was blushing, so she turned away, not wanting him to see her broad smile as well.

"Don't tease me," he warned.

She found his assertiveness attractive. It gave her a rush for a moment. "So," she finally said, taking a breath and gathering her courage to broach the subject. "You and Wolfram are a couple, I take it?"

Hans smiled at her. "Dulcinea, I like both men and girls. I have girlfriend."

"You do?"

"Yes, She's in college. Vassar, a girl's college."

"Oh."

"But I don't sleep with her."

"Oh?" Gretchen was surprised, but pleased. She decided not to hide her pleasure. She smiled at him. "She won't let you?"

"No, she won't let me make love to her. That is very frustrating. I am a virgin you see. It really bothers me."

"What does?"

"My virginity. It is embarrassing."

"It shouldn't bother you," she reassured him. It was amusing to her that virginity to a girl was important, but to a man, virginity was embarrassing.

"Aren't you a virgin?"

She blushed. "You should never ask a lady that question, Hans. It is not considered good manners."

He blushed now. "I'm sorry," he said.

She smiled reassuringly. "Apology accepted," she said.

Such a *strange* conversation, Gretchen thought, surprised that she could speak so openly with Hans. Lido taught her that. "Talk straight to a man, girl," he had instructed her. "They appreciate it. Men want sex. That's really all they want. Maybe some want a wife and children, but when a man has an erection, all he wants is sex. He doesn't think of the future or the consequences of sex, he just wants sex. It is his little head that is doing all the thinking for him." That was how Lido referred to his penis as his *little head*. He had also told her,

"I will teach you to like sex, my little kitten. I promise I will teach you to like sex as a man likes sex. It will be my gift to you."

Lido kept his promise. His lessons were a revelation to Gretchen. She not only liked sex, she craved sex, and she missed it. Lido was gone, but here before her was this handsome man who was still a virgin. It was a turn of events, she thought, for she had lost her virginity to Lido. Perhaps she should take this man's virginity. She was surprised to see a male virgin and even more surprised to hear him admit it. But she was charmed by his admission and decided she wanted him. Suddenly, the prospect of taking a *man's* virginity excited her, as did the whole situation.

She was alone with an assassin, a man who was probably going on a suicide mission. If he were successful in killing the damn Yid, Morgenthau, the wrath of Franklin Roosevelt would be upon him. There would be no escape for him. His probable death was exciting and romantic to consider. She might be his one and only chance to have sex with a woman. Oddly, she felt a duty to seduce Hans…if that was even possible. *How could a man love both men and girls?* She wondered. *What did he find so attractive in Wolfram?* Wolfram scared her. She saw nothing attractive in Wolfram. He seemed as hard as Krupp steel, as her Papa liked to say. Hans, on the other hand, showed her an uncommon vulnerability.

"Why don't you go see if your friend is asleep, Hans," she advised.

When he stood up, her eyes drifted to his pants. Her suspicions were confirmed. The bulge in his pants indicated at least the beginning of an erection.

Hans did as he was told, walking over to the first bedroom.

Hans had a nice rear, Gretchen evaluated. She liked a man with a nice behind. Her late lover, Lido, said a man's rear was an indication of male stamina. Lido had had a nice rump, and Lido had had stamina; Lido had worn her out.

Hans opened the door to the first bedroom very quietly and peeked in. Wolfram *was* asleep. He knew Wolfram was sleeping by the way he lay, on his side. The snoring was the final evidence. So often Wolfram had awakened Hans with his snoring, and it was difficult to wake him when he was deep in the arms of Morpheus, as Hans liked to say. Why did Dulcinea tell him to check on Wolfram?

He returned to the kitchen, but she wasn't there. He looked around the apartment. A hand was waving him to come hither from the doorway of the other bedroom. As he walked in the bedroom, the woman was lying naked on the bed. She was stretched out so invitingly, Hans thought, totally surprised and yet aroused by the situation.

"Come here, Hans. I want to teach you a few things," she said.

She didn't have to say it twice.

Gretchen thought she should feel like a whore for seducing Hans, but she didn't. It seemed more like a teacher and student, because Hans had no idea where her *love button,* as Lido had called her clitoris, was located. In fact, she had taken control of their sexual encounter by mounting Hans. She regulated her rhythm, going up and down slowly so he would not prematurely ejaculate.

From Hans' point-of-view, he had a sexual education with *Dulcinea.* She was a marvelous, experienced lover. Something like a courtesan, Hans thought, trying to remember famous courtesans from novels he had read. Suddenly, sex with Wolfram lost its charm. Sex with Dulcinea was a delight. At the same time, Hans feared that his own abrupt change to heterosexuality might bring out jealousy in Wolfram: violent jealousy. He realized his friend and lover from the Fatherland was unbalanced. The murder of Captain Carver and the delighted look on Wolfram's face when he hacked up the corpse with the chainsaw had convinced Hans. But Hans still loved Wolfram. It was a damnable situation.

Post coitus, Hans lay beside Gretchen/Dulcinea on the bed with her head resting on his chest. She took one hand and twirled a short strand of his chest hair. Then she removed her hand to light a cigarette. She took a deep drag on the cigarette and exhaled a puff of smoke.

"The British killed my brother," she said suddenly. "He returned to *Deutschland* when the war began in '39, and he was killed by a British sniper when the *Werhmarcht* marched into France in the spring of '40. I hate all British."

"I am sorry for your loss," Hans said, surprised at the sincerity in his own voice. "That is a terrible thing for you."

She smiled sadly and changed the subject. "How did you meet Wolfram?"

"Years ago in the German-American Bund," Hans replied. "It was a summer camp and by coincidence, Wolfram was headed for Yale in the fall, as I was."

"And you became lovers?"

"Not until the Madison Square Garden Rally on Washington's Birthday in '39," Hans elaborated.

"I remember that well. I attended the rally with my father," Gretchen said.

Hans looked at her and confessed. "We were both so moved by the evening that we took a hotel room and slept together."

"Which do you like better, Hans? Boys or girls?"

He smiled. "I think I like girls better today."

"Just today?" she asked coquettishly. She squashed out her cigarette in an end-table, cut-glass ashtray.

He looked at her sheepishly. "I can't sleep with you tonight, Dulcinea." he apologized.

She looked at him quizzically. "Why not, Hans?"

Hans looked at her, but hesitated.

She repeated her question. "Why can't you sleep with me, Hans?"

"Wolfram…he is a jealous lover. He is also very dangerous. If you and I are going to make love, it must be when he is either asleep or not here," Hans explained. "I don't know what Wolfram would do if he found out that we made love."

Make love, she thought. She hadn't *made love* to him. She had *fucked* him. She didn't love him. She just wanted him. She had never even used the word *fuck* until she met Lido. Now it ran through her thoughts. *Fuck, fuck, fuck, fuck!* Lido had used *fuck* all the time. But then, Lido was a man. *It was acceptable for men to use the word. Hans wasn't a man; he was really still a boy. It was sort of sweet that he used the phrase "made love."* She reminded herself that she was the first woman he had ever had sexually. Of course, he might equate his first *fuck* with love. While his first attempt was quicker than a Jesse Owens's dash in the Berlin Olympics, his second attempt showed great promise. And, on the third round, he inadvertently found what Lido had called her *trigger,* her *love button,* and she exploded with satisfaction. The third time was worthy of a shared cigarette. What did the fat Churchill say? It was their finest hour? *Well, fatso we just had ours.*

"I'd better get dressed before Wolfram wakes up," Hans said. He stubbed out the cigarette in a bedside ashtray. "Perhaps you should as well."

She shrugged and joined him in dressing.

Back at the kitchen table, Gretchen brought over another pot of coffee and sat down with Hans.

"I do not understand what Deputy Führer Hess was doing when he flew to Britain, Hans," she said. "Was he trying to get the British out of the war?"

"I think so," He said, "Or get them to join us in fighting the communists. When did you join the German American Bund, Dulcinea?"

She felt like she should tell Hans her real name, but something told her to hold back. She had abandoned caution in the bedroom, but a sixth sense kept her from disclosing her true identity. She had given her body to him, but suddenly, she felt safer if she kept her true identity her secret. After all, this was merely a fling, a fling which might only last for the length of the mission. When the mission was completed, Hans would be either dead or captured, and she would be back in New York. She had decided that after the mission, she would opt out of the espionage business. If she gave Hans her real name and he was captured, it was very possible the government would break him in interrogation. The F.B.I. would then find her as well. Her father would be dragged in and she couldn't have that happen to Papa.

No, she had decided that this would be her last mission. Espionage was no longer a romantic diversion for Gretchen; it was beginning to become very dangerous. Wolfram had put her on guard. While the danger of the two assassins and the mission increased her recklessness sexually, she had come to the conclusion that she wasn't willing to die for Adolf Hitler, after all. The sex had been the catalyst. She wanted to live, at least for sex. No, she thought, she would be better off back in New York with her *Vater*. Two dead men were staying with her. They just hadn't been buried yet.

Chapter 18

1939 had been the last time Tom Burk arrived at Union Station in Washington D.C. when he came for his mother's funeral. While the prewar Union Station had been a busy depot, Tom was hardly prepared for the throng of fellow travelers when he detrained in March, 1942. The giant terminal was a hive of activity with hundreds of people milling about the great concourse that ran beneath the canopy of a mammoth arched ceiling. Soldiers and sailors seemed to be everywhere, some waiting for trains, others frequenting the servicemen's canteen which was overseen by dozens of women volunteers. There seemed to be so much more for the soldiers in this war than there had been in the Great War. The servicemen obviously were better treated than he had been treated in the Great War. But perhaps these young men didn't have it so good in another way. For Tom feared that these boys were going to encounter a level of violence far beyond what he had experienced in 1918.

And what Tom had witnessed on the battlefields of Europe was enough for a dozen men. No, he did not envy these young men. Some of the young men, he was certain, dreamed of glory, that mirage of a mendacious militarism which deluded generation after generation of the young men of all nations. Glory, like the illusion of a non-existent oasis in a desert, had led many a young man to an early date with "that grim ferryman," as Shakespeare wrote.

Tom knew the ideal of glory continued to be one of the pernicious lies of war. Another falsehood was the politician's appeal to patriotism. How glorious, the politicians cried, to die for one's country. Cemeteries in Europe were filled with patriots from a score of nations, he thought. How insane was war. In battle, the reality of combat was that patriotism hardly ever entered into a man's mind, save perhaps, for a man's virgin charge after the shrill dirge whistle which signaled *over the top*. Men in combat did not fight for such lofty ideals as patriotism; they fought to survive and to save their buddies. The idea was to get the enemy to die for *his* country, not for you to die for yours. It was more important to remain alive than to become heroic.

Ironically, Tom Burk became a hero without thinking of heroism, but by just trying to save the men under his command. When someone was shooting at you or your friends, war became personal, very personal. The guy on the other side was trying to kill you, and when he pulled his Mauser's trigger, the German soldier was not thinking of the Kaiser or hearing *Deutschland Uber Alles* in his head, he was thinking of his own survival. Combat was kill or be killed. Combat was simple. It was primal, and it was brutal. Brutal beyond belief. The nightmares could haunt a man as they had Tom Burk. Rachel's love had helped to lessen the frequency of the nightmares, but they would still return from time to time. Headless bodies and splattered entrails were imprinted in his memory.

As Tom stood at the platform sorrowfully watching young men shipping off to their own great adventure. Images from the Meuse-Argonne flickered across his mind like the footage of newsreel. He looked out at the sea of uniforms paraded hither and yon in Union Station. The poor boys had no idea what lay ahead, what they would experience. If they didn't lose their lives or a limb, they would, at the very least, lose their innocence and their naive thoughts of glory. Tom Burk was glad he was old. Knowing what he knew of war, he would never be able to fight in a war again. There was refuge in old age, he smiled. Old age was as much a blessing as it was a curse, he mused.

Tom and his brother Walter agreed that Tom would wait by the arrival platform until Walter appeared. In this sea of humanity, it was a wise decision. Tom was nattily dressed in his black Sunday suit, silver cuff-links, and white shirt with red tie and tie clasp; his shoes were spit-shined black wingtips. On his head he wore a black Mallory fedora with a grey hatband. He was, he liked to tell himself, dazzling in his outfit, handsome in his haberdashery. The suit was the outfit Rachel had picked out for him for his mother's funeral, and the one that he rarely wore, except for weddings and funerals. Fortuitously, Rachel had sent it to the cleaners a few weeks before, and she was surprised, but pleased, when he said he was going to wear it to visit his brother. He lied to her about having to meet with a lawyer in Washington and said that he wanted to be presentable. *Presentable* was one of Rachel's favorite words. Using Rachel's word made his lie believable. He felt bad about lying to his wife, but he had no other choice. On the other hand, he was rather proud of himself for being able to lie to Rachel and not get caught. That was a first.

Still, Tom Burk felt guilty; Rachel deserved better than the fabricated fairy tale of his mother's *estate*. Technically there *was* an estate: his mother's house, the house where his brother and sister-in-law lived in Washington. To Rachel though, a settlement meant she was finally going to get some of her mother-in-law's household items, things that she coveted. Before he left for Washington, Rachel handed Tom a wish list.

"What is this?" he had asked.

"Things Mother Burk promised me," she had replied.

Tom scanned the list. "Her dry sink and her roll top desk?"

"Yes, I want you to get them from Mary," she said. "They were meant for me."

"I thought you women worked all of that out."

"I let her have Mother Burk's rocker...Just tell Mary you want those things, and bring them back with you. On second thought, have her ship them."

Tom remembered the day after the funeral when the women in the family descended upon his mother's home to lay claim to her possessions. He had read about that type of buzzard-like behavior among the American Indians. After the last man in a family died, the women of the tribe entered the tipi of the widow and took all of her goods. The Burk women were no more civilized than the Plains Indians, Tom thought.

At Union Station, Walter Burk found his brooding brother amid the masses of people by reading the arrivals board for the track location of Tom's train.

"Walter," Tom said to his brother with a warm smile. They shook hands. "Thanks for meeting me."

They began to walk side-by-side through the terminal. Walter raised his voice against the din of Union Station.

"Good to see you, Tom. Mary will have supper ready for us. We meet with President Roosevelt tomorrow morning. I hope you had a good trip."

"It was fine, Walter, even if it was second class."

"Yes, yes," Walter said, not wishing to talk about segregation on trains with his brother. Instead Walter

wanted to talk about positive things. He changed the
subject.

"What do you think of all the activity?" Walter asked as
they walked through the throng of travelers.

"It is really something," Tom said. "I have never seen
so many people, so many soldiers and sailors in uniform
since…"

"The Great War?"

"Yes," Tom replied. "Although I have a feeling this is
going to be a 'greater war' in many, many ways."

"Yes," Walter said. "That is how it is shaping up."

"I don't think I would want to be your boss, Walter,"
Tom said.

"I wouldn't want his job, either," Walter agreed.

They boarded a street car outside Union Station and
rode the electrified transit to Washington's Shaw
neighborhood, where their mother's home was within
walking distance of Howard University. The home's
proximity to the university made the late Victorian-era row
house valuable real estate. Tom had agreed that Walter
could stay in their mother's home until some future time
when they would sell the house and split the proceeds.
Three years later, that future time hadn't happened, and
Tom sensed Walter's wife, Mary, was not about to give up
what Walter nicknamed "Mary's Nest." The resolution of
what to do with their mother's house was a feminine
minefield that the two brothers would have to navigate very
carefully. Tom was in no hurry to sell his mother's house;
he didn't need the money, and he actually hated to see the
house sold to a stranger. Better to have someone in the

family living in the house as their mother had bought it in 1917 when she and Walter left Florida to take advantage of an increase in employment for colored folks in the District. If Tom could ever get Rachel to leave Florida, then they would need some money, but for now, it didn't bother Tom that his brother and Mary treated his mother's house as if it was their own. He was pretty sure Rachel would have acted just like Mary if the situation was reversed.

Tom was surprised to see colored boys of about nine or ten playing stickball in the street on this chilly March afternoon. When they were young, he and Walter played baseball in a rocky field in Florida without enough boys to have a right fielder. Hitting a ball to right field was ruled an automatic out; in addition, the batter had to retrieve the baseball, as they only ever had one lopsided, beaten-up ball for the game. Back in Florida, the white major league clubs were already in spring training, and the regular season would start in a month.

Tom knew that his brother was a big baseball fan, so he asked, "How does the baseball season look, Walter?" Tom Burk did not mean the American or National Leagues. He meant the Negro Leagues.

"Well, I read where they are bringing back the Negro World Series this year," Walter said. "So many folks are working in defense plants making good money because of Mr. Roosevelt that folks have money to burn. *Homestead Grays* will be playing a few games in the District this year."

"I guess you will go see them, huh?"

"You bet!" Walter said. Then he changed the subject. "Do you want to talk about Agent Kane, Tom?"

"Not today, Walter… if you don't mind. I certainly don't think we should say anything at all in front of Mary."

Walter agreed. "We won't. We will save it for the president, then. We agreed to keep our wives in the dark, and we will."

"Thank you."

They walked the remainder of the way in silence. Tom was impressed by the neatness of the neighborhood. Most of the homes in the Shaw section of Washington had a coat of fresh paint, curtains on the windows and well-swept stoops. On the stoop of their mother's row house, Walter called out to his wife.

"Mary, Thomas is here from Florida!" he shouted.

Walter's wife, Mary, a large woman wearing a polka dot dress and sporting a white apron, met them at the foyer of the house, nodding to Walter to wipe his shoes before going any further into her domain. Tom did likewise. The tantalizing smell of fried chicken permeated the whole home, and Tom realized Walter's wife was *putting on the Ritz* for him. Was she afraid he was in town to sell the house? Tom wondered, for Walter had told her the cover story of settling their mother's *estate.*

"Thomas, as I live and breathe, it is good to see you," Mary smiled. Her smile reminded Tom of the Cheshire Cat from *Alice in Wonderland.* Always had. She was as fat as that cat, he thought, cattily. Tom never knew what thought her enigmatic face hid.

Tom forced a smile back at his sister-in-law, wishing that Rachel were there to run interference for him. He never quite trusted Mary, but the two Burk wives communicated often by mail and occasionally by telephone. He never understood how Rachel could complain about Mary one day, and then write her a friendly letter the next. Women never seemed to stay mad at one another for long. He never understood women. What man did? Any man who said he understood women was either liar or a fool.

"Nice to be here, Mary, thanks for putting me up," Tom said.

"Think nothing of it, Thomas. After all this home is yours as well," she said truthfully, but he knew it was for his benefit. She didn't honestly believe it. Her belief would be more properly filed under *squatters' rights*. "Walter, please take your brother's bag up to the guest room for him, Dear."

"Yes Dear."

Mary took Tom by the arm. "Now you come in and sit a spell, Thomas. Did you remember to bring Rachel's wish list?"

Once again, Tom was surprised. Rachel had implied that Mary had no idea about the things she wanted, but she did. He was perplexed. Mary noticed his confusion. She smiled and, as if to answer his unspoken question, she said:

"Rachel and I spoke this morning on the telephone, Thomas. She called me long distance. Isn't that thoughtful?"

Great! He thought. *Long distance* charges. He dreaded the bill he would receive for that call, because he knew the two women wouldn't have kept it to three minutes. Gab, gab, gab, he thought. Rachel's long distance telephone calls to Mary were few and far between, but they were never short and thus never cheap.

"Oh," was the best Tom Burk could mutter to his sister-in-law. He brought out Rachel's list from his inside suit pocket and handed it to Mary. She took out a pair of horn rimmed glasses from her pocketbook, looked over the list and nodded.

"Yes," she said. "These items actually belong to Rachel now. Rest assured I will make arrangements to ship these things to her in Florida. You don't have to worry a thing about it, Tom," Mary said. She took his hand, patted it and led him into the living room, saying, "Now tell me of the children, Thomas. How are they?"

He went through the obligatory ritual of telling a family female the whereabouts of his son and daughter. It was a perfunctory performance, and he knew Mary was only trying to be polite, especially when she didn't usher any follow-up questions to his short summations. All of that, he realized, Rachel had probably already told her during their long-long distance telephone conversation. Thankfully, his brother rescued him, and they proceeded into dinner.

After dinner, Rachel asked the two men what their plans were for the evening. She was headed to church at Shiloh Baptist.

"I thought I might take Tom down to U Street," Walter said, thankful that his wife was headed out for the evening.

"Well, Walter, be sure you wear a tie if you are on U Street," Mary instructed. "Thomas is suitably dressed as he is. He looks very fashionable. I read in the *Washington Bee*, that Cab Calloway is at the Murray Palace Casino tonight. Perhaps Thomas would like to hear him. Just dress up, Dear," she smiled.

The Cheshire Cat image ran through Tom's mind again. Cab Calloway sounded promising though. He enjoyed his music, especially *Minnie the Moocher.*

Even Tom knew that social convention required colored men to dress up on U Street, the commercial hub of the forty-block neighborhood, sometimes referred to as Shaw. Shaw was a section of the city where colored people ran the show. It was also the name of the neighborhood school: *Robert Gould Shaw Junior High School.* The school was named for the white commander of Civil War 54th Massachusetts Volunteer Infantry, the first colored combat unit that made a valiant, if futile, charge at well-entrenched Fort Wagner in South Carolina in 1863. The charge may have been futile, but its attempt gained admiration and respect for the colored soldier as a fighting man.

The neighborhood was the pre-Harlem Renaissance center of African-American intellectual and cultural life. Before the Cotton Club in New York, there was Murray's Palace in Washington. Washington was the original home of Duke Ellington before he took *The A Train* to fame in Harlem.

The two brothers hadn't had the stamina to stay long enough to hear Tom's favorite, *Minnie the Moocher* sung by the famous Mr. Calloway. Walter didn't drink alcohol either, so the men only consumed *Coca Cola* and watched the younger people dance. Swing was the thing, but the two men left for home by nine-thirty, even before Mary returned from church. Their plan for the following morning entailed Tom accompanying Walter to work at the White House. That required the two brothers to be out of the house no later than 5:30 A.M. So they went to bed before Mary came back from Shiloh Baptist Church.

In the morning, while his wife still slept, Walter walked into the guest room and woke his brother for the early shift at the White House. The two siblings rode the *trolley*, as the electric street car was nicknamed. They exited the trolley at a transit stop near the White House. At the gate to the president's mansion, Walter introduced his brother to the guard, and Tom tagged along with his brother, the White House steward. Tom was proud of his brother's position; it was an enviable job, he thought.

Tom received a quick perfunctory tour of the White House before Walter led him upstairs to the private residence and watched quietly as Walter oversaw the breakfast operation. Walter explained that the president often took his breakfast on a tray in his bedroom, but Mrs. Roosevelt had asked him to join her this morning, bribing him with donuts. The Roosevelt's loved donuts, Walter said. There was a plate of donuts nearly every day for breakfast.

The coffee was ready, but the first lady requested that the staff not make breakfast for the president until Mr. Roosevelt was seated at the table and had a chance to glance at his stack of morning papers. The headlines would determine his appetite, the steward knew. He hoped it would be more than a grapefruit morning for the President of the United States. The president didn't eat much when the news was dire, sometimes not even a single donut. There had been too many grapefruit mornings lately.

"Does he read all of those newspapers, Walter?" Tom asked his brother.

"Scans them mostly, looking at the editorials and columnists in detail. He knows the war news better than they do. But it is the political news that really can upset his stomach. He is very fearful of the Republicans taking over the House of Representatives in the fall."

"Is that possible?"

"He seems to think so. He has to kiss a lot of cracker ass, Tom. He needs the southerners to control the House."

Tom was amazed at his brother's political knowledge, but he realized Walter had probably heard a hundred conversations of the president. "What about the war news in the papers?" Tom asked.

"Most of that is censored, Tom."

"Doing that with our little *Stuart News* back home."

"Seems to be the trend for sure," Walter agreed. "Helen," he said to one of the waitresses. "Make sure the salt shaker isn't sticking. Put a bit of rice in it. You know how he hates a sticky salt shaker," Walter said.

"He does?" Tom asked.

"Not that I know of," Walter whispered. "But I do." He smiled, and Tom returned the gesture with one of his own.

As Walter finished his instructions to the staff, the statuesque Eleanor Roosevelt, adorned in a simple blue dress, elegantly strode into the dining room. "Good morning, Mr. Burk," she smiled.

"Good morning, Mrs. Roosevelt," Walter replied. He didn't realize the first lady was waiting for him to introduce his brother.

Eleanor's smile reminded Tom of a horse. He shook the image from his mind. Cheshire Cat, horses. Sometimes his mind bothered him. The Meuse memories were one thing, but the other odd images- it was as if his brain processed frames of repressed images and brought them up for him to remember. Still, the repressed images could be a useful quirk; like that morning at the Hobe Sound railway station when the chauffeur pinched his cigarette. That repressed image of the P.O.W. had returned to him.

Tom realized he would have to introduce himself to Mrs. Roosevelt, as Walter had neglected that task. He smiled at the first lady, who was nearly his own height. She was a tall woman. Nearly six feet tall.

"Good morning, Mrs. Roosevelt." He said.

She looked directly at Tom and smiled anew. "You must be Mr. Burk's brother. Thomas, I believe?"

"I am, Mrs. Roosevelt."

She offered him her hand to shake. "Glad to meet you, Mr. Burk. Your brother does a first rate job for us."

"Yes, ma'am," Tom found himself smiling at the gracious woman. He felt a bit guilty that he had thought of her smile as horsy. It was just genuine.

"Won't you join me for breakfast?"

Walter intervened. "That won't be necessary, Mrs. Roosevelt. We ate already."

"Mr. Burk," she looked at Walter. She frowned and shook her head like a mother wanting her boys to eat before taking off for school. "I believe you only had coffee, if even that, and nothing more. Am I right, Mr. Burk? Mr. Thomas Burk?" asked the first lady, switching her head to him. She waited for his reply.

Tom Burk smiled, "Yes, ma'am."

"We must feed your brother, Walter," Eleanor continued. "I know you cannot sit at table with us, but your brother can."

"Yes, Mrs. Roosevelt."

She looked back to Tom. "Do you pay federal income taxes, Mr. Burk?"

"Yes, ma'am."

"Then I think you should get something back for your hard-earned money. Lord knows you should." She patted a seat beside her and said in an authoritative voice, "Sit down, Mr. Burk." Then she smiled again and asked him. "How about some ham and eggs?"

Walter Burk rolled his eyes. There was nothing he could do when Eleanor Roosevelt decided to intervene. Not a thing in the world. Even the president couldn't control her. The president had as much control over Eleanor as Walter had over his own wife Mary. He couldn't control his wife, and the president couldn't control his. The steward and his president had something in common after all, he smiled: the curse of being a husband with a demanding wife.

Eleanor was in the mood for gossip. "Tell me, Mr. Burk, did you really see Katharine Hepburn and Spencer Tracy together?"

What was it about movie stars that so interested white people? Tom Burk wondered. But he was polite to the first lady. "They stayed at the same house…Mr. Barry's house. He's a playwright, Mrs. Roosevelt." He was about to tell her about the enormous tip which Spencer Tracey had given him, but decided against it.

"Philip Barry, yes," Eleanor Roosevelt nodded.

She, of course, knew of Philip Barry. Tom realized that a bit too late. "You knew that of course," he added, smoothing things out.

"Yes, I have seen a few of Mr. Barry's plays in New York... I would like to ask you about Agent Kane who you knew as Captain Carver, Mr. Burk," the first lady began. "But I don't think that is a subject that should be broached before we eat, do you, Mr. Burk?"

"No ma'am. Mrs. Roosevelt?"

"Yes?"

"What was it like to fly with the colored pilot at Tuskegee? I thought you were very courageous to go up like that."

Eleanor smiled broadly. "Why thank you, Mr. Burk. It was the most exhilarating day of my life. I felt as if I were a bird. Chief Anderson is a wonderful pilot, so skillful. I was in safe hands all the time. He has more experience than most white pilots. I hope those Negro flyers will see some action in the war. We will need them. I believe you served in the First World War, Mr. Burk?"

"Yes, ma'am. With the French." Tom Burk noticed Mrs. Roosevelt's use of *Negro* in lieu of *colored* when she spoke to him, something Mr. Bartlett did, as well.

"Yes, such a slight to our Negro soldiers. Loaning our men to the French so the KKK wouldn't get upset. John Pershing was a coward for giving in to the Southerners, especially considering he cut his teeth with the Buffalo soldiers. Negro Soldiers led by General Pershing fought right next to my Uncle Theodore and his Rough Riders at

San Juan Hill in the Spanish War. Those Buffalo Soldiers never received the credit they deserved, although my Uncle Theodore spoke highly of them."

Having heard the first lady get up on her soapbox on many occasions, Walter Burk realized that Eleanor Roosevelt was about to give a sermon on race relations within the country. Suddenly, her impending lecture was interrupted as the president wheeled himself into the dining room.

Tom Burk stood up. It seemed the correct thing to do. Eleanor did not rise. Tom hoped his face hid his shock of seeing a handicapped president. He had never seen a photograph of F. D. R. in a wheelchair, but here he was. In a wheelchair. The President of the United States couldn't walk. He was crippled.

"Franklin," Eleanor said. "This is Walter's brother, Tom Burk, from Hobe Sound, Florida. I have invited him to join us."

The president offered his hand to Tom, who reached out and shook it. "That's fine, Eleanor. Sit down, Mr. Burk, please, sit down. May I call you Tom?"

"Yes, Mr. President," Tom replied. He sat down.

"We have a few things to talk about after breakfast."

Tom Burk nodded. "Yes, sir."

The president smiled and grabbed a donut. "Good," he said. "About Agent Kane...Captain Carver...another gentleman will be joining us, as well, a fellow named Frenchy Grombach. He's not really French, although his father was a French diplomat. Acquired the *Frenchy* moniker in school and it stuck. He has done a splendid job on some missions for me before. I hope that you will work with him to catch those fellows for me."

"Yes, sir," Tom Burk replied. What in the world did the president expect of *him?*

Walter Burk placed his brother's order of ham and eggs in front of him. Tom smiled for although he hadn't asked for "sunny side up," Walter remembered. "Thank you, Walter," he said.

His brother grumbled in response.

The president seemed to be hungrier for gossip than grapefruit. He wanted to know the scoop about the movie stars and the other Jupiter Island "high hats." "The swells of Jupiter Island," as F.D.R. referred to them.

It was odd, Tom thought; the president of the United States was waging a war on two fronts, and all he wanted to know about was what the rich people on Jupiter Island were doing and talking about and who was sleeping with whom. It was not what Tom Burk had expected of a president.

Franklin Roosevelt knew of Tom Burk's war record and was very complimentary of Tom's military service. He apologized for President Wilson's decision not to use colored soldiers for combat alongside white American troops in the Great War. F.D.R. served as the Under Secretary of the Navy during World War I during Woodrow Wilson's administration. From what Tom read, he realized that even though Wilson had been the governor of the progressive state of New Jersey, he had been born in Virginia and retained a Southerner's belief in segregation. Woodrow Wilson even called the inflammatory film, *Birth of a Nation,* an accurate portrayal of the Civil War and its aftermath. While by no means as liberal as his wife Eleanor, Franklin Roosevelt was ending racial discrimination in federal employment, which helped many a colored man get a good-paying job.

After breakfast, Tom Burk joined Eleanor and Franklin Roosevelt at the elevator for a trip to the Oval Office. Below, on the first floor, an aide stood waiting, tethered to the First Dog. Having completed his morning *business*, Fala waited patiently by the elevator for his master.

"You know, Tom," the president said as they descended to the first floor in the elevator. "Eleanor's Uncle Teddy caught a bit of hell for having Booker T. Washington at the White House for dinner."

Eleanor frowned. "You never really liked Uncle Theodore, Franklin. You know how he hated being called 'Teddy,'"

The president smiled at Tom. "He was a Republican, Tom. Republicans can get a bit stuffy now and then."

The first lady playfully punched the chief executive on his right arm. But she was smiling.

The elevator doors opened, and an unleashed Fala jumped into his master's lap.

When they arrived at the Oval Office, F. D. R. ceased his playful demeanor and wheeled himself around to his desk; Fala along for the ride. Eleanor indicated to Tom to take a chair. She sat on a couch. Miss Tully, the president's secretary, entered to ask if anyone wanted coffee. There were no takers.

"Hold my calls, Miss Tully," the president said.

"I thought he would be here by now," the first lady said.

"Frenchy should be here shortly, Eleanor," Franklin Roosevelt said. "He has never let us down." The president turned to Tom Burk. "Tom, would you show me the evidence you have on Agent Kane…of Captain Carver's demise?"

Tom Burk extracted his notebook from his suit jacket. He took a deep breath and addressed the president.

"The station master at Hobe Sound gave me the job of returning the Hoffman car to their home on Jupiter Island, Mr. President. When I arrived at the house, I noticed some blood stains on the porch. I knocked on the door, but no one answered. I wanted to leave the car keys. The door was unlocked, so I entered to return the keys. I called again, but no one answered. On a nearby table, I spotted a University of Texas class ring, Captain Carver's ring, I believed. I had noticed it on his hand when I drove him from Camp Murphy to Jupiter Island and I had shown him where the house was, where the two suspects were staying. So on a hunch, I went snooping around and found a diary, Mr. President. I copied down the important entry. Here it is:

My God, Hess killed an army captain. Wolfram scares me sometimes. I love him, but I don't know what he will do! Is he as unpredictable as his crazy uncle Rudolf? Has the war changed him that much? We had to cut up the captain and dump the body parts in the ocean. I am doomed. We are leaving in the morning for Washington to kill the Top Yid, Morgenthau. Wolfram is asleep, and I am tempted to- he is waking up…

And that is where his entry ends I assume because the other man came into the room."

"My Lord in heaven," Eleanor said. She hurriedly left the room with a handkerchief over her face, trying in vain to control her sobs.

Franklin Roosevelt's face went ashen. "Please excuse the first lady," he said. "She liked Agent Kane a great deal...we all did. I think she needed to well... you understand; she is a sensitive soul. Tom, I wanted you to know that Henry Morgenthau, Jr., my Secretary of the Treasury, is one of my two closest advisors, along with Mr. Hopkins. He and I have been friends for many years. I would be lost without him. We must find these men before they can harm Henry. I need you to help identify them."

"Yes sir. Whatever I can do."

"Did the diary just say Rudolf's Hess's nephew?" the president looked astonished.

"Yes sir," Tom replied. "Implied it actually, but I think it is the same Hess."

"Wow. Wait until I tell Winston about this," Roosevelt smiled. He was suddenly intrigued. "That would be a coupe, catching Hess's nephew."

"Yes sir," Tom agreed.

The president reflected for a moment then said: "Tom, are you certain these two men you saw were headed to Washington?"

"Yes sir, they took the early morning train the other day."

Refreshed, the first lady, came back into the room.

"Excuse me gentlemen," she said.

"No problem, Dear. Tom, I want you to know that it was Mrs. Roosevelt who suspected the plot against Mr. Morgenthau, and at first, I dismissed it because I thought, who bothers to shoot a *Treasury Secretary*? That was short-sighted of me, and I am sorry I doubted you, Eleanor."

"Thank you, Franklin," Eleanor said with a smile.

"You are welcome, my dear. Tom, I suppose I should have gone to Director Hoover, but I am not too keen about J.Edgar. I think he might be a pud-packer."

"Franklin!" Eleanor said.

Tom Burk was confused. "What is a 'pud-packer,' Mr. President?"

"A fairy."

Tom Burk drew a blank at the expression *fairy*.

"Please excuse my husband, Mr. Burk. The term 'fairy' is a vulgarity for 'homosexual," Eleanor explained. She glared at her husband.

Tom Burk grimaced. Once more his homophobia was coming to the surface. He was genuinely unaware of his intolerance for homosexuals. Had he not had such an ingrained cultural bias against homosexuals, he might have realized that they faced discrimination too. It was not just colored people who were ostracized.

"Like these two men who want to kill Secretary Morgenthau, Mr. President. I believe they may be homosexuals, for I found evidence which I won't discuss with the first lady present."

"Really, Tom? A queer Nazi?" the president laughed. 'You know they say that is why Hitler got rid of his good Nazi buddy, Ernest Rohm...because he was a queer. Queer as a three mark bill." The president laughed heartily at his own joke, a play on the nonexistent "three dollar bill." Tom managed to smile politely, although the discussion of homosexuality made him uneasy.

Eleanor, like a school marm, brought the two "boys" back to the task at hand. "Mr. Burk, Mr. Morgenthau received a hate letter postmarked from Hobe Sound, but I doubt if it was from either one of these two men," she said. "So, all of this may be a fortuitous coincidence, and we are very lucky to have inadvertently discovered the plot, thanks to you. The president originally assigned Agent Kane to Camp Murphy to check to see that the taxpayer money was being used properly. *We* gave him the alias Captain Carver. President Roosevelt and I made him your contact for anything you might discover, and you unearthed an actual plot to kill Secretary Morgenthau. That has taken us by surprise."

The president chuckled. "Never would have thought this would happen in a thousand years. Now, I wonder if somehow the German government found out about Morgenthau's plan to turn Germany into farmland after the war. We are all sick of Germany and their war machine, Tom. You saw what it was like in the Great War."

Tom Burk nodded.

The president's intercom buzzed. "Yes, Grace? Frenchy is here? Yes, please show him in."

Chapter 19

"Hello? Miss Tully?…yes, yes, I can be there in an hour. Please assure the president that I will be there. Thank you. No, Miss Tully, I won't need breakfast." Frenchy Grombach hung up the telephone. What an odd call from the White House, he thought. He wondered what the president required, for he knew the president would only contact him if he needed something. He saw the possibility of a quid pro quo. The president needed something from Frenchy Grombach, and Grombach required funding for his espionage inspiration, "The Pond."

Trim and fit in his early 40s, John V. Grombach had completed his early morning, four-mile run, as well as showered, when the president's secretary called. Currently in army intelligence with the rank of colonel, even though he remained in civilian clothes, Grombach was a man of action consigned to overseeing code communications for an organization known as the Coordinator of Information, recognized by its abbreviation, C.O.I. Chosen by M. Preston Goodfellow, who was selected by F.D.R.'s son, James Roosevelt, Grombach, or *Frenchy* as he was nicknamed since his days as a cadet at V.M.I., would much rather have been sent overseas on an espionage assignment. But that wasn't going to happen with the showboat William

Donovan running the newly minted Office of Strategic Services.

Donovan, no friend of Grombach, was similar to Herbert Yardley in one respect; neither man seemed to understand the importance of secrecy in espionage and counter espionage although Grombach held out hope for Yardley's reformation. He knew Herbert Yardley chafed at his ostracism. Yardley had learned his lesson, Grombach thought. Yardley could be helpful.

Frenchy Grombach found Yardley's book on the World War I super-secret intelligence outfit, *Black Chamber,* to be rather useful. Unfortunately, Frenchy's boss, Preston Goodfellow, informed Grombach that William Donovan had blackballed Yardley from further espionage work. "Wild Bill," as he was known, explained that both the departments of War and State loathed Herbert Yardley. Frenchy's task was to serve as a clearing house for intelligence. Keep everybody happy. Grombach wanted to use Yardley, but the former head of the World War I Black Chamber had ruffled too many feathers of the espionage elite with his best-selling book. The subsequent popular film starring William Powell brought to light too many intelligence practices best kept in the shadows. Hiring Yardley would be tricky, but once Grombach's "The Pond" was in play he would have carte blanche on hiring. He planned on secretly hiring Herbert Yardley.

Even though Grombach thought he might be able to use Yardley for "The Pond," a super-secret organization that Frenchy planned to run through the army's intelligence branch, he knew "The Pond" needed more funding, money that could not later be curtailed by that narcissistic asshole, "Wild Bill." The U.S. Army, thank heaven, wasn't too wild about "Wild Bill" Donovan, either, or his "Oh So Social" as the Office of Strategic Services was sarcastically nicknamed by jealous rivals. Too many fops and dandies in the O.S.S. for Grombach and the others.

Grombach was not an Ivy Leaguer like so many of the snobbish and clannish O.S.S. men, but politically, the O.S.S. was important to F.D.R. Many of the O.S.S. men had relatives who were large campaign donors for the president. Frenchy Grombach understood the politics of the situation and why the president had to please and appease so many different groups. Frenchy liked the president. He admired and respected a man who never let his physical handicap prevent him from running the country. Frenchy thought that F. D. R. had brass balls.

Raised in New Orleans, John Grombach was the son of a French diplomat stationed in *The Big Easy*. His family wasn't wealthy, and although John was multi-lingual, he was not a scholar. Rather, he was an athlete, an amateur boxer with a national ranking who would one day represent his adopted nation in the Olympics, for he had become a naturalized citizen after winning admission to West Point. He even managed to save his Roman nose from being broken in the ring. In profile, he looked as if his face might have adorned a Denarius coin.

Grombach was also a proficient fencer and a bouncer. Before entering West Point, after his stint at Virginia Military Institute, Grombach served as a bouncer in a house of ill repute. He liked to joke that he was probably the first whore house bouncer to compete in the Olympics, although he wasn't certain of it.

After the Olympics, Grombach became a member of the New York Downtown Athletic Club. Shortly thereafter, he became friends with Franklin Roosevelt, before F.D.R. went on to occupy the governor's chair in Albany and, later, the president's Oval Office in

Washington. He had, on occasion, managed a few off-the-record things for the president. As a result, the president put in a good word for Grombach with Henry Stimson.

The Secretary of War was interested in a clandestine spy agency apart from Donovan's O.S.S. Wild Bill, Stimson thought, was a publicity hound. And that was the last thing our spies needed: publicity. But Grombach's "Pond" would be something totally under the radar, and Frenchy was going to need more money than Stimson had allocated. A favor for F.D.R. could dramatically increase the project's funding. The president, master of all politics, understood the workings of a straight-up deal.

This would be Grombach's second visit to the White House. The first was when Frenchy met with Secretary of War Stimson, Henry Hopkins and the president. There, Stimson and the president listened as Frenchy roughly sketched out what he had in mind for a super-secret agency, apart from the O.S.S. It would be an agency unencumbered by bureaucracy for interagency squabbling, a truly independent agency. F.D.R. bought into the idea and wanted to fund it, but they hadn't really known what it would truly encompass. Nor had Grombach, who had underestimated the costs of such a clandestine outfit. Frenchy's opportunity to increase "the ducks in *the pond,*" was awaiting him at 1600 Pennsylvania Avenue.

When Grombach arrived at the White House, he was immediately ushered into the Oval Office. He was surprised to find Mrs., Roosevelt in the office, as well as a colored man, well-dressed in a beautiful black suit. Frenchy did not recognize the man, but he mistakenly assumed Tom Burk was an important political ally of the president, perhaps an emissary from the N.A.A.C.P. The first lady was sitting on a divan across from the colored man, who sat in a high-back chair. Frenchy was surprised when the colored man didn't stand up when he, a white man, entered the room. Surprised, but quietly pleased; he appreciated spunk in a colored man. Maybe it was Eleanor's doing, he wondered, thinking that perhaps the colored man was a friend of the first lady. She was always treating everyone as an equal. He had grudging respect for Eleanor Roosevelt, but he wasn't really fond of her. He thought her to be something of a nag. No wonder the president had mistresses, he mused.

"Frenchy," the president grinned. "Glad you could make it. I know you remember the first lady...'

"Mrs. Roosevelt," he greeted with a nod. He received her reciprocal nod in return. She was not *his* biggest fan, either. He had to work on that. Obviously Eleanor was part of this operation, whatever it was.

"This Negro gentleman is from Florida" said the president by way of introduction. "His name is Tom Burk. He is my steward's brother, and he has been working for us."

Grombach's eyebrows lifted. The colored man wasn't a politician after all. Sensing the proper move, at least for the liberal Mrs. Roosevelt, Grombach walked over to Tom Burk and offered Tom his hand. He knew how important it was to be on the good side of Eleanor Roosevelt. Woe to the man, who crossed "E.R." as her friends often referred to the first lady.

Tom Burk stood up and shook the white man's hand. Out of the corner of his right eye, Frenchy caught the first lady's smile. Bingo, he thought.

"Let's all find a seat," the president resumed. "Frenchy, it seems like there is a Nazi spy running around town. This Nazi killed one of my Secret Service boys and now is after

Henry Morgenthau. He came north from Florida after landing on Jupiter Island by way of a submarine would be my best guess. He came to Washington with an American citizen, a misguided boy from a very wealthy family. I am hesitant to use the word *traitor*, but I'm afraid the boy is in big trouble. *Big trouble,*" F.D.R. repeated for emphasis. "We know they came to Washington. Tom, for Mr. Grombach's benefit, would you read what you copied from that boy's diary."

Tom Burk hesitated a moment.

The president looked at his wife to see if she needed to leave the room again. "Eleanor, dear, would you like to…"

"I can deal with it now, Franklin," she assured him. "It just caught me off-guard, earlier."

"I understand, my dear…Please read the diary entry, Tom," F. D. R. repeated.

"Yes, Mr. President," Tom replied, and he began to reread the diary entry he had copied.

My God, Hess killed an army captain. Wolfram scares me sometimes. I love him, but I don't know what he will do! Is he as unpredictable as his crazy uncle Rudolf. Has the war changed him that much? We had to cut up the captain and dump the body parts in the ocean. I am doomed. We are leaving in the morning for Washington to kill the Top Yid, Morgenthau. Wolfram is asleep, and I am tempted to- he is waking up…

"Frenchy, it looks like the Nazis are intent on killing Henry Morgenthau," the president said. "Would you agree with my assessment?"

"I would, Mr. President. I would indeed. Did I just hear that Rudolf Hess's nephew is involved?"

The president smiled. He was delighted. "Yes, Frenchy. I would love to catch Hess's nephew. Kind of a competition I have with Winston."

"Wow," Grombach said.

"Frenchy, do you have any qualms about working with a colored man?"

Grombach couldn't care less what color a man's skin was, just as long as he wasn't a Bolshevik. "No, sir." A Black was fine, but not a Red, he thought. He hated communists.

"Good," the president grinned. "I want you to work with Tom Burk, Frenchy. He knows what these two look like, and he can spot them. The American citizen went to Yale so we will contact Yale for yearbooks from the last few years and see if we can get a photo of this Hoffman boy. His family is big in the beer business and used to be contributors to the American Firsters and Lindbergh's pro-German nonsense. But the young man probably looks different than when he was in college. Most boys do. So for now, Mr. Burk is our best bet to identify the two men."

"But why not the F.B.I., Mr. President?"

The president winced, but then smiled thinly. Eleanor interrupted.

"It is my fault, Mr. Grombach," the first lady said. "I wanted to give Franklin a little diversion from the war with some gossip about the rich fools on Jupiter Island. Secretary Morgenthau received a number of threatening letters, one of which came from Hobe Sound, where Jupiter

Island is located. Unsigned of course, and frankly fairly illegible. Horrible handwriting. So I assumed it was from one of those Jupiter Island men who were accustomed to dictating letters to a secretary, which would explain the terrible handwriting."

Frenchy was silently amused at Eleanor's assertions about handwriting. She struck him as a prissy Sunday school teacher. Totally irrational female, he thought, but he kept the thought to himself as the first lady continued:

"Walter Burk's brother Tom is a cab driver in Hobe Sound, so we hired him to watch out for anything suspicious."

"He found out that Spencer Tracy is sleeping with Katharine Hepburn," the president said with a smile.

"Franklin!" Eleanor chided.

How silly, Frenchy thought. There was a war on and they were interested in movie star gossip. Again, he held his tongue.

"Sorry," the president replied to his wife. Then he said to Grombach, "Frenchy, we sent Agent Kane to the new Camp Murphy to check on government contracts and later to contact Mr. Burk. Kane was under the name of Captain Carver, and he was checking to make sure that the government wasn't getting fleeced in building the new base in Hobe Sound, Florida. You know how Senator Truman is about such things. Harry is doing a fine job, though. Anyway, Mr. Burk was checking out if the threat to Morgenthau was real. It seems Mr. Burk found a Nazi. Tell him, Tom."

"Yes, Mr. President. Mr. Grombach, I saw a chauffeur smoking a cigarette like a German...or a European, at any rate. He pinched the cigarette instead of holding it between two fingers as an American does. I had seen that in the Great War with a prisoner I captured. Always thought it odd, and it stuck with me. A few days later I saw the same man, the chauffeur, playing tennis at the Jupiter Island Club. Chauffeurs do not play tennis at the club, Mr. Grombach. When he missed a shot, he shouted the German word for...excuse me, Mrs. Roosevelt... the German word for 'shit.' Sorry, Mrs. Roosevelt."

The first lady smiled. "I have heard the word before, Mr. Burk, in both English *and* German. As you are repeating what one of the men said verbatim, it is appropriate in this context. Please go on."

Tom Burk smiled. "Thank you, ma'mm," he said. "So, Mr. Grombach, I contacted Captain Carver, and he investigated. One morning, when I arrived at the station to await my first passengers, I noticed an army jeep in the parking lot. The station master asked me to take a car back to the Hoffman house, as young Hoffman and his companion had taken the northern train earlier that morning. When I got to the house, I noticed blood stains on the porch. I knocked, but no one was home and the front door was unlocked. I noticed a University of Texas ring, like the one Captain Carver had worn, and I looked around the house and found the diary. It was open and lying out on a desk. It seemed the two young men had left in a hurry. I copied the diary entry about the murder that I just read. Then I telegraphed my brother."

"Why didn't you notify the police?" Grombach asked.

"I am colored man, Mr. Grombach. I was told you were raised in the Deep South. You can understand my reluctance to contact the local cracker cavalry."

"'Cracker cavalry,' that is rich," the president laughed. "I must remember that the next time I entertain a Mississippi congressman."

Tom Burk allowed a brief smile to escape.

"So, what do you want me to do, Mr. President?" Grombach asked.

"Find the damned Nazi and the traitor, Frenchy. I want you to stop them from killing Secretary Morgenthau. I am rather fond of Henry."

"By any means necessary?"

"Yes, do what you need to do," F. D. R. said, staring over his glasses. "Then you and I can have a little private chat about your fiscal concerns," the president added. He broke into his campaign grin. Quid pro quo, Grombach realized. There was the carrot he needed from the sly, old fox.

Grombach smiled along. He didn't know how the president had discovered exactly what he wanted financially, but he knew that he never wanted to get into a poker game with the crafty F. D. R. The president could size a man up in five-seconds. He would know what that man was holding in his hand.

"Check with your old friend Herbert Yardley. The F.B.I. tells me his restaurant is a hangout for a number of suspected Axis agents. See if he noticed anyone or anything unusual. Mr. Burk can give the descriptions to Yardley."

"Really, Franklin, must we deal with that Yardley man?" Eleanor protested. "He is reprehensible."

"Of course he is, Dear," the president smiled. "He's a Republican. Let Frenchy handle it, Eleanor. Frenchy and Yardley go pretty far back. Frenchy, just don't tell Yardley you are working for me. I'm trying to keep the peace with the spooks, and it will be a bit difficult to keep the Pond's procurement off the books."

Tom Burk turned his head. The president used the term *spooks*. Did F.D.R. mean Tom and his brother? For *spooks* was cracker slang for colored people.

"Spooks? Mr. President?" Tom asked.

"Spies, Tom. *Spooks* is a nickname for spies," the president said innocently, not seeing any racial connotation in the word. "Tom, I want you to pretend that you are a diplomat from Haiti. That way, you can cross the color line in town if you need to. Did you know that Frederick Douglas was once ambassador to Haiti?"

"No, I didn't, Mr. President," Tom Burk lied. Tom had read a number of books on Frederick Douglas. He didn't know the president well enough to know if he could trust him. *If Rachel could see me now,* he thought. Too bad he couldn't tell her a thing. He thought he could act a passable Haitian diplomat; in fact, it would be one time he *could* be articulate among white people, for white people would expect a foreign diplomat to be intelligent.

They were forced to listen to the president give a short history lesson on Frederick Douglas in Haiti before Eleanor finally interrupted.

"Excuse me, Franklin," Eleanor smiled at her husband and stood up. The president acknowledged she wanted to leave.

"Mr. Burk, would you escort me to my office please?" She turned to Frenchy Grombach and said, "Mr. Grombach, Mr. Burk will meet you in a moment or two."

As the first lady walked out of the Oval Office beside Tom, she asked:

"Mr. Burk, do you know how to shoot a pistol?"

"Yes, ma'am."

"Have you ever fired one?"

"Yes, ma'am. In the war."

"What type of pistol?"

"It was a standard-issue French Model 1893 Revolver, Mrs. Roosevelt. The standard pistol of officers in the French Army. Eight millimeter."

They entered the first lady's office. She asked her secretary to leave for a moment so she could talk to Tom in private. "Have a chair, Mr. Burk."

She went to a filing cabinet and extracted a wooden box. She handed the box to Tom.

"Open it, please."

Tom Burk was surprised. It was a pistol. He said nothing, but the puzzled look on his face elicited an explanation by the first lady.

"It is a Colt OP .38 caliber special," Mrs. Roosevelt explained. "The gun is mine. A gift from the Secret Service in 1934 when I told them I didn't want their protection. So they gave me a gun and said good luck!" she chuckled. "But I'm afraid with the war on, Franklin insists I

take a Secret Service man with me when I travel. So I
would like to loan you my pistol. It is a very accurate
weapon. I fired it on a number of occasions."

"I don't think I need..."

"Mr. Burk, there is a Nazi agent running around
Washington, and a traitor as well. My idea is for you to
drive Mr. Morgenthau around as a chauffeur with Mr.
Grombach as bodyguard. That makes more sense than my
husband's goofy idea of a Haitian diplomat. But do go with
Mr. Grombach to see this Yardley fellow, and I will
convince my husband of a better role for you. Leave that to
me."

"Will he listen to you, Mrs. Roosevelt?"

"Yes, Mr. Burk. The president always listens to me. He
certainly will on this, trust me. Now you go off with Mr.
Grombach and see this Yardley fellow. When you come
back, I will have a chauffeur's uniform for you. I will
arrange to have a car for you so that you can drive
Secretary Morgenthau. Mr. Grombach will serve as his
bodyguard. Do you have any concerns?"

"My wife will be expecting me home in a few days,
Mrs. Roosevelt."

"We will need you here, Mr. Burk. You are the only
one who knows what these two men look like. If we only
had a *doppelgänger,* a look-alike for Mr. Morgenthau, but
he is so tall..." Mrs. Roosevelt ruminated.

"I understand, Mrs. Roosevelt, but what can I tell my
wife?"

"I will telephone her personally and ask her for
permission to hire you for a short while as the president's

driver. I will say that one of our drivers is ill. That should do it."

And after that phone call from Eleanor Roosevelt, Tom Burk would be the subject of discussion at the beauty parlor, Tom realized.

Tom was about to object, but he hesitated. It would be nice to be away from Florida for a week or so, and he was certain Mrs. Roosevelt would be able to smooth things over with Rachel for him. Frankly, he could use a bit of excitement in his life. Sometimes he felt his life in Hobe Sound was drudgery. He often wondered what his life might have been like had they stayed in New York after the war, or even moved to Washington instead of Florida. Maybe New York would have been drudgery, too. He didn't resent Rachel for their move to Florida; how could he? Rachel had saved his life. *And* his soul. But it would be nice having a vacation away from Florida, even if what he were about to do might be dangerous. His only fear was that Rachel would hop on the next train. But he doubted that. Her employer would not be returning north until after Easter at the earliest, so Rachel wouldn't be able to get away easily.

"So, what do you say, Mr. Burk? Will you work for us?"

Tom smiled. "Yes, Mrs. Roosevelt, I will," he said."

"Good," she said with a hearty smile. "Now, is your suit tailored or off the rack, Mr. Burk?"

"Off the rack, ma'am."

"Coat size? Pants, waist and length? Would you write them down for our tailor, so he can adjust a chauffeur's uniform to fit you?" She handed him a small sheet of white paper. Tom filled out his measurements.

"Excellent. We might even have an outfit that will fit you without alteration," she said.

She was a meticulous woman, Tom thought.

"There was something else I wanted you to have, Mr. Burk," the first lady added. She walked over to a closet and retrieved a shoulder holster for the pistol. "I never used this, Mr. Burk, even though they gave it to me. It is not too first lady-like. I kept the pistol in my pocketbook. Please try the holster on and adjust the straps."

Tom removed his suit coat and strapped on the shoulder holster. Then he put on his coat again. Mrs. Roosevelt opened the wooden box, removed the pistol. And satisfied that it was loaded, told Tom to put it in the holster.

Tom examined the cylinder. All six chambers were filled. He removed one bullet and spun the chamber so the empty chamber aligned with the barrel. She handed him the box.

"Why did you remove a bullet, Mr. Burk?"

"Safety, ma'am. Prevent an accidental misfire."

"Oh!" she said enthusiastically as if she had learned something new.

He carried the wooden box with him to meet Grombach on the first floor.

"What is that box for, Mr. Burk?" Grombach asked.

"It contained the first lady's pistol. She loaned it to me. Her idea is to have me be a chauffeur to Secretary

Morgenthau." He opened his suit coat to show Grombach the pistol in the shoulder harness.

Grombach smiled. "Good. I hope you won't need it though. That's my job. No offense, Mr. Burk. Hell, I'm just going to call you Burk, and you call me Frenchy okay?"

Tom Burk nodded agreement. "She also mentioned that she wished we had a doppelgänger for Secretary Morgenthau."

"A look-alike. I think I know a man who could fill in as a look-alike, Burk. Guy is as tall as Morgenthau."

"That might be good," Tom said. "What do you think of me being a chauffeur instead of a diplomat?"

"Chauffeur is a better cover than Haitian diplomat. For the restaurant though, be the diplomat, otherwise they won't let you sit down. You are from the South. I don't need to explain things to you."

"No, sir, you don't."

"Please drop the 'sir' shit, Burk. I'm from New Orleans. Seems like half the people in New Orleans are mixed race. C'mon, there's a car waiting for us outside."

Grombach told the driver to take them to the Rideau Restaurant. Then he began a conversation with his new colleague.

"First thing, Burk. In New Orleans, I knew lots of colored folks. I know colored guys watch what they say around white people. But if we are to work together, it can't be that way. I will treat you as I would a white man, and I want you to treat me as you would a colored man. We have to be honest with each other if we are to work together. This assignment could be very dangerous. Do you understand that?"

"Yes."

"We are on our way to meet a man named Herbert Yardley. He is an old friend of mine. Reports are that his restaurant may be a hub of Axis agents...or at least, where they come for lunch. I doubt it though. Sounds like another one of Hoover's witch hunts to me. I know he doesn't like Yardley. Hoover doesn't like anyone who is smarter than he...so he doesn't like many people," Grombach laughed.

Tom Burk didn't know how to take Frenchy Grombach. Could he be trusted? Grombach certainly had the president's trust, he realized.

"You have any questions, Burk?

"Why do *you* need *me*?"

"You are the only one who can identify these two Nazis, Burk. Simple as that. I think if our killers are here, they will be following Morgenthau, waiting for a chance to strike. If you drive him and I guard him, we might just flush them out."

"That sounds risky," Tom said.

"Squeamish, Burk? Weren't you in the last war?"

"Yes."

"From what I heard you were quite the hero."

"Not really. I just did my job."

"Germans shot at you, right?"

"Yes."

Grombach laughed. "Well, there you have it, Burk. Just like old times. Germans shooting at you again. If we see them, we will shoot them on sight. Got it. "

"No trial?"

"Hell, no."

Tom hesitated. Grombach caught his unease.

"Problem, Burk?"

"I think they should have a trial. Then you shoot them."

Grombach looked at Tom. "Burk, a colored man can't get a fair trial in the South...where are you from again?

"Florida."

"Did a colored man ever get a fair trial in Florida?"

"No.

"But you think a Nazi should get a fair trial?"

"Everyone should get a fair trial."

Grombach laughed: "You sound like Jimmy Stewart in *Mr. Smith Goes to Washington,* Burk."

Grombach liked this colored man. He was a man of convictions. He was no coward that was for sure. President Roosevelt had briefed Grombach on Tom Burk's war record after he left the Oval Office with the first lady. He had a commendable war record. Enviable, actually: a war record that any white man would envy.

Herbert Yardley was sitting alone at a table in the back
of the Rideau Restaurant, smoking a cigarette. It was only
9 A.M., but Yardley was going over that day's specials on a
menu insert. He didn't notice Grombach and Burk's
approach.

"Hello, Herbert," Grombach said to his old friend.

Yardley looked up from the menu and smiled.
"Frenchy Grombach, I'll be damned. You old reprobate!
What brings you here? Who is the boy with you, your
driver?" he asked in reference to Tom Burk's presence.

Boy, Tom thought. So much for the diplomatic charade.

Grombach shifted gears. He sat down at the table and
nodded for Tom to join them. "He's going to be the driver
for Henry Morgenthau. You have no problem with him in
your restaurant, right?"

"For you, anything, Frenchy," Yardley said. "Just don't
break bread with the colored man."

"Not here for a meal, Herbert. I am looking for two
young men, one American; the other, I believe, is a Nazi
agent. One of the men has a scar on his face."

"Like a fencing scar?

Now it was all coming together for Tom Burk. He
remembered that captured German soldier and how he held
his cigarette. But the man also had a scar on his face. It
was not a fencing scar, Tom thought: It was a bayonet scar.
He had seen enough bayonet scars in his time. The Nazi
agent had probably been in combat.

"I don't know if it was a fencing scar. What do you say,
Burk?

"I think it was a bayonet scar. I think the Nazi has seen combat."

Yardley looked at Tom Burk with respect then looked at Frenchy Grombach. "Okay, Frenchy, who *is* this guy?" he asked nodding at Tom.

"He's the man who can identify these two guys. The Nazi landed in Florida. The other guy is a Nazi sympathizer, an American. A traitor. My man Burk here came up from Florida to try and help catch the bad guys. "

"You said two men, right?"

"Have you seen a pair like that?"

"The other day…two men were here with a girl. One of the men had a scar on his face. I think he might have been foreign for the way he held his cigarette…like a…"

"German?" Grombach offered.

"There are British, French and Poles in town Frenchy, so I couldn't say what nationality the guy was. Lots of Europeans hold their cigarettes like that."

"A girl you say?"

"Yes."

"Do you know her name?"

"No," Yardley said. "I think she's just a nice piece of ass, Frenchy."

"Maybe. Maybe she is something more," Grombach said. "Do you get a lot of traffic from the Treasury Department, Herbert? For lunch?"

"Yes, Treasury is close by. Even Morgenthau came in the other day...yesterday. Yes, it was yesterday when I saw the two men and the girl. It was the same day that Morgenthau came in. After the girl and the two young men left. Yes, I'm certain of it."

"Thanks, Herbert, you've been a big help," Grombach said.

"Frenchy, I help you, you help me, okay? I've got to get back into the war, Frenchy. I'm sick of the restaurant business. Bill Donovan said Stimson blackballed me and that's why he couldn't hire me."

Grombach smiled. "You believed Bill Donovan, Herbert?"

"He lied?" Yardley asked, his face reddening.

Grombach shrugged.

"The bastard," Yardley went on. "Frenchy, you have to help me out. I am dying in this restaurant."

"I'll see what I can do, Herbert," Grombach promised. "Let's go Burk. We need to see the Secretary of the Treasury."

Frenchy Grombach led the way as Tom Burk walked beside him. "Yardley was one of our top men in your war, Burk. Ran a Black Chamber operation," Grombach explained. "Broke all kinds of codes that helped us beat the Huns. Some people in high places hate him, so he can't get a job in counter intelligence. Seems he wrote a book that bothered the spies, because he let the average reader know what we really do. He didn't win any friends with that."

"Sounds like our side could use him in this war," Tom Burk said. "Why didn't you tell him the Nazi was Rudolf Hess's nephew?"

"Because I wasn't completely honest with Yardley about Bill Donovan. Yardley was blackballed by Secretary of War Stimson, but if we capture the Nazis I will be able to help Yardley out. Get him out of the Spook Dog House. The Rudolf Hess nephew thing is a need to know, Burk, and Yardley didn't need to know. Our problem is: The president wants us to capture the man without fanfare, if possible. Capture is a long shot, but I'm not going to tell the president that. Looks like the restaurant isn't very far from the Treasury Building, is it?" Grombach asked rhetorically, as they stood at the base of the steps to the financial center of the government.

Rome, Tom Burk thought. Washington's buildings reminded him of pictures he had seen of Rome or Greece perhaps. Classical architecture. Inside the Treasury Building there was a buzz of activity. Grombach flashed his I.D., and a guard directed them to the Secretary's office. Having received a heads-up call from the White House, Morgenthau's secretary ushered the two men into the Secretary of the Treasury's office. Henry Morgenthau was a giant, Tom thought. He towered over them.

"Grombach, right?" Morgenthau asked.

"Yes sir…and this is Tom Burk from Florida."

Morgenthau nodded. "Sit down, gentlemen."

"Thank you, sir," Grombach said. He nodded for Tom to sit.

"Now, President Roosevelt and his wife say that someone is trying to 'bump me off,' as the say in the movies?" Morgenthau smiled.

"Yes, Mr. Secretary. Mr. Burk has seen the two men."

Morgenthau registered surprise. "Okay, so?"

"I'm here to protect you, sir. Mr. Burk will be your driver."

Morgenthau was puzzled. "One of my men can drive me."

"Yes, I understand, but Burk can identify the assassins. He is the only one who can. And you won't use Secret Service protection for yourself."

"That's correct. They are busy guarding more important people than a cabinet member," he replied.

"The president wants the men captured alive, if possible," Grombach said. "But I doubt if that *will be* possible."

"Hmm," Morgenthau murmured. "Go on..."
"One of the men is Rudolf's Hess's nephew."

Morgenthau raised an eyebrow. "As in Deputy Führer Hess?"

"Yes," Grombach answered.

"Is the whole Hess family loony?"

"I don't know, Mr. Secretary."

"So Franklin wants to use me as bait then? To try to capture Hess's nephew."

"He might, Mr. Secretary, but I don't know. I have a doppelgänger in mind."

"A look-alike...who?"

"An agent in the Social Protection Program. He resembles you very closely, although he is younger. With a bit of stage makeup, he can pass for you."

Tom Burk had heard a rumor of the Social Protection Program at Camp Murphy. The agents were trying to stop the spread of venereal disease at army camp. Servicemen had nicknamed them the "VD Boys."

"I see," Morgenthau said, smiling. "He will serve as my 'protection' so to speak?"

"Yes. But for today, we are going to ask you to ride along with us. I have to call the man's superior."

"I see," said Morgenthau.

"They may be watching you or following you already," Grombach explained. "A car will offer you some safety, and Mr. Burk will be able to identify the potential assailants."

Morgenthau smiled. "The old man wants you to catch Hess's nephew, doesn't he? Some sort of competition with Churchill, isn't it? Really...those two men are like little boys. You know what Roosevelt wrote Churchill? 'It's fun being in the same decade with you.' Like the war was a lark of two private school boys." Morgenthau shook his head and then smiled. He loved Franklin Roosevelt. He would do anything for him, but sometimes, he didn't understand the man.

"So then, when do we start?"

"We will go back to the White House and borrow a car. Essentially, we will drive you from Treasury to the White House or wherever you need to go."

"It's only a block to the White House. I enjoy the walk."

"Yes, I understand, Mr. Secretary," Grombach said. "But it is safer to go by car now that we know men are trying to kill you. It is too dangerous to walk even a block, sir. We will pick you up on the 15th Street entrance and drive around a bit to make sure we aren't followed. Then we'll take you to the White House."

"Sounds a bit ridiculous."

"Yes, it does, but I assure you, Mr. Secretary, the threat against your life is very real and these two men have already killed an army captain."

"I see," Morgenthau replied. "Okay, then gentlemen. I'll need a car for lunch with the president today."

"Yes, Mr. Secretary," Grombach replied.

As they left the Treasury Building to return to the White House, Tom Burk said to Grombach: "Who is the Doppelgänger?"

Frenchy smiled. "I played a pickup game of basketball against him. William Chandler. Blocked every one of my shots. You know, he might be even an inch taller than Morgenthau, come to think of it. But at a distance he can certainly pass for Secretary Morgenthau. Having the Secretary as bait in a car should smoke them out. They won't be able to tell it's a Doppelgänger. You aren't going to believe who his boss is, Burk?''

"Who?''

"Eliot Ness.''

"The guy who got Capone?''

"Actually, an accountant brought Capone down. But yeah, Ness should get some credit. He resigned his last job because he was drunk. That was in Cleveland and the upshot is in Cleveland he did put a lot of crooked cops and bad guys away. Anyway, the newspapers in Cleveland went after him for drunk driving and he fled to D.C. to head the VD Squad. There really is problem with what folks are calling 'victory girls,' or 'good time charlottes,' young women who think it is their patriotic duty to service the servicemen, so to speak. VD is up at camps all around the country. The joke going around is Ness has gone from the Untouchables to the Unmentionables as head of The VD Squad... Burk, the Old Man wants us to capture Hess if possible, but if I have to shoot to kill, I will. I think our assassins will figure out Morgenthau's routine. Then, they will take spots on his normal route to assassinate him. You know, you may have to use that pistol Mrs. Roosevelt gave you."

Tom Burk hadn't really thought of that, but now he did. "Yes, but I hope not."

"Do you think you can pull the trigger if you have to?"

Tom looked Grombach straight in the eye and said honestly, "Yes."

Grombach smiled. "Good. After all, there are at least two assassins, perhaps three if the girl that Yardley saw at his restaurant is a killer, too."

Chapter 20

After Wolfram awoke, he and Hans convened at the kitchen table to decide on where and when to assassinate the Secretary of the Treasury, Henry Morgenthau, Jr. Wolfram suggested that they should just walk into the Treasury Department with their guns blazing, but Hans argued that their mission was not some Jimmy Cagney gangster movie. They would never get beyond the Treasury Department guards to get a shot at Morgenthau. Hans thought it best they try to determine if Morgenthau had a daily routine, and when and where in that routine was a vulnerable area and vulnerable time of day to murder Morgenthau. He suggested that they take shifts watching the Treasury Department, starting the following day.

"What about her?" Wolfram asked, nodding to Gretchen as she stood making the men a sandwich.

"I suppose Dulcinea will be at work, except in the evenings," Hans replied. "It might look suspicious if she didn't show up for her job."

Wolfram nodded in agreement. "We don't need her," he said. "She can cook and do our laundry. That is what women are for."

Gretchen didn't care for Wolfram's dismissive, misogynistic, words. A sense of foreboding ran through her body. Was she as expendable as laundry? She suddenly considered taking the first train to New York and returning to her Papa's house. But then she stared at Hans a moment and realized she didn't want to leave. She wanted to be with him. Not because she loved him, but because she had missed sex, and sex was back. Orgasms were back. *You are a tramp, Gretchen,* she told herself, but she was smiling. *Strumpet!* She squirmed a bit, but otherwise, she listened attentively to the two conspirators' plan. After several minutes, she concluded that their plan was idiotic and would probably end in failure. They needed rifles instead of handguns. She doubted if they could even get close enough to Morgenthau to fire a lethal shot with a handgun. And, if they got lucky and shot him, there would be no escape. Neither of these guys was Lido, she realized. Her dead lover would not have come up with such a half-baked assassination plan. Lido would have booked a room at the Willard Hotel, slipped in a rifle, shot Morgenthau from an upstairs window, and made an escape from the hotel unnoticed. But these two? Again she said nothing. *Dummkopfs,* she thought in German. Her instincts told her to leave.

The men decided that Wolfram would take the morning shift, walking past the Treasury Building beginning at 7 A.M. That evening, Wolfram and Hans left the apartment to reconnoiter the area to determine if there were any possible ambush positions near the Treasury Department.

On the walk, Wolfram brought up the necessity of the woman.

"We should get rid of the woman, *Liebchen,*" he said.

"We can't do that," Hans replied.

"Why? Do you want to fuck her?" he asked in German.

Hans sensed he was blushing and was glad that it was too dark for Wolfram to notice. "No," he replied in English. "She is an agent, too. She is a spy for the Fatherland. She is valuable to the Führer." Did Wolfram suspect his infidelity? He knew he had to cover his tracks with Wolfram. He had to lie to him. Deception might be a matter of survival for him and for Dulcinea, as well. "I don't want to fuck her, I want you to fuck me," he lied. He *did* want to *fuck her* again. Again and again. Even at the kitchen table when they were planning the assassination, Hans had difficulty not thinking about making love to Dulcinea. "I want you to fuck me," he repeated to Wolfram although he was thinking of Dulcinea.

"I will, *Liebchen*, I will tonight." Wolfram promised.

Hans cringed. He knew he would be sore the following morning. He involuntarily contracted his sphincter muscle. "Don't be too rough, or you will have to stakeout the whole day if I can't walk."

Wolfram took Hans' comment as a joke, but Hans was serious. He realized if he didn't submit to Wolfram, his companion would realize that he *had* fucked Dulcinea. For him, the truth might lead to a beating, but for Dulcinea it might lead to the grave.

The following morning at the apartment, adorned in a robe, her hair in curlers, Gretchen walked out to the kitchen to fix breakfast, making a pan of a dozen scrambled eggs. Neither man had asked her to be a cook for them, but she fell into the part easily as she had cooked daily at her Papa's house. Wolfram was the first man to appear that morning, and he was dressed in his business suit, an outfit which, the conspirators assumed, would not attract any attention in Washington. Hans, also in his suit, followed behind, but he walked a bit gingerly. Hans took off his suit coat and placed it over his chair, nodding to Wolfram to do likewise. "You don't want to get food on your jacket," he explained. Wolfram nodded and placed his suit coat on a chair, as well.

Shortly after the trio's breakfast, Wolfram left the apartment to walk the area near the Treasury Building. He carried a little notebook to record when the Secretary arrived in the morning. Wolfram also kept a photograph of Morgenthau inside his suit jacket pocket. Hans had assured Wolfram that he wouldn't need to consult the photo, for Morgenthau would probably be the tallest man in any group of people entering the building.

Ten minutes after Wolfram left the apartment, Hans propositioned Dulcinea for a little morning coitus.

"I've got to get dressed for work, Hans," she protested. She was still in her curlers and robe.

"I won't take long," he pleaded.

That's an honest man, she thought, almost wanting to laugh.

"I'm in curlers," she replied.

"It's not *that* hair I'm interested in," Hans smiled. "Keep 'em in. I don't care. I bet you've never had curler sex," he teased.

She laughed. Damn his smile, she thought. He had a wicked smile, a grin like Errol Flynn. She sighed, "Okay, make it quick though."

"Sure…a quickie," he said.

He was a man of his word, she realized; he selfishly finished his business without considering her need or her desire, leaving her to clean up things for herself manually. It wasn't that the sex was so bad, but rather that it was too short. When he left her bed, she arose, took out her curlers, prepared her hair for the day and dressed for work. She was out the door by 7:50 A.M. for her walk to the Spanish Embassy, a trip which was a little more than a mile from her apartment. She was due at 8:30 and, at a normal pace, she was there by 8:15, at the latest.

As she walked past 15th Street on H Street, Gretchen glanced toward the Department of the Treasury. She wondered which entrance Morgenthau used; the White House side or the 15th Street side? If Morgenthau entered via the White House side, the agents might be better off watching for him from Lafayette Park. Certainly, it would be less suspicious for a man in the park to be sitting on a park bench reading a book or newspaper, than it would be for a man marching back and forth on 15th Street. Surely, after a time, such a man walking back and forth would draw suspicion. Perhaps if they were in uniform they would be less conspicuous, she thought. Or maybe they should follow her unspoken plan and book a room at the Willard Hotel across 15th Street from the Treasury, buy a rifle and just watch from a window. They could shoot Morgenthau when he came out of the building. *She* certainly didn't have enough money left for a suite at the Willard. She wondered if the men had any money.

Gretchen returned to the apartment after work and went immediately to the kitchen to prepare an evening meal for the conspirators. Neither of the men was at the loft when she returned, and she wondered what they were doing. Had they been arrested? Odd, the thought that they might have been arrested made her feel good. Why didn't she feel guilty for such a thought?

Wolfram was the first to return. He ignored Gretchen and went into the living room and turned on the radio. She was glad he ignored her, but she felt anxious being alone with Wolfram. A few minutes later, Hans arrived, and her anxiety lessened. She literally exhaled relief.

"Hello Dulcinea," Hans greeted.

"Hi, Hans," she replied with a smile. Something was missing though. She realized it was the passion. Strange, her desire for him was gone, completely gone. It was as if she was sated with sex and wasn't interested in any more intercourse. She had had her fill. For some inexplicable reason, Hans no longer appeared sexy to her. It wasn't that he was a bad lover, although he **was** terrible, it was just that suddenly, she no longer had a longing for him. She wondered if it was because Hans spent the night in Wolfram's arms. Was that it? Out of the corner of an eye, she noticed that Wolfram was watching them intently, as if he was checking to see if there was any attraction between the two of them. She sensed that any show of affection on her part could be very dangerous. Again, she considered leaving. She turned away.

At dinner, Wolfram's glances were uncomfortable for Gretchen. She tried not to make eye contact with Hans, who looked at her from time to time. As it turned out, the two men concluded that they needed to watch both the front and back entrances to the Treasury Department for Morgenthau. Hans told Gretchen how they rotated between walking up and down 15th Street and using Lafayette Park. They decided that they would avoid suspicion by alternating every half hour, and they did so for the entire day. Morgenthau arrived a few minutes before 9 A.M. He left Treasury and walked to the White House at noon, and he returned to Treasury about 2 P.M. He then left Treasury a bit after five via a cab.

The two men decided to stake out Morgenthau again the following day, and if everything was similar, they would kill the Secretary of the Treasury on the third day when he walked from Treasury to the White House around noon. It was only a block, but it would prove an adequate killing zone, and it would be so unexpected. Right in the middle of the capital of the United States, Roosevelt's Yid advisor would be shot to death, and Wolfram Hess would redeem his family's honor. Wolfram loved the plan. Hans had misgivings.

Gretchen listened attentively and tried to ignore Hans' foot beneath the table. She didn't feel comfortable playing *footsie* with Hans, not with his homosexual lover watching them so closely. Wolfram seemed suspicious, Gretchen sensed. That was the way Gretchen would act if she sensed her man was interested in another woman. *Was that possible with queer men? Schwuler:* that was the German word her father used. *Faggot.* She didn't care for the word, but the German word rattled around in her head as she thought of Wolfram.

Once again Gretchen felt unease, sensing that she was in mortal danger; she needed to plan an escape from these two men. The day of the assassination would probably be the best day, she believed. But she didn't think she could wait that long. Tomorrow would be a better day, she told herself. The men would go off to their stakeout positions before she went to work. She would calmly load a suitcase, walk to Union Station and take a train to New York. The men didn't know her true identity. Once back in New York, she would just vanish; she would disappear back into her Long Island world and find sanctuary at her father's home. It came as a revelation that she suddenly thought more of her own life than she did of her allegiance to Adolf Hitler. But frankly, she also sensed that these two men wouldn't survive the assassination attempt. They weren't really the brightest bulbs in the box, she realized. Shooting the Secretary of the Treasury on a Washington street in broad daylight was a suicide mission. Wolfram would be dead, and Hans and his cute little rear end would be dead as well.

After dinner, Hans helped her with the dishes while Wolfram went to the bathroom to relieve himself. He was surprised but pleased to find Gretchen's English language edition of *Mein Kampf* on a small table by the commode. He was delighted to read passages of Hitler's masterwork in English as he had his bowel movement.

While Wolfram was predisposed, Hans began a conversation with "Dulcinea."

"I want you," he said. That was obvious, she realized, as she glanced down at the erection growing in his trousers.

She put her dish towel down and looked him straight in the eye. "Not tonight, Hans."

"When?"

"When it is safe."

She could see he was frustrated.

"But I need you."

"No, you don't need *me*. You just need some pussy. Why can't Wolfram suck your dick for you?" Gretchen was surprised at her own vulgarity. Once again, her sharp tongue had betrayed her.

Hans was horrified by her frank language. He never expected that from her. Wolfram, yes, but not Dulcinea. She sounded like a tramp. He was repulsed yet at the same time attracted to the crudeness of her speech. Maybe she was just a whore after all. Maybe Wolfram was right; maybe they needed to get rid of her. She was certainly no Vassar girl.

"I'm sorry, Hans, she said, giving him a kiss on the cheek.

"I understand," he replied. But he didn't like her rejection, calling her *the little whore* in his mind. Maybe they didn't need to *kill* her, but they needed to keep an eye on her.

Gretchen thought he had accepted her rejection. At that moment, she heard the toilet flush. Wolfram would be out in a moment. She moved away from Hans. "Change the station on the radio, Hans. Jack Benny is on."

Hans did as she instructed and, from the ether, the voice of Jack Benny talking to his butler, Rochester, filled the room. A studio audience laughed at the repartee between Benny and his Negro servant. Hans laughed. Gretchen smiled, and Wolfram fiddled with his weaponry, unaware, at least Gretchen hoped, that his lover had been unfaithful to him.

Any second thoughts Gretchen might have had about deserting the mission disappeared after dinner as she watched Wolfram return to his weapons and meticulously clean his uncle's Luger and polish the dagger with the ornate handle and the skull insignia on its pommel. It seemed a bit surreal to her to look at a smiling cold-blooded Nazi agent cleaning his equipment while Jack Benny made jokes on the radio. Wolfram wasn't amused by the radio show, but rather by Gretchen's discomfort, she realized. He seemed pleased that she was bothered by his ritual. Gretchen wasn't smiling. She found nothing amusing about watching Wolfram. His smile changed to a glare at Gretchen when she seemed frightened. He slowly slid the dagger across his throat in a gesture that Gretchen understood all too well. Then he glared at her once again. This time his glare was like a winter wind; his cold eyes went right through her like a blast of frigid air through a thin coat.

"What do you want, *Fraulein?*" he demanded.

"Nothing. Nothing at all, Wolfram."

"Then what are you looking at *Du dumme Fotze?*"

"Hey," Hans intervened. "Don't call Dulcinea a dumb cunt, Wolfram."

Wolfram's head snapped to look at Hans. "You want *Fotze, Liebchen?*" he snarled at Hans. "You want *Fotze?*"

Hans blushed. Damn, Dulcinea thought. Hans gave it away. This was not good. His red face screamed infidelity. She suddenly felt vulnerable. Very vulnerable. She ran to her bedroom and shut the door behind her. She clicked the lock. She could hear the two men arguing in the living room.

"Did you fuck her?" Wolfram demanded in German.

"No!"

She heard a slap and a repeat of the question.

"No!"

Another slap.

"Please, *Liebchen*, please stop."

Hans was pathetic, Gretchen thought. *He is going to break! The weakling. Oh God, he is going to tell!* She was in mortal danger. She heard a thumping noise from the floor. It sounded like someone from the apartment below pounding on their ceiling with a broom handle or baseball bat. Then a male voice from the apartment directly below shouted: "Keep the noise down, or I'll call the cops!" She recognized Mr. Fabrizzi's voice.

The conspirators' voices lowered, but the snarling didn't stop. Gretchen could still hear it. The accusations, the pitiful pleas by Hans. *Disgusting!* Wolfram was swearing in German; Hans' pleading voice replied in English. At any time, the two of them could make up, and she would become expendable. Hans was too weak to stand up to Wolfram. Hans had a penis, Hans had testicles, but Hans wasn't a man. Now she even feared Hans, the man who she had so recently initiated into manhood. *When-* and it was only a matter of time- the sissy Hans admitted he fucked her, Wolfram might slit her throat with that knife of his. She sensed the bond between the two men transcended sexual attraction; Hans sincerely cared for Wolfram. Hans was bisexual, but Wolfram was certainly not. Wolfram was the dominate partner in the relationship, just as Lido had been the dominate partner in their relationship. Hans would do anything Wolfram ordered him to do. She could understand how threatened Wolfram must feel by her; it was how she would feel if the situation were reversed. She believed that if she were in a relationship with Hans, she would emerge as the dominate partner, as well. Hans was a weak individual. Wolfram, however, was not weak. Wolfram was scary as hell. She sensed a steel resolve in Wolfram. Hans would be afraid not to do what Wolfram wished. Her situation was precarious. It was perilous. She had to act. *Soon! Now!* She thought. She had to act now. At that moment, she had to flee. She could not wait another minute. *Now!*

She gazed out the bedroom window. Suddenly, she had an idea. She would throw some things into a suitcase, open the window and leave via the fire escape. She hoped Hans and Wolfram wouldn't realize that she was gone until the morning. By then she could be back in New York. She took the pink-handled revolver from her pocketbook and placed it beside her suitcase on the bed so that she could grab it in a hurry. She packed quickly.

She opened the window and climbed out onto the fire escape carrying her suitcase. Her pocketbook was strung over her shoulder. She released the ladder, and a clanging sound echoed in the alleyway. She winced, hoping that the men were still quarreling and they wouldn't hear her noisy departure. Quickly on the ground, she tried to remember what she had said to Hans when they were in bed together after they *fucked*. She had a bad habit of telling the truth after sex, a habit which might cost her dearly. What had she said to him? She searched her memory of their conversation.

She had talked about her childhood, her visit to Berlin for the Olympics. Hans knew she was from Long Island. If Hans realized she fled, he would think she was going back to New York. Suddenly, Union Station was not an option. That would be where they might track her down if they realized she had left the apartment. She could spend the night in the Spanish Embassy. She could tell the guard she had a fight with her boyfriend. She would show him her identity card, and she could sleep on a couch. She would be safe in the Spanish Embassy. The conspirators would never think of her taking refuge in the embassy, as she was only a dumb *cunt* after all. She hated the "c" word and hated men who used the word; rather, she *feared* men who used the word *cunt*. Those type of men treated women as objects, as "things."

With those two men, Gretchen found it difficult to
believe they hadn't already been captured. They seemed as
dumb as Amos and Andy. Dumb as those radio show
colored men. And the background report noted Hans had
gone to Yale! He thought with his dick, she realized. Lido
hadn't thought with his dick; he had known what his dick
was for. She smiled as she walked hurriedly toward the
embassy. She missed Lido. "Ulrich," she whispered, using
his real name. She missed him. He was not a boy, like
Hans; Ulrich was a man. The man she had loved. The man
she still loved. Even in death.

Back in the apartment, Hans suddenly stopped arguing
with Wolfram. "Did you hear that noise?" Hans asked.

"What noise?" Wolfram asked.

"It was a clanging. I'm going to check on her," Hans
said and walked over to Gretchen's bedroom door and
knocked. "Dulcinea?"

There was no answer. "Dulcinea?" he asked again.
"We want to talk to you."

No answer. He turned to Wolfram and looked at him
quizzically, as if to ask: *What do I do now?*

Wolfram knocked on the bedroom door. "Open up!" he
demanded. He turned the door knob. It was locked.

"She locked the door?" Hans asked rhetorically.

Wolfram put a determined shoulder to the door, taking
the wooden barrier off its hinges. The men entered the
boudoir.

"She's not here," Hans said stupidly.

"Window," Wolfram replied, pointing at the raised glass.

Hans peered out the window. "She went down the fire escape."

Wolfram said in German, "We can't let her go, she knows too much. She could turn us in."

Damn, Hans thought, Wolfram was right. "Union Station."

"*Wieso?*"

"Why? Because I think I know where she is going…she is from New York. I bet she is taking a train back to New York."

"We stop her, *Ja?*" Wolfram said.

"Damn strait, *Ja,*" Hans agreed. "Bring your dagger. No pistols, no noise; that brings attention." Hans said coldly. She was, he thought, just a whore after all. But she was a dangerous whore, a whore who could identify them, and Hans still had hopes of getting out of this alive if he could modify the assassination plan.

Hans and Wolfram hailed a cab and they were at Union Station within a few minutes, certainly faster than Dulcinea could have walked there, Hans thought. Even though it was the evening, the terminal was crowded with people, a sea of servicemen and civilians mingling about, waiting for a connection or loading a train for departure. The men decided to split up and watch the two most probable entrances for Dulcinea.

Had she taken a cab as well? Hans wondered. He looked at the arrival and departure board. A train for New York was loading and was due to leave in two minutes. If she was on it, she was beyond their reach. What did they have to fear from the little whore anyway? He mused. What would she tell anyone that wouldn't get herself implicated? No, she would keep her mouth shut, Hans assured himself.

When Dulcinea did not appear within the next twenty minutes, Hans convinced himself that she had escaped to New York. He walked over to Wolfram's location.

"Let's go," he said. "She made her escape. She won't inform on us. It would tie her in," he added.

"Ja," Wolfram agreed.

Hans rationalized he was actually glad that Dulcinea had made her escape. She was a whore, but she had taught him a great deal about women. He looked at Wolfram. Suddenly, Hans found his resolve. He would kill Morgenthau. But it had to be soon; he didn't know how long this burst of courage would last. He didn't have Wolfram's stamina. It was a now or never thing, Hans realized.

As they walked out of Union Station and were alone on the street, Hans said,

"I think we should do it tomorrow. Let's both be on the 15th Street side and shoot him when he goes in tomorrow morning."

Wolfram smiled. "*Ja*. Kill the Yid. *Ja*." He stopped on the sidewalk and embraced Hans. Then he kissed him on the lips.

A man and woman walked by them as they kissed. "Faggots," said the man. His female companion shushed him.

Wolfram reached for his dagger.

"*Sheiskopf,*" he muttered, which meant *shithead* in English.

"No," Hans warned him. He grabbed his lover's hand "Save it for tomorrow, *Liebchen*, save it for tomorrow."

Wolfram smiled. "*Ja,* " he said. *"Morgen."*

"We have bigger fish to fry."

Wolfram looked at Hans. He didn't understand the English colloquialism.

"Was?" Wolfram asked in German.

"Was? What?" Hans said, translating the German into English. "That American saying means that Morgenthau's death is more important than killing the swine that insulted us," he replied.

Henry Morgenthau arrived at the Treasury Department before dawn. He had a report to finish up before he met the president later than morning. He needed to get an early start as he had quite a few numbers to crunch. He didn't realize it, but this was the second time fate intervened and saved him from assassination.

Hans and Wolfram appeared before 8 A.M. on 15th Street and watched as dozens of Treasury Department workers entered the building. They walked up and down 15th Street until 9 A.M. when Hans sensed that they might soon attract attention.

Hans suggested they move to Lafayette Park and talk about an alternative plan. Wolfram agreed.

Chapter 21

When Tom Burk and Frenchy Grombach returned to the White House after their meeting with Secretary Morgenthau, Eleanor Roosevelt had a chauffeur's uniform ready for Tom to try on. Considering that Mrs. Roosevelt had taken charge, Tom wasn't surprised when the uniform was a good fit. Even the cap was the perfect size. There was something magical about the woman, Tom thought, as he strapped his shoulder holster beneath the chauffeur's jacket. The pistol and holster, however, made the jacket a tighter fit.

"A perfect fit, Mr. Burk," the first lady declared after he was dressed. "But I think you might want to carry the pistol in the glove box, as it bulges the suit."

'Yes, ma'am." He un-strapped the weapon.

"Have you ever driven an armored car, Mr. Burk?"

"Ah, no, ma'am." He didn't mention that he *had* driven a tank in France during the first war.

"Hmm. Well, I talked to the president, and he agreed you are much better placed as a chauffeur than a diplomat. But I insisted on the armored car…" she smiled. "The car you will be driving was once owned by Alphonse Gabriel Capone. You may have heard of him," she smiled again. "Imagine such an angelic middle name for such a hellion, but Mr. Capone didn't pay his income taxes, the naughty boy," she chuckled. "So now his armored car belongs to the United States of America. One other Capone car, I think it is a 1928 Cadillac, is on display in England.

What was going on Tom wondered? First it was
Eliot Ness and now Al Capone? What a crazy coincidence.
He didn't mention his feelings to the first lady, but replied,
"Al Capone's car, really?" Tom was as fascinated by
gangsters as much as the president was enamored by movie
stars.

"Yes. I don't want you going out in a plain car, Mr.
Burk. I certainly don't want Mr. Morgenthau killed either.
That just wouldn't do. I wish Mr. Morgenthau wasn't so
fussy about using the Secret Service for his own protection,
but there it is. He is a stubborn man. So I suggested to the
president that we let you have Mr. Capone's car. It is a
very safe vehicle," she said.

The president thought you might not have any practice
with an armored car, so we want you to drive it around a bit
before you pick up Secretary Morgenthau. I'm told it is a
bit slow on the acceleration, as it is incredibly heavy. The
president has a 1939 armored Ford on order, but Mr.
Capone's car was the car in which the president almost
rode to Capitol Hill to ask for a declaration of war, the day
after Pearl Harbor.

"The Secret Service agents were afraid of an
assassination attempt, you see," Eleanor explained. "After
all, the attack on Pearl Harbor caught us by surprise only
the day before, and there were rumors of assassins. The
Internal Revenue Service had impounded the car when Mr.
Capone was found guilty of tax evasion. So we going to
put Mr. Capone's car to practical use but my husband
refused to ride since he didn't want glorify gangsters. We
took our luck on the ride to the Capitol in a car that wasn't
bullet proof. Still I think it is nice to see that Mr. Capone is
going to do something for his country," Eleanor Roosevelt
said with a chuckle.

Frenchy Grombach was waiting for Tom Burk outside the White House when Tom appeared in chauffeur's costume.

"Looks good," he observed. "There's the car," he added, pointing to a vehicle. "I hope Al won't mind us using it," he laughed. "I wouldn't want a visit on Valentine's Day."

Tom caught the allusion to the St. Valentine's Day Massacre, and he smiled for his partner's benefit. Taking pride in his ability to identify makes and models of vehicles, Tom recognized Al Capone's car as a black 1930 V-16 Model 452 Cadillac Imperial Sedan. Unlike other 1930 Cadillac's, Scarface's sedan came with inch-thick, bulletproof windows. It also had a specially installed siren and flashing lights behind the grille, as well as a police scanner radio and 3,000 pounds of armor.

Tom had had the opportunity to drive the Renault FT-17 at the end of the Great War and that French light tank was a slow vehicle with a top speed of about five miles per hour and a weight of twelve thousand pounds. He had found a tank a bit difficult to maneuver, but he doubted Capone's car would be too difficult to drive. In fact, he thought he would be able to handle the Cadillac pretty easily.

To Tom Burk's delight, the Cadillac *did* handle easily. The armored car might not turn on a dime, but it handled well for a cumbersome vehicle carrying such additional weight. Of course, he was only steering the car around the White House driveway. Tom suggested to Grombach that they take the Cadillac out for a drive around town.

Frenchy hopped in the front passenger seat, and the two men in the Capone car rode through the White House gate and out onto the streets of Washington. Tom was pleasantly surprised that no one gawked at the car as he drove down

Pennsylvania Avenue. He assumed that the district's residents had seen more than their share of official cars from the motor pools of scores of foreign embassies. A Cadillac was hardly unique to a city full of Packards, Rolls Royce sedans and other luxury limousines.

"It is modeled on the Chicago Police Department cars," Frenchy explained. "It even has a police siren."

"I thought Capone was out of prison."

"He is."

"So why didn't they give the car back to him?"

"I guess if he ever pays all of his back-taxes, maybe they will. But I doubt that will happen. This car should be helpful for our mission, Burk."

"Yes," Tom agreed. "Don't you think this is weird, Frenchy...Capone's car and Eliot Ness's agent?"

Grombach laughed. "Yeah, it is come to think of it. But hey, if Ness hadn't gotten drunk and screwed the pooch in Cleveland he wouldn't be head of the VD Boys. Look at this way, Burk. Both Capone and VD are social diseases and Ness fights social diseases. An epidemic of clap can destroy an army...didn't they tell you that in the first war?"

"Yes," Tom replied, remembering his training on venereal diseases as a young officer at Des Moines.

"We have to pick up Morgenthau in an hour for lunch with the president. Anywhere you want to go?"

Tom thought a moment. "I would like to see the Lincoln Memorial," he said.

Grombach smiled. "Sure, do a U-turn."

"Hang on," Tom said and turned the wheel sharply, hit the brakes, and was suddenly going the other way.

"Nice move, Burk."

"Thanks."

"Hope you don't have to use it."

"I hope not too."

Grombach added softly. "You never know though. You never know."

Frenchy Grombach accompanied Tom Burk up the marble steps of the Lincoln Memorial. When they reached the top of the steps, Tom took a moment to view the statue of Abraham Lincoln. The statue appeared to be peering out toward the George Washington Monument. To Tom, it seemed like Abe was seated on a throne, like Zeus at Olympia. Indeed, Lincoln was like a god to the country, Tom thought. He really was: *Father Abraham*.

"You know when the Lincoln Memorial was dedicated, his son Robert Lincoln was here," Frenchy said.

"Yes I know," Tom replied.

"You knew that?"

"I was here that day, Frenchy," Tom replied. "Twenty years ago. I came to hear Dr. Robert Russa Moton speak."

"Never heard of him."

"He was a protégé of Booker T. Washington," Tom explained. "He took over as head of the Tuskegee Institute. The colored flyers in Alabama train at Moton Field,

Frenchy. The airstrip is named for him. He died two years ago."

Grombach stepped back a moment as to appraise his partner. "You are a very surprising colored man, *Mister Burk.*"

Tom Burk smiled. He felt comfortable around this white man. He felt like saying to his companion: *you are a very surprising white man, Frenchy,* but he held his tongue.

Having grown up in New Orleans, Frenchy Grombach had met many educated colored men, but he realized colored men, except for radicals like W. E. B. Du Bois, didn't reveal their intelligence to most white men. For a colored man to let his guard down, as Burk was doing with him, showed a great deal of trust. Grombach was not about to abuse that trust. He liked this colored man. Hell, he liked most colored men and assumed that he had colored blood running in his veins. There had been too many rascals among his ancestors who had owned plantations in French colonies during the 18th and 19th centuries. He was fairly certain he had some colored cousins somewhere in the Caribbean.

"So what did this Dr. Moton say that day?"

Tom Burk smiled. "He upset a few of the white folks. He compared two ships sailing for America, the Mayflower, which promised religious freedom, and a slave ship en route from Africa to Jamestown. He talked about two principles contending for a nation's soul: bondage and liberty."

"How did that go over?"

"The white newspapers glossed over it, but the colored newspapers applauded him for his honesty. The white folks wanted to talk about how Lincoln saved the union. They didn't want to be reminded of slavery. Maybe someday another black speaker will stand on the steps and give another great speech," Tom said. "But I won't hold my breath."

"Yeah, maybe. Were you here for Mahalia Jackson?"

"No, but my brother was. Quite a day, he said."

"It was," Frenchy agreed. "She has the voice of an angel."

Tom walked around the marbled martyr and read Lincoln's words which were carved into the walls. He preferred the *Gettysburg Address* with its line of a *"new birth of freedom."* The white folks could say all they wanted to about Lincoln saving the union, but in truth, the war was about slavery, and Lincoln freed the slaves. It was right there in his 2nd Inaugural address inscribed on the wall: *Every drop of blood drawn with the lash shall be paid by another drawn with the sword, as was said three thousand years ago, so still it must be said "the judgments of the Lord are true and righteous altogether.*

Tom Burk doubted that Lincoln would be pleased about how the modern colored people were being treated throughout his nation. At least, Tom Burk hoped Lincoln would be upset. Lincoln was a man of his time, but then Tom recalled how close Frederick Douglass was to the *Great Emancipator,* and how Lincoln had ordered colored troops into combat. Douglass pressured Lincoln on that. The irony, which the white folks overlooked on the day of the Lincoln Memorial dedication ceremony was that Lincoln saved the union by ending slavery and letting the colored men fight.

Grombach interrupted Tom Burk's reverie. "We should be going," Frenchy advised.

"Okay," Tom replied. "Did you ever read *The Soul of Black Folk,* Frenchy?"

"No."

"DuBois wrote it. He talks about the double-consciousness of my race and the ability to deal with both black and white worlds. You might like it," he smiled.

Grombach shook his head in admiration. Who *was* this guy? "I'll have to pick it up someday," Frenchy replied.

Outside the Treasury Department on 15th Street, Tom Burk kept the engine of Capone's car running as Grombach went in the building to retrieve Secretary Morgenthau. By habit, Tom watched the people on the street, a gallimaufry of humanity, a hodgepodge of hoi polloi, civilians and servicemen, file clerks and enlisted men, secretaries and able-bodied seamen, all headed one way or another. Two civilian men in business suits, one carrying a briefcase, caught Tom's eye in his rearview mirror, one of the men, smoking a cigarette, held it European-style. Certainly, there were enough Europeans in Washington, Tom realized, but his senses made him wary. The Holy Spirit might be trying to tell him something. *Pay attention,* he told himself. *It might be a God moment.* He also wondered if there was something more to the coincidence of Eliot Ness's man and Al Capone's car? That was so weird, he thought.

As the two men walked north on the sidewalk across the street, Tom instinctively pulled his chauffeur's cap down to hide most of his profile. The two men stopped.

They were furtively looking toward the Treasury Department. Then Tom noticed one man's facial scar.

Good Lord, Tom thought. It was them, the two men from Hobe Sound who killed Captain Carver. *Agent Kane,* he remembered.

Slowly, he reached into the glove box and retrieved the first lady's pistol. *What is taking Frenchy so long?*

The passing seconds dragged on. The two men moved on up the street, toward the park and out of sight. By the time Frenchy Grombach escorted the lanky Morgenthau down the Treasury Department steps to the waiting armored car, the two assassins were long gone.

Morgenthau took a seat in the back, and Grombach rode "shotgun" in the front passenger seat. When Frenchy noticed Tom holding a pistol in his hand, his puzzled face asked his partner for an explanation.

"I saw them, Frenchy. The two men who killed Captain Carver…Agent Kane. They just walked by a few minutes ago," Tom said.

"Really…did they notice you?"

"No, it is one of the advantages of being colored," Tom Burk said with a smile. "I am

invisible."

"What's going on?" asked Morgenthau from the backseat.

Grombach turned his head to the back seat. "Mr. Burk spotted the two Nazi agents, Mr. Secretary."

"Really? Well done, Burk."

"Thank you, sir," Tom replied. "They seemed to be checking things out, Mr. Secretary. They walked past the Treasury Building from across the street. They stopped and looked across at the building as if they were looking for something or someone. "

"A recon mission," Frenchy evaluated. "That's what it sounds like to me. Burk, take us for a short ride around town before we take the Secretary to the White House," Grombach advised. "Just in case those two men saw us."

"I don't understand how we missed him this morning," Hans said to Wolfram as they sat together on a bench in Lafayette Park across from the White House. "I wonder if he is out of town."

Wolfram just frowned and lit another cigarette.

"Well," Hans said, trying to be more cheerful. "It is almost noon. Morgenthau should be walking from Treasury to the White House any minute. We should be ready for him. All we have to do is cross the street and shoot him."

"I am ready," Wolfram said. "I will take the first shot."

"*Ja*," Hans said in German. "You get the first shot, *Liebchen.*"

Hans opened his briefcase and retrieved a pair of binoculars. He assumed a pair of binoculars was not a suspicious item for a tourist, although in his business suit, he didn't appear to be a tourist. He decided they needed other outfits, something less like tourists. If they missed their chance today, they would purchase uniforms. They had his father's money. Why not buy some clothes? Why not buy uniforms? Yes, he thought. They would dress up as soldiers, soldiers on leave. Many of his classmates at Yale who joined the service and were commissioned as officers had to purchase their own uniforms. They could do it as well. It would provide a good cover. Dressed as soldiers, they would blend in easier in wartime Washington.

He put the binoculars up to his eyes and scanned the capital's panorama. Pausing at the White House, he noticed a black sedan drive up the front gate. The car stopped, a chauffeur got out and opened a passenger door; a very tall man in a blue suit emerged. That car seemed familiar. Where had he seen it? It quickly came to him. That car had been parked across the street by the Treasury Department entrance on 15th Street when they walked by the building. "Son of a bitch," he said aloud. "We missed the bastard!"

"*Was*?" Wolfram said in German.

Hans pointed at the White House and passed the binoculars to Wolfram. "What? What? Look," he said.

Wolfram looked through the glasses. He saw the tall man. "Morgenthau?" he asked.

"Yes, damn."

"That car…the same as we saw?"

"Yes. They picked him up. He didn't walk to the White House." Then Hans added, "They may be on to us."

"*Nein*," Wolfram replied, dismissing the idea.

Now Hans became paranoid and wondered if somehow someone had traced Captain Carver to his family's Jupiter Island house, and if so, had someone found his diary? Why hadn't he packed his diary? That was a stupid mistake. He didn't want to think about it. He asked Wolfram: "Do you think Dulcinea betrayed us?"

Wolfram thought a moment. "*Ja,*" he said.

"Damn. The bitch! You were right. We should have killed the cunt."

"Too late, *Liebchen,*" Wolfram said.

"Maybe not. I will contact Klaus."

"*Ja,*" Wolfram agreed.

Hans thought about the uniforms again. "We need to purchase army uniforms, *Liebchen*. We will be second...no, first lieutenants. We will be less conspicuous in uniforms if we are walking around the town."

Wolfram took a pair of captain's bars from a suit pocket. He had taken another grisly souvenir from the dead man Hans realized, a bit nauseated.

"I will be cap-i-tan," he said. He smiled at Hans.

Hans felt a shiver run through him. "Okay," he agreed. "We will both be captains then."

On the way to get fitted for uniforms, the conspirators stopped at a Western Union outlet. Thinking that Dulcinea double-crossed them, Hans sent a telegram to Klaus at the Spanish Consulate in New York City.

Dulcinea deserted us. Stop. No idea where she is. Stop. Think she sang. Stop.

HH

The tailor asked Hans and Wolfram which insignia they required for the uniforms, and as Hans hesitated, Wolfram quickly said, "Infantry."

The two conspirators called it a day after they picked up their uniforms. The collar sported the double bar and the crossed rifle insignia of the infantry. They had decided to wait at the shop, as the tailor found two uniforms that merely needed a few quick alterations. Thankfully, he was a taciturn man who didn't attempt to converse with either of them. Because of his reticence, Hans gave him a handsome tip, which made him merely smile. Did he know more than he should? Hans wondered. Did he know they were phonies, not real officers? Maybe this wasn't the first time he made uniforms for impostors. The inscrutable tailor kept his thoughts to himself; had he said anything to Wolfram about his misgivings, Wolfram would have cut the man's throat.

Back at Dulcinea's apartment, Wolfram found leftovers in the refrigerator and was able to make some sandwiches for the two conspirators. Hans made a long-distance call to New York, a station-to-station call to his contact number.

"Hello?" a voice said.

"Klaus?"

"*Ja.*"

"It is Hans. What about Dulcinea?"

"I took care of the problem," Klaus said coldly.

Hans felt sick to his stomach. He had only sent the telegram four hours before. He needed to vomit, but instead, he controlled his gag reflex and asked, "Was that absolutely necessary?"

"Yes," Klaus said in English.

"I don't think..."

"It is done. I did *my* duty, now you do *yours,*" said Klaus succinctly as he ended the call. Hans knew by the tone of Klaus's voice that he had no way out. Any thoughts of abandoning the mission were gone. He knew that Klaus would find him and kill him, should he try to quit the mission.

Before Hans talked with Klaus long-distance, Gretchen Schwartz, AKA Dulcinea Martinez, after a peaceful, uneventful journey from Washington, walked through Grand Central Station in New York toward the connection with the Long Island Railroad. She bought a one-way ticket to Mineola. With the ticket in hand, she felt free. Safe. She was convinced she had made the right decision. She could hardly wait to see her Papa. It would be so good to be with her *Vater* again.

In Washington, she left her brief career in espionage behind. Her courage had deserted her, replaced by cowardice mixed with sanity. Her life seemed suddenly more important to her than her duty to Adolf Hitler. The revelation surprised her. She wanted to live more than to die as a martyr for Germany. Sex with Hans *and* fear of Wolfram had changed everything. Sex with Hans, as bad as it was, was good enough to change her *Weltanschauung*, her world view, her conception of life. Fear of Wolfram had activated her survival instinct. To survive and to love seemed more desirable than to die a martyr for *Herr* Hitler. Sex renewed her hope; she hoped for marriage, a family and domestic future which would provide the perfect cover for a former spy. A name change would help hide her past.

Women were lucky that way. All she had to do was find a husband, preferably a service man about to go overseas. That way, she could pursue other men while her husband was away. She felt she was oversexed. She had read about being oversexed in a women's magazine, and she sensed she was a "nymph."

If she were lucky, the poor man she married would die and she would receive the ten thousand dollars in death benefits. She was an awful girl, she told herself, but she smiled. It was a wicked world, and the cards were stacked against women. Life wasn't fair for a woman. Men had all of the power; women had only their feminine wiles.

Her papa could help her find a husband, but she didn't want anyone pro-Nazi; she wanted a fresh start. Perhaps a good, English-American man, maybe even a Canadian. Heck, even an Irish man would do. No one would suspect the wife of an Irishman to be a spy for the Nazis; maybe for the I.R.A., but not for the Germans. She ruminated as she changed trains; perhaps she would be better off in Canada. Any association with the Nazis would be even that much harder to trace if she were the wife of a good Canadian. She had no desire to end up like Mata Hari: taken out and shot.

Hans and Wolfram would muck up the assassination attempt. Of that she was certain. They were a pair of losers, and Wolfram was a psychopath, Gretchen thought. She doubted that Hans would live long enough to experience sex with another woman. That was too bad; he certainly could use some practice. Even if they succeeded in killing Morgenthau, the two nitwits had no escape plan. While Gretchen admitted to herself that she was pro-Nazi, she decided she was not pro-suicide. She valued her own life too much to sacrifice it, even for the Führer whom she still admired even though she remained puzzled with

Hitler's alliance with the racially inferior, mongrel, Japanese. She was glad she was a woman, now. Perhaps that was the only advantage a woman had over a man; no one expected a woman to die for her country. That was a calling reserved for men. She was safe now.

Only Lido had known her true identity, and he was dead. The agent who had given her the assignment at the Spanish Consulate in New York didn't know Gretchen's true identity. Or did he? Hadn't Klaus worked closely with Lido? She dismissed that thought. They would all assume when the two nitwits died that she had died, as well. There would be no publicity about an attempted assassination of a cabinet member, not with the censorship which was being practiced. Gretchen settled back and enjoyed the ride out to Long Island.

Feeling secure, Gretchen had forgotten about Klaus. But Klaus hadn't forgotten about her. She felt free as she stepped from the train at the Mineola station. It was only a half mile walk to her Papa's house, and it was a lovely day for a walk. She felt like singing. She was happy.

When she arrived at her father's house, she was surprised to find the front door ajar. Papa had forgotten to close the door, Gretchen thought. He was getting forgetful in his old age. She swung the door open.

"Papa!" she called. "Vater?"

She set her suitcase down. She put her purse down on a glass coffee table. Perhaps he was down in the basement listening to the Führer on the short wave. She had to go through the kitchen to descend to the basement. Papa was in the kitchen. His head was down on the kitchen table. Was he asleep? A sudden fear overcame her. A heart attack! She ran to him and lifted his head. There was a bright red stain on the tablecloth. She held up her Papa's head. He had been shot in the forehead. She was stunned.

Gretchen scream was primal. "Vater!"

She heard footsteps rapidly ascending the stairs to the basement. Her heart raced. Three men, two young, large, blond men and a small man in a grey fedora and trench coat, carrying an armload of her Papa's souvenirs, burst into the kitchen with guns drawn. Klaus!

Why was Klaus here? Oh God, why is <u>he</u> here! She was frightened. *Oh God, why is <u>he</u> here?*

She didn't have a chance to ask what Klaus was doing with her Papa's things or why her Papa was dead. The three men quickly surrounded her in the kitchen.

She remembered the pistol in her pocketbook. It was in the living room. She turned to dash to retrieve her mother's pistol. A man blocked her path. Her legs turned to rubber, and she didn't move. She peed her pants.

"Kill her," Klaus ordered.

The two men leveled their silencer-tipped guns at Gretchen. She closed her eyes.

"Heil Hitler!" she shouted, a desperate cry for help or a plea for mercy more than any salute to the German leader. She prayed it might save her.

It didn't.

Gretchen never heard the two *'pips'* that followed. She fell to the kitchen floor at the feet of her Papa. One shot had entered her heart, the other her brain. She had been dispatched with Teutonic efficiency.

"I think we have everything," Klaus said clinically.
"She will be untraceable to us now. I won't have another
Lucy Boehmler," he stated, referring to the female spy that
had turned state's evidence in the Joe K Spy Ring trial.
Klaus could not afford another screw-up like that. He had
no desire to be sent to the Russian front.

Chapter 22

Tom Burk pulled Al Capone's Cadillac up to the entrance at the White House. Like a good chauffeur, he opened the rear door and Henry Morgenthau emerged from the back seat of the armored car. Grombach accompanied the Secretary of the Treasury into the White House. Tom, staying in character as a chauffeur, assumed he should stay with the vehicle. He reasoned his importance to the mission was essentially the identification of the suspects. Feeling totally secure on White House grounds, Tom placed Mrs. Roosevelt's pistol back in the glove box and sat in the driver's seat to await Morgenthau's return.

He began to daydream of Rachel as a young woman: it was a summer evening, there was a gentle ocean breeze, and she was wearing a polka-dot cotton dress; the two of them were together, hand-in-hand on a Florida beach, looking out at the ocean as if the water could foretell their future. There was music playing in the background of his memory, Scott Joplin's ragtime music. *The Entertainer.* But the tune and his reverie were interrupted by a knock on the bulletproof driver's side window.

"Burk?" said Frenchy Grombach. "What are you doing out *here?*"

"Huh?" Rachel's smiling image disappeared to be replaced by a growling Frenchy Grombach. "I thought I was supposed to stay with the car, Frenchy," he replied. "I'm the chauffeur."

Grombach shook his head, but smiled. "That's your cover, Burk. You are *pretending* to be Morgenthau's chauffeur. You are my *partner*, not my driver. C'mon, let's go. Mrs. Roosevelt has set two places for us at lunch. I'm hungry."

Upstairs at the White House, Tom's brother Walter was supervising the lunch table setup. While in Washington, Walter had been very accommodating to his only brother, but Tom realized his presence in the White House was wearing on Walter. *Fish and visitors smell in three days,* Tom thought, remembering a Benjamin Franklin epigram. Tom Burk suddenly hoped they could capture the assassins quickly, and he could leave Washington and return to Florida. He was surprised how much he missed Rachel. He kept thinking of his wife throughout the day. Without Rachel, Tom felt as if he was missing a hand. An arm. His heart.

He had a nightmare the previous night, but he hadn't told Walter about his dream. How could he? Walter couldn't understand. Walter wasn't in the Great War. The nightmare was set yet again in the Meuse-Argonne of 1918; the devastated French forest that had turned into a "no man's land," as trees were torn asunder by artillery and craters formed by exploding shells that pock-mocked the desolate hell of the terrain, a landscape that was Tom Burk's nightmare world. Again in his dream, he was replaying the oft-repeated scene where he handed a cigarette to a German prisoner; but this German prisoner seemed different than in previous dreams. In this variation of the nightmare, the German prisoner had a scar on his face, an identical mark to the Nazi they were hunting. This time, the German prisoner spoke English, not German, to him. In this variation of his dream, the English-speaking German prisoner said he was going to "kill the Yid." Those were his exact words. The prisoner also bragged that was also going to kill Tom Burk and Frenchy Grombach.

Tom had awoken from the vivid nightmare in a cold sweat; he rolled over and reached for Rachel in the dark, but his lifeline wasn't there for him to cling to. He turned on an end table lamp and looked at the clock beside the bed in the guest room at his mother's house. It was 4 A.M. There was no sense in going back to sleep or turning off the light. He had no desire for darkness, only dawn. He didn't want to fall asleep again and possibly return to the Meuse-Argonne. Walter would be knocking on his door to wake him in twenty minutes anyway.

Tom just lay in bed and thought of Rachel, the Rachel of their youth, when she was young, before she bore their children. He had wished Rachel was there, that she had been sleeping next to him; she would have calmed him down. Such a strange dream.

He stood in the White House remembering the nightmare when Mrs. Roosevelt entered the room. She smiled when she saw him.

"Mr. Burk, Mr. Grombach. So nice of you gentlemen to join us for lunch," the first lady said. "Mr. Morgenthau says you spotted the assassins, Mr. Burk?"

"Yes, ma'am. Walking on 15th Street."

"Really? What did they look like?"

"Two men in business suits, Mrs. Roosevelt," Tom replied. "They seemed to fit in with the pedestrians, but then they stopped and stared across the street at the Treasury Building. I found that rather odd and conspicuous, ma'am. I wouldn't think too many tourists gawk at the Treasury Building, Mrs. Roosevelt. That's when I became suspicious and looked again. After a moment, I recognized them."

Frenchy Grombach spoke up. "We will stop them, Mrs. Roosevelt," he assured her. "Now that we know for sure they are in town."

"I hope so, Mr. Grombach. My husband can't do without Mr. Morgenthau. He is crucial to the war effort."

"Did I hear my name mentioned?" Henry Morgenthau said as he came into the dining room, trailing the president's wheelchair.

"Yes, Henry," Eleanor said. "I was just talking to Mr. Burk and Mr. Grombach about your potential assassins."

"'Assassins,' an interesting word," Franklin Roosevelt interjected. "Marco Polo wrote about a Persian prince, Al-Hassan, who gave his murderers hashish before they went out to murder someone. Apparently the word derives from that era. Etymology is interesting. Of course, there are some bankers out there who think a New Dealer is synonymous for assassin," the president joked.

Henry Morgenthau laughed. The others smiled at the president's attempt at humor. The first lady, however, frowned at her husband.

"Franklin, this is nothing to joke about," Mrs. Roosevelt said.

"Relax, Eleanor. We didn't invite the assassins to lunch with us," he smiled. "Everyone, please take a seat. Your president is famished. It's time to eat. So, Mr. Burk, one of the men has a scar, is that correct?"

"Yes, sir."

"Is that the Nazi?"

"Yes, Mr. President."

F. D. R. smiled. "Dueling I bet. You know the year Hitler and I both came to power, the Nazis rescinded the German laws against dueling. Suddenly, the Germans started dueling again. That's why so many of them have dueling scars."

Tom Burk wondered if the president was making that up. He was beginning to have some misgivings about F. D. R. The president certainly liked to be the center of attention, Tom realized. But perhaps all politicians were like that.

"Franklin," Eleanor interrupted. "It is time to call Mr. Hoover and let the F.B.I take over."

Franklin Roosevelt scowled at his wife, but didn't answer her. He preferred to ignore her. The president turned to Grombach. "So Frenchy, how do you plan to capture Rudolf Hess's nephew?"

Frenchy Grombach cringed. "I don't know if capture will be possible. If he shoots at us, I will shoot him, Mr. President."

"I understand, Frenchy, but I would love to have him alive," the president said. "Young Hess captured would be good for morale."

"If we can take him alive, I will see to it, Mr. President. But I can't promise he will surrender if he is cornered."

"I understand, Frenchy. I understand."

The president nodded and changed the subject to Mrs. Roosevelt's daily newspaper column, praising the first lady for her latest commentary. It was his way of apologizing to his wife for ignoring her by quickly placating her. It was a strange marriage, Tom thought. Tom felt like a spectator at this lunch as the conversation turned to politics, the fall elections and the need to keep the Southern Democrats happy, lest F. D. R. lose the House of Representatives and his ability to fund the war.

Midway through lunch, the president prattled on with another story about a naked Winston Churchill startling the servants who brought brandy to his bedroom during the British prime minister's stay at the White House the previous December. While the president held center stage, Walter Burk silently slipped a note to Frenchy Grombach. Agent William Chandler, Grombach's Morgenthau 's look-alike had arrived.

"Send him up, Walter," he whispered to the steward.

A few minutes later, Agent William Chandler made his entrance into the dining room. He stood next to Walter Burk.

"What a tall drink of water," the president said upon seeing the Morgenthau look-alike. "Why, Henry, the man could be your son. The spitting image. Is there some woman you never told me about, Henry?" the president quipped.

Morgenthau laughed and said, "I feel like I'm looking into a mirror…a mirror of thirty years ago, Mr. President."

"Mr. President," explained Grombach. "This is agent William Chandler from the Social Protection Program."

"The VD squad?" the president asked. Eleanor's face turned red at the mention of "VD."

Tom thought it inappropriate to talk about venereal disease with the first lady present.

After a moment of awkward silence, Grombach resumed.

"Agent Chandler has agreed to serve as our bait. We don't have to risk the Secretary at any time from here on in. Now that we know the assassins are here, we will make it easy for them to find us. It is hard to miss Al Capone's car."

Tom Burk thought the resemblance was uncanny, although agent Chandler was much younger than his look-alike. But certainly the resemblance should be good enough to fool the two assassins, at least at a distance. Plus, Agent Chandler would be armed. The only difference in the initial appearance of the two men that Tom noticed was Chandler's suit was brown, whereas Morgenthau was blue. They would be sure to match the suit color tomorrow.

Chapter 23

Captain Hans Hoffman dressed in a phony United States Army uniform, had taken *Dulcinea's* place in the apartment's kitchen and was busy scrambling a dozen eggs for breakfast, as Wolfram finished dressing. After a few minutes, his lover appeared outfitted as another counterfeit U.S. Army captain. Wolfram gave Hans a kiss on the lips and then sat down. Hans placed a plate of scrambled eggs before Wolfram and sat down to join his lover and fellow assassin.

"I don't think we should try to shoot Morgenthau in the morning." Hans began. "He's too unpredictable in the morning. I think we should shoot Morgenthau when he leaves the Treasury Building for lunch. Right there on 15th Street. In broad daylight."

"*Ja,*" Wolfram said as he buttered a piece of toast.

"Then we shoot his driver, and we steal his car for a getaway," Hans added. He was surprised at his own bravado. A part of him still thought of abandoning the mission like Dulcinea had futilely and *fatally* tried to do. *The poor dumb tramp,* he thought. He recalled Dulcinea's naked body spread-eagled on her bed; her hands beckoning him to enter her bedroom and her body. He felt a momentary pang of guilt for Dulcinea's demise, but it was a brief pang. Survival was a stronger instinct than guilt. To flee from the mission was to risk the same fate as the little whore. That was certain death. Strangely, Hans realized his chance for survival might actually *be better* by assassinating Secretary Morgenthau.

If they could just escape Washington and get to Hampton Roads, Virginia. At Hampton Roads, a boat would be waiting for them to take them to a German submarine off the coast. That's what Klaus promised: an escape by submarine and a trip back to Germany, where they would be celebrated as heroes. He imagined being given a medal in Berlin, a city where his older brother had failed to win a medal in the Olympics. Hans smiled at the image. *He*, not his older brother, would shake the hand of Adolf Hitler. *He,* not his older brother would receive a medal in Berlin.

But Hans wondered if escape by submarine was feasible. Had Klaus merely made up a story to satisfy him? Were he and Wolfram expendable? Would they even be able to make it out of Washington? Where would the sub moor? Off Hampton Roads? That was implausible. The naval base at nearby Norfolk, Virginia was well-guarded from submarines. Hans was dubious of the escape plan's success. Virginia was not Florida, a peninsular state with miles of unguarded stretches of beaches. Stealing a car seemed the most reasonable getaway plan. But then what? Maybe not Hampton Roads. But where?

He remembered reading of John Wilkes Booth and his escape to Maryland after he assassinated Abraham Lincoln. Most people thought Lincoln's assassin would have headed to Confederate Virginia. Booth fooled his pursuers by riding off to Maryland and to Dr. Mudd's home, where the physician set his broken leg and consequently wound up with a lengthy prison sentence for his troubles. Only later would Booth and his accomplice cross the river into Virginia. There John Wilkes Booth would die a couple

weeks later after a shootout in a barn. Hans remembered
that the dying Booth looked at his hands and muttered,
"Useless, useless."

West Virginia. They could escape to *West* Virginia, but
then what? Hide out in the mountains. Rent a cabin in the
woods. Pretend to be hunters. They would need to buy
rifles and other sporting gear for their disguise. They would
grow beards. Beards would help. They had plenty of cash.
Then, when things calmed down, they could make their
way to Mexico. Hike down the Appalachian Trail. Yes, he
thought. That was it. No one would look for two fugitives
on the Appalachian Trail.

The Appalachian Trail would take them as far as
Georgia. From Georgia they would somehow make their
way to Mexico City and the safety of the German embassy.
Hans was a bit vague on the geography of the escape once
they made it to Georgia. But he knew that if they made it to
Mexico, they would travel by ship to *Deutschland.* Hans
would say goodbye to the United States, but he would be a
hero in Germany. He smiled when he thought of the look
on his father's face when the great brewer realized his son
wasn't coming back; that his son was a traitor to the United
States. Hans would be as famous as Benedict Arnold. He
would have the satisfaction of topping his hated brother and
disgracing the father he resented, as well as serving the
Führer. The thought brought a smile to his face.

Wolfram concurred with the plan to assassinate Henry
Morgenthau when the Secretary of the Treasury went to
lunch. Wolfram also agreed Morgenthau was too
unpredictable with his arrival schedule, but it seemed he
lunched at the White House on a regular basis. They would
shoot him as he walked down the steps to his awaiting car.
Right there on the steps of the Treasury building. Not
inside the Treasury Department building. There were too

many guards. Rather, the two assassins would shoot him on the steps of the building, in broad daylight. It was bold. Wolfram loved it. The Führer would admire the boldness of the plan. The Hess family name would be restored. Perhaps even his incarcerated uncle would learn of his heroic nephew. Wolfram did not expect to survive; he expected to die, but to die gloriously for the family and for the fatherland.

Hans noticed Wolfram's pants. Wolfram was becoming erect. The thought of murder stimulated his lover, Hans realized. And, as his lover became stimulated, Hans became stimulated as well. They had plenty of time before the assassination. Hans sensed he hadn't needed to dress now that they had decided on the later time for the Morgenthau murder.

Hans cleared the table after breakfast and put the dishes in the kitchen sink. There was no need to wash the dishes; they wouldn't be coming back to the apartment. He walked over to the bedroom. Wolfram was already on the bed; it only took Hans a moment to remove his uniform.

Chapter 24

In the afternoon, their day completed, Tom and Walter Burk rode the street car together to their late mother's house. Walter's wife had supper on the table when they arrived: pork chops with rice with gravy. The dinner table conversation was pleasant and the food was tasty. Mary kept the banter at banal, chit-chat level. She was not about to upset her guest and have him sell *her* house. Mary had no intentions of leaving *her* home.

After dinner, Tom and Walter took a walk through the neighborhood and passed the Howard University campus.

"Do you think you will catch the Nazis, Tom?" Walter whispered as they walked a deserted city street, side-by-side.

"I don't know, Walter. I have no idea. All of this seems strange to me. I mean... really, why am I here? Couldn't they catch the spies without me? Mrs. Roosevelt wanted the F.B.I. to step in for us, but the president didn't like that idea."

"Yes, Tom. The president doesn't like Mr. Hoover, and what you and Colonel Grombach are doing is off-the-books, as they say. Your mission isn't sanctioned, and the president does not want Mr. Hoover to learn about it. And, well you know what they look like, Tom. You see, I know

how much the president would love to capture Rudolf
Hess's nephew. It's some type of game he has with the
British Prime Minister."

"Seems awfully silly to me," Tom said. "Childish,
really."

"I think it is a way for him to relax, Tom. Churchill too,
I think. To have some type of competition between the two
leaders. Things aren't going very well. For either of them.
The president has a heck of job, Tom. He really does. I
wouldn't want his job."

"I wouldn't either," Tom admitted.

"Mary was wondering…"

Tom smiled, "When I am leaving?"

Walter couldn't hold back a laugh. "Yes."

"As soon as I can, Walter, I want to get back to Rachel."

"You miss her, don't you?"

"Good Lord, yes. I didn't realize how much I needed
that old woman until I left her. So, I guess this trip was
useful in that regard."

"We take our women for granted, don't we?"

"Yes. Yes, we do."

"I wouldn't know what to do without Mary, Tom. I
understand what you mean about Rachel. You live with a
woman for all of those years, you get used to them, as odd
as they are."

Tom smiled. "*As odd as they are*, Walter. They *are* odd
creatures."

"That they are, Tom. That they are."

"You assure Mary I will be gone soon, Walter."

"I will, Tom. Tom, I want you to stay out of the line of fire. I don't want to have to explain anything to Rachel."

"I'm no hero, Walter."

"You were once," he said.

"That was a long time ago. I'm not that man anymore."

Walter smiled. "I'm not so sure about that, Tom. I think hero is in a man's blood. Either he has it, or he doesn't. You do. You have hero blood. I think you were born with it. You always had the courage I lacked, even as a boy."

Tom Burk shrugged. He hoped he wouldn't have to be a hero. He'd had enough of that a long time ago.

Chapter 25

Tom Burk dressed for another day as chauffeur and once again rode the street car trolley with Walter to the White House. He was surprised to see Henry Morgenthau at breakfast with the president and first lady. The first lady stood up and walked toward Tom. Tom stopped in his tracks.

"Mr. Morgenthau was our guest overnight, Mr. Burk," Eleanor Roosevelt explained as she saw the perplexed look on Tom's face. "In fact, until you and Mr. Grombach capture these two assassins, we think it prudent that he remain here and conduct the Treasury Department's business from the Lincoln Bedroom."

The president's spoon arose from his poached egg, and he chimed in, "You see, Tom, Abraham Lincoln's ghost is going to protect Mr. Morgenthau." He laughed alone at his own joke, although Morgenthau came forth with a subordinate's obligatory smile.

"Huh?" Tom mumbled.

F. D. R. continued, "Lincoln had a premonition of his own death, Tom. He talked about it the week before he was shot. He saw his own coffin in the White House. So there are a good many people who think Honest Abe haunts this old house."

Eleanor Roosevelt frowned and said to Tom, "Don't pay any attention to my husband, Mr. Burk. The ghost story is just a legend. Did you have breakfast, Mr. Burk?"

"Yes, ma'am, my sister-in-law fed my brother and me this morning."

"That's nice. Mr. Grombach should be arriving any time now, Mr. Burk. Make yourself at home."

"Do I have your permission to roam about, Mrs. Roosevelt?"

"Certainly, Mr. Burk. This is the people's house. The president and I are merely its latest tenants. There will be others, after us."

Tom's self-guided tour of the White House was abbreviated by the appearance of Frenchy Grombach and Agent Chandler; the latter dressed in a blue suit which matched the same suit that Morgenthau wore for a second day.

"Okay, Burk. Here's the plan," Frenchy explained. "We drive Agent Chandler over to Treasury at the 15th Street entrance. I'll walk him in slowly, so if our friends are watching, they can see him. Then you and I come back here to the White House. If they have been watching us like I think they have, and realize we have a car for Morgenthau, they may strike when we return to pick up Chandler for Morgenthau's lunch with the president."

"But Mr. Morgenthau is here already."

"Yes," Grombach said. "But the assassins don't know that. We can't let them know that. The secretary is going to spend the day at the White House. So he is safe from any would-be assassins. On the other hand, we keep our eyes out for our two pals in business suits, and we nab them before they get off a shot, if possible. If you see a gun, you shoot. Don't bother with the niceties. It may not be sporting, but shooting first and asking questions later is highly recommended for survival," Frenchy smiled. "So let's get cracking. The president really wants us to capture Rudolf Hess's nephew alive, but it wouldn't break my heart if he wound up dead. Do you understand, Burk? " He gave Tom a conspiratorial wink.

"I understand, Frenchy."

"Good, please go get the car."

Tom Burk brought Al Capone's car up to the entrance of the White House. In case there was a Nazi spy watching, Frenchy Grombach made a show of opening Agent Chandler's car door before jumping in the front seat with Tom.

"Let's take Agent Chandler to Treasury just like he's Morgenthau," Grombach said, repeating the plan like a teacher using repetition with a class until the lesson sank in. "Keep an eye out on 15th Street for our Nazi friends," Grombach suggested. "Maybe they already know about the car and might make their move when they see it. Think Boy Scout motto. Be prepared, gentlemen."

Tom didn't see the assassins on 15th Street when he pulled up in front of the Treasury Building. Grombach walked up the steps with Agent Chandler then returned to Tom Burk who sat with the motor running.

"Well, it was worth a try, Burk," he said. "We'll come back and pick him up at noon. Let's go kill some time in the Smithsonian."

Tom Burk enjoyed the exhibits in the *Castle,* but he was beginning to feel a bit apprehensive, not unlike the apprehension he felt before battle in the Great War. Their plan for capture of the two men was vague, at best, and Tom realized Frenchy Grombach was determined to shoot the assassins on sight. They might be too dangerous to try to capture. To Tom Burk, capturing the two spies seemed a bit farfetched anyway. He really didn't care if the president bagged a human trophy to show off to Winston Churchill. Tom Burk would shoot them, if need be. For the first time, Tom determined that he really *would* shoot the spies if he had to. He was a bit surprised at his own resolution. He also came to realize that shooting the Nazi and the traitor might be the only way he would quickly return to Florida and to Rachel.

Tom Burk parked the armored car by the curb at the Treasury Department and kept the motor running, as Grombach entered the building to retrieve their doppelgänger for Morgenthau's regular lunch with the president. He thought nothing of the two army captains who stood on the steps of the building, smoking cigarettes. Their insignias denoted the young men's rank to be captain; they seemed young for the rank, but then again, in war young men climbed up the ranks over the dead bodies of senior officers. Was that one captain *pinching* his cigarette? Sitting in his driver's seat, Tom squinted to see. The doors to the Treasury Department swung opened; Grombach and Chandler walked out. The two captains tossed their cigarettes and suddenly turned. Tom Burk saw the man's scar.

"My God!" he shouted. It was them! In uniform!

He blew the horn and then cut the motor. He grabbed the first lady's pistol from the glove box and sprang from the car. In two-seconds, he was around the front of the car. "Lord, help me," he prayed. "Thy will be done."

"It's them!" Tom Burk yelled, but his voice was lost in the sound of gunfire. He watched Chandler take a bullet and stood helpless as the tall man fell forward, his jaw cracking as his face met the cement. Chandler's body slid down a few steps, before its momentum stopped, and the body came to a halt. A pool of blood formed on the cement and dribbled down the steps, as well.

"Heil Hitler!" Wolfram Hess shouted ecstatically, thinking he had killed the Secretary of the Treasury, Henry Morgenthau. Wolfram didn't have time to switch his weapon to his left hand and give the right arm salute, for a Treasury guard, responding belatedly to the gunfire, burst through the door. Wolfram put three bullets from his Uncle Rudolf's Luger into the hapless guard.

Grombach had taken a slug, as well, from the gun of Hans Hoffman, but remained standing *and* cursing. "You motherfucker! You goddamn, fucking motherfucker!" Frenchy screamed at the rich boy, returning the young man's fire with deadly force, dropping the assassin with a shot to his heart. "You traitorous little fuck!" He added a second bullet to Hans Hoffman's throat.

As the bullet pierced his skin, Hans Hoffman felt as if a sledgehammer hit his chest. His throat burned. Images flashed before his eyes, like the photos of a fast-turning picture album. Some invisible hand flipped impressions; memories of his boyhood rapidly clicked by. His father. His doting mother combing his long locks of hair when he was a little boy. The other little boys teasing him about his long hair. His older brother thrashing him in a fight.

Madison Square Garden. Wolfram in the hotel. The
passion. The feelings.

Instinctively, he tried to call out his lover's name, but
his throat emitted only a gurgling sound, the blood
bubbling up to his mouth. His knees buckled; his legs were
rubber. He never felt his face smack the pavement or heard
the crack of his front teeth as they broke on the cement.
Then, no more images in the picture album, only blackness.

Hans had tried to shout "*Ich sterbe!*" as he fell.

The wounded Frenchy Grombach crumbled to his knees
on the pavement, like a pillar struck by a wrecking ball.

"*Liebchen!*" It was a primal scream. Wolfram turned
away from the guard and looked at Grombach. Anger
morphed the Nazi's face into a twisted visage of horror.
Wolfram was consumed by rage.

The man with the scar pointed his Luger at Grombach.
"Die!" He shouted in English, as if he wanted to make sure
the American understood his command. The Luger
jammed. "*Sheiss!*" he screamed and scurried to pick up
Hans' pistol which was lying beside its dead master's
corpse on the pavement.

Instinctively, Tom Burk knelt to a knee and assumed a
firing position: right hand on the stock of the pistol, left
hand supporting the barrel. Suddenly, Tom Burk was back
in the Argonne Forest. It was there that he first killed a
man, a "Hun," an evil "Kraut," as the Doughboys
nicknamed the German soldier in the Great War. He had
felt so ambivalent that day when he killed that first
German. But he felt positively wretched when riffled
through the dead man's pockets and found a photograph of
his wife and three daughters, little girls dressed in what he
had assumed were their Easter dresses. He had killed the

girls' father. The dead man wasn't an inhuman "Hun," he was a daddy. Tom Burk had vomited on the spot.

He felt no such ambivalence this day as he took dead aim at the back of the head of the man with the scar. But Tom Burk didn't want to shoot him in the back. Even if he was a Nazi. He wanted to look the Nazi in the eye and send him straight to the devil, where he belonged. He knew he was being reckless, but he wasn't going to shoot a man from behind. He considered shooting a man in the back to be dishonorable. *Got to play the stupid hero, don't I?* He asked himself. *Dumb ass!*

"Hey! *Sheiskopf!*" Tom Burk yelled in German, and Wolfram Hess turned to the voice. "Fuck Adolf Hitler!" He yelled, glad that Rachel wasn't there to hear him use profanity.

"You? *Was?*" *What?* Wolfram mumbled in German as he suddenly recognized the African cabdriver from Hobe Sound. He seemed puzzled as to why the cabdriver was there. Tom's surprise appearance caused Wolfram Hess to hesitate for a fatal moment, as if not knowing which man to shoot. Grombach or the cabdriver? Wolfram Hess's last thought was a question in German: how did the cabdriver get here?

Tom Burk calmly aimed and fired one round. In the one, hesitating moment, when Wolfram Hess was distracted by the sight of the African who had first unnerved him at the railroad station in Hobe Sound, Tom Burk squeezed the trigger.

His shot was true; a bullet split the Nazi's forehead sending a sizable chunk of the Aryan assassin's brain outward, splattering the steps of the United States Treasury Building with gooey, grey matter that stained the pavement with a small pool of blood and tissue fragments. In his last involuntary moment of life, Wolfram Hess staggered and fell beside his lover; his left arm draped itself over his deceased companion. Captain Carver's hat fell off as he hit the cement.

Slowly, Tom Burk progressed up the stairs, pistol at the ready. He watched intently for any movement from either of the assassins' bodies. He was ready to shoot again, if need be. Grombach was in pain and swearing profusely. A non-mortal shoulder wound, Tom assessed, having seen a fair share of such wounds in the Great War. Tom Burk smiled at his partner. "It's not a fatal wound, Frenchy. Your profanity is unbecoming," Tom chuckled.

"Fuck you, Burk," Frenchy smiled. He added, grudgingly, "Nice shot."

"Thanks."

"Fuck you," Grombach repeated with a grimacing smile. "Check the others, Burk."

Tom checked on Chandler and the Treasury Guard. The lack of pulses indicated both were dead. He double-checked their necks. They were gone. He walked back to the Nazi to double-check that he was dead. He leaned down and picked up the United States Army olive drab hat. Inside the brim he noticed the name: *Carver.* The Nazi bastard had worn Agent Kane's captain's hat, Tom realized. He suddenly felt good that the Nazi was dead, that he had avenged the agent's death. He would have to ask the Holy Spirit for forgiveness, he realized. But not just now. His blood was still up.

"You saved my life, Burk," Grombach said. "God, this hurts. Shit, shit, shit! How is Chandler?"

"Chandler is dead, Frenchy," Tom said. "You killed one of the assassins, and I shot the other."

"Damn fine shot, Burk," Frenchy repeated. "Damn fine shot."

Tom Burk didn't say anything. He didn't feel "fine" at that moment. He suddenly felt sick for killing a man. It didn't matter that it was kill or be killed. *Thou Shalt Not Kill.* He asked the Holy Spirit for forgiveness. Again, in his mind he saw the face of the first man he ever killed, the face that sometimes still haunted his dreams. And the other faces, too, the faces in the photograph he found in the dead man's pocket, the photograph of the young woman with the three little white girls.

Tom bent down to examine Wolfram Hess's corpse. He went through the dead man's pockets and found a black-and- white photograph of a smiling Rudolf Hess standing beside Adolf Hitler. He also found a news clipping photograph of Henry Morgenthau. There was no identification. Into his mind came an image of Hitler with horns on his head, as if the Holy Spirit were telling him that Hitler was the devil and that this killing was justified. Maybe he could live with that feeling. He needed Rachel to hold him, to comfort him. He needed to get back to her. A tear ran down his face. He wiped it away. He gathered himself.

What irony, Tom Burk thought; the dead Nazi never realized the man he killed wasn't the Secretary of the Treasury. The assassin had probably died a happy assassin, thinking he had succeeded in his crazy mission for his crazy, evil Führer.

The whole exchange of gunfire hadn't lasted one minute, but for Tom Burk, the time slowed. For that one minute, Tom was in the moment, and he remembered his training. He ignored his older body with a rush of adrenaline and reacted like a young man. For that one minute, he was a soldier again. Adrenaline had worked like an elixir from the Fountain of Youth, allowing him to do things that surprised him. Now, the crisis over, he suddenly felt exhausted. It was emotional exhaustion, he realized. But he also felt physically spent.

Finally, three other Treasury Department guards arrived on the scene from inside the building.

"Drop your gun, nigger!" one yelled at Tom. It was a Southern accent.

Surprised, Tom did as he was ordered. He was all too familiar with that Southern cracker accent.

"Put your hands up, nigger!"

Tom complied.

"On your knees, boy!" the guard continued.

Tom complied.

Another of the Treasury Department guards went over to Frenchy Grombach who was still a bit groggy. "Did that nigger shoot these soldiers, Colonel Grombach?"

The fog lifted from Frenchy Grombach's mind. "What the fuck are you talking about?" He shouted. "These are fucking Nazi spies, you idiot. They dressed up as our soldiers. Mr. Burk shot one, and I shot the other. Jesus, you twit, the colored man is my partner. Hey, douche bag!" Grombach yelled to the guard standing over Tom. "He's my partner, and he's a hero. Let him up, or I'll have your ass, you dumb ass motherfucker.""

"What?" the guard replied. "You're working with a nigger?"

"He's no *nigger,* you fool, and he's a hell of a lot smarter than you are, you stupid asshole," Grombach snarled. "Get on the phone to the White House and tell Secretary Morgenthau that Colonel Frenchy Grombach says the mission is complete and successful. He'll know what I mean. Tell him he can return to his office now. Then take the bodies inside."

The chagrined guard with the Southern accent said, "Anything else?"

"Yes. Get me a doctor!"

"Yes, sir. Right away, sir."

Frenchy Grombach turned to Tom. "Give me your arm, Burk. Let's go inside and wait for Secretary Morgenthau."

"Sure, Frenchy. You're going to be okay."

"Think so? Have you seen many shoulder wounds, Burk?"

Tom Burk smiled wistfully. "Too many, Frenchy, too many… but that was a long time ago. Hurts like the devil, doesn't it?" Tom asked as he helped Grombach up the steps and into the

Treasury Building.

"Damn straight it does," Grombach replied. "You were wounded in the last war, weren't you?

"Yes."

"How did you manage your pain?" Grombach asked as Tom Burk helped him up the steps.

"I kept telling myself how lucky I was to be alive…and I was. Too many of my men were dead, Frenchy. I *was* lucky to be alive. You are too. Look what happened to Agent Chandler and the guard. They weren't so lucky. "

Grombach grimaced, but said. "I see what you mean, Burk. Just a matter of luck."

"Yes," Tom replied. Survival was a matter of luck and sometimes, grace, he thought.

Inside, on the lobby floor, the four dead bodies were laid out, side-by-side. A crowd of Treasury workers was gathering, including female secretaries and female switchboard operators. Gawkers, Tom Burk realized, like the people who slowed down or stopped to look at traffic accidents.

"Christ!" Grombach shouted. "Put a sheet over our men. No…not a sheet. Find two large flags for our men."

Tom Burk felt his stomach churn when he stared at the mangled face of the Nazi agent he shot. He was unrecognizable. Then he looked at Agent Chandler's corpse; his face was frozen in a startled stare. He must have died instantly. Tom had never even talked with the man. He hoped Chandler was a bachelor and didn't have any children. Then he looked at Hans Hoffman and wondered why a boy from Jupiter Island would betray a country that had made his family so rich? Was it some strange, sick bond between queers that made them willing to die for their lovers? Was that it? He didn't understand queers; they were sick, he thought, his homophobia reinforcing his prejudice. The stupid boy; a wasted life. Tom took off his chauffeur's jacket and placed it over

Agent Chandler's face. The white faces in the crowd seemed startled to see a colored man with a shoulder holster that carried a loaded weapon. Tom heard the murmuring, but he ignored it when Frenchy Grombach said,

"Help me get my suit jacket off, Burk."

Gingerly, Tom Burk helped Grombach out of his blood-stained coat. "Place it over the Treasury guard's face, Burk, will you?" He asked. Then Grombach turned toward another guard and shouted, "Where are the fucking flags!" The agent took off running.

"I think you need to sit down, Frenchy." Tom Burk turned to another Treasury guard. "Get Colonel Grombach a chair now," he ordered. A female switchboard operator moved swiftly and quickly found a wooden folding chair.

"Here you are, colonel," she offered.

When a guard returned with the flags, Tom retrieved his jacket. The guard draped the stars and stripes over Agent Chandler and the dead guard. Behind him was Secretary Morgenthau, his head above his entourage, as his group followed him. He was accompanied by a doctor in a traditional white coat; a physician who sported a black handlebar mustache and carried a fat, leather medical bag. A blond nurse followed behind the doctor with a wheelchair. The crowd parted to allow Morgenthau to pass through.

"Okay, everyone," said Morgenthau. "The show is over. I want everyone to get back to work now. We still have a war to win. There are a lot more Nazis out there besides these two dead ones."

The crowd dispersed, and the doctor came over to the folding chair where Grombach sat, grimacing in pain. The physician injected a shot of morphine into Grombach's wounded shoulder and ordered, "Take him to the infirmary, nurse. We have to extract the bullet."

"In a moment, Dr. Mendelson," Morgenthau intervened, placing a hand on the wheel chair to prevent the nurse from following the doctor's order. "I need to speak to Mr. Grombach and Mr. Burk. Tell me what happened, Grombach."

Grombach took a deep breath, exhaled, and said, "The two assassins were disguised as army officers, Mr. Secretary. They fooled us. We thought they would be in civilian attire. At the last second, Burk recognized them. Mr. Morgenthau, if it hadn't been for Burk, I'd be dead. And if it hadn't been for Agent Chandler, you'd be dead."

Morgenthau nodded his head and turned to Tom. "Good work, Burk. I'm sorry about Agent Chandler and our guard, Harry Robinson."

"Thank you, sir. It was a privilege to work with Frenchy," Tom Burk offered. He wondered if he should say that the Nazi's Luger jammed. He decided not to. Praise from a white man was rare indeed. Why spoil it?

A Washington D.C. police officer came through the front door of the Treasury Department and walked over to the Secretary. "Mr. Secretary, excuse me, sir," the cop said. "We received a report of a shooting." The officer followed Morgenthau's eyes as the Secretary of the Treasury nodded to the floor. "Holy shit!" the officer said.

"Yes, officer, 'holy shit,' indeed," Morgenthau echoed. He pointed to the two uncovered bodies on the floor. "Two dead Nazi spies dressed as army officers, and, I'm afraid, two dead of our men. Two brave Americans gave their lives."

"I see, Mr. Secretary. I shall have to file a report."

"No, you will file no report, officer," Morgenthau corrected. "It happened on federal property, and this has to remain secret. I don't want the press to find out, either. We have to censor this until we find out where the other spies are."

"Other spies?" the officer asked.

"It's a spy ring, officer," Morgenthau lied. "We don't want the ring to know these men were killed by us. Do you see, sergeant?"

"I'm only a corporal, Mr. Secretary."

Morgenthau smiled at the officer and winked.

"Ah yes, yes, sir," the officer stammered.

"We will take it from here, officer. I thank you for coming by," Morgenthau smiled.

Tom Burk was amazed. The Secretary of the Treasury had just lied to a police officer and dangled a promotion before the man if he cooperated in a cover-up. Amazing. Tom understood the need for censorship. The public didn't need to know that there was an assassination attempt in the middle of the nation's capital. They didn't need to know there were Nazi spies in Washington. The nation didn't need hysteria in the capital city. The war was going bad enough without spreading fear that there were Nazi spies in Washington D.C.

"I want some photographs. Get a camera," Morgenthau said to an aide who was standing beside him. "The president will want to see these men. Have the photographs developed and sent to Miss Tully at the White House."

'Yes, Mr. Secretary."

"Okay nurse, you can take Mr. Grombach. Mr. Burk, I would appreciate if you would take the armored car back to the White House. I won't be needing it, thanks to you two men. Please tell the president that the photographs will be ready soon."

"Yes, sir," Tom said.

"And, Burk?"

"Yes sir."

Henry Morgenthau offered Tom Burk his hand. Tom took it. No words were needed.

The "Captain Carver" hat hadn't moved from its resting place outside the Treasury Department Building where it had fallen during the shootout. As Tom Burk descended the steps he stopped, bent down, retrieved the hat, and walked to Al Capone's armored car.

Tom Burk drove the vehicle back to the White House. He would catch the evening train to Florida, he thought. But first he had to meet with the president and first lady for a debriefing.

Chapter 26

In the upstairs residence at the White House, Walter Burk welcomed his brother's safe return with a manly handshake and a pat on the back. Tom smiled and gave his brother a hug. It was an odd feeling.

"I'm glad you're all right," Walter said. "Lord knows I wouldn't want to explain all of this to Rachel if you weren't."

Tom smiled. "You're not as glad as I am. It was pretty nasty. I'm ready to go home, Walter," Tom said. "I'm exhausted. I'm too old for this."

Walter read the exhaustion on his brother's face. "I don't get off for a while, but if you want to take the trolley…"

"No, I don't mean to our mother's house, I mean I want to go home to Rachel."

"You want to return to Florida? Today?"

"It isn't just Florida, Walter. It's Rachel. This trip has shown me my home is with Rachel. Wherever she is, is where I want to be."

Walter smiled. "I understand, brother."

"Rachel is the heart that gives life to my family, Walter. Please make sure Mary ships Mom's items to Rachel."

"I will, Tom. I don't want to start a war between our women. Aren't wives always the heart?" Walter asked rhetorically. "So, you are ready to leave?"

"Yes, I did what the president wanted."

"Okay. He's waiting for you in his office. Mrs. Roosevelt is in there with him."

In the Oval Office, Mrs. Roosevelt rose from a chair as Tom Burk entered the room. The handicapped president remained seated at his desk. "Mr. Burk," she said effusively as Tom Burk walked into the Oval Office. "I am so relieved that you are okay."

The president added, "So am I. I just want to thank you, Tom. You did your country a wonderful service."

"Thank you, President Roosevelt," Tom replied as he handed the president agent Kane's *Captain Carver* hat. "The Nazi was wearing agent Kane's army hat, sir."

"I see," Franklin Roosevelt replied, placing the cap on his desk. "Too bad you men couldn't have taken young Hess alive, though."

The president's remark irritated Tom Burk, but he masked his emotion as he normally did when speaking to a white man. He simply nodded and replied, "He had already shot Agent Chandler, Mr. President, and he was about to shoot a wounded Frenchy Grombach. He did not offer to surrender, sir."

Franklin Roosevelt seemed a bit taken back by Tom's comment. "True. You and Grombach are lucky to be alive," he conceded. "I certainly am thankful for that. I'm afraid we can't let this out though, Tom" the president went on. "I want to keep a lid on news coverage of spies, especially in the nation's capital. I'm not sure how people would react to spies and assassins in Washington."

"I understand, Mr. President."

Eleanor Roosevelt looked at her husband and said: "Pish posh, Franklin. Be honest with the man. Mr. Burk needs to know the real reason." She looked at Tom and said, "What my politician husband won't admit, Mr. Burk, is that if our Southern friends find out that we employed a Negro as a counter-intelligence agent, they might vote for the other party in the fall. My husband would have a hornet's nest of Republicans in the House of Representatives. The Republicans might not fund the war as he wants. They might cut Lend-Lease. That would hang the Russians out to dry. It has nothing to do with censorship, although my husband doesn't want Mr. Hoover to find out and hog the headlines. As Sir Walter Scott wrote: *Oh what a tangled web we weave when first we practice to deceive.*"

Tom Burk was startled. Franklin D. Roosevelt was blushing. He was caught in his own mesh of mendacity, but it seemed to be the Scott quotation that drew the redness to his face.

"I understand, Mrs. Roosevelt, I truly do," Tom said. "I live in the South. I understand how difficult it is for the president to win the war keep the white Southerners happy. I just hope that things will change for my people in the South after the war. I would like to vote."

"You should vote, Mr. Burk. It is a travesty that you cannot cast your ballot. You are a very gracious man, Mr. Burk," Mrs. Roosevelt observed. "After this war, I will make sure that my husband does right by your people. Starting with voting."

Franklin Roosevelt glared at his wife.

"Thank you, Mrs. Roosevelt," Tom Burk said, but he wondered if they would really follow through on the promise. He didn't doubt Mrs. Roosevelt's sincerity; he doubted Franklin Roosevelt's resolve. In the past few days, the president's luster had dimmed for Tom; Franklin Roosevelt was no Lincoln. But then, who was? F. D. R. was a wily politician, with a winning smile. Tom was suddenly wary of trusting the man.

"Tom," the president said, his glare gone and replaced with his *Happy Days Are Here Again* smile. He handed Tom a thick, business-sized white envelope. "Mr. Morgenthau and I got together and decided we wanted to give you a little token of our esteem. Something to help out you and your family."

Tom looked at the fat envelope in his hand and wondered if he was supposed to open it in front of them.

As if answering the question in Tom's mind, President Roosevelt said, "Please open the envelope."

Tom looked inside the envelope. There was a stack of fresh one hundred dollar bills. Hush money! Should he count it right there? No, he thought. That would be bad manners. However, it reminded him of how Rachel received her Christmas tip from her Jupiter Islander employer: cash in an envelope for the help.

There was no need to count the money as a smiling
F.D.R. explained: "Two thousand dollars, Tom. For your
time and trouble. And...your silence. Do you understand?"
Roosevelt gave him a full campaign grin worthy of
Movietone News. "I don't want you talking to anyone
about what you did here. And, for good measure, you can
have my wife's revolver."

Tom smiled. F.D.R. was the consummate politician.
But two thousand dollars was a fortune to Hobe Sound cab
driver. "Yes, sir," he said. He flipped through the bills and
noticed they were in numerical sequence. Straight from the
United States Treasury, courtesy of Treasury Secretary
Henry Morgenthau? He wondered. If that were so, how
would the Treasury Secretary account for missing money?
File it under "Miscellaneous Expenses?"

"That means your wife, too, Tom," F. D. R. added.
"You tell a woman, and she will tell her friends."

Eleanor Roosevelt frowned at her husband, but F. D. R.
continued.

"We just can't let this story get out. So don't worry
about declaring this on your income taxes either. Let's just
keep this between us. Yes, I admit I need the Southerners in
the fall elections, or I will lose the House, Tom. If I lose
the House, I can't govern. At least, not in the way I need to
win this damn war. We might lose the war, Tom. I can't let
that happen. *And* if our little secret comes out, you will be
forced to pay income taxes on the money."

Tom Burk wondered how much of what Roosevelt said
was exaggeration. It didn't really matter. He would keep
his mouth shut. Two thousand, *tax free* dollars. He would
tell Rachel that the other chauffeur recovered from his
illness, or better yet, a new chauffeur was found since he

said he wanted to go back to Florida. That's why he was coming back so soon. Yes, he thought, he would tell Rachel the latter lie. That would make her feel better. He would lie to his wife, because it was for the good of the country. That was a lie in itself; he would lie to his wife, because it was for the good for his bank account.

"Please keep the uniform too, Mr. Burk," Mrs. Roosevelt added. "Perhaps it will be useful for you in your taxicab business."

"Yes, ma'am." It would be useful to have a uniform, Tom admitted to himself. The Jupiter Islanders would like it and probably so would the officers at Camp Murphy. With the war on, everyone seemed to be getting in uniform, anyway.

The president gave a nod to his wife, and Tom Burk realized it was F.D.R.'s signal for her to show Tom the door. The president had no further use for him. He was dismissing his servant, just like any Jupiter Islander. The president had more in common with the rich folks of Jupiter Island than he wanted to admit. "Miss Tully, show Admiral King and Colonel Doolittle in now, please."

"I expect you would like to see your brother before you leave, Mr. Burk," said Eleanor Roosevelt as she stood up and walked Tom to the door. They passed a naval admiral and a lieutenant colonel entering the Oval Office as they exited the most powerful room in the United States. The lieutenant colonel was carrying a large map of the Pacific Ocean.

"Good luck, Tom," the president shouted as Tom passed Doolittle and King. Tom Burk put the envelope inside his suit jacket.

Tom paused at the door and said, "Good luck to you, too, Mr. President." But F.D.R. had already moved on and was conversing with the two military men. Tom Burk truly felt like a servant.

Outside the Oval Office, a man in civilian dress addressed the first lady.

"Hello, Mrs. Roosevelt."

"Hello, Mr. Early. Cleaning up our mess today?"

"Yes, ma'am."

"Thank you, Mr. Early."

"My pleasure, Mrs. Roosevelt."

"Your job…" Eleanor mumbled with a sigh, but she smiled at him.

As they walked up the stairs to the residence to meet up with Walter, Tom asked Eleanor Roosevelt, "Who is Mr. Early?"

"Mr. Stephen Early? He is the White House Press Secretary. It seems the press corps found out about the little shootout at the Treasury, Mr. Burk. Even with censorship, it doesn't look like we can keep it quiet."

"But the president told me to be quiet."

"Yes, the president is going to make Frenchy Grombach the one who shot the Nazi, if the press ever gets wind of it, and then he is going to censor it totally."

Tom smiled. "Is it because Frenchy is a white man?" Then he laughed, realizing he had asked a rhetorical question.

Eleanor Roosevelt blushed. "Yes, that and he's from Louisiana; he's a Southern boy. Killing a Nazi might help the fall campaign if the president decides to release the information. But I doubt that he will."

"Frenchy will play along with the charade?"

"Yes…he wants funding for The Pond."

"What's that?"

"Some spy outfit Mr. Grombach wants to start. That's about all I know about it. I'm not among the King's privy council, as they say."

"So, the papers won't write about any of it?"

"No, no. If Mr. Grombach had taken Rudolf Hess's nephew alive, my husband might have him get the credit in the newspapers. The president is a bit irritated he wasn't captured alive. Dead, he is useless propaganda, so he will bury it. He doesn't want citizens to know there are spies so close to the White House."

Tom was skeptical. "Because Mr. Morgenthau is Jewish? Is that why the president changed the story? I mean, should it ever come out…even after the war?"

Mrs. Roosevelt blushed again. "The Southerners don't like Jewish people, either, Mr. Burk. Especially the Ku Klux Klan. I have no idea what will happen when the war is over. I hope the truth will come out."

"Niggers and kikes, please take a hike," Tom Burk muttered.

Eleanor Roosevelt stopped walking as they neared the dining room. "Excuse me?" she said.

"I'm sorry, Mrs. Roosevelt. It is just a saying I've heard."

"That's terrible, Mr. Burk. I wish there was something I could do about it. But I'm afraid as a woman I could never be elected president. You and I have that in common. No woman and no Negro will ever be president."

"Yes, ma'am."

She offered Tom her hand. He shook it. "Thank you for all that you did for your country and your president, Mr. Burk. I won't forget you. I promise you that."

Then she was gone and Walter appeared.

"How did it go, Tom?"

"Fine. They paid me off," he replied.

"Really?"

"Yes. Seems they can't give a colored boy credit for killing a Nazi, because that would upset the rednecks and the crackers in the South. So, if they have to they are going to make Frenchy Grombach the hero. He has the proper skin color. But they don't even want the story out at all."

Walter shrugged. "That's how it is, I'm afraid. Now, what do you plan to do?"

"Go back to Mom's house, pick up my things and head for Union Station. Buy a ticket

home."

"What about Mom's house? Do you want to sell it?"

"You stay there for now, Walter. It's a bad time to sell. Maybe after the war is over the market will improve. People will want to start families then I think."

Walter Burk smiled. "That's white of you, brother," he said.

It was a cynical statement that both men had used when they were teenagers and watched how white folks actually did business. They also learned in history class in their segregated school that white men had broken all the treaties they ever signed with Indians, but "Indian Giver" was a phrase for someone who double-crossed someone. The two Burk boys changed "Indian Giver" to "white man giver." Tom knew his brother was kidding and that Walter appreciated Tom's reluctance to sell the house, although he had a right to demand just that.

They both laughed. Tom looked his brother in the eye, held out his hand and then decided to hug him one more time. This trip had changed him from a hand-shaker to a hugger. Who knew when he would see Walter again? Who knew what this war would bring?

Later that evening, the gun and holster in his suitcase, Tom Burk boarded a train for Florida. He entered the segregated colored car and walked the aisle searching for a seat. A mustached, younger man in a grey business suit with matching vest, smiled at Tom Burk, picked up his briefcase from the adjoining seat to his and offered the seat to Tom.

"Harry Tyson Moore," he said by way of introduction. He offered Tom his right hand.

Tom shook it. It was a firm handshake. He looked the younger man straight in the eye. He didn't flinch.

"Tom Burk," Tom said to the younger man.

"How far you headed, Mr. Burk?"

"Hobe Sound, Florida," Tom replied. "What about you, Mr. Moore?"

"Florida as well. Little town called Mims. Ever heard of it?"

"Don't think I have."

"Brevard County. I'm the principal and fifth-grade teacher at Mims Colored Elementary School."

"Oh, you are a teacher. That's wonderful. We could sure use a few more good teachers in Martin County."

"Uh-huh. Are you registered to vote, Mr. Burk?"

"No. The white folks discourage colored voting where I come from."

"Really?" the younger man smiled. "I am registered. So is my wife." He handed Tom his business card.

"N.A.A.C.P.?"

"Yes. Are you a member, Mr. Burk?"

"No."

"Well now, let me tell you about our organization and how we plan to register our people to vote, Mr. Burk. We could use a few good men to join us. We are going to change the world, Mr. Burk. We are going to change the world."

It was a long ride to Florida, and the young man was certainly talkative. Tom Burk figured he might as well hear the younger man out. He had an evangelical zeal, a passion for colored people obtaining the rights they had been promised in the U.S. Constitution. Tom Burk sat back and listened attentively until Harry Moore suddenly asked:

"Mr. Burk, do you remember Rubin Stacy?"

"Of course. Who doesn't? He was lynched. A hungry man in Fort Lauderdale back in '35. They put a grisly picture of the lynching on the front page of many, too many newspapers. I think it led to the idea of the Anti-Lynching bill. President Roosevelt made a speech against lynching. I remember that. But nothing ever came of it becoming a law."

"Yes, and Mrs. Bethune and N.A.A.C.P. leader Mr. Walter White lobbied the president. Even Mrs. Roosevelt tried to get her husband to back the anti-lynching bill. But F.D.R. didn't back the bill because of the 1936 elections and fear that he would lose the South and he would not get reelected."

Tom smiled. That sounded familiar. "Uh huh," he replied.

"In fairness though, F.D.R. did to a great deal for equal employment."

"He's just not keen on colored folks voting, or stopping lynching," Tom replied sarcastically. "Mr. Moore, don't you see how ironic it is that the poem *Strange Fruit* which was made into a song by Billie Holliday was written by a Jew in 1936? Abel Meeropol? Don't you see any parallels between Nazi Germany and the American South? Nazis kill Jews, Kluxers kill us. Only difference is the Kluxers wear hoods instead of swastika armbands.

"It's different," Moore replied lamely.

Tom Burk merely smiled. He waited to see if Harry Moore could wriggle out of his comment. Finally, Moore said. "Perhaps you are right, Mr. Burk."

The two men conversed and, at times, argued, respectfully, for the first few hours. By the time they passed into Georgia, Thomas Burk was a registered member of the National Association for the Advancement of Colored People, promising to send a check for his dues, as Mr. Moore did not want to take cash from a member while on a train. Harry Tyson Moore was charming as well as persistent. He was also a darn good salesman. But Tom Burk was not about to do anything more for the N.A.A.C.P. until the war was over. Then, perhaps, he would become involved, he promised Harry T. Moore. But not until the war was over.

Harry Moore told Tom about his background, his birth in Houston, Florida in Suwannee County. He was an only child, but when he was nine his father died. His mother tried to get by working in the cotton fields, but she sent Harry to live with his aunts in Jacksonville. Jacksonville had a well-established colored community and his aunts were educated women (a nurse and two teachers) who emphasized a need for Harry to get a good education. At the age of 19 he graduated from Florida Memorial College with a "normal degree," a two year program designed for teachers. In 1925 upon graduation, he was offered a teaching position in Brevard County where he began by teaching the fourth grade. He met his future wife there. At the time they met, Harriette Vyda Simms was selling life insurance. She and Moore married and Harry was promoted to principal of the Titusville Colored School which went from the fourth through the ninth grade. While he was principal he also taught ninth grade and supervised six teachers. Two daughters later, in 1934, Moore started the Brevard County chapter of the National Association for the Advancement of Colored People. He led the fight for equalization of pay for white and colored teachers, but his teaching vocation began to take a backseat to his civil rights avocation and his work with the N.A.A.C.P.

Tom Burk listened attentively to Harry Moore's life story. He certainly was a driven man, an idealist. Tom didn't say much, but he listened as Moore shared his vision for the future, a hopeful picture of a modern South where Jim Crow was dead, where integration replaced segregation and colored men and women exercised their right to vote as was guaranteed by the 15th and 19th amendments to the United States Constitution. Harry Tyson Moore had a lot to say until the train made a stop in Florida. Tom thought Harry Moore must certainly be a fine teacher because he certainly liked to talk.

Tom Burk said goodbye to his new friend when the train stopped at Mims. He assumed that when this war was over, and colored servicemen returned to Florida, the colored veterans could lead the push for voter registration. That would be the time, not now with the war on. He felt confident that things could change after this war. After all, he thought, if a colored man could kill a member of "the master race," as he had, perhaps the world could indeed change. He would love to vote for president, although he wasn't sure that he would vote for Franklin Roosevelt. Eleanor Roosevelt though, he would vote for *her*.

The train stopped at Hobe Sound. From the front cars, a few Jupiter Island winter residents exited and waited at the side of the train as red-cap colored porters carried their bags down the train steps. Tom Burk simply grabbed his suitcase and descended the train steps and walked from the station down Bridge Road, across Federal Highway and into Banner Lake. Rachel didn't drive, so there was no one at the station to pick him up. Besides, having been sitting for so long, he needed to stretch his legs. Two thousand dollars in his suit pocket, and he preferred to walk rather than take a cab. Who was he kidding? He *was* the cab, at least among the colored in Hobe Sound. It was doubtful that a white man would ever offer him a ride.

In Harry Tyson Moore's future paradise, Tom wondered if whites and colored would ride as equals in the same railway cars or buses.

Tom wasn't home twenty minutes before Rachel had the two thousand dollars snapped securely inside her pocketbook, safely under her control. Within thirty minutes, she had also learned that Tom shot a Nazi spy on the steps of the United States Treasury Building. But Tom knew that his tale would go no farther, for he had told her that it was classified. While he couldn't keep a secret from Rachel, *she* could keep a secret from the rest of the world. Telling Rachel was like making a deposit in a safe. She would listen, commit it to memory, and then seal her lips, like a banker closing a vault. She was an uncommon woman that way, Tom realized. Most women couldn't keep a secret. Heck, Benjamin Franklin had written: *Three can keep a secret if two of them are dead.* But Ben Franklin had never met his Rachel.

Rachel, who had listened gape-jawed as her husband told the story of working with Frenchy Grombach to stop an assassination in the nation's capital, smiled with pride and relief after he finished the story. "They don't want to give a colored man credit is all, Thomas " she said when he had finished.

"The president is worried about the elections in the fall."

"Hmmmph," Rachel said. "That's a lot of baloney."

Rachel never cursed. Tom had never heard her swear. *Baloney* was about as strong a word as she ever uttered. But *baloney* to Rachel was *bullshit* to everyone else. Tom Burk laughed when his wife used the term.

"You think it is bullshit, Rachel?" he smiled.

"I said 'baloney,' Thomas Burk, and you know it," she protested, but she was smiling at her husband, her eyes twinkling in their sockets. "But your days of shooting Nazis are over, you hear?"

"I love you, old gal," he said.

"You'd better," she replied and took him by the hand and guided him slowly to their bedroom.

Chapter 27

Christmas Day 1944 was a lonely day for Tom Burk. Rachel was working Christmas dinner at her employer's house on Jupiter Island and he was alone. Daughter Phillis was involved in war work in Washington D.C. and Tom Jr. was in Europe with the 333rd Field Artillery. Tom Sr. knew from news reports that his son and his unit were involved in a battle in the Ardennes Forest that the newspapers were calling the "Battle of the Bulge." His son was fighting about fifty miles from the Meuse-Argonne, the battlefield where Tom Sr. had fought in the Great War. How ironic, Tom thought: The same earth. The same terrain nourished by the red blood of hundreds or thousands of young men on both sides. Deja vu. As his old friend Gene Bullard had often said, "All blood runs red."

Two nights before Christmas, Tom awoke from a dream with a start. In the dream, Tom Jr. had come to him. His son was missing part of his face, yet he still spoke clearly, distinctly. But he was speaking French. Or at least a few words of French. Tom couldn't remember many of the French words after so many years, but he remembered *Au revoir,* French for "goodbye." When Tom awoke, his nightshirt soaked in sweat. Had something happened to young Tom? No, he told himself, that wasn't possible, was it? He looked at Rachel beside him in the bed. She was asleep, smiling peacefully. Tom slipped out of bed and changed into a dry nightshirt. There was no reason to disturb Rachel.

The following morning, not wanting to upset his wife, he said nothing to Rachel about his dream. He was thankful that he hadn't awakened her. He had returned to the Meuse-Argonne in his dreams. And here was his only son, not fifty miles from where Tom Burk had fought not thirty years before. Unlike the Meuse Argonne, however, this time the Germans had caught the Americans unprepared and were threatening to break through the allied lines in Belgium. Just when it appeared the war in Europe would soon be over, Hitler counterattacked. It was, Tom admitted, a bold move and a gamble. But it appeared that Hitler's plan was succeeding.

Tom had clipped out a European battle map from a newspaper and posted it on a wall in his home. He and young Tom had worked out a pre-arranged code in their letters so that Tom Junior's letter could pass the censors who screened the "V-mail" that was exchanged between troops and their families. The Burk men never referred to France, but rather the place that Papa visited when Tom Sr. was a young lieutenant in World War I.

Young Tom and his all colored artillery unit arrived in France shortly after D-Day and fought their way across France along with their white counterparts. By a few clues in his letters, Tom Sr. deduced that his Tom Jr. was close to Belgium. From there, Tom concluded, the U.S. Army would drive to, and across, the Rhine River. They could race the Russians to Berlin.

Tom and Rachel had gone to Christmas Eve service at church and come home to open their presents in their annual Christmas ritual. But Christmas Day he spent alone and Tom Burk decided to take his fishing rod and try his luck at Banner Lake. In the twilight he returned to his house as Rachel arrived from her hard day's work. They passed an uneventful evening listening to Christmas music on the radio.

On the morning of the 29th, a special delivery telegram arrived from Western Union informing Mr. and Mrs. Burk Sr. that their son, Thomas, Jr., had been killed in action on December 23rd. Rachel fainted on the spot, but Tom was able to catch her before she fell to the floor. He placed her gently on the living room couch. When she awoke, she awoke sobbing, crying uncontrollably, inconsolably. Tom felt as if he had been kicked in the stomach. Then he felt numb. His legs felt shaky. His eyes watered profusely, but he held back the sobs. He was angry, terribly angry.

By the evening of the 29th, Rachel had regained a bit of composure. She went to her keepsake drawer and withdrew a gold star. She walked to the living room window and removed the service flag with the white field and red border and replaced its blue star with the gold star, which symbolized a soldier killed in action. If the neighbors didn't know the bad news already-and they probably did considering the Western Union operator was a terrible gossip-they certainly knew when they walked by the Burk household that young Tom had died in service to his country.

Rachel and Tom barely spoke to one another over the next two weeks. The silence between them was deafening. If Rachel wasn't working she seemed to always be at church. Tom, on the other hand, took his fishing gear and walked alone to Banner Lake, where he took a seat on a short wooden pier and cast a line into the water. He reminisced about his son at different ages in of the boy's life. It was a bittersweet reverie.

Then, out of nowhere, Tom suddenly remembered the conversation he had with Harry Moore on the train and the reference to Rubin Stacy, the colored man who was lynched in Fort Lauderdale less than a decade before. Tom recalled buying a newspaper with the horrific front page picture of the deceased Rubin Stacy and showing it to his son as a warning to stay clear of white women. Rubin's "crime" had been to ask for some food from a white woman. But the body hadn't caught his son's eye. What had puzzled his son was why the little white girl in the picture was smiling. She was only a few feet from the murdered man. She could almost reach out and touch Rubin's dead body hanging from the tree. The little white girl appeared happy, even excited; did the little girl sense her power to have a colored man killed? Young Tom had asked his father. Tom Sr. had had no adequate answer to his son's question.

Into Tom's mind came the image of his son from the night before. It was clearer now and young Tom had lost a piece of his face, but in Tom's mind, his son was speaking to him again, this time strictly in English. "The mail has come, Papa," he said. "There is a letter for you and Mama."

A chill went through Tom Burk's body. The voice was as clear as if Tom, Jr. was standing right there.

Ever since the Holy Spirit spoke to Tom Burk in the Meuse Argonne in 1918, he had not discounted the advice of voices that spoke to him in his mind. But no voice had ever been this Clear since that first voice on the Meuse-Argonne battlefield in 1918. It was the voice of young Tom Junior sending him a last message, he realized. He didn't need to go to Cassadaga and use a medium; young Tom had spoken to him. He picked up his fishing gear and trundled back to his house to find a piece of V-mail in the family mailbox.

It was dated 22 December, 1944, a day before his death: Inside were two letters, a sweet thank you note to his mother for the knitted wool socks that Rachel sent and a note addressed to Tom.

Papa:

Six days ago, eleven colored soldiers surrendered to a German S.S. unit. The men were taken out and shot because they were colored. I can't tell you where this happened, but I certainly will tell you more when these monsters are finally defeated. I am so tired of the discrimination in the army, but I am outraged at what the Nazis did to our men. I kept thinking of the picture you showed me of Rubin Stacy, that piece of "Strange Fruit." And I wondered: if we don't do something in Florida are we going to wind up like the Jews of Europe?

23,5,18,5,20,8 2/5/12

The numbers at the end of the letter were a simple code from Tom Jr. to his father to say where the soldiers were captured. Decoding it, Tom arrived at: *Wereth, Bel.* Wereth, Belgium.

The first thing Tom thought was that young Tom getting the letter through censors was remarkable, even miraculous. Especially their rudimentary numerical code which was based simply on the order of letters in the English alphabet. But in his mind, his dead son was smiling at him. He was right there a few feet away.

Young Tom nodded his head to his father as if there was someone behind him. "He helped a bit," young Tom explained with a smile. "He also says hello. He remembers you from a long time ago in France."

Those words were a comfort to Tom Burk for he believed his son was walking side by side his old friend, the Holy Spirit.

Chapter 28

On Easter morning 1948 Tom accompanied Rachel to church and sat beside her in the second pew on the left side of the sanctuary. Tom liked Easter service as the increase in music decreased the length of the minister's sermons. As he opened his church bulletin, an insert fell out. It slipped to the wooden floor and Tom picked it up.

The N.A.A.C.P. invites one and all to hear Harry T. Moore speak at Lincoln Park Academy....

Tom's thoughts were taken back six years. He saw the smiling face of the young, well-dressed man on the train from Washington to Florida who persuaded him to join the N.A.A.C.P. for a year. Tom had not renewed his membership as he had simply forgotten to send in a check. The insert in the church bulletin was part of a membership drive. Tom decided to drive up to Fort Pierce and once again listen to the man who was going to change the world. The world hadn't changed that much for the colored man and Tom wondered if the world had changed Harry T. Moore or if Mr. Moore was still an optimist.

Lincoln Park Academy, built in the 1920s to accommodate colored students on the east coast of Florida, was one of only four colored high schools in the state when it was constructed. The school was the pride of the colored community in Fort Pierce. In the years since their chance meeting on the train from Washington D.C., Tom had often read about Harry T. Moore and the N.A.A.C.P. But that evening, Moore was representing the Progressive Voters League. The P.V.L began as a reaction to a U.S. Supreme Court ruling, *Smith v. Allwright,* which declared whites-only Democratic primaries in the South to be unconstitutional. Since, Republicans rarely, if ever, won elections in the Deep South, colored voters were disenfranchised by segregation. The

Progressive Voter's League was the brainchild of Harry Moore and had helped to registered colored people to vote in Florida. Moore and his group had registered more than 100,000 voters, the greatest percentage of Negro voters in any Southern state.

Harry Moore stood before an audience of about two hundred people, including twenty or so high school students. He introduced himself. He spoke of the importance of voter registration as Democrats. He spoke of the importance of the upcoming 1948 election. He reminded his audience that Truman had integrated the military.

As he spoke, Moore's head swiveled from person to person, making eye contact with people on a one-on-one basis. Finally, Moore's eyes made contact with Tom Burk. Moore smiled. It was the same winning grin he had used on the train in 1942. When he came to the end of his speech, Moore answered questions for a few minutes. After half an hour, having answered everyone's questions, he came over to Tom.

"Mr. Burk, I believe."

"Hello, Mr. Moore."

"Here to pay your back dues?" Moore kidded.

Tom smiled.

Moore continued. "I remember what you said on the train a few years ago, Mr. Burk. You would get active after the war was over. Well, it's over. They tell me we won." Moore added with his winning smile. "Is that true?"

Tom laughed. Moore's recall amazed him. Moore was, Tom realized, a very bright man with a politician's gift for not forgetting a face.

"You have a good memory, Mr. Moore."

"I want to express my condolences to you and your wife for losing your son in the war. I cannot imagine such a loss."

"Thank you...how did you know?"

"Mrs. Roosevelt told Lawyer Marshall and Thurgood told me. I think your brother told her? Didn't he work at the White House?"

"Still does," Tom replied. That made sense, Tom thought. Walter would have said something to Eleanor Roosevelt, but Tom had never received a condolence from her.

"How would you like to help me get our people registered to vote, Mr. Burk? It can be a bit dangerous, but freedom never descends upon a people. It is always bought with a price, like the price your son paid."

Tom looked at Moore, but in his mind his son was saying: *Do it, Papa. Do it. It is what you and I fought for. Our freedom. Do it, Papa.*

"I'll do it," he said to Harry Moore. "It's time. Maybe it is even past time."

"Amen to that," Moore replied. "Welcome to the Progressive Voters League, Mr. Burk."

Chapter 29

One evening in early September, 1949 while Tom
Burk was at home with his wife Rachel listening to the
radio, the telephone rang. Harry Moore was calling from
his house in Mims. Tom hadn't heard from Harry since the
1948 presidential election when they worked hard to ensure
Truman won Florida's eight electoral votes which helped
the president upset Thomas Dewey. Enough Negroes voted
for Truman to prevent Strom Thurmond and the *Dixiecrats*
from stealing the state. It seemed too soon to start the
registration drive for the 1950 Florida governor's election.
As it turned out, Moore's phone call was not about voter
registration. It concerned something even more serious.

Harry Moore had a job for Tom, a paying job for a
change. It wasn't a paying job with the Progressive Voters
League, but rather something which might prove
dangerous. Moore wanted to hire Tom to shuttle two
N.A.A.C.P. lawyers between Orlando and the town of
Tavares, the site of the Groveland Boys trial. It wasn't safe
for the colored lawyers to stay in Tavares overnight, Moore
explained. It was an unnecessary explanation as Tom had
already met Lake County Sheriff Willis McCall.

"Tom, the N.A.A.C.P. wants me to hire a dependable
driver for attorney Franklin Williams from New York who
will be working on the Groveland case. You have a rather
new car which

I believe is rather fast. Only a few years old?"

"Yes, Harry. It is a Buick Roadmaster Super 50, 1946."

"Can it go 80?"

"I wouldn't know," Tom lied.

"I think you would," Harry T. Moore laughed on the phone.

Tom chuckled. "She'll go a lot faster than that. She can do a hundred or a hundred and ten. Downhill," he added with own laugh. "The manual says her top speed is 90, but she can go faster."

"Can I count on you then, Tom?"

"Yes."

"Can you pick up Mr. Williams, Horace Hill and *New York Post* reporter Ted Poston at the Orlando airport tomorrow?"

"Sure, Harry. Ted Poston, really?"

"You've heard of Ted?"

"Are you kidding. Poston was the first Negro to work for a white newspaper. I remember his articles about the Scottsboro boys when he wrote for the *Amsterdam News.*"

Moore laughed. "Poston dressed up as a farmer, sat in the Negro balcony then went to the restroom which had only a partition separating from the white and slipped his story into a stall where a white editor retrieved it. He is our insurance policy."

"Insurance policy?"

"It will be tougher for the KKK to harass Williams if a reporter for a big white newspaper covers the trial. He should be on the plane with the lawyers. He's an old friend of Franklin Williams"

When he returned to the living room. Rachel looked at him suspiciously. "That was Harry Moore on the phone wasn't it?"

"Yes."

"He wants you for something doesn't he?"

"Pick up lawyers from the N.A.A.C.P."

"Are you the only colored cab driver in Florida, Thomas Burk?"

Tom smiled. "No, but I have the fastest car."

"Why do you need a fast car?"

"We might have to get out of town quickly."

"Orlando?"

"Tavares."

"Tavares?"

"It's where the trial is taking place."

"Trial?" She murmured and then she gasped as she realized where Tom was headed. Lake County, the White Trash county, Ku Klux Klan county. The Groveland Boys trial. Was that it? It had to be. Lake County was a cauldron of racial hatred. After the young men were arrested, angry whites burned colored homes. Dozens of them. People were beaten. Most of the Negros fled the area, fearful for their lives. Tavares was a tinderbox. White trash, white trash, she thought.

Rachel had read a great deal about the Groveland boys in the *Miami News,* the Negro newspaper. Who hadn't? There had been national publicity about the four young men. One of the accused had already been hunted down in the swamps with dogs and killed and the other three were in custody. Two of the *boys* were veterans. They had been accused of raping a 17 year-old married white woman. From what Rachel heard through the beauty shop grapevine, the Groveland Boys were innocent and the girl and her husband were clay-eating crackers, low down, white trash. But that wouldn't matter to an all-white jury. Even white trash rednecks were viewed above the most well-educated colored man, especially in Lake County. Justice hadn't mattered for Claude Neal or Rubin Stacy. They'd been innocent and they'd been lynched. When Tom read about the Groveland case in the newspaper and learned that two of the men were veterans, Rachel feared he would do something noble because of Tommy. "It might have been our son Rachel," He told her after reading about Groveland.

She knew the N.A.A.C.P was getting involved, but she doubted if it would do any good. Harry T. Moore was a righteous man, Rachel realized, but a righteous man could be a dangerous man in Jim Crow Florida. A righteous man got people killed. Well, she thought, remembering her husband's 1942 trip to Washington and his work as an agent, at least Thomas was telling her upfront. She suddenly regretted that she had made him return Mrs. Roosevelt's revolver.

"You'll be going into a hornet's nest, Thomas Burk," she said. "It's one thing to register voters, but the

Groveland trial, you have to be crazy, old man. Those crackers are worse than those Nazis."

Tom might have argued the point about the Nazis, but he kept quiet. He had to let her vent. She realized what he planned to do was a good thing, a Christian thing, a 23rd Psalm thing, but she was fearful for him. He was going to walk through the valley of the shadow of death, and while Tom feared no evil, Rachel did. Sometimes her husband amazed her. She was the good churchgoer, she prayed twice a day. She never saw Tom pray, but why did he have more faith than she? Why did he not fear evil and she did? Why had he heard the voice of the Holy Spirit? She hadn't. *Why, Lord?* She asked. Sometimes it seemed like the Holy Spirit was Tom's fishing buddy!

"Your luck will run out some day, Thomas Burk," she often warned. But this day, she could only whisper a concession to what she knew in her heart was right, "Go, Thomas, our son would want you to."

Tom rarely shared with Rachel the conversations he had with the spirit of their dead son. He had told her that he had spoken to their boy, but Tom had not told Rachel the frequency in which they conversed. Perhaps a doctor would have labeled him mentally ill, but Tom knew he wasn't crazy. He had been hearing voices since the Holy Spirit spoke to him in 1918. He knew his church-going wife was envious of his relationship with the Holy Spirit so there was no sense rubbing it in and making her feel even worse. Tom had no idea why the Holy Spirit had chosen him.

"Yes, Rachel. You are right. Tommy would want me to help them and I can help by picking up the lawyers and the reporter at the airport and being their chauffeur."

The following morning, Tom drove to Orlando to meet the flight from New York. He was a few minutes late and two-well-dressed men, one in a dark blue Brooks Brothers suit, both sporting fedoras; the lawyers might have been mistaken for models for a men's wear advertisement in *Ebony Magazine*. A third man, slight in build and wearing black frame glasses and a rumpled suit, seemed a strange companion for the nattily dressed lawyers. They were standing outside the terminal, their luggage beside them. They were drawing attention. Instinctively, Tom pulled his car to the curb. A number of white people passed the two dapper colored men and gave them a glance assuming the men must be Negro ministers, Tom thought. No one seemed to pay much attention to the third man. Tom rolled the passenger window down, scooted over and leaned his head out. He had seen that face before in a newspaper photograph of an N.A.A.C.P. press conference. Franklin Williams had stirred up the state of Florida for declaring the defendants in the Groveland rape trial were repeatedly beaten to obtain confessions. And now here he was in Florida: Franklin Williams. He had a lot of courage, Tom thought, or else he was incredibly naive.

"Mr. Williams?"

The man smiled. "Yes, Mr. Burk, I presume?"

"Yes," Tom replied. He quickly exited the car, took their luggage, and deposited the bags in the Buick's trunk. The men were already in the back seat. Franklin Williams was the lead attorney and he introduced the other young lawyer as Horace Hill. Then he introduced the most famous Negro journalist in the country, Ted Poston.

Tom drove and listened along with Ted Poston as the two young lawyers discussed the defense of the Groveland Boys. They were realists. They knew there was no chance that the young men would receive a fair trial. Not in Florida, and certainly not in Lake County. However, they hoped that there would be some mistake that the prosecution or the judge would make which would serve as the basis for an appeal to a higher court and a guilty verdict might be overturned. An acquittal for black men accused of raping a white woman would never happen in the segregated South.

Tom listened to the men and grew angry. Not at the lawyers, but at the legal system. What had he fought for in the Great War? What had his son died for? Certainly not for unequal treatment before the law.

Harry Moore had said that the key to equal justice was to integrate juries and jury integration lay in the ballot box as jurors in Florida were selected from the pool of registered voters. Only with integrated juries, Harry said, would Negroes get fair trials. Getting the vote was the first step to equality, Harry liked to say, since the jurors were derived from voter lists. As it would turn out in the Groveland trial, there were only three Negroes in the jury pool and two were too fearful to show their face. They had been visited by the Ku Klux Klan and dissuaded from appearing in court. A burning cross on a colored man's lawn was a powerful deterrent. The third Negro was an old man who the district attorney called a "fine nigger," but the man was dismissed anyway when the prosecutor used one of his challenges. The jury, to no one's surprise, would be composed of all white men, primarily farmers who, Tom feared, would be irritated by two well-dressed "nigger lawyers" in town to stir up trouble among *their* coloreds.

Tom took a seat in the colored section, in the balcony of the courthouse. How strange it seemed to see two well-dressed Negro lawyers at the defense table with their white associate. As Tom had learned, the white lawyer would do the cross examinations as the white jury members would resent a colored man asking a white man any questions. The white attorney, Alex Akerman, was a courageous lawyer for taking the case as he would be ostracized by the Lake County whites. Harry Moore told Tom that it had been difficult to find a white attorney in Florida who would risk his career to take on the Groveland case. And it was suicidal for the colored attorneys to cross-examine a white woman. In fact, it was difficult for Alex Akerman to enter evidence. A physician had examined the *victim,* Norma Padgett, and concluded that he doubted a rape had taken place, but Judge Truman G. Futch, denied a defense motion to enter the doctor's avadavat that no rape had occurred into evidence. The judge declared he believed the white woman. He wasn't going to subject the poor woman to being disputed. Poor woman, indeed. When Norma Padgett was called to the witness stand she sashayed through the courtroom like a high school homecoming queen. She held her head high and sported a dark dress with a hip corsage and a large white belt. She had drawn the attentive eyes and lecherous leers of hundreds of Lake County men as she took the stand. It was Norma's moment in the spotlight and she followed the rehearsed testimony that the prosecutor had coached her on. And when prosecutor, Jesse Hunter, asked Norma to point out her assailants, she took a theatrical pause and then pointed at the three defendants and said dramatically, "The nigger Shepherd, the nigger Irvin, the nigger Greenlee." The boys were as good as gone, gone to the electric chair. It didn't matter that the boys were innocent or that Norma Padgett had committed perjury, it was a white girl's word-she was no woman, Tom thought- and her word was enough to send the Groveland boys to the electric chair.

Tom Burk thought the "trial" was surreal. The judge rejected a defense motion to throw out the defendants' *confessions* even though they were obtained under torture. Franklin Williams later explained to Tom that the defense team brought up these motions not believing the judge would accede to the motions, but rather to serve as a basis for possible appeal. The trial was, in a sense, no more than a "legal lynching." The Groveland defendants never had a chance. The defense lawyers, black and white, thought the best they could hope for was a guilty verdict and a sentence of life in prison. The white lawyers for the prosecution and Mr. Akerman for the defense made their closing statements and the jury adjourned. A colored lawyer addressing an all-white jury had never happened in Lake County and would not have helped the defendants.

At the defense table, Franklin Williams turned his head around, made eye contact with Tom Burk and nodded. It was the prearranged signal for Tom to meet the attorney outside the courthouse.

Tom huddled with Franklin Williams outside the courthouse on the lawn. Darkness was descending. Thank heavens for a bright moon, Tom thought. The two moved away from nosy white men and whispered to each other.

"I don't expect the jury will be out too long, Tom," Williams said. "Have your car ready to go out back of the courthouse in a few minutes. It is getting dark and we do not want to be in Lake County after dark. I've been warned."

Tom Burk wasn't surprised, although he didn't think Sheriff McCall would be that brazen to threaten an agent of the court. Rather, the threat to Franklin Williams had come from a couple of tough looking, large, white thugs who, Williams had learned, were members of the Ku Klux Klan.

Tom remembered the noose left on the hood of his car when he had been working on registering Negro voters in Lake County and the warning he had received from Sheriff McCall. Tom had no reason to believe that the six foot one inch, two hundred and forty pound, sheriff wouldn't just as soon kill him as look at him. What may have saved Tom that day was that McCall wanted to send a message to Harry Moore.

"You take the rope to your head nigger Harry Moore," McCall said. "Tell him this is what waits for him if he ever shows his black ass in Lake County."

At the trial Tom watched Sheriff McCall stare at Franklin Williams. He sensed that if a Harry Moore wasn't in Tavares, Franklin Williams might be a good substitute at a lynching. Oddly enough, Sheriff McCall hadn't recognized Tom Burk and Tom was thankful for that small favor.

Tom looked at the sharply dressed New York attorney, so out of place in backward Lake County. He asked. "Any chance at all for the boys, Mr. Williams?"

"As I said, Mr. Burk, the best we can hope for is life in prison."

"What a sham."

Franklin Williams smiled weakly. "We have another journalist beside Ted Poston joining us for the trip to Orlando. Her name is Ramona Lowe and she is a reporter for the *Chicago Defender.* No one wants to spend the night in Tavares, Tom. Can you manage one more?"

"Yes, "Tom said.

"We are going to want to get out of her as quickly as we can, Tom." Williams advised. "so be ready."

"Okay, I'll get the car running. I'll be waiting for you in back of the courthouse."

As Franklin Williams returned to the courthouse, Tom spied Ted Poston leaning against a tree. The journalist seemed to be going over his notes. Tom remembered what Harry Moore had said about Ted Poston masquerading as a farmer during the Scottsboro Boys Trial. Tom was curious how Poston pulled that off.

Ted Poston smiled and told him. "I played the shiftless nigger fool, Tom. Sat in the balcony and wrote my notes on a reporter's notebook that I concealed with a coat over my lap."

"Clever. How do you think this trial will go?"

Poston shook his head. "Tom, I once had an affair with a white lady. I worked in her house tending the fireplaces. I was a teenager. I wanted to break it off but she said if I did she would claim I raped her."

Tom was shocked. "What did you do?"

"I kept tending fireplaces and tending her," Poston laughed. "One day, the woman found another Negro, a bit more handsome than yours truly, and moved on. Happiest day of my life," he added with a grin.

"That's amazing," Tom said.

"What I'm saying is, maybe Norma Padgett had an affair with one of the men, but she is claiming rape to cover her tracks. Excuse me, now, I need to get back in there."

Five in the car, Tom thought. The Buick was spacious enough for Franklin Williams and the other attorney, Horace Hill, plus Ted Poston of the *New York Post* and Ramona Lowe of the *Chicago Defender*. For the first time in years, Tom was sorry he had returned Mrs. Roosevelt's pistol to her, but it had been at Rachel's request. He had a feeling he might need a revolver before the night was over. He kept the car idling and didn't make eye contact with the white people who passed his Buick. He also paid no attention to the racial slurs directed his way. He was alone with his thoughts.

How in good conscience could even a dumb cracker think the boys were guilty? Norma Padgett, the alleged victim, was not credible. But because she was a white woman, she was believed. It astounded Tom that when the defense tried to introduce physical evidence to show no rape took place, the judge denied the motion, preferring to let the word of the "victim" go unchallenged. The boys never had a chance for a fair trial.

The judge was a travesty. Tom wondered if the three boys would even make it out of Tavares alive. There was a mob mentality in the town. He remembered the Claude Neal lynching in Marianna, Florida. Neal was accused of killing a white woman, Lola Cannady. The authorities had even moved Neal to a jail in Alabama, but the crackers discovered his location and a hundred men stormed the jail, snatched Neal, and returned him to Marianna. Then the mob leaders announced Neal would be burned at the stake on that Friday night at 8 P.M. The announcement even went out on the Associated Press teletype to the entire country. The Florida governor didn't intervene. Ten thousand people appeared at the designated spot. The mob leaders held off on killing Neal in the hope that the crowd might disperse. The crowd was even larger than they had expected and the crowd was on the verge of being out of control. But the audience didn't disperse as the crackers had come for blood. So the mob leaders took Neal into the woods, severed his penis and made him eat it. Then the mob leaders cut off his testicles and made him eat them. They sliced his sides and cut off fingers. Then they applied red hot branding irons to his whole body. After they finished with the irons his mutilated, nude body was dragged to the farmhouse where the rape victim had lived.

Then, men, women and even small children, girls as well as little boys, stuck Neal's disfigured, naked body with sharpened sticks. When Neal finally, mercifully, expired, they hanged his lifeless body from an oak tree and started taking photographs, which were later sold as postcards for fifty cents apiece. Then the mob leaders took the corpse down, tied it to the hood of a car and drove the car to Cannady's farm. George Cannady was upset that he hadn't been the one to kill Neal, so he fired three gunshots into Neal's lifeless forehead.

Neal's lynching led to a cry for an anti-lynching bill, a fireside chat by Franklin Roosevelt and a few newspaper editorials, but the lynching's continued. Watching the angry white faces in the courthouse and on the streets of Tavares, Tom Burk feared for the safety of the defendants. He also feared for the lawyers, the Negro journalists, and for himself. He began to fear that he might not see his beloved Rachel again.

Attorneys Williams and Hill came out the back entrance if the courtroom, stopped for a moment with a state troop to ask for protection.

"The trial is over, my job is done," the state trooper said and then he casually walked away, leaving the attorneys unguarded.

Williams and Hill picked up their pace. Journalists Ted Poston and Ramona Lowe, visibly shaken, were right behind them. The journalists were frightened. No, the journalists were *terrified*, Tom thought. They made it to the idling car.

A crowd of scowling whites was ominously gathering.

"Let's get out of here, Tom," Williams suggested.

Tom gunned the engine. Even with a full car load of passengers, the Buick accelerated quickly. Tom didn't need to ask about the verdicts; he read the verdicts on their forlorn faces. He surmised that all three had been sentenced to die: two young World War II veterans and a sixteen year old boy. He was surprised to learn that the teenager, Charlie Greenlee, was sentenced to life in prison. Still, he wondered if any of them would make it to prison alive or whether they would wind up like Claude Neal, disfigured and hanging from an oak tree. Again, Billie Holliday's sang *Strange Fruit* began playing in Tom's mind. But they would have to catch Tom Burk. His Buick would give them a run for their money.

Tom pointed the Buick toward Orlando on State Road 19 that would take him to Route 441. In the rear view mirror, he saw a car, its headlights growing larger. He pressed the accelerator to the floor. The following car was still gaining on them. Ahead, in the middle of the road, a man waved a white handkerchief for Tom to stop. Tom kept his foot on the gas. When the man realized the car wasn't going to stop and would just as soon run him over, he ducked out of the way just in time to avoid joining a road kill armadillo a few yards away.

The car was still behind them.

"Jesus, help us," Ramona pleaded. The men were stoic until Poston said as if realizing the precariousness f their situation for the first time, "They *really* mean to harm us, don't they?"

"No, Mr. Poston," Tom replied, calmly. "They mean to kill us... See the big Stetson hat of the man driving the car. That's Sheriff McCall."

"Shouldn't we stop for the sheriff?" Ramona asked naively.

"No!" Horace Hill replied. "He's the one that wants to kill us."

"The sheriff wants to kill us?" Ramona asked.

"Yes!" Said a chorus of male voices.

"Cars ahead, Tom, blinking lights," Franklin Williams warned.

"Roadblock," Tom evaluated. Fearing gunfire, he turned off the Buick's headlights to make the vehicle a

334

more difficult target. He could drive by the bright
moonlight. How he wished he had Al Capone's car this
night. He pushed the Buick to 95 MPH. Thankfully, the
two cars with the blinking lights straddled the road and
Tom zoomed between them. Those two cars waited for the
sheriff's car to pass, then joined in the pursuit.

Tom Burk smiled. In his mind his son was
laughing. *You are having fun aren't you, Papa?* Suddenly
there was a gun shot, followed by another. By going 100
MPH, Tom put some distance between the Buick and its
pursuers and the bullets missed their marks. Ahead were
the lights of Mount Dora. He slowed the Buick to sixty,
running a red light in the middle of town and barely
avoiding a collision at an intersection. Surprisingly, his
pursuers slowed their cars lest they run over white people.
Leaving the city limits of Mount Dora, Tom gunned the
engine and never slowed down until the Buick crossed the
county line between Lake County and Orange County. As
the crossed into Orange County their pursuers stopped and
turned their cars around. Sheriff McCall had no
jurisdiction in Orange County.

When the Buick arrived in the colored section of
Orlando its passengers finally exhaled. They were finally
safe. *Nice driving, Papa.* He heard his son say. *I thought
you might join me tonight.*

"Not tonight, son, not tonight," Tom said aloud.

"What's that, Mr. Burk? What's not tonight?"
Williams asked.

"Tonight's not the night we die." Tom said.

Chapter 30

December 25, 1951

Tom Burk packed an overnight bag for his trip to the Brevard County whistle-stop of Mims. Rachel was scheduled to work a large Christmas party at her employer's Jupiter Island winter home. The remuneration from the upper class soiree was worth her while to work on Christmas Day, as she nearly always brought home fifty to a hundred dollars in tips from the wealthy and, often, tipsy, party-goers.

Rachel and Tom celebrated Christmas, as they always did, on Christmas Eve. This year, Rachel had tried to dissuade Tom from his Christmas visit to Harry T. Moore and his wife, Harriette. She had no luck.

"The Kluxers are after Harry Moore, Tom," Rachel warned her husband. "Worse than ever, I tell you."

"Oh, they talk a lot," Tom replied. "Groveland needs the light of day, that fat white sheriff killed those boys. Harry's just trying to prove it. Sheriff Willis McCall killed those boys as sure as Jesus died at Calvary. Harry's the man who is going to prove it."

"He'll never do it, Thomas."

"Thurgood Marshall thinks he might."

"Thurgood Marshall? Thurgood Marshall? What good is he? He's up in New York in his fancy law office. He's not in Florida. He's safe in New York."

Tom did not tell his wife how close Thurgood Marshall had come to getting lynched a number of times; Thurgood Marshall faced down death in the South. So Rachel was wrong. Thurgood Marshall didn't confine himself to the safety of a New York office. He risked his life for the cause of Civil Rights. Tom Burk had as well, especially the night he and four others escaped from Tavares after the first Groveland trial.

Tom had met Thurgood Marshall through Harry Moore and once, during a conversation with the famous lawyer, Marshall told Tom:

"You know, Mr. Burk. Sometimes, I get awfully tired of trying to save the white man's soul." Then he had smiled.

"Let Thurgood Marshall come down here," Rachel went on in protest. "You've helped Harry Moore enough, Tom. Almost a third of colored folks are registered to vote in Florida. It is the best percentage in the South. Harry Moore couldn't have done it without you. But Harry is stirring up trouble trying to get that cracker sheriff arrested. Groveland is not your business any longer. It is over. You barely got out of Tavares alive."

"It is Christmas Day, Rachel. Even the Kluxers don't kill us niggers on Christmas Day," He said the word with a smile for he knew she hated the term "niggers." "We have to talk about next year's voters' drive. To plan it. Two-thirds of the Negroes *aren't* registered, Rachel," Tom Burk explained. He had begun using the term *Negro* more often after working with Harry T. Moore who thought the term *Negro* was more respectful than the term *colored*. "Our son fought and died for this country, Rachel. He thought he was fighting for a better world, for democracy, for freedom for all the people. He was one of the few Negroes to see combat in the war. Aside from the airmen from Tuskegee, of course."

"Don't you bring our Tommy into this, Thomas Burk. Let our son rest in peace with Jesus." She glared at her husband.

Tom ignored her glare. "Tommy was proud of his service, and I was proud of mine. Tommy won a bronze star and earned a purple heart. He was a hero."

"I wish he hadn't been so special to see combat, Thomas," she said. "I wish he hadn't been a hero. That is not what a mother wants for her boy...or her husband. But if you are going to go see Harry Moore go, you foolish old man... Go! I can't stop you. That Groveland is still a hornet's nest, Thomas, and Harry Moore is sticking a pitchfork into it."

Two years after the verdicts were rendered in the Groveland rape case, the United States Supreme Court declared the need for a second trial due to the irregularities of the original proceedings. But after the Supreme Court ordered a new trial for the two men sentenced to death, the two defendants were shot "trying to escape," as they were being transported from prison to the court house. The two men were shot by Tom Burk's cracker nemesis, Sheriff Willis McCall. Harry Moore was attempting to have the sheriff indicted for murder. Miraculously, one defendant survived his wounds and contradicted the sheriff's account of the attempted "escape."

Harry Moore, Rachel claimed, was a marked man. The Kluxers were out to silence him. But that was just when

Harry Moore needed people to stand by him, Tom argued.
A man didn't desert his friends or his platoon when danger
arose. Rachel would never understand that about her
husband. His blood was up. He couldn't let Harry Moore
down, no matter what the cost. Tom heard Harry's voice
say, "Freedom never descends upon a people. It is always
bought with a price." Harry Moore was willing to pay that
price, Tom thought. *Am I?*

Tom hadn't been able to let his men down in the
Meuse-Argonne. His brother Walter told him he had "hero
blood." If he did, unfortunately, he had passed that blood
down to his own son. Thomas Jr. had had hero blood, too,
and that *hero blood* had cost his son his life. Tom's pride
for his son's valor paled in comparison to the ache in his
heart at his death. He dearly missed his boy. There was
never a day, that Tommy didn't enter his thoughts. In
rational moments, Tom knew the conversations he had with
his dead son were imaginary, but he wasn't always rational.
Spirituality, he reminded himself, was not always rational.
It relied on faith.

Tommy had been such a wonderful little boy, so joyful
the day that he caught his first fish with his tiny cane pole;
he was only five years old. He hooked a good-sized
catfish; little Tommy struggled, but he brought him in.
Rachel cooked his catch especially for him that night
although she had confused things a bit for the little boy by
saying that someday perhaps Tommy would be a fisher of
men. Five year-olds were not too keen on metaphors.

Tom preferred to remember how Tommy beamed with
pride at his dad when he caught his first fish. He recalled
how he had hugged his little boy and congratulated him,
praising him effusively. Oh, how his little boy had beamed
with pride!

Tom Burk smiled wistfully at the memory of Tommy as a child. The boy even snuck out of first grade at recess to go fishing. He got into trouble for that, although Tom didn't spank him for his misbehavior. Only once did he spank Tommy, when his little boy innocently whistled at a white woman. Tommy was only practicing his whistle, but the white woman might have made trouble for his little boy. Had Tommy been over ten, instead of six years old, he might have been strung up or taken out to the glades, tied to a saw palmetto, and left for the mosquitoes overnight. Tommy had cried when his father spanked him, but he never whistled at a white woman again.

In his mind, Tommy was waving to him, and a wave of grief overcame Tom Burk like a wave from an ocean of sorrow, causing him to choke up. The waves of grief had lessened over time and these days, years after Tommy's death in battle; they were not generally the overwhelming waves that caused such sobbing as they had shortly after Tom and Rachel learned of Tommy's death.

In a way, Harry T. Moore was like a surrogate son to Tom. Harry needed his help. Tom hadn't been there to save Tommy, but maybe he could help save Harry Moore. Yet, Rachel might be right. Maybe he was just a foolish old man. It was too late for the old dog to learn a new trick, though. Of that Tom was certain.

Rachel was angry with him, but she knew he was determined to see Harry. She accepted the fact that her husband's creed would not allow him to desert a friend. It just wasn't in his nature. What good was a man who wouldn't go to the aid of a friend? He had asked her.

"Do you always have to be a hero?" she had responded. She listened to him as he explained doing the right thing wasn't heroic; it was just the right thing. Then he smiled at her and gave her a wink.

"I do have a little time if you want a little Christmas cheer," he had offered, nodding toward their bedroom.

She couldn't help but smile at him, the old fool. They had engaged in sex the night before and the prospect of her husband's ability to provide an encore at his age was about as remote as a colored man being elected president, she thought. Still, she knew he was trying to tease her and she did love him when he teased. She knew that was his way of showing her his love. She wished he would tell her more often that he loved her; she wished he would use the words, but he rarely did. When he used the words "I love you," it was wonderful. But she hadn't run out of fingers counting the times he had told her that over the years.

"Don't let your mouth write a check your body can't cash," she said to him about his allusion to a sexual encore, but she could not hold back a smile. It was her standard statement to him, a phrase that she had picked up at the beauty parlor one day and adopted as her own. "Go on now, Thomas. I'll see you tomorrow morning then."

As he drove off, she whispered, "Please God, if it be Your will, keep my husband safe in Mims".

Tom Burk's old Buick died a year after the Second World War ended, but he had managed to squirrel away enough money from wartime Camp Murphy fares to buy the blue, 1946 Buick *Roadmaster* on clearance when the 1947 Buicks arrived in the showrooms in the fall of 1946 after the car dealers discounted prices to move the previous year's models. The drive to Mims wouldn't take him much more than three or four hours as there was little Christmas Day traffic on U.S. Highway 1. And he certainly hoped it wouldn't be as harrowing as his escape from Lake County after the Groveland Boys trial two years earlier.

He drove into Stuart and crossed the Roosevelt drawbridge across the St. Lucie River. He proceeded north on Federal Highway through the lightly inhabited St. Lucie County until he finally came to a stoplight in Fort Pierce. The town of Fort Pierce seemed asleep as well. North of Fort Pierce in Indian River County, the orange and grapefruit groves began, accompanied by roadside stands that provided the tourists with the famous Indian River Fruit which was shipped all over the country. Harry Moore had a little orange grove on his Brevard County property, and Mims had a reputation for its citrus.

Tourism and fruit were the two main industries of Florida, although as he drove into Mims and looked to the east, Tom sensed the future: Cape Canaveral. The site had been chosen for missile tests, and the military had already launched a number of Nazi V-2 rockets out over the Atlantic Ocean. It seemed ironic to Tom that the United States was experimenting with the type of German rockets that had terrorized London at the end of the war, killing or maiming so many British citizens. And, no sooner had that war ended than a *Cold War* between the Soviet Union and the United States began. Suddenly, our wartime ally was our enemy.

Now, the United States was fighting communists in Korea. Negroes and white soldiers were fighting side-by-side in integrated units, unlike in World War II, when the units were segregated by race. In another irony which the Cold War brought, the United States even employed the German scientists who built the Nazi terror weapons, because now we were afraid of communists, Tom thought. What next? Hire former S.S. as spies? Would we ever run out of bogeymen? Enemies to fear? What would the white man do without someone to fear or hate? He still had us niggers, Tom thought. He still had Negros to hate.

On unpaved streets east of U.S. 1 set the colored section in Mims: row upon row of shotgun shacks, many of the small houses lit with small strands of Christmas lights, some strung amid the thorny bougainvillea. Other homes sported wreaths on front doors or candles in the windows in celebration of the savior's nativity. Tom noticed a small portrait of a brown Jesus hanging from a mailbox, as well as cutout letters strung together wishing one and all *Merry Christmas.*

Tom passed St. Missionary Baptist Church, but the Christmas services had ended earlier that afternoon, as the church marquee announced the last service at 11:30 A.M. Congregates, he realized, had gone home for their Christmas dinners, although Harry said that the Moore family would be having a late afternoon dinner at Harriette's parents home, about a half mile from Moore's house. He was invited to join them and celebrate not only Christmas, but Harry and Harriette Moore's wedding anniversary.

Tom turned into a white-sand driveway that disappeared into a citrus grove. After a quarter mile, a one story frame house, resting on cinder blocks, appeared in a clearing. A blue Ford sedan was parked on a scraggly small lawn. The front door opened, and a middle-aged man with a thin mustache, wearing a powder-blue business suit and a silver tie that accented a pressed white shirt. As he walked over to where Tom parked his car, Tom noticed the flecks of grey hair on Harry T. Moore's head.

"Merry Christmas, Tom," he offered and gave Tom Burk a big hug.

"Merry Christmas, Harry."

"We have a lot to do today, Tom, but that can wait for later. Harriette!" he called toward the house. "Tom is here." Then he asked Tom, "Where is Rachel?'

"She had to work."

"Oh, that's too bad. Harriette will be disappointed. Peaches is here from Ocala," Moore said, using the nickname for his twenty-three year old daughter, Annie Rosalea, home for Christmas vacation from her teaching position in Ocala.

"Where is Evangeline?" asked Tom about Moore's youngest daughter who worked in Washington D.C. in the Department of Labor."

"She'll be on the morning train, tomorrow," Moore replied.

Harriette, a woman in her mid-forties and Annie Rosalea, a beautiful, young woman who reminded Tom of his wife Rachel as a girl, appeared and greeted their guest.

"Leave your car, Tom. We're going over to Harriette's folks for Christmas dinner. Peaches, take your momma in the car to grandma's. Mr. Burk and I are going to walk over. We have some things to discuss along the way."

"Yes, Daddy."

As the Ford took off down the rutted driveway to the path's end in the grove, Tom and Harry Moore began the walk to the in-laws. "I taught my daughters how to drive," Harry said proudly. Then suddenly, he turned serious.

"You might want to turn around and go home, Tom," Harry said.

"Why?"

"You know I'm a marked man. Sheriff McCall has vowed to get me, I hear. He's a Kluxer."

"Quite a few white men in Florida are members of the KKK?"

"True enough."

"Harry, I don't desert my friends. I'm not that type of man."

"I know, Tom, I know. Still, I started carrying a pistol in my glove box. A .32-caliber when I travel. I keep it in a paper sack by the bed when I'm home."

"That's pretty serious."

"Yes...as much as I travel...you know, some of my friends have said I'm pushing too fast for our cause. I'm going to do it even if it costs me my life."

"What about the 'boom-stick boys'?" asked Tom, referring to name given to the perpetrators of a number of dynamite bombs which had been exploding across the state.

"I'll take a few of them with me, if it comes to that," he said.

"It's Christmas Day, Harry. Even the Kluxers won't do anything on Christmas Day. They go to church like everyone else. I'm not sure what God they pray to, though. Now, tomorrow? Tomorrow, they might try to kill you." Tom smiled. "But today you are safe. That's why I'm here. It's safe," Tom smiled.

Harry Moore laughed. "That's why I like you, Tom. You are so reassuring. You're not afraid of them either, are you?"

"Don't see any reason to be. I've had a good life. Rachel and The Holy Spirit saved me." Tom smiled and added, "Of course, they had to work together, because I was a pretty hard case. Harry, if my time is up, my time is up," Tom smiled wistfully. "And if my time is up, I'll see my son again."

Harry Moore nodded then said, "Look to the east, Tom. I wonder if our new wise men are going to be there, over there at Cape Canaveral. Maybe someday, a man will go into space. Maybe someday a Negro will be in the White House."

Tom smiled. "My brother has been in the White House for over twenty-five years, Harry," Tom said.

Harry Moore laughed at Tom's humor. "No, I don't mean as a steward, but as a president."

"You are a dreamer, Harry, you are a dreamer."

"*We are such stuff as dreams are made on, and our little life is rounded with a sleep.*"

"*Othello?*"

"*The Tempest.*"

"You are the teacher, not me," Tom said.

"I *was* a teacher. They fired me."

"For getting equal pay for Negro teachers. They get the same pay as whites because of you, Harry."

"So much for *all men are created equal.*" Harry laughed. "We should start the day after New Year's registering voters for the '52 presidential election. This could be a pivotal election, Tom. Someday, maybe after we are dead and gone, a Negro will run for president and win Florida in the election. That is my dream."

"When pigs fly, Harry. When pigs fly."

Harry Moore smiled at Tom. "If Dumbo can fly, Tom," Harry said, referring to the Disney movie's flying elephant. "Maybe Porky Pig will fly one day, too."

"Those are cartoon characters, Harry. They aren't real."

Harry Moore only smiled. "Did you ever think how your life would change when you sat down beside me in that train nine years ago?"

"No, I sure didn't."

"You've been a good friend, Tom," Harry Moore said nostalgically. "You have been a great help to the cause of civil rights."

Tom didn't like the look on Harry's face. He had a distant look. Tom called it Harry's *Moses Look,* remembering the Biblical story of how Moses could see the promised land of Canaan, but couldn't cross over himself. He remembered a passage from *Deuteronomy: And the Lord said to him, "This is the land which I swore to Abraham, to Isaac, and to Jacob, I will give to your descendants. I have let you see it with your eyes, but you shall not go over there."* Like Moses, Harry was leading his people, but to Tom, it seemed Harry didn't think he would arrive there with them. That was Harry's *Moses Look.* To Tom, Harry T. Moore was a hero; Harry T. Moore was a man with hero blood, too. Every day Harry

T. Moore risked his life to make the words of the
Declaration of Independence become reality: *that all men
are created equal.*

But today was Christmas, Tom thought, and Harry T.
Moore didn't have to worry. This was the Savior's
birthday, no one would debase Christmas with violence, not
even a Kluxer. Tom didn't have time to dwell on the Ku
Klux Klan for the two men were at their destination. Inside
Harry's in-laws' house, Harriett's mother, Rosa, was
leading a chorus of *Silent Night.*

Later in the evening, before Tom, Harry, Harriette and
"Peaches" returned to the Moore home, a late-model
Chevrolet clicked off its lights and rolled slowly onto the
sandy road. The car turned down the driveway that ran
through the orange grove. Four white men were in the car.
As the car came into the clearing, the white men were
heartened to see that there were no lights on; no one was
home. A man in the backseat fiddled with a brown paper
package, setting a timer for 10:20 P.M. The timer was
attached to four sticks of dynamite. He rewrapped the
paper on the package.

"Nigger's Christmas present is ready," he laughed.

The other men chuckled, as well. "Ho ho ho," one man
said. The others laughed again.

"Whose car is that?" A man from the backseat asked
about the blue Buick. "That ain't Moore's car."

"Some dumb nigger that's company, I guess."

"Bad luck for him. Hey wait! I know that car. We
chased a car like that out of Lake County two years ago.

The son of a bitch could drive like a bat outta hell. We didn't catch that Buick that night."

"Well, looks like that nigger's luck done run out. We git another dead nigger. I say a good night's work. Give me the bomb; I know where Moore's bedroom is."

"I don't know about killing him on Christmas, Earl."

"Cox, you coward. We paid off your mortgage. That's the deal. You made the bomb. I'll plant it. Don't you worry. Chocolate pudding tonight."

Earl J. Brooklyn and Tillman Belvin, two Klansmen with violent reputations, exited the car as Joseph Cox and Edward Spivey remained in the back seat. Brooklyn, the driver, left the car idling.

Belvin began singing, "Deck the Halls with splattered niggers, fa la la la la la la la la. Tis the season for dead niggers, fa la la la la la la la la."

Brooklyn planted the bomb between cinderblocks and walked back to the car.

"Time to go, boys," Brooklyn said. "Sheriff McCall won't have to worry about this nosey nigger no more."

"Hell, all Willis did was shoot a few niggers and save the county money on a new trial," Belvin said. "Saved taxpayers' money."

Brooklyn laughed along with his fellow Klan member.

"When that bomb goes off, they'll hear it in Titusville," Belvin bragged.

Tom Burk never heard the explosion. He was in the middle of a dream. Tommy was talking to him. *It is time, Papa, it is your time. Come with me, Papa. Come with me.* Tom took his son's hand and turned to look at the charred body. He wondered if there were enough remains to identify him. He didn't want to give Rachel any false hope. *Mama will be along directly, Papa, it will only seem like only a moment.*

Chapter 31

In her office at the United Nations, delegate Eleanor Roosevelt was reading an article in the *New York Times*. On the wall in her office was a laminated copy of the United Nations' *Universal Declaration of Human Rights* which the former first lady of the United States had helped shepherd to passage in the United Nations General Assembly not quite three years before.

NAACP Leader Killed in Florida

The headline grabbed Mrs. Roosevelt's attention. Once again, the American South had made a mockery of Article 3 of her precious United Nations resolution: *Everyone has the right to life, liberty and security of person.* Unless one is a Negro, Eleanor thought.

She read the article:

Harry T. Moore and another unidentified Negro man were killed in a bomb blast at Mr. Moore's Home in Mims, Florida, on Christmas evening. His wife Harriette remains in critical condition at a local hospital. The explosion was heard in Titusville, a town five miles away.

Seeing Harry Moore's name, Eleanor Roosevelt felt a gag reflex, the bile backing up in her throat. She kept from regurgitating by sheer force of will. She knew Harry T. Moore. She had met him at Thurgood Marshall's home.

She knew his wife, as well. This was terrible. This was an abomination. An assassination on Christ's birthday! What kind of monsters were capable of such a heinous act?

Eleanor Roosevelt knew all about the racist sheriff of Lake County, Florida: Willis V. McCall. She knew all about the Groveland rape case. So much like the Scottsboro Boys. Harry Moore had been playing with fire in his attempt to have McCall indicted for murdering defendant Samuel Shepherd. Walter Irvin had barely survived a gunshot wound and survived by pretending to be dead. Eleanor was certain that McCall killed Samuel Shepherd in cold blood, that the sheriff concocted a fabricated story about an attempted escape to cover his murder. This was a terrible, terrible outrage. This shouldn't take place in the United States of America, she thought. Murder of a helpless defendant, the assassination of an official of the National Association for the Advancement of Colored People.

Her secretary walked into her office. "Mrs. Roosevelt, there is a reporter for the *New York Times* on the line who wishes to speak to you about Mr. Moore."

"Put him through," she said.

"Yes, this Eleanor Roosevelt... Yes, I have a comment: That kind of violent incident will be spread all over every country in the world and the harm it will do us among the people of the world is untold. Read it back to me," Eleanor instructed and listened as the reporter repeated the comment to her. "Yes, that is correct. You may quote me. Goodbye..." She hit her intercom button. "Dear, get me the White House. I need to speak with President Truman."

Even after six years, it felt odd to Eleanor Roosevelt to call anyone other than her late husband "president." At least she no longer called Mr. Truman *Harry* though, she smiled. At least not all of the time. Five minutes later, her secretary said,

"The president is on the line, ma'am."

Harry Truman's nasally Midwest twang came on the line. "Mrs. Roosevelt…is this about Harry Moore?"

"Yes it is, Mr. President. What is being done?"

"The F.B.I. is investigating. But you know how hard it is to get a conviction in Florida."

"Yes, I do. Do they know the identity of the other Negro man?"

"Yes. It was withheld until his wife could be contacted. I am told he was the brother of the retired White House steward Walter Burk."

"Thomas Burk?"

"Yes, I believe that was his name. Did you know him?"

A cold shiver went through Eleanor Roosevelt. "Yes, I knew him."

"In what capacity?"

"He saved Henry Morgenthau's life."

"You must be confused, Mrs. Roosevelt. Frenchy Grombach was the man who saved Henry Morgenthau. President Roosevelt told me that after I became Vice President. I had thought it was an attack on the Treasury, but the president told me how sensitive the Southerners were to Jews."

"Franklin deceived you, Harry," Mrs. Roosevelt. "Just like he deceived you about the atomic bomb and me with his paramours. Franklin Delano Roosevelt was a master of deceit, Harry. He couldn't allow it to get out that we used a Negro as a counter-intelligence agent. Let alone one who saved a Jewish Treasury Secretary. Remember how close the '42 elections were?"

"Yes. We almost lost the House. The South saved us."

"Yes, yes. We made a Faustian deal with the devil by placating the South, Harry. Will you keep me apprised of the F.B.I. investigation?"

"Yes, Mrs. Roosevelt."

Their conversation ended, Eleanor Roosevelt clicked her intercom once again. "Book a sleeper car on the Miami train for me tomorrow. I am going to Hobe Sound, Florida. But we will tell everyone that I am headed to Miami Beach to see my son, Elliott, and his latest wife, Minnewa or Minnehaha, or whatever her name is."

"Minnewa, ma'am."

"I know her name, my dear, I'm just not fond of the name. Nor am I fond of her. She sounds like she is Hiawatha's sister."

Eleanor Roosevelt was instantly recognized when she detrained at the Hobe Sound railway station, but as the people of Hobe Sound were accustomed to seeing famous people coming to Jupiter Island during *the season;* no one made a fuss over her. She carried her own small overnight case, and a colored man approached, doffed his cap and said,

"Excuse me, Mrs. Roosevelt, do you need a cab to Jupiter Island?"

She smiled at the man. She wondered if the man was Thomas Burk's successor in the cab business for the Negro community.

"No, I do not desire to go to Jupiter Island. Do you know where Rachel Burk lives?"

"Yes, ma'am. But I believe she's in church at the moment. Her husband was killed on Christmas. She is at his funeral service this morning, I believe."

"May I hire you for the day?"

"Why, yes, ma'am."

"Will twenty-five dollars be fair?

"Yes, ma'am. More than fair."

"What is your name?"

"Theodore Lincoln, ma'am."

Eleanor smiled brightly. She assumed the man had been named for both her Uncle Theodore and Abraham Lincoln. She would have to give him a good tip. "Mr. Lincoln, would you please be my driver today?"

"Yes, ma'am."

"So please take me to the funeral, then."

The cabdriver drove west on Bridge Road, crossed U.S. Highway 1 and then turned south into the colored section known as Banner Lake. He stopped the car in front of the Allen Temple African Methodist Episcopal Church. The funeral service was over. Only a few stragglers remained in the parking lot. Asking the cab driver to wait, Eleanor Roosevelt left the car and walked over to a group of mourners. The small group of women dressed in solemn black was surprised to see a white woman in their neighborhood. A tall white woman. Then an older lady in the group recognized the tall white woman, or thought she did.

"Mrs. Roosevelt? Eleanor Roosevelt?"

Eleanor smiled. "Yes. I am Eleanor Roosevelt."

"Excuse me, ma'am," the woman continued. "May I help you?"

"I came to pay my respects to Mr. Thomas Burk," she said.

"Really?" another woman asked. "You knew Old Tom Burk?"

"Yes. He did a favor for my husband and me during the war," she replied.

"Old Tom Burk? He did a favor for President Roosevelt?" asked another woman. "In the war, really?"

"Yes, yes, he did. Is Mrs. Burk inside the church?" Eleanor asked.

The older woman, who recognized Eleanor, intervened. "Mrs. Roosevelt, you come with me. Rachel is at the cemetery with Thomas, just across the way. It's just a short walk over to Banner Lake Cemetery," she said, pointing to a nearby necropolis that wasn't more than fifty yards in the distance.

On the short stroll to the cemetery, the older woman and Eleanor walked side-by-side in respectful silence. Banner Lake Cemetery was a neat, well-maintained, burial ground reserved for colored bodies only. Even in death, the people of Florida were segregated, as if the segregationists believed the hereafter contained two heavens: a colored heaven and a white heaven.

A file of mourners was leaving the cemetery, walking from the graveyard back to their homes nearby in Banner Lake. Eleanor Roosevelt was the only white person present, and many of the mourners who left the cemetery recognized the former first lady of the United States. They murmured to one another without saying hello to Mrs. Roosevelt, although two or three smiled at her. *Do not speak unless spoken to;* Eleanor knew the code for the Negroes in the South. She smiled as she walked by them, nodding at many of the mourners, as her guide led her to the fresh gravesite of Thomas Burk.

There were two mourners remaining; two women dressed appropriately in black. One of the women appeared to be in her early thirties, and the other seemed a few decades older. They stood silent vigil over the freshly turned earth.

When Eleanor Roosevelt was about ten feet from the grave, she stopped and said, "Excuse me, Mrs. Burk? I knew your husband. I am Eleanor Roosevelt."

The tear-streaked face of Rachel Burk looked at the tall white woman and immediately recognized her. She remembered the phone call she had received from Eleanor Roosevelt during the war, the ruse to keep her husband in a dangerous position. She hadn't cared for the way the Roosevelts used Thomas. They had taken advantage of his patriotism, Rachel thought bitterly. Thomas would do anything for his country, even if his country would do nothing for him. Rachel was bitter about how her husband's life had been risked once again in a second white man's war. She smiled politely though, in recognition of the former first lady, and her manners immediately kicked in.

"Pleased to meet you, Mrs. Roosevelt." It was an effort for Rachel not to use the word *baloney.* "I am so sorry for your loss. You husband was a fine man." Eleanor saw the sorrow etched on Rachel's face and also noticed the tears streaming from the eyes of the younger woman. Her thoughts were cast was back to April 1945 when Franklin died, although many of her tears then were tears of rage, for her husband had been with his mistress, Lucy Mercer Rutherford, when he passed away at Warm Springs, Georgia.

Thomas Burk, on the other hand, had been by the side of Harry T. Moore, the champion for civil rights. This Negro lady's husband had a finer death than her own husband; the Negro man's demise was a much more dignified exit than that of the philandering Franklin Delano Roosevelt, the president of the United States. Franklin Decadent Roosevelt, she thought, although she had hidden her fury at being a woman scorned from the public. Her husband was a hedonist; this Negro woman's husband was a hero. But Thomas Burk, not Franklin Roosevelt, was the forgotten American. They had even put her late husband's face on the dime after his death to honor his efforts with the March of Dimes, an organization dedicated to the eradication of polio, a disease from which F. D. R. suffered.

Rachel Burk replied, "Thank you, Mrs. Roosevelt. Your husband was a fine man, too. Allow me to introduce our daughter, Phillis Wheatley Burk."

Eleanor offered her hand to the younger woman.

Phillis was a bit surprised, but took the white woman's hand.

"What did my father do for you, Mrs. Roosevelt?" Phillis asked.

"He was a hero."

"A hero?" Rachel asked.

"He never told you?" Eleanor asked Rachel.

"Told me what?"

"That he shot a Nazi spy on the steps of the Treasury Building?"

Rachel feigned amazement and then anger. She turned to the fresh grave and addressed it as if the hill of dirt was alive. "Thomas Burk, you never told me about shooting a Nazi spy! Thomas Burk, do you hear me?" She held back a smile. Finally, she thought, someone was going to acknowledge her husband. But Franklin Roosevelt hadn't, and she was still angry at the late president for the oversight.

"Mama," Phillis said as she took her mother's arm. "Daddy's not there, he can't hear you. He's with Jesus and Tommy."

Rachel smiled and looked at her daughter, giving her a quick conspiratorial wink. "He can hear me, honey. He can hear me. It's good thing you are gone, Thomas Burk, because if you were here, I would give you a what-for." She turned to the former first lady. "Ain't that just like a man, keeping secrets from his wife?"

Eleanor smiled wryly. "Yes it is," she agreed.

THE END

For Further Reading (non-fiction)

In 2006 the Florida Attorney General Charlie Crist released the results of the investigation of the murders of Harry and his wife Harriette Moore (she died of her wounds shortly after the blast) on Christmas night 1951. It is available to the public to peruse. The KKK conspirators are listed by name.

The seminal work on the Groveland Boys trial is Gilbert King's Pulitzer Prize winning *Devil in the Grove: Thurgood Marshall, the Groveland Boys and the Dawn of a New America (Harper-Collins 2012).*

Q Gary Corsair's *The Groveland Four: The Sad Saga of a Legal Lynching* (Author House 2004) gives a full account of the trial.

Henry Morgenthau, Jr.: The Remarkable Life of FDR's Secretary of the Treasury by Herbert Levy (Skyhorse Publishing 2010), may appeal to some readers.

Before His Time: The Untold Story of Harry T. Moore, America's First Civil Rights Martyr. By Ben Green (University of Florida Press 2003).

Information on John V. Grombach and *The Pond* can be found on the Central Intelligence Agency website. Just *Google* John V. Grombach "The Pond."

For Viewing

Rendezvous, the 1935 film which was based on Yardley's book, *The Black Chamber,* was last shown on *Turner Classic Movies* in 2012.

Made in the USA
Coppell, TX
06 July 2024

34301015R10197